SO-AGJ-218

also by Elizabeth Gundy

NAKED IN A PUBLIC PLACE

BLISS

CAT ON A LEASH

Love,
Infidelity
and
Drinking
to Forget

Love, Infidelity and Drinking to Forget

by Elizabeth Gundy

The Dial Press
Doubleday & Company, Inc.
Garden City, New York
1984

Library of Congress Cataloging in Publication Data

Gundy, Elizabeth.
Love, infidelity and drinking to forget.

I. Title.
PS3557.U483L6   1984   813'.54
ISBN 0-385-27760-1
Library of Congress Catalog Card Number 83–2076

Copyright © 1984 by Elizabeth Gundy

All rights reserved
Manufactured in the United States of America
First printing

1

The houseplants were spread on the sidewalk like a flower show, along with a mounting collection of unessentials that wouldn't fit in the truck—picture frames, floor lamps, kitchen table, wok, and his armchair.

He strapped her easel and paintings on top of the truck. She kissed her friends good-bye one last time.

"Carol . . . Vito . . . Judy . . ." she cried.

"Sara . . . Daniel . . ."

He got behind the wheel. Sara extended her arms through the truck's open window.

"Call," cried Carol.

"There aren't any phones up there . . ."

"If you need anything . . ." wailed Judy, forcing the wok through the open window onto Sara's lap.

He started the motor, and the truck moved down Christopher Street. "Write," cried Sara. "Keep us up to date . . ." They headed toward Hudson Street, out of sight, out of earshot.

She's sad, thought Daniel. But she's prepared to the teeth. Her purse bulged with papers—Canadian immigration certificates, birth certificates, dental X rays, the cats' rabies inoculation declaration, her Bloomingdale's charge plate, and the master code of their cartons which would now have to be changed to delete the floor lamp, kitchen table, and his armchair.

He piloted the truck across the Village, and east on Fourteenth Street; the Triborough Bridge was the goal; until you were off the FDR Drive, the long arm of New York could reach out at any time —in the form of a berserk cabbie, a psychotic killer, a frustrated teen-age gang, or any other of the piranha fish in the school of the city—and leave you by the side of the road with your truck stripped down to the wheel rims. But once you were over that bridge . . . once, he thought, I have my belongings, my cats, and my wife on the wide open road . . .

He glanced beside him. Sara was dressed for the move in a rural extravaganza of red checkered shirt, trousers with many pockets, cowboy hat, and riding boots, in which she looked as much like a farmer as had Dietrich in *Rancho Notorious*. Tawny hair was sleeked back, elegant cheekbones gleamed, emerald contact-lensed eyes were hidden behind large sunglasses; it was inconceivable that this dyed-in-the-wool New Yorker would soon have her manicured hand on the plow.

She'd grown quieter with each passing block, and now was hunched over the wok; he saw her worries clicking off: She'd just given up an incredibly cheap rent-controlled apartment in the chic West Village; had parted with treasure it'd taken a lifetime to collect; was putting miles between herself and all friends and business acquaintances; had let her prize-winning pedigreed cats loose in a second-hand panel truck whose springs were trailing the gutter, engine sighing, multigrade petroleum leaking out of the oil pan, marking their trail to the wilds of the north woods and a house which may have fallen down since they bought it.

He had his books on Taoism, Buddhism, and twenty-four-volume *Home Handyman Encyclopedia* to guide him and was ready for anything, but she, Daniel suspected, didn't believe it was happening. It had started with an innocent country vacation, then aimless drives through New York State and northern New England, where farmland grew progressively cheaper, until they'd found the area cheap enough for even their budget, Atlantic Canada.

Patches the cat had settled himself in back of the van, on top of *The Egyptian Book of the Dead,* and was gazing out the rear window like a calico sphinx, face pressed to the glass, watching the fleeing city bubbling with summer heat, the desperate frenzy of the eight million, through which Daniel steered like a liberated being; true he'd given up an almost-profitable antique store on Bleecker Street, but could start another in the country. The two passions were similar; walking through the woods gave him the same feeling as walking through attics filled with art nouveau lamps, old stereoscope cards, castoff furniture, and Buck Rogers rings, or through the aisles of his favorite occult bookstore perusing dusty tomes from long-defunct publishers, printed in alleyways of Bombay or privately struck in little-known mews of London, dealing with astral projection, flying Tibetans, whirling dervishes, survival of bodily death, and acupuncture for the millions. The aisles of tall pines seemed to whisper mystical secrets.

And somehow he'd convinced Sara that she too was a lover of nature; after all, her apartment with its hundred houseplants cascading over marble, wicker, and delicate objets d'art bore a striking resemblance to the stately gardens of Lady Mountbatten; and she definitely doted on animals; filling several file drawers in the van were seven years of photographs she'd taken of cats, on marathon walks through Manhattan every Sunday, portraits of felines basking alone in locked shops, a collection ready to be culled and published. Publishing, in fact, was her field; she painted jackets for historical romances of passionate scoundrels and fair maidens, a career she would have to continue long-distance.

Glancing past her worried profile, he noticed a canvas of a fair maiden dangling down from the roof. Following his gaze, Sara turned and saw it too. "Oh my God."

"Nothing to worry about. The load's shifted." The home handyman swerved into a gas station, stopped the truck, and climbed out. Now she has immediate concrete insecurity on top of her nameless fears of wilderness destruction and poverty. What kind of confidence can she possibly have in a husband who can't even tie a fair maiden to the top of a panel truck? What sort of provider is this?

"Having some trouble?" asked the gas station attendant.

"I was sure I had those paintings tightly roped."

"Rope?" The mechanic took hold of the rope. "This ain't rope. It's string."

Daniel raced across the street to the hardware store, purchased four hanks of rope suitable for lifting pianos, and roped the maidens as if he were Simon Darkway tying them to a railroad trestle. His task was made no easier by the cynical stares of the gas station attendant and Sara, standing together and watching his antics; his thumbs did not seem to be operating in proper opposable fashion, but he never could work well with people watching, which was why he'd done it wrong in the first place; he could only work in the cool darkness of his late lamented antique shop . . . or in Atlantic Canada, he thought triumphantly, tying the last huge knot. Let's see those maidens get away from this one.

He climbed back into the truck, avoiding the ropes which wound round and round it like a cocoon, and resumed progress, onto the FDR Drive.

What a beautiful escape. We're going from prison to paradise. At this time tomorrow, I'll be walking through my own forest, on the brink of illumination, satori, revelation, ejaculation, and the winning lottery ticket. What could possibly go wrong in a little old farmhouse that a home handyman with a twenty-four-volume encyclopedia can't, eventually, fix?

"What," asked Sara in a doomed voice, "if my art directors won't work with me through the mails?"

"They said they would."

"But suppose they're all fired? How will I cultivate new ones? I'll be too far away. I'll lose all my accounts, and have to get a job picking potatoes."

"Relax. All of your art directors aren't going to get fired. And even if they do, what's wrong with picking potatoes?"

Immediately he perceived he'd said the wrong thing, watching her plunge more deeply into anxiety.

A busload of children bound for camp waved as they passed the panel truck.

"That was friendly," said Sara glumly.

"I think they were waving at Patches."

She turned around to admire her cat, and Daniel saw the quiver of a smile touch her lips; then her hollow voice: "I don't see Alice."

"She's hiding."

"How do you know?"

"She must be if you can't see her."

"Are you sure you packed her?"

"Don't you remember how we opened her case and let her loose in the van?"

"Maybe she got lost at the gas station."

"We didn't let her out at the gas station."

He sensed further inner gnawing; the hollow voice: "Am I supposed to ride for sixteen hours with this wok?"

The wok, the wok, he'd have to do something about the wok. He paid the first of the tolls, and they were swept onto the Expressway —a space ship caught in the next gravitational field—he and she jettisoning their past as astronauts jettison the stages of their space ship. "We'll throw the wok overboard."

"There's a fine for littering," she replied dully. "Hundreds of dollars."

The Bronx fled by on both sides of them and the huge apartment dinosaurs of the outer city; through the heavy haze of pollution, the sun burned down on the roof of their truck. "Once you're safe at the farm," he said, "all your troubles will be over. No more heat, no more smog, no more crowds . . ."

His psychology didn't seem to be working; her elegant form and the wok were joined in one miserable slump. "Just think," he said, "this is the last time we'll ever have to make a long trip."

He continued chatting aloud, a one-sided conversation on the happy move they were making. On the parkway, apartments and factories gave way to green trees; a cool breeze cut through the heat, but the haze still hung in the air. All these expensive homes in the suburbs, he thought, but the pollution is still around them. He felt how he and she had done admirably well for their money—two hundred acres of abandoned farm for nine thousand dollars—and tried to share the good tidings with her; but she wasn't overly communicative.

Connecticut was upon them, and the series of tolls that you have to pay to make your escape. "You could spend hundreds of thousands of dollars for a place here," he said, "and what would you have?"

"Access to New York."

They stopped for gas; the oil leak seemed to be getting worse, and her spirits not much better. He could feel her total immersion in all New York had to offer, the culture, the striving for greatness, the rich weave of immigrants, the restaurants, the museums; everything was at one's fingertips in the city—the best in art, opera, or whatever one's pleasure; and now he'd torn her from it, just so he could walk in the woods.

By mid-afternoon, they'd jettisoned Connecticut and were in Massachusetts' gravitational field, the traffic less dense, the sky more clear. They passed a farm by the side of the road, a couple of cows, some picturesque barns. Her voice grew more resigned; her posture, now that they'd jettisoned the wok in Howard Johnson's parking lot, was more erect. She began to take an interest in her maps.

"We've made terrible time."

"We had to stop for oil," he explained. "And to tie up the paint-

ings. And that turnoff we missed. And chasing Patches around
Howard Johnson's . . ."

He glanced toward the cartons in back; the rare male calico and
the chinchilla Persian lay upside-down in the heat, arms and legs
spread as in flight, twitching through dreams.

Outside, the monotonous movement of cars and scenery continued; he turned on the radio and got some peculiar news about a
church supper planned for tomorrow evening; it appeared that
beans would be featured. He switched the station and encountered
a minister offering a complete prophecy package for only ten dollars.

A sound of pain came from the passenger beside him; he quickly
shut off the prophecy salesman. "We'll get the world news at six,"
he assured her. "Everyplace has the world news at six. The world is
the world." How he could be sure of this assumption he didn't say,
and she didn't ask. Because suddenly, an incredible perfume blew
over their faces, wafting in through the truck's open windows;
alongside the road was an enormous field with a man on a tractor
dragging something and people shaping pale golden cones of dry
grass.

Could this possibly be the proverbial *making hay in the country*?

"They're haying," she stated definitively, from the wealth of her
super-thorough, conscientious, all-encompassing research of gardening books, back-to-the-earth magazines, and seed catalogs.
She'd sent away for rubber knee pads for weeding; a patented
shears which would revolutionize pruning; a plastic cylinder for
measuring rainfall; a pamphlet reissued from the turn of the century on cultivating ginseng for gullible Chinamen. "Doesn't it smell
good?"

It made the Bloomingdale's perfume department smell . . .
superficial. This was the scent of life. This was reality. This was
what they were moving into. How could it be a mistake?

He saw her smile for the first time all day, saw her beginning to
remember why they were doing it.

"No matter what happens," he said, "you can always grow food in
the country. It's the fundamental thing of life. It's the primal situation. How can it ever do us wrong?"

Her smile faded; he was laying it on, perhaps, too thick. The
thing to do, he realized, is let the land speak for itself. Let the

scents waft, let the birds sing, let the hills roll, and let them make hay.

"And," he added, in the cool of nightfall, as they jettisoned New Hampshire and entered the pine-perfumed gravitational field of Maine, "it isn't as far as a trip to the moon; nor of such dubious value; it's simple and real."

She nodded sleepily, sniffing the pine. He felt that he and the scenery and exhaustion had worn her down; she'd commented favorably on several old farms, had spoken of root cellars and crop rotation, had raised several points in favor of goats over cows.

"I'm falling asleep," she murmured.

His eyes were crossed from driving, but they couldn't afford a motel, and they had the cats, and they had to push on.

The farms became pinpoints of light, and gradually the points of light became fewer, and then there were no points at all. He listened to the radio, but finally even the last disc jockey—a solitary voice carrying the lonely flame of jazz out across the dark sleeping night—began to fade, grew disconnected, and was swallowed up in the vastness.

"Sara," he said softly. "I think we're coming to Customs."

The little border station, bureaucracy's seat in the wilderness, manned by a skeleton night shift, glowed dimly at the edge of the forest.

A young customs inspector came out of the low building; behind him on the wall of the office hung a portrait of Queen Elizabeth.

Sara opened her purse, drew out her numerous certificates and lists, and filled out the forms; the officer signed them through with only the most cursory glance at the van. We could be bringing in half a ton of valuable contraband, thought Daniel, if only we had some.

They wended their way along the dark country road, and his eyelids kept falling shut; his dreams had begun, flitting vaguely across the road. He nodded off and jerked back up, blinking at the patchwork of animated shadows before him. "I'm hallucinating."

"So am I."

"What're you hallucinating?"

"Tempestuous sagas of forbidden love."

His own fuzzy amorphous visions now took definite shape. The first pale light of morning was coming up as they rode through the valley; in a meadow by the roadside, a dainty shepherdess had risen with the rosy-fingered dawn to take her rosy-footed sheep to pasture; driving closer, Daniel could see the romantic look in the heroine's eyes as she glanced over her shoulder at the devastatingly handsome hero painted pastorally in the background; then as the truck was almost upon her, the dainty shepherdess abruptly changed to an old woman in raggedy nylon nightgown and furry backless slippers, cigarette dangling, tits hanging, carrying two buckets of water. The devastatingly handsome hero was losing his suspenders, pants slipping past his protuberant belly, cap jammed on sideways, and he appeared to be drunk.

Quickly, Daniel rolled down his window, drank in several large gulps of oxygen, and steered out of the valley with his head stuck into the breeze.

Sara took out the agent's directions, and they clocked the miles . . . five . . . ten . . . fifteen . . . sixteen . . . seventeen . . . until the forest turnoff appeared and the twisted signpost pointing to the Hills of New Jerusalem, the ghost settlement with a name like a cemetery.

They struck off onto the dirt road and drove up the tortuous hills, which were green with summer, lusher than he'd remembered. After four miles, they came upon the first abandoned farm, then the second, now fallen down; his eyes met hers with a question; we'll know soon enough, he thought. He drove on, to the derelict church, past the boarded one-room schoolhouse, and made the turn to their lane, densely framed by bushes and wild flowers, narrower than it had been in winter, more secret, more lovely, and at the end of the lane was the field, stretching to the infinite green hills, and the gray ramshackle house was still standing, surrounded by tall yellow blooms.

It does feel like landing on the moon.

They opened the doors of the truck, and stepped out; the perfume that had blown in the truck window was now all-pervasive; the flowers growing wild in their field could fill all the florist shops in Greenwich Village.

He sank into the blossoms, wondering how it could be real— hundreds of miles of woods, mine to walk in. What was the fly in the ointment?

Patches cautiously climbed down from the van, stared around, and leapt off through the meadow as if it were wall-to-wall catnip, as if he'd always lived in a meadow and his years as a city cat locked in four small rooms had been a single night's dream.

Alice's silver face appeared at the door of the truck, gazing with green worried eyes at the immensity.

Vast unbroken wilderness, he thought, drinking in the hills' panorama; the silence was complete, except for the birds and wind in the leaves and bees in the blossoms, and he imagined the many animals roaming through the forest, and he was now part of their world. He would spend all his days wandering the woods, as he'd dreamed his whole city life; he would swim in Jerusalem Creek; he would sleep beneath the stars.

"It's much more than I remembered," she said, standing in the flowers without a hint of worry, the fair maiden in her field.

They turned to the house.

It looked strangely bald.

Hadn't there been lightning rods on the roof?

His eyes traveled from the roof to the ground; in the house's lower left corner gaped a huge hole that seemed to have been blown out by a cannonball.

He took out his key, hoping she hadn't noticed the hole, or absence of lightning rods.

They entered the woodshed, which had been piled high with wood when last they'd seen it; now only a small stack remained. No doubt old Suttle, the rollicking octogenarian they'd bought the farm from, figured city people wouldn't know the difference between one cord and eight; hopefully Sara didn't.

"I'll get the bedding," he said, and went out to the truck. The timid Persian was finally making her careful entrance into the wide world, but his return addled her, and she scurried back into the truck among the cartons. He pried free the sleeping bag, and took it into the house.

Sara was sweeping a space to sleep in the center of the living room. "Do you know that under this ratty linoleum there are hardwood floors? In excellent condition."

He felt it as a personal compliment. Hardwood floors. Excellent condition. He laid down their sleeping bag, and they followed, stretching out on the hardwood floors.

"Weren't there lightning rods on the house?" she asked.

"Were there? You must be thinking of another house we looked at."

"Did you see the big hole in front?"

"One of the sills simply caved in. All I have to do is look up *sills* in my twenty-four-volume *Home Handyman Encyclopedia*."

"Or *holes*."

There was a scuffling sound on the shed, and the screen door swung open. Patches, covered with hay and twigs, marched in and joined them on the floor in his tricolored pajamas; a baritone purr started up.

"He's taken to the place like a duck to water."

"We will too," answered Sara sleepily.

Did she really say that? he wondered. Is she really contented? She snuggled tiredly into his arms; and, satisfied, he gazed at the sun through the window, stroking the spotted cat and listening to his soft breathing, and Sara's soft breathing, feeling the cool silence of the place, feeling its peace start to fill him.

■ ■ ■

New York City.

Traffic jam.

Horns beeping, beeping, beeping.

He opened his eyes, perceived he was in a strange house, and felt somehow as if he'd lived there except he wasn't sure in what lifetime.

Sara opened her eyes beside him; Patches gave a tuna fish–smelling yawn. And the beeping continued.

"I think," said Sara, with an amazing grasp of the situation, "there's somebody outside."

"How could there be?"

The beeping grew more persistent.

He got up and went outside; coming toward him in the sunlight was a tall smiling apparition with a face like a used bar of soap.

"Wendell Bubash," said the soap-faced man, extending his hand. "*Comfort Furnace*. We got her, wood, coal, or oil. You'll be needin somethin."

"No furnace needed."

"That's jes where yer wrong," said the gentleman conversationally, taking out cigarette papers and tobacco, settling in to a sociable talk.

"It's kind of you to come," said Daniel, "but I haven't had much sleep."

"Sleep? We'll have to pry you out of yer sleep with peaveys, that ice'll be so thick. Why Christ, I seen freeze-ups in this here field you wouldn't believe. I seen it so cold that chickadees was fallin dead out of the air in this very dooryard. Only thing between this here field and the North Pole is a barbed wire fence." He puffed on his cigarette. "But mostly, 'tis the fault of them ice birds."

"Ice birds?" inquired Daniel.

"Yer right, ice birds. Bigger'n that mountain out there, floatin about sixty mile off shore and about hundred mile to the east of us and producin them there winds I was tellin you about."

Sara glided out to join them, dark glasses hiding her exhaustion, her cosmopolitan charm glittering oddly against the gone-to-ruin old farmhouse.

"Bubash is the name, ma'am," said their guest, stepping forward; before Daniel could get in a word, the soap-faced man told her the entire story of chickadees, ice birds, and the fierce polar winds which Daniel already saw numbing her delicate skin.

"But how will I paint?"

"Paint?" said Bubash. "You gonna paint the place? She sure can use it."

"I'm an artist. I draw."

"No, by Jesus, you won't draw. Not with forty below hangin off the end of yer pencil." He winked at Daniel. "But don't you worry, ma'am. Me and yer man here been talkin about it. We're gonna put you in one sweet burner, and I'd say mebbe two hundred-gallon tanks of oil. The price'll surprise you."

■ ■ ■

The home handyman is often confused by the terms "cement," "mortar," and "concrete" . . .

He read by the light shining in through the hole at the top of the cellar wall; before he replaced the *sill,* he would have to close up the hole underneath it with *stone* and *cement* (or *mortar* and *concrete*). He sat on a pile of fallen stones on the dirt cellar floor, and read: *Hurried construction will lead to quick collapse of the wall.*

It was apparent this wall had been hurriedly constructed; how-

ever, you couldn't call a hundred years quick; unless the editors of
the *Home Handyman Encyclopedia* had extremely high standards.

A shadow fell over the book. He glanced up to see a piebald face
in the hole; Patches dove lightly into the cellar, ears back, nose
quivering. Alice's silvery face now filled the gap, and after much
nervous preparation, she too leapt in, looking like a walking junk
heap, her long Persian fur dragging cobwebs, burrs, and moth
wings. Daniel was amazed how fast they'd adapted, though of
course they had finer senses to adapt with than he did.

He took up his pickax and resumed leveling the wall's surface,
after which he could begin cementing in the stones. From upstairs
came the sound of Sara scraping twelve coats of wallpaper off the
living room walls. And all around them stretched the great peace;
he could feel it even in the damp dark cellar, coming in on the fragrant breeze, and in the stealthy steps of the cats; for an instant he
seemed to hear the magic rushing of the stream. A car horn
honked.

He put down his pickax, made his way to the stairs, and climbed
out. A rotund gentleman with spectacles held together by tape was
walking toward him, shaking his head.

"Boys, I wish you'd talked to me before you bought this place."

Daniel felt he ought to protest that he hadn't known the man
well enough to talk to him, or at all, in fact, had never set eyes on
him before. The stranger continued: "Did you ever get taken?
These old farms ain't worth a dime. They're sellin them fer
nahthin, seizin them fer back taxes and givin them away. They're
all over the place."

The peaceful day turned suddenly gray. Taken. Our life's savings. For nahthin.

"But the worst of it," said the stranger, "and moreover the most
dangerous, is the wirin in these old houses is sub-standard."

Having not gotten to *volume w—wiring,* Daniel inquired,
"Meaning . . . ?"

"Meanin the goddamn place is liable to burn down one night
while yer asleep in yer bed."

Going to bed in the country seemed to be fraught with dangers.
How, he wondered, did the families who lived here before escape a
century of ice and fire, forming on or consuming the bedposts?

"Y'see," began the stout fellow, adjusting his taped together
glasses which angled across the bridge of his nose making it seem

as if one eye were high on the side of his forehead; with this sagacious mien, he peered in through the doorway at a light bulb hanging from the shed ceiling. "Y'see, that there wire is frayed and of a quality that is not mouse-proof neither. You will notice that there are mice teeth marks all alongst that wire. Mice likes to chew wire, appear to favor the taste of it. And one fine night they'll chew right through, and there she'll go. This place'll flame like a tinderbox. She's only insulated with sawdust." He tapped on the wall; half his glasses fell off and he caught them, gazing at Daniel through his now-monocle. "A spark catches in that there sawdust and you'll have some fine barbecue."

". . . How did old Suttle manage to survive with this wiring?"

The gentleman spat and adjusted his monocle. "Jes Suttle's luck. Now you take a look around this settlement. How many houses you see left standin? None. Where's all the others? Burnt up. That's where. Standards has changed. Electric wire. You want a first-class wirin job if yer gonna live here."

I suppose we do, thought Daniel, it'd be a shame to burn in our beds. "Can you recommend a good electrician?"

The gentleman fiddled with the two halves of his spectacles. "There's Randolph Pinsies. He's a pretty good electrician."

Daniel took out pencil and paper, and wrote the name, with the help of his new friend who spelled it for him, slowly, torturously, phonetically.

"And how do I get in touch with Mr. Pinsies?"

"Ain't no need fer you to get in touch. Randolph's hayin now. He wouldn't have no time fer you. But, there's Jephthah Waggons."

Daniel wrote down Jephthah Waggons, spelling it as it sounded. "And how do I contact Mr. Waggons?"

"Waggons's hayin too. Bad time of year fer an electrician."

"Aren't there any non-haying electricians?"

"Now, there's where I can save you quite a piece of money. Cause though I ain't got the license, I got the know-how. And I got the wire, and the boxes, and so forth."

"Don't you need a license?"

The gentleman laughed loudly. "Who in hell needs a license way out here? Who's gonna know? There's the power comin in on that pole. There's the box goin into yer house. We jes tap right into her with the new wire. We'll do it ourself. You and me. I see yer a handy feller."

Daniel realized he was dealing with a perceptive man. A handy feller. He'd do his own goddamn wiring, he and his friend here. And he'd have a new skill to show for it.

A rustling from within the house heralded the appearance of Miss Bonwit Teller, whom neither absence of makeup, nor painter's overalls, nor coiffure twisted back in a knot could make a jot less sophisticated.

"Afternoon, ma'am. Jes talkin to yer man here, about yer wirin."

"We're going to wire the house," explained Daniel.

"But isn't it wired?" she asked in surprise.

"Tain't safe," said the gentleman, putting on half his spectacles, as if in a lady's presence one ought to put on at least half one's spectacles; or maybe, thought Daniel, he just wants a better look at her.

■ ■ ■

He knelt on the shed roof, tacking tarpaper. *Leak no more,* he said to the shed in a challenging tone; he'd figured the entire procedure out for himself—you unroll a sheet of tarpaper and nail it. The sun blazed down on his good work, on his warm back, on the oily fragrant tarpaper, and the two cats who were stretched out on the new-papered end of the roof; they both looked ten years younger, two cats who'd never before basked in the sun; he often felt the best part of the move to the country was the metamorphosis of Patches and Alice; whatever he would have to pay for a furnace and rewiring, at least Patches and Alice would be warm and fireproof. As for himself, he liked nothing better than kneeling here in the sun, hammering tarpaper on the shed, doing a nice neat job, and afterwards he could look up and say, *There's my tarpaper shack.* And there are my cats, basking on top of it. And there are my fields and forest and orchards and barns and it's all mine, all paid for, forever.

■ ■ ■

It was evening when they went to call on the plumber. They drove over the Hills of New Jerusalem, and onto the highway, along a narrow river where cows stood in the shallows cooling their legs; grazing land stretched beyond, dotted with white calendar farms; beneath a bridge, children swung from green iron girders and swam alongside the contemplative cows.

"He lives on the other side of the bridge," she read from her notes.

The opposite side of the bridge boasted several small summer cottages set on stilts above the high-water mark.

"The house is supposed to be brown."

He parked by a likely-looking brown cottage, climbed the steps of the house, and knocked.

"*Eh?*" bellowed a voice from within.

They knocked again.

Heavy footsteps approached, and the screen door was opened by an old bum with a repellingly cunning glint in his eyes and the hint of a leer on greasy lips; he'd been eating something with rank fat in it.

"I hope we didn't disturb your dinner," said Sara.

"Who're you?"

"We bought Suttle's old farm in Jerusalem."

"Are you Angus Deake?" interrupted Daniel, thinking this fact should be established before they hired on an inexperienced if willing old hobo.

"Come on in," said the hobo, cleverly not answering, and they followed him onto his veranda, decorated with fishes and animal heads nailed to the wall and a single row of unmatched chairs lined up for a view of the half-dry river.

"What d'you think of my view?"

"Lovely," said Sara.

He pointed proudly to an early Morris chair. "Genuine bird's-eye maple. Got it from an old house I worked on. Folks who owned it didn't know what they had, so I offered to take it off their hands fer five cents."

I've come to antique dealer's heaven, realized Daniel. The country's crawling with antiques for a nickel for the unscrupulous. Could I be as unscrupulous as Angus Deake? If this is Angus Deake.

"Lemme show you the rest," offered their host, leading them into the heart of his home, dominated by the fiery woodstove on which sputtered his noxious dinner.

The old man followed their eyes to the malodorous frypan. He gave a sly wink.

"Mr. Deake," said Sara, "I must say you have beautiful things."

He smirked, explaining how he'd obtained this antique and that, by wile, deviousness, and outright theft, including a Tiffany wisteria lamp that would've given the poor old innocents he'd wangled it from a comfortable old age if they'd sold it to an honest dealer. Am I, wondered Daniel, that honest dealer?

"Do you think," asked Sara, "you might be able to come out tomorrow?"

"Lady, I'll come when I come."

■ ■ ■

The last rays of sunset streamed through the kitchen window with the cool green scent of evening and the music of the crickets; a fire glowed in the stove; his rocking chair made a faint creaking noise; the kettle steamed; and he read in a yellowed newspaper about milking machines.

He also read about pig troughs, alfalfa, silage, watering systems, and numerous other recondite subjects from 1940 issues of *The Farmer's Friend* left behind by Suttle; the articles were incomprehensible and, in all probability, he'd never need to construct a 1940 milking machine, but it gave him a good feeling to read about such things; it seemed what he ought to be doing in the evening after a long day's work.

He'd recently purchased a pair of heavy work pants and button-on suspenders, and the suspenders holding up his baggy pants, along with the yellowed newspaper, the yellowed walls, the wood fire smell, the creak of his rocker, the sounds of insects and birds in the field, all seemed to contribute to a feeling of the old time, the old farm, its spirit.

Sara sat at the table making bright labels for old canning jars she'd brought up from the cellar. They'd hung barn-board shelves on the wall for the jars, and some of the iridescent containers were already filled with fragrant herbs which they'd picked and dried and hoped were edible.

Ferns from the forest hung in the windows, and the walls were decorated with old seed posters; the charm of the place was finally starting to be revealed; he and she were starting to lock in with the pattern, the work of years that permeated house, barns, and fields. He felt in stride with *The Farmer's Friend*. The sunset streamed across the worn wooden floorboards; the cats basked in the warmth of the woodstove, curled in a purring circle of calico and silver. He rocked back in his chair, and turned a fragile page, feeling indescribably deep with milking machines, pig troughs, silos, button-on suspenders, hay moisture, forage, and apple maggots.

■ ■ ■

A horn blew in the driveway, and soap-faced Wendell Bubash led his charge of furnace installers across the lawn.

"Mornin," said Wendell, with the takeover confidence of a man about to be paid cash for a twelve-hundred-dollar job. His troops were fanning out around him; like commandos they began scaling the sides of the house and chopping holes in the roof, while Bubash looked on from below.

"Can I help?" asked Daniel in a humble voice, feeling his inadequacy against these pros, graduates of *volume f—furnace, volume r—roof, volume s—scaling the sides of a house.*

"No, my boys know what they're doin. She'll be a tight little house when we're done. The little woman'll be warm as a hot bun." He appeared to be looking around for the little woman.

Above on the roof, the men were hammering, banging, scurrying around in a feverish pitch of activity, as if they had a dozen more furnaces to install before nightfall. The generalissimo ducked into his truck for liquid refreshment, and Daniel wandered off to do more low-caste work.

As the morning sun moved high over the trees, the cellar became an octopus of iron ducts; the rooms upstairs erupted in metal grids; chunks of hardwood floor were torn up and replaced by hot-air squares; pieces of ceiling were demolished to make space for a stainless steel chimney. Daniel tried to keep out of the workmen's way. Going down to the cellar to get a tool, he stopped short on the steps, above a gentleman who was nonchalantly raining a great gush of piss on the wall. Could it be a time-honored tradition to piss on cellar walls in the country?

Daniel snuck back upstairs; another van was coming down the lane—*Angus Deake, Plumber.* This is really something, he thought, all these fine professionals converging at once.

The old bum stepped grinning from his truck, followed by an enormous young man so shy he had trouble maneuvering his feet.

"This here's Rolly," said Angus.

"Pleased to meet you," said Daniel, as the plumber's assistant scraped his troublesome feet and Daniel wished he'd ascertained how much Angus intended to charge, with assistant versus without. Although it's possible Rolly's some kind of idiot genius—thought Daniel, consoling himself, avoiding the boy's strange shifty eyes— and probably dirt cheap at the price.

"The old well's gotta be dug up," said Angus.

"Maybe Rolly could do that," suggested Daniel.

Rolly blanched; Angus spit a wad of phlegm on the ground. Obviously this was a skilled apprentice and not a lowly ditch digger. Daniel said quickly, "I'll dig the well."

He escaped down into the cellar for his spade; Patches and Alice were wrinkling their noses and tiptoeing daintily away from the area where the gentleman, or gentlemen, had been pissing. The cats followed him upstairs, and supervised his digging of the well, which was purportedly six feet under hard clay.

Wendell Bubash, who'd been taking much liquid refreshment, was issuing garbled and voluble instructions to his men. "Shift her a little to the right, boys," he called, pointing to someone he saw on the roof, though Daniel could see nobody, either upon the surface, nor under the eaves. "She's comin now," said Bubash to Daniel, his face of soap looking more used than ever, his voice more confidently booming.

"She is?"

"Everythin's fallin into place." Bubash himself looked about to fall into place in the soap dish.

However, in at the soap dish, that other master craftsman, Angus Deake, was bringing plastic pipe through the walls, while his dodo-footed assistant stared out the window at a porcupine slowly crawling up a tree, a creature to whom he bore a strong resemblance in style of mobility.

The old bum greeted Daniel from the back of the bathtub. "The beauty of this pipe is the way she goes together jes with glue. Hand me that there glue, Rolly."

The apprentice did not respond, his dreamy eyes still riveted on the gnawing porcupine.

"Rolly, hand me that glue afore I thrash you with a pipe." Angus winked at Daniel. "It's ruttin season fer moose. Ain't that right, Rolly?"

Rolly's moronic eyes registered no answer. Automaton-like he handed the glue to Deake; the glue disappeared behind the bathtub, and Deake's face again appeared, as he sat back and lit up the stub of a foul-smelling cigar. "We almost got her licked. Jes a couple more elbows."

Feeling the bathroom was too small for a cigar like Deake's and any other living being, Daniel went back out to his well hole.

"Interested in plumbin, are you?" asked Bubash. "With that there oil furnace, you'll have all kinds of hot water." How many kinds of hot water are there? wondered Daniel, returning to his digging.

As the afternoon wore on, from time to time, Sara appeared at his side. ". . . Angus stole two antique bottles."

Daniel continued to dig, taking off his shirt in the heat.

". . . Angus took the old pickle crock."

Around four o'clock, the furnace operation was being finished; Daniel watched with satisfaction as the workmen put flashing and caulking around the new chimney; he knew that *flashing* and *caulking* guaranteed a *watertight seal*. It was all being done according to the encyclopedia; this wasn't just some primitive piss-in-the-cellar outfit, but sophisticated workmen who knew all twenty-four volumes. Pissing in the cellar was merely a cultural quirk, and no reflection on their work.

The men tossed their tools into their trucks, and Wendell Bubash, his soap face by now half dissolved, handed Daniel a contract and accepted his check.

The house was fully furnaced, for only twelve hundred dollars. And halfway to running water.

"Be back tomorrow," said Deake, as he and his somnambulant assistant drove away; the words followed Daniel into his dreams, where he saw gangs of workmen hammering into the night, transforming his house, himself, his wife, his cats, into . . . what? The question was left unanswered, but morning brought, as promised, the leering face of the old bum and his slothlike apprentice.

With the confidence of a master craftsman, Angus hooked up the heavy vent pipes, the drainage pipes, and hummed to himself as he pillaged the house for valuable antiques. When found with stolen objects in hand, somehow he made it appear you had given them to him, a ruse he stretched as far as it would go, until by the time he was leaving, it seemed you'd accepted him as a beloved member of the family and showered upon him all the things he had stolen.

"She don't leak. She won't freeze. There ain't the least bit of a shudder to them pipes. And near as I can tell it's jes a perfect job. It should never give you no problem. But should one develop, you go down and get hold of Rolly and he'll come right up here and straighten her out."

They both looked at Rolly, who was standing like a wooden Indian on the avenue, holding out his can of glue as if it were a tin of cigars.

"I'm sure it won't come to that," said Daniel.

"If yer satisfied then," said Angus, climbing into his truck, laden with antique bottles, crocks, and other plunder which Daniel didn't have the heart to call back. This was a man he'd worked side by side with; what if he did have this cultural quirk? You just had to overlook it. In New York, if you took your eyes off your plumber, he'd steal the bathtub.

As the dust settled in the wake of Angus's van, Sara made the announcement:

"I'm going to take a hot bath."

They marched ceremoniously into the bathroom, Patches and Alice bringing up the rear.

"With that oil furnace you'll have all kinds of hot water," said Daniel, taking his seat in a chair to watch her prepare for the great occasion.

The bathroom was the first completed room in the house—the walls were stripped to their plaster and painted white; potted plants stood in the window; and a luxurious blast of brand-new oil heat came up through the grid in the varnished oak floor. Elegantly, she took off her clothes, fluffed out her towels, placed soap and loofah and sponge in the tub, and turned on the hot . . .

"WATCH OUT!"

"SHUT IT OFF!"

"I CAN'T GET NEAR IT!"

He lunged over the fleeing cats, ran across the kitchen, yanked open the cellar door, tumbled down the steps, raced to the hot water valve, and shut it off with fiendish frenzy.

By the time he got upstairs, the towels and chair, the varnished oak floor, the fresh-painted walls, all were dripping and soggy; the leaves of the plants in the windowsill had collapsed like parachutes. And the hot water pipe from the cellar was one single unit no more, but had burst into its two original independent identities, producing a ceaseless flow of all kinds of hot water.

"Rolly," she said, "and his glue."

"I'll mop it up."

"Maybe I won't take a bath." She stood lobsterlike in her skin, gazing sadly around the wrecked room and at the deflated plants; Patches and Alice peered excitedly in from the kitchen.

"You'll have a bath," declared Daniel, striding out of the bathroom and going for his twenty-four volume *Home Handyman Encyclopedia.*

In the middle of the night, he switched on the bedroom light; he was still in his work pants, dirty, tired, triumphant. "You can take your bath now."

She opened one sleepy eye. "Would it be all right if I waited until morning?"

She shut her eye; there was no question of getting her up. He walked to the bathroom, and took off his clothes; a bath would be had tonight, no matter by whom. He filled the tub with hot water, and sank into the princely brew; the luxurious sensation she'd anticipated was now his; in spite of Angus Deake, they had running hot water. Lying back in the steam, he contemplated the drooping plants. A noise from the shed indicated that Patches or Alice, or both, were hunting; Patches had become an outstanding hunter; Alice caught an occasional moth, mice being more than her nerves could handle; but after all, this was just the beginning; they both had many years ahead of them in the country. And he, stepping out of his wonderful tub, was experiencing the wonderful country night at a time he'd usually be unconscious. He toweled himself off, grateful to Angus Deake for leaving a piece of the job, so that he could enjoy the stillness of midnight.

He turned off the light, and stared out over the field. Two shapeless fluffy piles of paleness were stalking the moon. And as he watched his cats, a faint pitter-patter touched his ears—which he immediately recognized as your famous country rain on the roof—that marvelous tinny sound you never grow tired of, that peaceful tune that wakes you and lulls you to sleep, that delightful primitive music of the spheres. He put on his pajamas, and slipped into bed beside Sara.

In the morning, when he awakened, the living room was flooded.

He gathered his encyclopedia, sheets of tin, hammer, nails, caulking, ladder, and climbed up onto the roof. As he patched the numerous holes made by workmen's boots, he did not feel grateful to Wendell Bubash for leaving a piece of the job. It was raining in torrents, he was soaked to the skin, getting colder by the minute, and worst of all the ink was running in *volume r—roof repair.* However, by mid-afternoon, he had, incredibly enough, stopped the leaks. He stood in the living room, and looked up at the ceiling with an almost embarrassing feeling of satisfaction. As a home handyman, he was indubitably growing.

A horn sounded; she went out through the shed.

An official-looking truck pulled to a stop in the lane.

"Come to change your meter," said the man stepping out. "J. Nutting's the name."

"How do you do, Mr. Nutting?" she replied.

"I do fine," he grinned, revealing gums as bare as a baby's and two long pointy dog teeth. He edged over until he stood quite close to her. "Ain't a little girl like you afeared to live by yerself in the woods?"

She drew a step away and gave a careless laugh. "What's to be afeared of?"

He went on grinning, the length of his cuspids producing a feeling in her that there might be much to be afeared of. "'Scaped convicts fer instance."

"Surely there aren't any . . . 'scaped convicts way out here?"

"This is zactly where they would be. A 'scaped convict will hightail it into the woods and make his way durin the night until he comes to an old abandoned farmhouse out alone by itself . . . Course, I suppose you got a shotgun handy to yer piller and know how to use it."

"Why . . . no, I don't."

"I wouldn't stay here without a shotgun meself, but everyone's dif'rent I guess."

Patches dropped from an apple tree, and skulked by them.

"Plenty of game round here," remarked Nutting.

"That's not game, it's my cat."

"Still and all, you wanna keep him tied durin huntin season."

"Nobody would shoot a house cat. Would they?"

"You wouldn't think so, but folks who don't look afore they shoot might take that spotted feller fer a raccoon." On this note, the vampirish gentleman marched back to his truck and brought out the meter.

She followed him around the outside of the house, feeling the beginnings of panic. "Have you really heard of hunters shooting house cats?"

"Cats get shot, caught in traps . . . Them leg-hold traps will tear the leg right off a house cat." He took down the old meter and began to put up the new one. "Betimes they starves to death. Betimes they chews their own leg off. Three-legged cats is common round here."

She glanced toward the orchard, but Patches had disappeared. And, she realized with alarm, she hadn't seen Alice all morning.

Nutting looked up from changing the meter, and gazed into the bathroom window, sharpened cuspids hanging out over his lips. "You wanna get curtains on them there winders."

"Why?" she asked, perceiving instantly that if she looked up from her bath to see the face of J. Nutting, Hydroman, and his yellow drooling dog teeth, she would know why.

"Because there's some funny people around. Fer an instance, there's that old imbostyle with the red hair creeps about farms zactly like this one." J. Nutting, Hydro employee, turned toward the forest as if hearing at that very minute the footsteps of his red-headed imbecile. He snapped the new meter shut. "Guess I'll be leavin you now, all alone out here . . . Where's yer man?"

"Don't you hear him chopping wood?"

"Is that what 'tis? I thought 'twere someone creepin round with a hammer, testin."

"What would they be testing?"

"Entrance into the house," said Nutting. "You might wanna get yerself one of them burgal alarm systems."

"But no one would hear it."

"That's the trouble." He shook his head as if to say there was nothing to keep away red-headed imbostyles, 'scaped convicts, or fanged-tooth hydromen.

He strolled amicably toward the sound of Daniel's chopping. "You'll be needin that ax one of these fine nights."

Daniel laid down his ax, and stared at the hydroman.

"Fer splittin somethin more'n jes wood," said J. Nutting.

■ ■ ■

"Watkins, ma'am. World's finest collection of quality extracts, spices, and products fer the home since 1868."

"I don't need any, thank you." She attempted to close the door and get back to papering the bedroom wall.

"Mebbe you didn't hear me. I said I sell Watkins—lotions, potions, vittamins, makeup, you name it, we make it, we sell it, the best in the world since 1868, and I ask you would we have lasted this long if we wasn't no good?"

"I am rather busy."

"I see yer lookin at my sandals. I'd rather wear shoes, but I must wear sandals because of my condition. Severe metatarsal problems plus I cannot bend my big toe."

Had she really been staring at his sandals? Guiltily she averted her gaze to the upper portion of his person; unlike the other men she'd met in the country, who dressed casually and colorfully in work clothes, he was carefully, blandly attired in neat jacket and tie, with a very wide and relentless smile that made her think of her wallpaper paste. Perhaps in view of his metatarsals, she ought to buy something from him. "I guess I could use a cake of soap."

"We used to have soap. Good soap too. We never had a lot of soap, but what we had was good. A lot better'n the soap you get from a lot of other companies. I don't wanna put down other companies by name, but Watkins ain't no company. It's a family. We don't like that word 'company.' Y'know what I mean? Watkins don't have no board nor shareholders fer to answer to. Jes a family-owned corporation, and that's how we keep it quality. But we ain't got no soap." He eyed her meaningfully.

". . . Shampoo?"

"Let me open my van and see."

He opened both front and back of his van, discoursing on this item and that stacked inside it. "This here hair conditioner hasn't changed its price in ten years."

She shook her head in awe; if people were paying that much for hair conditioner ten years ago, they had to earmark a fair percentage of their salary to hair conditioner. "It was shampoo I wanted."

"What people forget is we're originally a spice company. That's why I carry my spices up front. To remind people. Because they forget." His tone carried a moral burden, his service in reminding people of a precept forgotten. "Ain't nahthin better'n Watkins. Fer an example, Watkins's pepper is granulated. Do you know of any other pepper that's granulated?"

"But isn't all . . ." She broke off; he was gazing about him, his eyes sweeping over the orchard, barn, field, and distant hills.

"This is what I like," he declared. "The beauties God has created, not the works that man has destroyed."

"I beg your pardon."

"You follow the Scriptures?"

"Not closely."

"Scripture is jes as pert'nent today as twas two thousand year ago."

Were Bibles, perhaps, included in the Watkins line?

". . . Fer it says in the Scriptures to love and respect yer feller man, and I as a Watkins represent'ive have ample opportunity to do so, irregardless of race, color, creed, or what have you."

"Shampoo?"

"I notice you ain't wearin no lipstick."

She had to agree.

"When we got married, I asked my wife not to wear lipstick. And she has not done so since. Except jes fer gardenin when nobody can't see her, then she wears a very incornspicuous Watkins lipstick to protect her from the sun because she has thyroid problems. Watkins lipstick is pure oil of glycerine, no oil of tar like other lipsticks I don't wanna name. I don't wanna talk against Avon, but Avon ladies themself have bought lipstick from me because Avon has more coal tar than any other brand. The list was published, and who was at the top? Avon. And tweren't alphabetical, mind you. Them there Avon ladies told me it made their mouth break out into pimples, blisters, scales, canker sores . . ."

"If you can't find the shampoo, I'll take lip gloss."

"We don't sell lip gloss. Fact is we don't sell lipstick anymore neither. But Watkins didn't warn me in time they wasn't goin on with their lipstick and I got stuck with five hundred dollars worth of the stuff. So now if somebody buys somethin, anythin, I don't care what 'tis, I'll give them ten percent off what they bought toward a lipstick. How's that sound to you? Here they are, five hundred lipsticks minus the ones I sold. Fashion shades fer the most part. Look at that, there 'tis right on the box: *Since 1868*. Stands to reason, don't it, if I sell you somethin and you don't like it, you ain't gonna buy from me in the future?"

"What if I just took some hand cream . . ."

"I been to every province in this country, and nahthin in this world has ever bored me. I done a lot too. I didn't alluys sell Watkins. I was a seafarin man until the wife asked me to give it up. Then I had a little business buildin boats and then I had to give that up. Then I went into paintin—pref'ably churches and steeples—till me eyes got too bad fer the heights. Only then did I turn to Watkins. No, I done a lot of things and I met a lot of people and I ain't never been bored . . ."

"I'll take this hand cream," she said desperately.

"Gotta check my price on that one. Sure you don't want this other hand cream too?"

"Yes, yes, give me both of them."

"I save a lot of time with this here shorthand system I invented. See, I write *h. cream*, instead of *hand cream* . . ." The time-saving shorthand system took fully ten minutes to do and explain, but finally she had her cream, and he had her money. Fondly, he jingled the coins in his leather bag. "I jes use a bag fer my money. No cash register." He laughed in advance of his joke. "I ain't Jewish."

■ ■ ■

She strolled through the farmer's market, filling her basket with turnips, beets, apples, squash, and potatoes. Making her way along the stalls, she came upon a familiar figure addressing himself to a head of cabbage.

"Hello, Mr. Bubash."

The furnace man looked up from his tête-à-tête, his countenance indicating perhaps a weekend-long binge. "How's yer furnace?"

"Good. At first the roof leaked . . ." She left off speaking; he wasn't listening, but staring at her as if her words were another language.

Slowly, she continued down the echoing hall, examining handmade quilts and cozies, embroidered pillowslips, stuffed toys, and heavy-knit socks; she felt akin to the country ladies seated behind the counters; this was her way of life now, her people. She bought some potted plants and homemade pickles and in among the jellies, she met their unlicensed electrician.

"How's the new wirin?"

"It seems okay . . ." she began, then saw he wasn't listening either, but looking at her as if she were another jam jar.

My people, she thought, walking on; she bought some freshly baked bread and fresh buttermilk, and bumped into Wendell Bubash conversing with a rutabaga.

She went outside, and piled their van with vegetables, plants, and preserves. An autumn wind ruffled her hair.

The clean crisp air and old houses drew her along; she found herself wandering the snug homey streets; the backdrop of forest made it feel like a frontier town. From the windows, jack-o'-lanterns grinned; paper skeletons swung from the doors, along with witches on broomsticks; while in New York, she thought, Halloween means poison candy and razor blades in apples.

A gentleman with carrot-orange hair and a bizarre pielike countenance was staring at her; a phrase clicked in her brain—she'd recognize him anywhere—the famous red-headed imbostyle. She hurried around the corner to Main Street. How quaint and simple everything was; everybody seemed to be dressed out of mail order catalogs. Another gentleman with carroty hair and squashed pie face passed her; which was the real red-headed imbostyle? The town appeared to be filled with red-headed imbostyles.

She checked the numbers on the doors. That must be the art store on the corner. A gentleman entered before her, a pot-bellied, handkerchief-hanging, cap-askew, torn-trousered rural gentleman, and she thought how wonderful it was that art had gotten to the grass roots; it gave her a warm feeling to think that such a man, whom you'd superficially judge as not having the slightest artistic inclination, was on his way into the art store. She followed him in.

It seemed to be not an art store, but an arts and crafts store, and the main craft was home brewing equipment. Shelf after shelf was stacked with malt, hops, vats, tins of fruit extract, tubing, beakers, ferments, and concentrates.

On the sidewalk, her friendly unlicensed electrician was bending over and picking up half his glasses.

"Howdy."

"Howdy."

A horn honked, and Daniel pulled up alongside her in their van. They drove home through the darkening countryside.

Passing the bridge that led to Angus Deake's cottage, she saw that his light was lit, and pictured him inside, surrounded by his plunder. The van turned the corner, and they entered the tiny village which nestled at the foothills of New Jerusalem.

The door to the post office swung open. In the lampglow, the village postmaster called to them.

They pulled up, and climbed the post office steps.

"I got some bad news fer you," said the old man. "Yer house burnt."

■ ■ ■

The field swarmed with ancient figures, like a canvas by Brueghel; she saw the embers still red in the pit and Daniel standing alone; she saw the fantastic bloody sunset against the ridges, reflecting back on the crowded smoky field, bathing the primeval figures in a ruby glow, and it was only a painting, and she caught her breath at the beauty.

"Tomorrow's another day," said a woman taking her arm.

Sara faced the woman, and the beautiful painting became platitude, then reality. "Do you think," she asked softly, "that my cats got away?"

A spectral villager, a man made stiff and crippled by some disease, stood before her in the drifting smoke, his pained figure like that of the gatekeeper to a secret realm. "I'm sorry," he said.

The woman's assured voice interrupted. "You must put them out of yer mind. It says so right in the Scriptures. Animals don't have no souls."

Sara backed away and found Daniel beside her, his arm on her shoulders. She shouted again for the cats. Daniel said gently, "They probably won't come back for a couple of days."

Another pair of arms came around her—an elderly woman dressed in gray with a white minister's collar; Sara burst into tears.

"They smothered, my dear," said the minister. "They didn't feel anything."

A tall slender man walked toward them, nodding casually. "You may as well stay at my place. I'm jes rattlin around by meself." He tilted his head back, gazing into the smoldering cavern. "Same thing happened to me t'other year."

Sara looked at the tall strange man; the other villagers were surrounding them in silence, circling, drawing closer, staring with morbid interest as at Martians; eyes shone dully in the red glow; mouths hung open.

"Let's go to his place," she whispered.

The tall man walked to his car; they climbed into their van and followed him up the lane. They drove through the rolling smoke, past the schoolhouse, church, and falling-down barns; through the veil of the ghost settlement's landmarks, she saw Patches and Alice in flames, struggling, running here and there through the house, trying to get out. The hills appeared, and Daniel steered slowly into the village; she replayed the scene: They leap through the flames. A wall collapses, a window breaks, they escape.

The car before them stopped at a large dark house.

They got out. From every dooryard and window, eyes stared at them.

"You ought to eat," said their host, leading them into a sloppy bachelor's kitchen piled with dirty dishes. In the light of the bare bulb hanging from the ceiling, she saw that the man's narrow face, which had looked young and hard in the dark, was creased with many lines.

She sat at a table pushed haphazardly against tattered curtains and a cold windowsill. "Do you think they could've gotten out?"

"I had a cat at my place when it burnt. Come back a week later. He must've run fer miles."

"How'd he get out?"

"He was on the shed." He laid a griddle across his stove and sliced some potatoes onto it, with large pieces of onion.

"Was he locked inside?"

"I say, he was on the shed."

She looked toward Daniel, and saw her calculations pass over his face. "They might've," he said in answer.

"Prob'ly still runnin." The man waved his chopping knife toward the cupboard. "Best set the table."

She got out some dishes.

"Was it insured?" asked the man.

She closed her eyes. All my paintings. My photographs. Daniel's collections.

"I say, was it insured?"

"We insured the house when we bought it. But we've been so busy. We never got around to insuring the contents."

The man reached in his pocket, brought out a wallet, and held out two ten-dollar bills. "You'll wanna buy a few things."

". . . We don't need it."

"Take it," he said sharply. "And anybody else comes round here with anythin, take it too. Don't matter what 'tis. If you don't want it, you can alluys throw it in the woods."

The man offered them cigarettes, and lit up his own. "I smoke three packs a day. Keeps me fit."

"How did your cat get out?" she asked.

"A cat'll get out," said the man. "Leave them dishes."

"We've got nothing else to do," said Daniel, and they cleaned up in silence, Daniel washing, she drying, and the man putting away. When the kitchen was cleared, he led them into the living room, where he turned on the television, not bothering to bring up the sound; he didn't bother to look at it either, just sat in a dilapidated stuffed chair, smoking another cigarette, in the manner of a man used to solitude.

They sat apart from each other in three old chairs, the only sound the hum of the flickering television.

The doorbell rang. Their host rose, and a young man and woman entered, carrying a box. "Here are some things fer you," she said to Sara. "I dunno if they'll fit."

"Thank you," said Sara, putting her hand to the box, but not opening it.

"There's some of my husband's clothes in it too. A few shirts and pants and a jacket."

The husband stood, embarrassed, looking at the floor. "If you need anythin else . . ."

"We got four kittens," said the woman, "if you want one."

"You can have all four," said the husband, still nodding at the floor, and backing toward the door.

The young couple left. The television hummed on, beaming its unwatched picture to the walls.

Through the window, they could see some little Halloweeners passing in the street. The man raised a large powerful hand and brought the edge of it down into the palm of the other with a loud crack. "That's what I got fer Halloweeners—a judo chop behind the ear."

"They're only children," said Sara.

"The hell they are. Is it children burn people's barns down?"

"You don't think . . . ?"

"I don't think nahthin," he said, pulling another cigarette from his shirt pocket. "But if they try somethin with me, I may kill five or six of them." He lit his cigarette with vengeance, and smoked it with ferocious elegance in his long fingers, plunging back into furious silence.

"Surely," she said, "no one would burn a house with animals in it."

There was no answer.

"I can't believe that anyone would do such a thing," she said.

Darkness took the street outside, and the living room was lit only by the soft light of the soundless television.

They went into silence again, letting the night go by, the man smoking one cigarette after another. Finally he got to his feet, and led them up the rickety stairs to the second floor of his big empty house. He opened the door to a bedroom, bare except for an old iron bed, then closed the door and went back down the stairs.

They undressed in the strange bedroom; the images gathered around her again, and she found herself rocking back and forth on the bed, tears flowing down her cheeks. Alice's button-nosed face and green eyes rose before her; and Patches in his coat of many colors, his chocolate mouth. Through her tears she gazed out the window toward the two-lane road that ran through the village. A car passed, trailing taillights into the abyss. A street lamp, hidden by the trees, cast a patch of light on the pavement.

Daniel left her and went downstairs, then came back in, softly. "He's sitting in the living room with his hat on, smoking. In the dark."

She nodded. "Waiting for Halloweeners."

■ ■ ■

She turned restlessly on the bed, falling into thin films of forgetfulness, only to emerge once more in the fire. It felt like a nightmare she couldn't wake up from, and she went down again into feverish whirling images of faces and forest, each image shifting and quickly dissolving, a frenzied tumult of half dreams. She passed into sleep and a dream of fire engines coming from four directions, all converging on Christopher Street; hoses were pulled out, and ladders; men in shiny black slickers jumped off the fire trucks with axes. Sitting in the middle of the street, looking calmly around, were Patches and Alice.

2

The three women sat in a huddle around their woodstove, daughter, mother, and ancient crone.

"We understand," he said, "you might have some information for us."

"About the cats," prompted Sara.

The woman in the middle spoke. "We only got there at the last. But we heard a howlin. Everybody heard it." She turned to her daughter.

"A terrible howlin."

"Did it come from the woods?" he asked.

"It give us the creeps," said the younger woman. The old crone rocked back and forth, unspeaking; she'd clearly not been anywhere but her kitchen for many years.

"Eldon was the first to get there," went on the middle woman. "Seen a big cat," he said, "throwin hisself at the winder again and again . . ."

Sara let out a sort of a moan.

The old woman spoke, for the first time, in a cracked ancient voice. "Listen to me, girl. Eldon never seen no cat. You hear? Eldon never seen no cat."

■ ■ ■

"Why the hell didn't Eldon, whoever he is, throw a rock at the window?"

He and Sara stood overlooking the foundation, and Pike stood with them, lighting a cigarette with vengeance. "Because he's a cruel son of a bitch."

The foundation still smoked, but less than last night; twisted pieces of their possessions could now be discerned, bits of silver and glass melted together into shapes of teardrops. Pike pointed to a great heap of white ash which had settled over one half of the cellar. "What was all that?"

"Books," said Daniel. "Drawings . . . photographs . . ."

"Listen!" said Sara.

". . . What was it?"

"I thought it sounded like a cat."

They listened. A crow called, far away.

"They won't be back fer a week," said Pike, "same as my cat. But I'll help you look."

They spread out into the woods, Daniel making for the avenue of little spruce where the cats often played.

He heard Sara calling, "Patches . . . Alice . . ."

He walked on, and her voice grew further away, echoing across the lonely morning. Out through the trees, out over the valley, through the emptiness, he heard her calling.

■ ■ ■

"They'll survive," said Pike, cutting potatoes. "Two cats together like that can alluys hunt in a team."

They spent much of their time in Pike's kitchen, the rest of the huge haunted house being unheated and for the most part unfurnished; hollow rooms rambled off dingy hallways, and weapons and boards stood in shadowy corners.

"You'd be surprised how animals will hunt in a team. One year I was stayin back in the woods in an old porc'pine den so small you had to stick yer arm out the door to flip a pancake, and I seen two crows hunt together. They was huntin rabbit." He hunched up his shoulders and wrinkled his face in what Daniel supposed was a crow imitation. "The one crow'd drop stones down out of the sky fer to flush out a rabbit, and then t'other crow'd catch him." As he spoke, he hurled chunks of potatoes onto the griddle, like stones, eyeing his invisible quarry across the stove, and then he became the second crow, pouncing with spatula. "Funny thing about a fire where you lose all you own," he said, serving potatoes. "Even after all these years, I find meself reachin out fer things that ain't there."

Daniel toyed with the food on his plate. "Where was that por-cupine den you stayed in?"

■ ■ ■

Pike opened the door of the shack. "That's all there is to her. I wouldn't advise nobody but a woodchuck to stay here, but if you want her she's yours."

It was the most inhospitable-looking place Daniel'd ever seen, with cobwebbed pots on the wall, stacks of broken dishes, a rusted stove, and buckled floorboards. But he was too numb to care, and he saw she felt the same; a porcupine den was enough. It was a place they could be by themselves, and it was near the farm in case Patches and Alice were still alive and would return.

"I don't suppose it's too bad," said Pike. "Better'n sleepin in a ditch."

■ ■ ■

There were two chairs in the shack; the reverend sat on one and the oldest ambulatory citizen of the village sat on the other.

"More tea?" asked Daniel.

"No thank you," said the reverend.

"I do believe," said old Burpee, "I stayed in this camp meself. Twas back a good many year now . . ." He'd been talking for close to an hour, fruitlessly embarking on numerous lengthy and compli-cated stories which had long ago lost their meaning, if they'd ever had any to begin with. "Trappin . . . used to be a lot of good trappin out here in Jerusalem. You ask Pike, he'll loan you some traps." The old man's watery eyes twinkled; he turned to Sara. "Li-able to ketch yerself a bear. Make an awful nice rug. And bear grease too."

The minister spoke. "Burpee, I think it's time for us . . ."

"I do believe we hung some deer back here. Many's the deer we hung right in this dooryard. You'll prob'ly find a skull back of the house. Make a lovely ashtray."

"I'm glad," said the minister, as if summing up their rambling visit, "you're managing all right."

"Why shouldn't they be?" asked old Burpee, who appeared to be under the impression Daniel and Sara had lived in the shack for years and he and the minister had just come out for a cup of hot tea. "Did I ever tell you about me wristwatches?"

"I suspect," suggested the minister, "that Daniel and Sara are busy."

"I daresay they'll be busy. Busy? Sports! Many's the American sport stayed out here. I'd take them out, lead them up hill and dale. Used to take a bath in a great big barrel." He gazed out the window. "Ain't that it over there? All busted up. 'Tis a wonder this place is still standin. Wonder them snowmobilers ain't shot her all full of holes." He spat in the stove, and lapsed into a contemplative silence that seemed so close to prayer the minister dared not disturb him.

So they sat in the shack like four shadows, and Daniel felt the grotesqueness of the situation, but he couldn't cope; nor did he care; what if he wasn't the perfect host? or any of the other things he'd tried being, like the happy farmer relaxing by his stove; he supposed when it came down to it, he was a refugee; and no one seemed to expect him to say anything anyway, no more than they expected from each other. He felt physically adrift, as if he were floating up at the ceiling looking down at himself. It was nice of old Burpee and the minister to come, but he himself didn't have to express it; he was adrift and cold as Burpee's warmed-over stories.

The minister stood, preparing to go.

Burpee attempted to get up, sank back down, and resumed his reminiscences. "Did you ever hear tell of a feller called old Mushrat Bobkins?" He paused, as Mushrat's story drifted out of his eyes, and he didn't elaborate on old Bobkins, only stared at the table in his strange timeless dream that matched Daniel's own feeling; there was nothing to mark time with anymore, not even Mushrat Bobkins.

"We really must be going." The minister took the old man by his elbow. He struggled out of the chair and hobbled across the room. "I helped build this camp. Still standin. She'll be here after I'm gone. After we're all gone."

He stepped out into the sunlight. "Porc'pine goin. You'll have to shoot that feller."

Daniel looked to the woods where the porcupine was rustling.

"All right, reverend," said Burpee, "let's you and I move on out of here." He hobbled over to his vehicle, an ancient Ford in mint condition. The minister drew something out of her pocket and handed it to Daniel as if it were an afterthought; then she got into the car with Burpee.

The antique puttered away through the woods.

Daniel opened the envelope, and handed its contents to Sara—a long list of names and what looked like around three hundred dollars in bills and change.

■ ■ ■

He crouched in front of the box-stove, blowing at the embers to help them catch, but it wasn't much of a stove; or maybe the problem lay with the wood, which was green and wet; or maybe with him; the fire smoldered sulkily, radiating just enough heat to make you want more. He shut the stove door, and straightened up; the tiny room held cot, table, nails on which to hang clothes, and for decoration and inspiration some former inhabitant had posted a sign which said OUR MOTTO: NEITHER A SCROOGE NOR A PATSY BE.

He went to the table, where Sara was trimming the wick on the kerosene lantern; she got it straight, lit it, and put on the glass chimney; a pale yellow radiance spread over the table, making the rest of the cabin fall more deeply into darkness.

He sat down in the kerosene glow and felt his aloneness with her. It seemed they'd never been alone until this cabin; least of all at the farm, where there'd been so much to do, so many material plans and demands, so much to fantasize over; now, stripped of everything, the worst having happened, he felt nakedly confronted by her personality.

All the paraphernalia of her glamour had gone up in smoke, along with her work and her worries; he'd expected her to fall apart at the seams, but she'd voiced no regrets, no complaints; she trimmed the wick and did what had to be done and was, he sensed, as intensely aware of him as he of her.

In the shadows, a mouse tightrope-walked across the clothesline behind the stove. Mice rattled things in the walls at night and stockpiled his and Sara's boots with beans. He watched the flame dance on Sara's face, and recalled how theatrically she used to arrange her apartment as a backdrop for her personal glitter; the kerosene's flickering diffusion worked its own will on her features, capturing the slow procession of her stillness.

The mouse leapt from the clothesline onto the cupboard; the fire smoldered and hissed. Outside, the silence extended forever. He'd thought the farm lonely, but this camp was the last outpost of loneliness.

OUR MOTTO, he read: NEITHER A SCROOGE NOR A PATSY BE. It was his only reading matter. He read it a hundred times in a day, until he was ready to think the philosophy as good as any.

■ ■ ■

In the darkness he circled the cabin, its beam the one light in the forest; round and round he trudged, like an animal on a treadmill.

Winter had come with sudden cruelty; the night wind swept through the trees and bit his skin. Through the window of the shack, he saw Sara bending over the cupboard, washing the supper dishes in a pan. A porcupine rustled nearby in the bushes.

There's got to be something else up ahead for us, he thought, something other than this jinxed ghost settlement at the end of nowhere.

As far as he could see, it was blackness unalleviated, just one big black empty hole up to Alaska and on to the North Pole. Now he appreciated how Sara had felt when they first thought of moving to such a remote location; it was finally coming home to him; the wilderness was oppressive and hostile.

He glanced into the dimly lit cabin; Sara's figure bent over the panful of dishes was that of an old woman. This kind of life aged a woman faster than anything.

He continued circling the cabin, keeping within range of its light, unwilling to strike out into darkness; but finally he picked up his waterbucket and flashlight, and trudged the winding path through the woods to the stream, which slithered cold in the moonlight. He dipped in, filled his bucket, and started back up the trail, with icy water splashing over the sides of the pail onto his trousers and into his boots. Through the treetops, a cold gust of wind shuddered. Everything was alien, everything difficult. What we need is a nice warm hotel room and a deep hot bathtub.

He kicked open the door of the shack, and entered with his bucket. "We've got to get out of here."

She was seated at the table in the glow of the lantern. "We'll go to a hotel," he said, "where it's civilized, human, and warm."

She looked up. "I don't want to leave here."

He stared at her pale face. "But it's horrible. It's the worst place I could think of."

"We ought to be able to handle it."

"What in God's name do you mean?"

"A hotel's an escape. It's temporary. But if you stay in a place"— she gestured around the dim room—"after a while, you can get on with life."

"We'll get on with life somewhere else. With running water. We could get an apartment somewhere."

"We didn't come this far to get an apartment in a small town."

"We didn't come here expecting to lose everything either. Doesn't that change the situation?"

She lowered her eyes, and stared into the lantern's flame in her quiet denuded way, and it seemed to him her entire past had dissolved, her whole familiar feminine image. He didn't know what to say or to do.

■ ■ ■

He opened his eyes, and gasped with cold.

Steam rose up from his nostrils, billowed above the bed, and floated.

He lifted the burden of blankets, so heavy it was like sleeping under another person, and moved his aching limbs off the sagging back-breaking cot; he stepped into his boots—he was already wearing socks, as well as long-johns and hooded sweat shirt—and tried to walk; but his boots, wet with ice from the night before, were frozen to the floor.

He pried them up, and hobbled to the stove, which had burned out hours before. The thermometer on the wall by the cupboard said seven degrees Fahrenheit; the wall was white with frost; and in the water bucket, a dead mouse hung suspended in ice, drowned and frozen. "This is it," he said.

Her head came out of the blankets. Steam floated up from her mouth, her nostrils having apparently frozen shut in the cold.

He ran his fingernails down the wall, scraping off five tracks of frost, and held his hand up in front of her like a trump card. He gestured beneath her pinched nose, and the frost from his fingers fell on the blankets. "Do we need this?" he asked.

"We'd better get the fire going."

"We're leaving. This morning."

"I don't want to."

"There's a mouse in the water bucket. Frozen solid," he said, delivering the coup de grâce. With her sensitivity to animals, her mania for animals of any kind, the sight of that mouse would do it. She climbed out of bed chugging gusts of steam, looked into the bucket, and walked on by.

She's tougher than she used to be.

"We're not staying here," he repeated.

"The place will be warm in an hour." She gathered wood from the cupboard, and laid it in the stove.

Does she want to freeze to death? He had the awful feeling, watching her bent over the wood, that he wasn't arguing with the Sara he knew, but with a blind, stubborn, immovable thing he'd never suspected existed.

"Sara, be reasonable. We can't spend the winter here. It'll take all our energy just to survive. Do you call that getting on with life?"

She snorted in reply, a strange crude sound. She picked up the kerosene can, poured a dribble of oil into the stove, and struck a match. The papers inside caught with a roar.

"Sara," he said gently, "there's no reason for us to live in a porcupine den. It's masochism."

"It's where we happen to be."

"We're going," he said firmly. "We're going to take the insurance money and travel."

"No we're not."

"Do you actually like it here?"

"That has nothing to do with it."

He gazed at the hated frost-lined room. OUR MOTTO: NEITHER A SCROOGE NOR A PATSY BE. "Only a scrooge *and* a patsy would stay in a place like this."

His eyes met hers across the room; she was wearing her thick-lensed wire-rimmed glasses and her sweat shirt hood was tied tight about her face; she looked like a white bespectacled rabbit in long-johns. "Pack our things," he said. "I'm going out to warm up the truck."

He opened the door; a blinding blast of coldness engulfed him. Hurriedly he stepped out and shut the cabin door behind him. The outside thermometer said thirty below.

He climbed into the van, and turned the key.

There was no response from the motor.

This van, he realized with the sinking sensation of a man at the end of a very frayed rope, has never experienced thirty below. It wasn't built for experiencing thirty below.

He gazed out over the frozen treetops and felt the icy hand freezing him in, a mouse in a bucket.

In the silence, a faint sound came to him . . . the sputtering of a motor . . . drawing closer.

He looked down the long logging road, and saw a vehicle chugging toward him.

Help was at hand. The heavens want us to make it to town today and have a hot bath.

The old truck pulled up alongside him, ground to a stop, and two strange figures stepped out, emerging from the dark ages, or further back in time, from a cave where they'd been gnawing on bones; their teeth were worn down to stumps. They wore ragged flannel shirts unbuttoned to the killing north wind, and peaked caps over heads which grew without indentation from gargantuan necks. They weren't as tall as modern man, nor did they walk erect, but swayed forward, guffawing.

"Havin trouble?"

"My van won't start."

The younger one spat. "Build a fire underneath her. That'll warm her up in a hurry." His cap was ripped at the back, giving it the shape of a court jester's hat, and a huge dagger hanging at his waist intensified the feudal flavor; since his beer belly made it impossible for him to wear a belt, he'd fastened the dagger's sheath to his pants with a giant horse blanket pin; his boot laces hung open, with boot tongues falling over; and thus attired, he was ready, casually, for thirty below zero.

"Now you jes wait a second," said the elder, a darkly grizzled individual, with caved-in lips and sunken eyes, one eye a good deal brighter than the other. "Sun'll be beatin down by afternoon and you can start her up then. What's yer hurry? Anywhere you gotta go can wait." Daniel could see that a stalled automobile was not an intense experience for either of them.

Sara came to the door.

"Mornin," said the old man politely. "How you makin out here?"

"It's cold."

"I got a little kerosene burner that'll keep you warm. It'll cost you twenty-five dollar. Or you can jes have her."

It seemed to Daniel a sound proposition. "Want to come in?" he asked the two gentlemen, who lumbered into the shack, removing their caps as if they were visiting not a porcupine den, but a neighbor's house.

"You got her fixed up nice," said the old man.

Daniel gazed around him; the dishpan set on the counter, the mouse floated in the bucket, and it was exactly the way it had always been.

"Looks quite comfor'ble," agreed the younger.

Daniel felt the deck of cards being slowly shuffled and a new hand being dealt.

"Ought to get a fire goin in that there stove," remarked the old man. Daniel saw that Sara's kerosene fire had been a flash in the pan, a quick roar and nothing. The old man leaned over, and the fire burned briskly. Daniel blinked; was it some kind of magic trick? The old man seemed to have just gestured, and the flames responded.

The younger man rolled a cigarette. "Grampie Amos used to live here."

"Aye," said the older. "Father spent fifteen winters in this camp."

Everybody seems to have lived here, thought Daniel, and he felt something circling around him, enclosing him, settling along with the wreaths of smoke from the men's ragged cigarettes.

". . . We'll put an elbow in that there stovepipe, and a damper over there, set the oil burner back of yer table . . ." The old man described the logistics of making the place warm, and then the two visitors got up to go. "Nor don't you worry about yer truck. Soon as the sun gets high, she'll start."

"And if she don't," said the younger, "we can alluys set a fire under the son of a whore."

"I wanted to thank you for the stove . . ."

"Down, Festus," said the woman to a mongrel who was barking berserkly and leaping at Sara's throat.

"We live nearby," explained Sara, dodging the dog. "Your husband gave us an oil stove . . ."

The woman gazed at her as if wondering why the explanations, when all was already known—not only exactly where Sara lived, but about the house burning down, the cats, the furniture she'd brought up, and how many letters a week she got from New York. The woman stood unsmiling in her doorway, wearing a thin flowered housedress suitable for summer, her short arms and legs bare to the freezing wind. "Well, are you comin in?"

Sara followed her through a rough dirt-floored shed into a very warm and clean kitchen. The dog, subdued, accompanied them, sticking close to the woman, who looked in need of protection, with her naked pink flesh, flimsy unseasonable dress, and childlike plumpness. Her gray hair was butchered off short, she'd probably never worn makeup, and yet there was something disturbingly, femininely exposed about her; her expression, as well as her plump pink skin, was curiously defenseless.

Sara sat in the old kitchen chair the woman offered her; the other chairs had lost their backs. Light streamed into the room from three big windows, whose distorted glass produced a sun-spattered effect on the yellow flowered paper, dark wainscoting, linoleum floor, and especially on the woodstove, a gleaming altar of rose-colored porcelain trimmed with highly polished nickel and a black iron surface which shone like a mirror; the oven was blasting forth fresh bread and buns.

"Cup of tea?"

"If you're having one."

The woman set a polished aluminum teapot on top of the stove, and sighed. "Feels like Sunday, don't it?"

". . . I guess it does."

"Days are short."

"Yes, they are."

"Yesterday was awful short, wasn't it?"

"Awfully."

The woman continued where she'd left off, removing the loaves and buns from their pans, pans so fire-blackened and brittle with use that holes were worn through their bottoms. She painted the newly baked loaves with melted shortening and their fragrance filled the bright kitchen.

"Snowstorm tonight or tomorrow likely. You can tell by the way the bread rose. Should snow five or six inches." She poured the tea, and buttered a couple of hot buns as crisp as croissants. "I'll put some in a bag fer you to take home. Ain't no one here to eat them. Jes me and Murvyle and Hilton." She tossed a bun to the dog who lay by the stove. "And Festus."

Festus swallowed the bun whole and yawned.

"He don't get one bit of pleasure from it."

"Surely he must."

"Betimes I break them into pieces fer him, but do you think he cares?" She sighed, and her sigh expressed her utter aloneness. Her men were no doubt out working. The rest of the neighborhood was uninhabited wilderness.

"How long have you lived here?" asked Sara.

The woman looked surprised. "All me life."

"Always all alone?"

For the first time she smiled. "Twas all of us in here at one time. The whole settlement was farms and fields."

They both gazed through the blistered windows at the endless stretches of woods.

"About how many people?" asked Sara.

"Mebbe two or three hundred."

It seemed unbelievable that such a large community had shrunk down to one family and a dog. "But why did everybody leave?"

"One follered t'other."

Sara noticed that the woman often glanced toward the windows, as if she were wondering where everyone had gone.

There was a long sigh-filled silence.

The woman spoke: "How do yous like it back at the camp?"

"The most difficult thing's not having water."

"Yes, you gotta go all the way down to the stream. I go right over the hill there." She gestured vaguely past the trees, rose to her feet, banged out of the kitchen, and left Sara alone; a moment later, she returned with a battered enamel dishpan, which she set on the stove; then she banged out again, and returned with a bucket of water, which she poured into the pan, adding some soap flakes. The whole production had a remarkable symmetry, like a painting with very few elements, each perfectly placed, and the economy of the woman's scene suddenly seemed extraordinary; she had so few things—a fire to tend and water to haul, plus a couple of sticks of furniture, stove, and dishpan—all old, well used, and gleaming.

The woman returned to her backless chair and resumed her vigilant watch out the windows, waiting for the dishwater to heat. Once Sara met her eyes, and they both turned away, Sara shaken as if her pain had been touched and was pulsing again; the flames of Halloween eve had blazed as clearly as words in the mute naked sympathy of the lonely woman's gaze.

The woman heaved to her feet. "Don't you stop eatin. I'm jes gonna make some pies." She uncovered a giant washtub of thinly sliced apples, sighing at the immensity of it. "Ain't no good me makin only one or two."

"I guess not," said Sara, unsure why one or two pies wouldn't be any good, why it had to be at least a dozen.

Expertly, the woman rolled out the dough, gazing through the bubble-glass windows.

"There's Dad, comin up the road."

Sara turned and looked out; all she could see was forest and hills. After ten minutes, she asked, "Isn't he coming?"

"He died in the homes."

"But I thought you said . . ." Sara pointed to the road.

"He alluys comes when I'm rollin out pies." She offered her rolling pin for inspection; it was old, like everything else in the place, rough-hewn from one piece of pale golden wood. "He made this fer me."

"So when you use it you think of him."

"Tain't so much me," she said apologetically. "It's Dad."

"You mean you saw him as clearly as you see me?"
"He alluys was an awful hand fer my pies."

■ ■ ■

She stirred the beans, tasted them, added more salt, then lowered the blackened shortening can back into the box-stove's fire; in
the second circle of the stove hung a shortening can filled with rice.
Eyeing the hobolike arrangement, she thought of her Le Creuset
pans in New York, and her life in New York . . . She sensed he
was coming before she looked out the window. He walked slowly
across the clearing, came round the cabin, and stomped wearily in,
covered with sawdust and smelling of pitch pine.
"I hired on with Murvyle, Hilton, and Anson, cutting pulp."
"You know how to cut pulp?"
"I work the horses."
"You know how to work horses?"
"I was wandering around and heard the chainsaws and I walked
over and they hired me."
"But is it safe? Those aren't ordinary horses. They're like ele-
phants."
"Have you seen an old bottle around here somewhere called
horse liniment?"
"Does the horse need liniment?"
"I do." He limped to the cupboard, and came out with an ancient
prescription written for a turn-of-the-century animal named *Fred
Biddle's Horse.*
An overpowering odor flooded the room as he took out the cork
—an eye-burning herbal mix. She opened the door to let out the
fumes. "Does it pay well?"
"No." He flopped down on the cot, heaving a groan. "But I will
soon have a thirty-inch neck and be able to enter the Mr. Olympia
contest."

■ ■ ■

They backed up, revved the engine, and their tires raced in
place. They got out and shoveled, climbed back in, and tried again,
but the snow was still too deep.
Across the frosty morning, she heard the jingling of bells; round-

ing the bend up ahead, there appeared a mythical creature, a
Homeric god-horse of old, topped with a high, shiny, gondola-
shaped bridle, with a mad tricolor dog bounding behind him. Murvyle's sawed-off form followed; the old man had a lurching uneven
gait, and his brown leathery skin seemed grained with decades of
woodsmoke and grit. Hilton brought up the rear, shirt open to the
storm, cap ripped, fly unzipped.

The chestnut horse high-stepped toward them, tossing his mane
and snorting.

"Thought I heard wheels whirrin," remarked Murvyle laconically.

Hilton steered the horse around, and hooked his traces to the
van. They're not, she thought, going to make that horse pull a
truck; she felt she ought to step out in the snow and protest; as a
lifetime member of the International Humane Society, National
Wildlife Federation, Audubon Society, Sierra Club, Fund for Animals, and Cat Rescue League, she couldn't allow a fragile living
creature to haul half a ton of inert iron.

The animal's muscles rippled, tensed, and quieted; he's going to
kill himself, she thought, as Daniel turned on the motor, Murvyle
yelled "Gee-yup," the horse lifted his tail, gave a thunderous fart,
and calmly twitched the van forward out of the snow. The dog
barked and the horse started to run, pulling the truck through the
snow as if it were no more than a log.

He slowed down when they reached the road, and they rolled
easily along behind him up to Murvyle's house; the horse stopped
in the barnyard, and casually turned his head around and eyed her.

They stepped down from the van; Daniel disconnected the
traces, while she patted the steaming animal, stroking his face; he
drew back his great lips and sneered.

"Are you comin in?" called a voice from the doorway.

She walked to the house, brushed her boots off with the broom
Phoebe handed her, and followed her into the kitchen.

"We had another horse once looked like that one," said Phoebe.
"Had his tail bobbed short, and when that tail stuck straight out,
the horse was pullin with all he had." She pointed to a faded snapshot on the wall, of a gray blur, presumably the look-alike horse.
"Ain't too often you get a pitcher like that of a horse when he's
movin."

Boots thumped on the shed, and the three men entered. They

gathered round the table, pulling up backless chairs. Hilton leered affectionately at the dog. "Wonder what he'd do if I hit him in the head with a piece of wood."

■ ■ ■

"You can't outrun a bear." Pike viciously lit a match to his cigarette. "You can't outclimb a bear." He puffed ferociously. "Way I cal'ate it, the only thing you can do if a bear attacks is set yer shirt afire."

She glanced out the cabin window at the ice-covered trees which caught the bright rays of the sun in enormous refracted stars; here gold, there red, now blue, the big crosses hung from the branches, and then the light moved, or your eye, and the illusion passed; she painted quickly, trying to catch each colored ornament before it dissolved.

"A bear is afeared of fire. 'Bout the only thing he is afeared of. Jes t'other day an old mother bear attacked me and I had to set me shirt afire."

"I wonder why she attacked you," said Daniel.

"I was playin with her cubs. I never could resist a bear cub. So when I seen these two little cubs . . ."

She frowned at her canvas; all those crosses on the trees tended to make the painting look like a Christmas card.

"Used to keep a cub on my shed. Fed him bread and molasses. One time I fed him ice cream." Pike's tale wound on behind her; he sat on the cot opposite Daniel, the two of them ignoring her struggle with the sun on the trees; you learned to ignore a lot when you lived in one room. ". . . I held out the cone and he reached fer it. Then I pulled it back jes to tease him. When I held it out the second time, he drove the goddamn ice cream right in me face."

It was actually worse than a Christmas card. It looked like one of those inspirational books they sold in town at the Gift & Bible Shop.

"Whack! Whack! I karate-chopped him right in the head. He karate-chopped me back. Whack! Whack!" Pike's demonstration had lifted him up from the cot and was drawing him gradually closer to her table and canvas. She felt his eyes on her painting. "Funny thing about bears, ain't it?"

"What happened to the cub?" asked Daniel.

"Some circus man come around, offered me a thousand dollar fer that cub. But I didn't sell him. No sir. A thousand dollar, do you believe that?"

She wasn't sure if she did.

His voice was hovering steadily around her chair now. "The old mother bear she come back. Dug a hole right under the shed. Crept in, and off they both went."

He fell silent, while she tried to make the crosses less corny.

"Funny thing about paintin," he offered slowly. "I had a job paintin once. Me and another feller. Down in the basement of a big store. Partitions, we painted partitions."

He and Daniel discussed partitions, basements, and stores, and she turned her efforts to the snow that thickly carpeted the ground.

". . . I never told this to nobody before. I guess I figgered they'd laugh at me. Wasn't none of their business anyways. I say, twasn't none of their business. Not about the partitions. 'Bout the pitcher. We done a pitcher. A great big whore of a pitcher of Mussolini. Filled a whole partition with him. You would've thought he was standin in front of you, that's how real twas. Thing was so real it would've scared you. Real? We even pasted buttons onto his jacket. We done it at night so nobody knowed. Me and t'other feller." His voice rose in fury. "And then some goddamn son of a bitch stole him from us."

He was hard at her elbow. "That sky ain't green enough."

"Where do you think it needs more green?"

A long nicotine-stained finger appeared before her eyes; he pointed to the middle of the sky.

She touched some green to the edge of the cloud.

The finger appeared again, further down.

"Do you want the brush?" she asked.

He drew back as if shot. "I don't know nahthin about paintin."

"It's no good anyway," she said. "If you want to try and fix it, you can."

"I'd only wreck it."

"Why don't we all work on it?" suggested Daniel.

"You two go ahead," said Pike. "I gotta go home."

"I think I'll make supper," she said, laying her brush on the palette, and getting up.

Daniel drifted over. "Where does it need more green?"

There was a short hesitation over which of the men would take the brush, until Pike, grudgingly, ended up at the helm. "I know I'll wreck it."

She filled the kettle with water, surreptitiously watching as Pike scowled and slapped brush to canvas.

He stood back. "I've ruined it now."

Viciously he stepped forward and attacked again with the brush.

Daniel silently joined her at the stove, stirred the embers, and added a log. They found themselves tiptoeing about their tasks.

"Bad," muttered Pike, "that's bad." He was seated in her chair, slashing away at the landscape; he lit a cigarette, yanked it forth from his lips, and renewed his assault with blind hatred, glaring from canvas to window and back.

She and Daniel made supper. They ate it alone on the cot. Then they lit the kerosene lantern for the evening, and cleaned up.

At length, Pike flung down his brush. She and Daniel edged over to look.

In the dim glow of the kerosene lamp, the sentimental landscape she'd trapped herself into was now almost totally green. In the foreground, where her Christmas lights had mawkishly hung from the trees, tiny stick figures dangled, a mass execution by hanging. It would make, she thought, a nice Christmas card for the Ku Klux Klan. "Still," said Pike, "it needs a little more green."

■ ■ ■

"I trimmed the tree," said Phoebe.

"May I see?"

Rather ceremoniously, they crossed the threshold from kitchen to curtain-shrouded living room, where Sara had never been. From the center of the murky ceiling hung a single bare bulb, unlit; on the original deco couch were souvenir pillows brought back by traveling relatives from as far away as Perry's Nut House in Maine. A framed reproduction dominated the wall, entitled *The Return of the Dog*. A small television sat on top of a large television. And in the furthest darkest corner of the room towered the great gloomy tree, decorated with one short garland and five strands of tinsel.

"Aren't there any lights?"

In answer, Phoebe pulled the overhead string, letting the bare bulb illuminate the whole lugubrious scene.

"It's big," said Sara.

"It's got a nest into it."

They crouched on their hands and knees and searched for the bird's nest which lurked deep within the lower branches, a tiny cup-shaped thing which surely raised the tree well above the ordinary gaudy light-and-ball-spangled breed.

They got to their feet, and Phoebe pursed her lips as if deciding on something big. Then, having brought Sara this far into the house, she let all caution fly to the wind, and opened the door to an even more recondite room, a narrow chamber whose temperature was just above freezing and whose contents consisted solely of boxes.

"This is what Charlene give me last Christmas." She lifted one of the lids. Inside was a brand-new, unused, pop-up toaster.

". . . From Anson and them two Christmases ago." An electric teakettle.

"Bertha's kids give me this on my birthday . . ." An electric frypan.

One by one, they went through the boxes, everything sparkling new and unused, in sum representing most of the tools required for bringing Phoebe into the Twentieth Century.

Without comment, they closed the Freezer of the Present behind them, and made their way through the dark gloom of the Thirties back into the bright ageless warmth of the wood-fired kitchen. Phoebe sank down onto her hard backless chair with a sigh of relief. "Nice to have them there anyways."

■ ■ ■

She gazed at the path piled under with three and a half feet of snow.

She gazed at the toboggan heavy with groceries and laundry.

She thought of her snowshoes, which were in the cabin at the other end of the impassable road.

"What are we going to do?"

He lifted one end of the toboggan, climbed over the drift, and she followed, sinking to her waist in soft snow. She tried to lift her leg, and managed to take a single step.

He was moving ahead by inches.

She plunged forward once more, raising her leg against the weight of the snow, and listening to the thump of her heart. It was like swimming through glue. She was sweating inside her snow-filled clothes. *This is the hardest thing I've ever done.*

Surely it will improve me.

Slowly, she lifted her other leg, stepped forward, and gently collapsed. *How could you do something so hard and not be improved?*

Wearily, she straightened up, and attempted one more impossible step. But how? *In what way will it improve me, flailing a mile through three and a half feet of snow? Artistically? Spiritually? Physically? It seemed to be no on all points.*

Laboriously, she raised her right leg. *Dear Sir,* she wrote. Correction: *Dear Minister of Highways . . .*

She lifted her left leg and pushed forward through the heavy mass.

It is well known by the road crew in our area that we live back in the woods. However, after plowing out the whole rest of the settlement . . . Sounds like persecution complex. Better reword it.

Dear Minister: After the great Boxing Day storm, as we were coming home . . .

She followed the deep holes of Daniel's boots in the snow and the drag of the toboggan. *Dear Minister: As you know, this past Boxing Day, we had a storm . . .*

If she stepped *exactly* in his tracks, she saved herself an infinitesimal, but important, amount of energy, which she might need if they lost their way and ended up wandering for days.

Dear Minister: As a taxpayer, I am entitled to be plowed out in winter . . .

She came upon a sack of potatoes in the snow. "You dropped the potatoes!"

"I'm lightening the load!"

She continued on, profoundly impressed by the sack of potatoes. It was like a sinking ship, where you tossed the weak and helpless overboard. Her heart, she noticed, was now sounding like a bass guitar, amplified, and her face and body were drenched. And the potatoes had been thrown overboard.

Dear Minister: I narrowly escaped dying this weekend as a result of negligence on the part of your road crews . . .

She toppled over her pink pillowcase of newly washed laundry.

First the potatoes. And now, the laundry.

To the honorable Prime Minister Trudeau, she wrote. *I thought*

*you would like to know that my laundry had to be sacrificed as a
result of . . .*

■ ■ ■

"Come in, come in," said Pike. "You better have some tea." His
welcome had the ring of a warning, implying that the night outside
was filled with ominous forces, against which, if they were to stand
any chance, they'd best, all three, begin their counteroffensive with
tea.

He led them through the wind-swept living room, abandoned for
the winter, into the blazing heat of the kitchen, which had under-
gone a radical transformation. Sink, drainboard, and all cupboard
surfaces were cluttered with brushes, tubes of oil paint, cans of
hardware paint, turpentine, and linseed oil; the dining table served
as a palette, its wooden surface smeared with mixtures of color; the
paintings themselves, done on plywood, were hammered directly
onto the blue flowered wall with spikes which protruded mur-
derously top-center of each picture; and Pike was wearing a red
beret, slung low on his forehead and uncompromisingly tugged to
one side.

"I'm into the paintin business now," he announced. "No tellin
where it might lead a man."

"You've come a long way fast," she said.

"I don't care what any of them bastards say. Let them laugh if
they want. I alluys had the idea I might paint and now I'm doin
it."

His paintings were of woodland, field, and village, where little
stick figures writhed in torments suitable to the specific scene—
death by rifle, fire, drowning, or automobile.

"I got some peaches here." He swung open his cupboard; it was
filled with more paint and brushes; he snatched out a can of
peaches, pierced the lid as though giving the death thrust, and
dumped the fruit furiously into a glass mixing bowl. "Better have
some." He slammed the bowl on the table, the peaches another
veiled threat against the forces or characters lurking outside waiting to do the three of them in.

"They'd like to try some funny business with me." He hinted
with his peach spoon at how he would deal with any such attempts.

As they ate the peaches and Pike explained how the only way to deal with a bobcat was to tear its jaws apart, she studied his paintings. The content of course was preposterous; nor did he have any sense of design; she suspected he was red-green color blind; he had obviously no technique or even ability; but whatever he had was exactly what she lacked.

He followed her eyes, and asked, almost humbly, "I figgered you might have some pointers fer me."

God knows she had. But would it help? She shook her head.

He seemed satisfied. "Seen a panther up yer way t'other day."

"A panther in New Jerusalem?" asked Daniel.

"You wanna carry a gun when you step out of that cabin."

"I've never seen tracks that large," said Daniel.

"They're cagey with their tracks. But they're around."

What is it? she wondered, staring at the nightmarish paintings. What does this sixty-year-old maniac have that I don't?

"Don't kid yerself," Pike was saying, "if them French in Quebec gets too funny, the American Marines will come in and shoot every one of them." His left cheek bulged with a knowing tongue; he nodded significantly; his new job, washing floors in City Hall, had made him privy to innermost international secrets. "Canadian Army's a joke. Sons of bitches couldn't defend Prince Edward Island."

And where, she wondered, in two hundred miles, did he ever find a red beret?

He suddenly jerked to his feet, as if he'd heard the noise he'd been waiting for . . . enemy aircraft . . . the French . . . American Marines. He sidled along by the wall and at the crucial moment flung open the cupboard door.

She expected a prowler to fall out. Instead, Pike grabbed a can of peas, muttering, "Half the stuff a man buys, he don't know why he bought it," the implication being that the peas had somehow been foisted on him, were just what he despised, a millstone round his neck. The brand, she noticed, was R-A-D-I-O, with radio tower zigzags pulsating out of the letters as if celebrating a new-fangled invention; has he been hoarding these peas since the days of Marconi?

He beheaded the offending can with vengeance, dumped the peas into a pot on the stove, and said, "It's a funny thing about rat poison. I say, it's a funny thing about rat poison." He stared at them hard. "Used to be a banty rooster in this village. One day he got into the rat poison. Warfarin. You know that there Warfarin rat poison? Warfarin. That banty rooster was like an old man comin down off a drunk, staggerin and fallin, we cal'ated he was done fer. And then . . ." Pike crouched by the stove, and sprung. "Up in the air he went. Flyin all over the place. Flew over every damn house in the village, and slept fer two days afterward." He dished out the boiling forty-year-old peas. "Couldn't keep the son of a bitch out of the rat poison a'tall after that."

She watched while Pike ate a spoonful of peas, gave him several minutes to succumb to botulism, and then began to eat some herself. A suspicious noise came from the door; was the enemy now trying to scratch its way in?

"That brown bastard from next door," explained Pike, getting up and letting in a large pink-eyed dog, who took his apparently accustomed seat on the floor and stared ahead of him.

"We'd better be going," said Daniel, peas finished.

Man and dog accompanied them out through the kitchen, into the ice-cold living room, where scattered about, along with rough lumber, lay jars of homemade preserves; bear traps grinned with steel jaws in the corner, and rifles of assorted sizes leaned against the walls; the overwhelming impression was of an armed camp, and after the door closed behind them, it was a shock to find the village quietly sleeping under the stars. Who, she wondered, gazing at the peaceful scene, would suspect that in one of these quaint village houses sits a warrior, an artist, raging through his dream.

■ ■ ■

". . . So she took the three kids to the shack where her husband and his new woman was stayin, and when they opened the door, she pushed the kids forward and says to the woman: *You took the stud, you may as well take the colts.*" Phoebe giggled. "Pretty good though, ain't it? Dumpin yer kids on yer husband's new woman?"

"Not bad," said Sara, thinking it would make an effective book jacket—the moonlit doorway, the children, the two passionate and beautiful rivals. "Was she pretty?"

"Ain't you never seen Daisy? She's a nice-lookin woman, 'ceptin fer where the dog bit her nose off. But what I don't like is how it's alluys the children who suffer."

Sara nodded; it was one of Phoebe's maxims: It's alluys the children who suffer.

"Noreen now, she's an awful nervy woman. Eats aspirins steady."

"I suppose," said Sara, "her head hurts."

"It's jes a habit. A way to pass the time." Phoebe sighed, gazing out through the bubbly windows at the endless white stillness that blanketed the crystalline woodlands. Sara felt herself sinking too, into the deep hibernation, the long closed-in months in front of the stove, and the eternal pulsation. "More tea?"

"If you are," said Sara.

"Nahthin else to do." Phoebe sighed, then jumped up from her seat. "Clock stopped."

The brown-faced clock on the washstand said three fifteen; Phoebe shook it, and set it forward. "Poor Aunt Idella was nervy too."

Aunt Idella, Noreen, Daisy . . . Sara wondered if she'd ever get a grip on the infinite blood links that connected Phoebe's family with Murvyle's family with all the other families in the surrounding villages. The network of relationships formed a tower which rose to a unified peak, but the swirls of the spiral had no beginning or end you could cling to and they circled round and round too fast for an outsider to grasp.

"Old Uncle Firmin, see, he put dinnamite in the barrel where Aunt Idella alluys throwed her ashes. But he never thought to tell her about it. So when she throwed out her ashes, the barrel blowed to pieces." Phoebe sighed deeply. "Poor Aunt Idella."

"Hurt?"

"Dinnamited. Tits here, legs there . . ."

". . . What was Uncle Firmin doing with dinnamite in the first place?"

"Fishin fer salmon."

"Was he convicted?"

"They never did catch him with no salmon."

"I mean about Aunt Idella . . ."

"Poor Aunt Idella."

"Did anything happen to Uncle Firmin?"

"Dif'rent things. Same as the rest."

"Was he a lumberjack?"

"He worked fer the Jews."

Sara sucked in her breath. *Worked fer the Jews* meant Uncle Fir-

min worked in the junkyard; it wasn't the first time the expression
had been used. The problem was how one could work it into the
conversation, casually, without any implied criticism, that junkyard
and Jew were two different words and that there were numerous
Jews (oneself for a casual example) outside as well as inside
junkyards. But how do you come out and give a speech like that
casually—to someone you've spent so much time with, someone
who's fed you, lent you their mailbox, their barnyard to park your
truck in, and discussed with you such intimate things as a grandchild's first menstruation or who's the putative father of whom?
Someone who's offered you the use of her own private chamberpot
under the bed to save you walking in the snow to the outhouse.
How could you possibly accuse such a friend of something so petty
as race prejudice? The solution was probably to bring it up on a
day when neither Jews nor junkyards had been mentioned . . . perhaps in a general discussion of religion.

"Murvyle comin," remarked Phoebe. Sara looked out the window, but the crest of the hill was as still as it had been for the last
half hour; nor could she hear anything.

"He'll want his tea, likely," said Phoebe, going for the big box of
Red Rose. Sara pushed the kettle over the firebox and helped pull
out the table to seat five people. It seemed she'd never eaten so
much in her life as this winter, and only the energy she expended
shivering with cold was keeping her slim.

At the crest of the hill, Murvyle's truck finally appeared.

In the barnyard, Daniel and Hilton put down their snow shovels.

Phoebe stepped out to the shed, in twenty below, in her sleeve-
less housedress, bellowing, "Come in fer yer tea!"

Festus bounded across the yard first, snow flying off his nose,
and Daniel and Hilton followed, as Murvyle's truck pulled into the
driveway.

Phoebe returned to the kitchen, pointing meaningfully at Hilton
weaving along the frozen lane to the house; his voice boomed
drunkenly over the valley.

"Tsk, tsk," sighed Phoebe.

Boots stamped on the shed, Daniel's, then Hilton's; Murvyle was
coming toward the house behind them, his stumpy form bedecked
in an antique serge suit of blindingly vivid blue, complete with
striped shirt and tieful of galloping horses.

"Holyo-peena!" said Hilton in greeting, an expression whose

derivation and meaning Sara could only wonder at. Murvyle, bringing up the rear, remarked, "Damn cold day fer to bury a man."

"Are you coming from a funeral?" she asked.

"We should've jes drug him under some pine boughs and left him there till spring."

"I hate a fooneral meself," said Phoebe.

Daniel and Hilton drew up their chairs.

"Our Bertha now," said Phoebe, dishing up the donuts, "loves a fooneral."

They dug into their diet of white flour and sugar, supplemented by shag tobacco and boiled tea, the secret apparently of their superb health, extraordinary strength, and history of extreme longevity.

"Who died?" asked Daniel.

"Old Birdie Carlyle," said Phoebe. "Drunk a bottle of Javex, wasn't that it, Murvyle?"

Chlorine bleach? thought Sara, stunned. "He committed suicide?"

Hilton snorted. "Birdie thought he was reachin fer the good stuff. He weren't lookin, that was his problem." Hilton's tone of contempt indicated that he himself when confronted with the dilemma of drinking Javex or the good stuff would always choose the good stuff, but there was also a certain breadth in his statement that showed an appreciation of the continual problem the ordinary person faced in making this choice on a daily basis and that you had to be on your toes every minute to avoid laundering your esophagus.

"Still'n all," said Murvyle, "you wouldn't have thought it'd kill him."

"No, you wouldn't," said Phoebe. "Remember that moldy bread he used to eat?"

"Clear blue."

"And them eggs?"

"Now there's a story," said Murvyle, removing his spectacular tie. "Them eggs of old Birdie Carlyle's."

"You listen," Phoebe advised Sara in undertones, obviously considering Old Birdie Carlyle's Eggs one of Murvyle's choicest stories, and she leaned her own head forward to hear her husband tell a tale she must've heard a hundred times before. Sara gazed at the two old tea-drinkers, and for an instant saw, superimposed on Mur-

vyle and Phoebe, a snapshot from the family album—of a powerful
young man and splendid girl with the wind pressing her faded
summer dress against her curves—and then Murvyle said, "Birdie
Carlyle's old woman was queer in the head. She'd put a great big
platter of eggs out fer us men who was workin fer Birdie, and some
of them eggs'd be new and some'd be old, and you never knowed
which you'd get, but you wouldn't get nahthin else, and she was as
likely to put out five-month-old eggs as she was to put out the good
ones. I used to like eggs before them eggs of Birdie Carlyle's, but
thems were the last eggs I ever ett. How long has it been now?"

"Twenty year anyway."

"Now Birdie, he could eat rotten eggs."

"But appurently he couldn't take the Javex."

"Well," said Hilton, wiping crumbs from his chin and shoving his
chair clear of the table, "I guess I'll go fuck the Frenchwoman in
the ass."

Phoebe pursed her lips and silently went, "Tsk, tsk."

Hilton slung on his flannel shirt, and stomped out to the shed.

"You can't say a thing to him when he's drinkin," whispered
Phoebe.

"Have some more buns," said Murvyle. "Don't be shy."

Sara cleared her throat. "Is there a Frenchwoman in New
Jerusalem?"

All heads were cocked to the sound of Hilton's car pulling away.
Eventually Phoebe answered. "You know Francine in the village,
don't you?"

"No, I don't," said Sara, consumed with curiosity over the image
of a petite Edith Piaf bent over her woodstove, singing in pain,
while the barbarian heaved behind her.

"He jes talks," said Murvyle.

Daniel gave her a wink. Had Hilton told Daniel about it? Daniel
had a habit of not telling her the most interesting stories. Or maybe
he didn't know she'd be interested? His close friendship with Hilton was a mystery to her. Not that Hilton wasn't kind-hearted and
convivial, but he was sort of medieval; when he ate, she always
thought of Henry the Eighth ripping apart raw meat, drooling,
blood dribbling down his chin.

"Was it a good fooneral?" asked Phoebe.

"Poor sermon."

There! thought Sara: A religious discussion.

"I was dreamin 'bout old Birdie too," said Murvyle, "t'other night. Never thought we'd be buryin him today. He was crawlin up the hill, through the snow on his hands and knees. You know where the graveyard is? That's jes about where I seen him, crawlin along slow and tired. As I recollect, we didn't talk very much. I says, *Birdie, how're you doin?* And Birdie, he says, *I can't make her any further, Murvyle.*"

Through the dense whirling snowflakes, the jingle of bells drew closer, and gradually the shape of two horses appeared in the white moving veil; behind them came Hilton, standing upright, gliding on some sort of board. His laughter bellowed in the wind. "Are you comin fer a sleigh ride, Dan'l?"

Daniel jumped on, and the horses moved forward, the rusty runners of the flat sled hissing through the snow. Hilton's head swiveled around; he pointed to a big shiner circling his eye. "See what they done to me at the Legion last night?"

His words echoed in the snowstorm . . . *see what they done to me . . . done to me . . .* and Daniel felt himself plunging violently backward in time, to the dark ages where Hilton still lived, a world of cudgels and maces, powerful horses and dark ignorance, and as the horses picked up speed and the snow swirled around them, he felt himself to be nothing but a citified idea of a human being.

For some time, he had fantasized teaching his friend how to read, and then one night he had a dream where Hilton said to him, *The soul is secretly satisfied.*

Hilton gave a yell as they rounded the bend in the road, snow flying in their faces. Daniel felt the intimate pull of horse and riders, the texture of the forest, the field spreading out before them; they skimmed over the snow toward the barns, where Murvyle stood with his ax and Phoebe was hanging her wash out in the middle of a snowstorm in bare arms and legs.

Daniel waved. Hilton shouted, "Snow, shit, and rain," snapping the reins and urging the horses on through the storm.

The farm disappeared behind them and they plunged ahead

through the white fluttering curtain, dark-aged dream horses with their Gothic driver lifting his blackened eye to the veiled sun.

■ ■ ■

"I seen the moon dancin," said Pike, seated in the midst of his paintings. "Twas the night before Easter. Mother got us out of bed. *You may never get another chance to see it,* she said, and led us downstairs to where twas dancin on the wallpaper in the parlor. I've told dif'rent people and they wouldn't believe me, but once I told a feller, and he said he never seen it hisself, but twas the truth accordin to Scripture. The moon. I didn't see the sun," added Pike scrupulously, pouring their obligatory first-line-of-defense cup of tea, followed by a box of Oreo cookies which he thrust on the table as if it might, for all he knew, be fused with explosives inserted by one of the enemy agents who disbelieved his tale of the moon, were constantly attempting to kill or malign him, and who had just fired him from his job.

"So you weren't harassing politicians?" asked Daniel, carefully opening the suspicious Oreo box.

"They was harassin me. But I wouldn't take it from them. When I'm cleanin the floor, I don't want nobody walkin over it, don't care who he is, mayor, premier, or the goddamn pope, I'm doin me job, and if he can't wait till it's dry same as anybody else, he knows what he's gonna get." Pike didn't specify, but made a motion implying that a hurled bucket of dirty water had something to do with the aggression that had led to his dismissal.

He narrowed his eyes. "Anybody been botherin you back at the camp?"

"No."

"Nobody's been comin back there?"

"I don't think so," said Daniel, no longer so sure.

"They might've come without our noticing," admitted Sara nervously.

"I'll run the bastards off fer you," said Pike. "They won't know what hit them."

Good thing Pike's on our side, thought Daniel, envisioning the menacing figures lurking around the camp and the intrepid form of Pike running them off. But if there were menacing figures, wouldn't they have left tracks in the snow? "I'm pretty sure nobody's been back there."

"They will be."

I guess they will.

Or will they?

"They been tryin to buy me out again," snarled Pike. "Sons of bitches. *I know what yer after,* I told them. I says, *Afore you can look at this house, I want three-thousand-dollar down payment. Cash on the barrel.*"

"What exactly are they after?"

"They can't bluff me," replied Pike, leaving it open for Daniel to wonder: Was it his bear traps . . . his treasures . . . his soul itself that they wanted to trick him out of? Whatever it was, the source of his vitality seemed to seesaw back and forth on veiled threat and response to threat, by which he apparently kept himself well and fluid.

"Can I give you somethin else?" he threatened.

"No thanks."

He slammed down a can of Lyle's Golden Syrup. "You better have some of this." It sounded like a doctor's prescription, given at gunpoint.

Daniel spread syrup on bread.

". . . So he says to me, *This dog of mine will tear the heart out of any livin creature.* He was a nice-sized dog, but I had me doubts and I says so and I laid him a little money on it. After a while, we come to a stream, and there was a bear fishin fer salmon. You ever seen a bear fish fer salmon?" Pike stooped on the floor, scooping imaginary fish and gazing around maliciously. "That dog he made fer the bear, and twas as I bet would happen. Dog ups in the air and comes down stone dead. Back broken." He gustily performed both roles, the swatting bear and the ill-fated dog, flung and broken, mouth open, eyes rolling, then looking up and noting Sara's horror-stricken face, he remarked, "I was sorry to see it happen."

■ ■ ■

Sunshine polished the snow with hard gold lacquer, and melted a narrow path round the cabin. He set out an aluminum lounge chair for her to sunbathe on.

"For the first time in my life," she said, "I'm going to get a good tan."

He gazed out over the glittering expanse of burnished snow. His breath, used to the crystal-hard purity of the cold, unexpectedly met no resistance, and it felt as if he were drinking the soft air; the blue jay's harsh winter cry turned liquid, falling from the warm sky in raindrop-shaped notes.

She took off her clothes. "Snow's a fabulous reflector. If I start early and lie out each day, by summer I'll be black." She arranged her naked white limbs on the lounge. He sat down beside her. "Did I tell you," she asked, "I finally worked it into the conversation with Phoebe, about my being Jewish."

"Was she dumbfounded?"

"Not at all. And I gave quite a lengthy speech. She was rolling dough. Her roller didn't miss a beat."

"You see, they're really not bigots. They just haven't had much contact . . ." His incipient lecture on the salt of the earth was interrupted by a faint buzzing sound which grew steadily louder.

She sat up and stared around.

"They're not coming here," he assured her.

"It sounds like they are." She jumped off the lounge, and flapped for the cabin, just as a speeding snowmobile swerved down their lane and smashed headlong into a tree.

Daniel ran to the wreck.

Hilton lay in the snow, out cold, spittle running down chin, having flown like a bird over the handlebars.

Sara rushed over in boots and bathrobe. "Is he hurt?"

"Not as bad as the snowmobile is."

She looked at the unconscious figure. "What fool would lend Hilton a snowmobile?"

"It's his. He bought it."

"How do you know?"

"I lent him the money."

She gazed at the heap of junk metal.

"You what?" she inquired.

"He kept asking me. I couldn't stand it. And then this second-hand machine came along, and it was the buy of a lifetime . . ."

The injured sportsman slowly opened his bloodshot eyes; a leer spread over his swollen features. He held out his paw to Sara. "Francine . . ."

"It's Sara, Hilton, you got hit on the head."

Hilton fumbled in dismay for his head. "Holyo-fuckeye, what a lump."

"Easy does it," said Daniel. "On your feet . . ."

Hilton groaned like a moose horn, and staggered upright in several stages. His hair stuck out in short angry cowlicks and snow patched his disarrayed clothes; the buttons of his shirt had burst at the belly, which protruded like a great pink bowl. "Me back is out," he declared in stunned outrage, as though someone were badly at fault, and would pay, most likely the government. He glared at the world through woozy eyes that dared whatever he saw to lend him one more blow. An enormous imprint marked the snow where he'd sprawled.

His eyes finally focused on his pancaked snowmobile, which had wrapped itself around the pine tree. "We'll have to chop down that son of a whore."

"Maybe we can lift the snowmobile out," said Daniel.

"I don't think it." Hilton rubbed his head and winced, looked around for his cap, and gingerly placed it on the side of his head.

"Let's give it a try," said Daniel.

They crouched down to pry the entangled machine from the tree; Daniel gave it all he had, and at the other end, felt Hilton's superhuman strength; the injured man lifted the snowmobile free with a primeval grunt, looked over the mashed-up crunched-in frame, and said, "She'll need some body work."

They examined the disaster more closely. "Them fuckin handlebars are on crooked, that's what's wrong with the son of a whore. Did you see the way she come round the curve? I had her wide open and she wouldn't hold. Jesus Christly handlebars are on crooked."

Unsteadily he climbed on, and the crushed motor started, the way motors, no matter what their condition, always did for Hilton, as if fearing their master's wrath. He shouted above the roar, "You comin fer a spin, Dan'l?"

Spin seemed to sum up the condition exactly; Daniel gazed at the twisted-up wreck and said, "I have some wood that needs chopping."

"All right," hollered Hilton, throwing the machine into gear and hurtling off, sideways, down the logging road, to what further adventure Daniel didn't know, he only knew that Hilton would be carried far into the day, through numerous crashes, hat backwards, shirt open, scenery rushing past him in the blur that was his normal state; a hero of the north woods. The sound of the snowmobile grew faint, faded into the distance, and ceased, though Daniel could not be sure whether it had crashed into another tree, through an open barn door, or was hurtling, gloriously, into the sunset.

■ ■ ■

Wind, sun, rain, all joined to level the great white mass of winter, bit by bit, but there was so much of it, the leveling seemed endless. The brooks rose and rushed to the rivers; the owl called and birds arrived in vast flocks; creeks appeared in the deep, soft, impassable white forest; and still, spring kept coming, month after month, and would keep on coming until there was no more snow and the whole forest world would be melted into one passionate streaming, so huge and profound it would sweep everything in its creation, as it was sweeping away his last cold resistance to building the home Sara wanted.

"We've no place else we'd rather be," she persisted. "We're living cheaply . . ."

The eternal feeling kept evading him, slipping away under his feet, a feeling compounded of soft mud and hot sunlight and the slow endless dripping of trees and the drip drip of shrinking snowbanks and the rushing sound of rising streams. He felt if he could understand it, he'd understand everything, and the centuries-old mud road would open up under his boots, and he'd find himself standing on the soft black brink of truth. Gazing up at the sky and ahead toward Murvyle's farm, gazing around at the dripping forest and down again at the road, he felt the mysterious lure of painted scenes that beckon you into them like dreams.

"Just a small house," she said, "nothing grand . . ."

As winter sloughed off its skins, shedding layer after layer of snow, the same thing seemed to be happening in him, as if what had frozen over the long cold months had been his conceptions, and now with the thaw, he was slowly sloughing them off. Conceptions of how one should live, ideas about people, travel, needs . . . all a person needed was spring.

Up ahead, Murvyle's farm looked like a junkyard, with husks of old cars peeping up through the snow, tin oil barrels and tires emerging like flowers. By the barn, the steaming manure pile lifted its moist hay smell to mingle with the other perfumes of spring, and through the big open door, the two horses stood chained to their stalls, staring at space, while beside them, also motionless and staring, like a third horse, stood Hilton.

Sara walked toward the house.

Daniel entered the stable, where Hilton, leaning up against his pile of hay, eyes drooping, nodded, patted the closer horse on the flank, and said, "What this feller wants is a good curry-combin. Make him shine, by Jesus." He patted the horse again tenderly, reached over to a shelf in the wall, and came out with a bottle; he unscrewed the top, took a swig, gasped, sputtered, and passed it to Daniel. "By Jesus, that's a good drink of rum."

Daniel took a swallow, and handed it back.

Hilton took another long swig, staggering up against the hay. The horse who needed the curry-combing looked at him balefully. "I'm gonna pull out of her one of these days. Go up north somewhere. Get a job on a goddamn big diesel. Tractor." At the moment he appeared anchored in horse manure and not about to pull out of her for a while; he let out a large liquid belch; rum and other spiritous fumes made the horse blink its eyes. Hilton ran his hand affectionately up under its mane. "Yer a good old foolish fucker. I guess you'd like some oats, wouldn't you, you foolish fucker, alluys lookin fer somethin to eat." He maneuvered around to the oat barrel, walked on past, subsided into the hay, and vomited.

Daniel fed both horses, while Hilton retched in the hay and the horses exchanged knowing looks; then philosophically they began grinding their oats.

Leaving his friend to his purge, Daniel headed for the house. In the kitchen, high tea was in progress.

"Well," remarked Phoebe.

Festus thumped his tail.

Greetings, Daniel was learning, were casual in the country, which had its own etiquette—surly hellos, terser farewells, and never a thank-you; if you were grateful, you gave money instead; one day, after having eaten himself into a stupor on Phoebe's baking, he'd hauled some water for her and been offered a quarter.

"Sit in and eat," said Murvyle. "There ain't much, but there's lots of it."

"Don't get up," replied Daniel, going into the pantry for a cup.

In among the saucers and plates was the family pharmacopoeia, which had evidently served well for some generations: an ancient bottle of British Troop Oil; a venerable container of Mother Seigel's Syrup for dyspepsia; a box of Blaud's Tonic Capsules containing both arsenic and strychnine, excellent it said for anemia and run-down conditions; could arsenic and strychnine be the secret of the family's sanguineness? There was Olajen Restores, A Builder from Childhood to Old Age; Eucament Liniment for internal as well as external complaints; Dr. Thomas' Electric Oil; and Kellogg's Asthma Remedy, depicting a man or a boy burning some kind of powder and inhaling the conflagration; Daniel was often tempted to steal a pinch of Kellogg's Asthma powder, or pinch the entire collection to sell on Bleecker Street. There was also a more contemporary collection of empty Moosehead Beer bottles; and Murvyle's lower teeth, grinning up from an earthenware bowl, handy for Phoebe to bring to the table with apples or other hard delicacies.

". . . Yessir," said Murvyle, picking up a thread he'd left dangling earlier somewhere, "I was eleven when I begun to work in them lumber camps."

"Did you see my beer bottles?" Phoebe asked Daniel. "I'm gonna sell them to the Jews." His eyes met Sara's.

". . . We slept on pine boughs," Murvyle continued, "spread out over the dirt. Cold? I'll say twas cold."

"Five cent apiece," said Phoebe. He could only conclude that she was emotionally incapable of absorbing the knowledge that Sara was Jewish. Jews are remote junkyard beings, not somebody sitting in your kitchen.

". . . I'd get into bed," said Murvyle, "and ask meself, *What's goin on down there?*"

"You know them young folks," asked Phoebe, "boardin with Uncle Burpee? They wouldn't get out at the last, so he called in the Mounties on them. Dunno why they wouldn't pay their rent. Where else could you stay fer twenty dollar the month, even if you do have to take care of old Burpee who wets his bed?"

". . . So one night," went on Murvyle, "I pulled up them boughs and looked."

"Got a new young couple stayin with him now. French people he met in hospital. Bein French they might not know about Burpee's ways."

". . . No sir," said Murvyle, "you never seen so many snakes."

The outer door banged open and Hilton's heavy tread announced itself on the shed; a belch pronounced his presence at the inner door; he stepped through, a stupefied smile on his face as if he were seeing everyone there for the first time that day. "By fuck, I'm hungry," he said, and laid himself down on the cot behind the stove.

". . . So," said Murvyle, "I built a new bed up in a tree. But even them trees was filled with snakes."

Hilton snapped up on his cot like a jack-in-the-box, leering at Sara. "Be a snake in yer bed, one of these nights."

Even Festus joined in the laughter that rocked the kitchen. Daniel's eyes met Sara's; she wore the pained expression she reserved for the jests of his boon companion Hilton.

Phoebe, after hooting the loudest, pursed her lips and went, "Tsk, tsk."

"I had a snake hit me in the face once," remarked Murvyle.

Hilton muttered and again rolled over. ". . . son of a whore." Like the Eskimo with five hundred words for snow, his *son of a whore* had infinite gradations of meaning.

"Murvyle," said Phoebe, "when you gonna fix that leak up attic?"

"I'll get to her tomorrow."

"You been sayin that fer fifteen years."

Murvyle winked at Daniel. "Perhaps I have."

Silence resumed, and they gazed out the windows, listening to the snow's slow endless dripping.

■ ■ ■

"Line 'er up," advised Uncle Burpee, licking snuff, and pointing a tremulous finger at the footing course of cement being poured atop the thick stone wall; the foundation hole was patched with snow, the woods still wet and spongy, but mayflowers and trillium bloomed on the trails, and beside the old foundation, fragrant white narcissus clustered.

Daniel gazed down at the stones. The old cellar hole was a small one, several hundred yards away from their original house; they'd chosen this small foundation over the other because the stones were flatter, perfectly fitted, laid to last forever; and the ghosts weren't theirs.

"She's straight as a die, boys," croaked Burpee, in his bright blue overalls, swaying over the hole like a raucous old blue jay about to take off. Each time he swayed, Daniel held his breath, and all work stopped, as he and Murvyle and Hilton watched to see if they'd lose Uncle Burpee. "Straighter'n an arrow," said Burpee, catching his balance and spitting blood-colored snuff into the snow-white foundation. "The eye knows."

The old stonemason had voluntarily come out of deep retirement to supervise the foundation of the first home to go up in the Hills of New Jerusalem in fifty years; when he'd opened the ancient cigar box holding his incredibly work-worn pumb line, Daniel had known that getting Uncle Burpee was a stroke of luck. "I've put 'em up straight in St. John's, I've put 'em up straight in Moncton, I've put 'em up straight as far as Calgary," he said hoarsely, standing stiff as a board, in his vivid blue overalls. "Easy there, boys. Yessir, we put 'em up in the old days without no levels, no rulers. The eye knows, boys, the eye will tell you right every time."

Warm breezes swept in from the fields, ruffling Burpee's snow-white hair, and drying the cement they poured in the wooden forms.

Each final touch was done by the master, with a bent and pitted trowel that had served him well no doubt in Calgary, Moncton, and St. John's. Teetering, but with one eye closed, like the artist he was, he sighted and struck with his antique trowel, cackling at every corner: "Straight as a star . . . Straight as a comet . . . Straighter'n the prick on a billy goat."

They spread their lunches out on the grass which was dry and mossy around the roots of the spruce trees, and Burpee told them tales of jobs he'd worked on, in the long distant past, and of the chickadees, seventy years ago, who'd picked his teeth clean for him.

He dozed off after lunch, but woke with a start, admonishing them to "Line 'er up straight."

By evening, the job was done to his satisfaction, and Daniel, in a burst of artistic appreciation, slipped the old mason twenty dollars.

"That's too much, Dan'l," said Burpee, then pocketed the money; eyeing Murvyle and Hilton, he added under his breath, "You don't wanna spoil yer workmen."

The workmen all left, and Daniel sat by himself beside the finished foundation, thinking about Uncle Burpee.

Twenty dollars was a lot. But not too much. It wouldn't be auspicious to stint with old Burpee. It'd be like haggling with a Zen master.

■ ■ ■

The carpenter rubbed his beet-red bald pate. "How in Jesus," he asked, "are we gonna build a straight house on this here yee-hawed foundation?"

"Yee-hawed?" asked Daniel.

"Look here at my level. There ain't a straight line from one corner of this thing to t'other."

"But we had Burpee!"

"Tain't that Burpee's old," replied the carpenter. "Burpee's jes no good. He wasn't no good in his prime. He's built 'em crooked down to Moncton. He's built 'em crooked up to St. John's. He's built 'em crooked out to Alberta. Burpee builds crooked. It's his style."

■ ■ ■

A loud roar brought him out of his sleep. He got up and raced to the door.

Outside, overhead, in the dawn, flew three World War Two fighter planes, dropping a thick vapor on the cabin and forest.

His eyes streamed; he couldn't breathe.

"Close the door," cried Sara.

He stumbled back in, pulling the door shut.

The vapor came down the chimney and in through the windows, and then the roar passed into the distance, and he and she stared at each other, with streaming bewildered eyes.

■ ■ ■

"You'll get used to it." The carpenter took out a handkerchief and wiped his red shining head. "They do it every year."

Daniel was having trouble coordinating his movements, and his head was still stuffed and fuzzy.

"It's fer to kill the spruce budworm. That's the idea. Course, it's jes a money grab. The more they spray, the more they need to, fer the budworm gets worse every year."

Daniel rested on the sawhorse. "But what about the people?"

The carpenter laughed. "You should've been here when they used that there DDT. Now that was the good stuff. Sick? But none of it hurts nobody."

Daniel noticed the carpenter's movements too were erratic; his hand trembled with the level. Several times he teetered like Uncle Burpee.

They stopped for lunch, and ate beneath the trees.

The woods were quiet and still; just a single bird appeared, a tiny goldfinch. The carpenter tossed a crumb to it.

The chartreuse bird glanced at the crumb, then went on stalking a bug, a small white moth, which it caught in its beak; holding the moth in its beak, the bird toppled over.

The carpenter grunted. "That's funny, ain't it?"

"It's dead."

"Appears to be."

Daniel picked up the still-warm bird, and walked to the woods. He sat down on a stump, and listened for the teeming life he'd felt around him all through the spring, surging and multiplying as the days grew warmer, in the bark of the trees, under foot, in the leaves, and deep in the earth, but the whole forest seemed stunned to silence at what had happened to it.

She stuck a bean in the earth, covering it with dirt, then moved three inches, and put in another. It was taking longer than she'd imagined it possibly could to plant beans, compounded by frequent dizzy spells from being sprayed on three consecutive days.

"I wonder when Waldo will get here," said Daniel.

She glanced up the lane, but there was no sign of the carpenter's truck, and so she turned back to admiring the neat gridwork of her garden. Would it ever come up? It felt like a reckless act of faith, putting little seeds in the ground and expecting a plot of bare earth to turn into vegetables. "Daniel, a toad!" The toad stood in mottled gray and brown bumps like a petrified fossil, withered and old, without moving or winking, perhaps hoping he could still blend in with his camouflage skin and become invisible. "Isn't he cute?"

"He seems a pleasant enough toad."

"He's shy."

"I'd say he's terrified."

"I'm going to build a house for him. I read all about it in a magazine, if you want to keep a toad in your garden, you've got to give him a place with shade and a dish of water. They suggest an overturned flowerpot, but I can make something much prettier with stones."

"I wonder where Waldo is."

"And I'll paint on it, *Toad Hall*. Here's a good rock to begin with . . . Frenchwomen *pay* for toads. They buy them at market and put them in their gardens to eat destructive insects."

She went to the barn, found an old broken cup, filled it with water, and carried it back to Toad Hall.

"Next row?" he asked.

"Three of corn interspersed with pumpkin. Pumpkin and corn

are companions." A little stone castle, secret and cool, with an overhanging rock terrace . . . maybe she should divide it into rooms, in case more toads arrived. "And you know how thrifty the French are, so they must really be worth it." Perhaps she'd photograph the completed Toad Hall, with tenants, and send it in to *Organic Gardening*. Or had she read about the Frenchwomen in *Vogue?* Or *Toad? Toad Magazine* . . . dedicated to the appreciation and welfare of toads.

"I guess," he said, "there's no more point in waiting for Waldo."

"What do you think of Toad Hall?"

He surveyed the little cavern of stones, wiping his eyes and blowing his nose. "I'd like it if I were a toad. Shall we go back to the camp?" He struck across the field toward the woods.

She hurried behind him, her thongs falling off. "Why don't we go on the road?"

"You'll enjoy it more in the woods."

The woods were still wet; her feet squished through mud. Her bare legs were getting scratched. And her head ached from the spray. What if the people from *Toad* should come along to photograph her beside Toad Hall, with her legs scratched and her thongs falling off?

He plowed into marsh, and she followed, sucking through mud on one thong, the other having torn. "Are you enjoying this?" she called.

"Aren't you?"

A woodpecker on a dead tree gave his Woody Woodpecker cry, followed by a sharp ra-ta-tat as he banged his beak on the bark; the sound echoed over the forest. How does he keep from getting a headache? Mine is splitting.

"I can't understand what happened to Waldo." His voice rose up from the canyon. She clambered down over stones and ferns to the rushing brook, which had flooded its banks, obliterating the path that usually ran by it.

He grabbed a branch hanging over the edge, and swung forward, propelling himself along the bank like Tarzan.

She hesitated. To her right was fast-flowing ice water, to her left unfathomable jungle. She grabbed a branch, dropped her other thong in the freshet, and teetered forward, hand over hand.

They swung toward the bend.

And there, at the crook of the brook, up ahead, was a bright red ball glinting with sunlight—a bald pate—a fisherman standing in the stream.

"Waldo," called Daniel.

The carpenter turned and gazed at them. "Lovely day," he remarked, giving his head half a twitch as if he knew the beauty they were sharing was ineffable.

"Catch any fish?" asked Daniel.

"They don't appear to be runnin."

Since he didn't budge from his spot, they made their way over and stood at the edge of the water as close as they could to where he was rooted in his waders.

"Did you put in yer garden, missus?"

"Yes."

"That's nice. Good to get a garden in early."

"Is your garden in?" asked Daniel.

"Can't say 'tis."

"What're you fishing with?"

"Flies. I tie them meself." He brought out his line, and Daniel admired the fly. They spoke further on the subject of tying flies, the weather, and crops. At length, she realized no one had any intention of mentioning the house.

"Waldo," she began, "we were sort of hoping you'd work on the house today."

"Plenty of time. Got all summer."

"Plenty of time," agreed Daniel.

She dug her toes in the mud. "What do you think you'll be doing tomorrow?"

"I might try another stream."

"We'd appreciate it if you'd work on the house. I don't mean tomorrow. But what about Friday?"

"Friday . . . Friday . . ." He rubbed his red pate, studying the bumps on his scalp, pondering long and deep, and finally gave his dome the half twitch. "I guess I'll be free fer you Friday."

A splashing noise came toward them upstream.

They turned to see Hilton emerge from the trees, maneuvering the far bend of the brook in waders. He waved his fishing pole at them, performed a peculiar dance, lost his step, struggled, sank, and bobbed downstream toward them, holding his pole aloft.

"Fuckin near drowned," he sputtered, arising in their midst, his hip boots overflowing.

"Tain't easy to drown in three foot of water," remarked Waldo.

"Son of a whore." Hilton glared at the brook as if daring *it* to respond.

"Catch anything?" asked Daniel.

"Wanna see what I caught?" he leered; Sara was keenly aware of her very bare skin and skimpy sunsuit and had a flash of the Frenchwoman bending over her stove.

He opened his soaking creel, and drew forth a bottle of Moosehead Beer, which he stuck in his mouth and attempted to decap with his teeth. In horror, she watched as he grimaced with his poor stumps, panting, heaving, and finally, hideously, achieving his goal; contemptuously, he spat the bottle cap into the stream, along with a few chips of teeth, and flashed his black-gapped grin.

■ ■ ■

"I wanna buy a pitcher from you," said Phoebe formally.

"I'd be happy to give you one."

"No, I wanna pay fer it. How big would a five-dollar pitcher be?"

Sara gazed around at the calendars on the kitchen wall, and pointed to a good-sized year, wondering which of her paintings Phoebe wanted.

"Can you paint me a pitcher of the New Jerusalem graveyard?"

"Sure," replied Sara, hiding her dismay. Giving away a picture she'd already painted was one thing. Having to take five bucks on top was an acceptable insult. But to be offered such a commission to paint a cemetery, one of her least favorite places on the face of the earth . . .

Phoebe disappeared into her bedroom; Sara heard mattress springs squeaking; and, presently, she was handed five neatly pressed dollars.

■ ■ ■

What is this godawful life doing to my skin? In the cracked mirror, she searched for disaster, warding off she knew not what: *the competition,* she suspected, though whether competition referred to unknown girls they passed on the street without speaking once every two weeks in town, or the Frenchwoman she'd never met bending over her stove, or more dangerously lovely ladies lurking in more hidden wings of life, or some far-off future competition should she and he ever be hurled back to the city, or some dreadful unspeakable day when he might leave her and she find herself undesirable, outcast, gone to wrinkle; a thousand unknown terrors lurked, for which you had to be prepared, with Nivea, mouse-bitten soap, and a dishpan of water.

Cleaned, creamed, and combed, she packed her paints, locked the shack, made her way out of the woods, and hiked up the hill to the graveyard.

The little peeling white church sparkled in the hot sun; above the steeple, a few lazy clouds floated by; the forest ended at the edge of the graveyard, which was sadly in need of mowing, grown over with tall grass and weeds, a few straggling hardy flowers, and some faded plastic posies.

She circled the desolate spot, trying to figure out where to position her easel. Would Phoebe want the church or just the yard? No doubt for five hard-earned dollars she'd want as much as possible; but she'd specifically asked for the graveyard; perhaps the church itself might just hulk in the background.

Birds sang in the trees bordering the cemetery; bees buzzed in the few scraggly flowers; the grass was soft; she settled down at the end of the graveyard where she could get all the markers and the white church behind them.

Dully, with pencil, she roughed in the unhappy scene; it would be an uninspired picture, but what did it matter? Phoebe and Murvyle couldn't see the difference anyway. To them the clumsiest scrawls of their grandchildren indicated an artist's colony of budding Saras. Where all people were backward and deprived, all were equal; and all works were equal.

She put down her pencil, and walked toward a stone to check out its shape.

In memory of Faithful Luvina, consort of Elisha Jarvis, who departed this life in the sixteenth year of her age. O, how untimely was the stroke! And how severe the blow. The lettering was almost obliterated, but it gave her a strange feeling to think of the young bride lying under her feet this warm summer morning. The stonecutter had chiseled grasses and wheat around the words, graceful symbols of his trade. The gurgling of a brook rose in back of the churchyard, and she noticed an overgrown lane leading into the woods. Once this was all field, she thought, and these graves looked out over fields to a stream, and to more fields, and busy farms; men and women cleared the land, worked it, lived, multiplied, died, and now it's all been reclaimed by the forest. *They rest from their labors and their works do follow them. Ebenezer Wood, departed this life in his 75th year.*

She returned to her canvas. How had it been, this settlement, when the Jarvises and Woods and Carlyles and McGivneys had lived here? The names on the stones were the same as the men and women who lived now in the nearby villages; but only Murvyle and Phoebe and Hilton were left in Jerusalem, on a farm growing up in pulp and brush and wrecked automobiles.

Uncapping a tube of paint, she thought of the animals, the chickens and pigs and horses, and the cows that had roamed over the bright flowered fields, gently chewing their cud; ghostly cowbells sounded in the forgotten distance. *Shadrack, son of Shadrack and Rebekah Aikens, age 7. Young children all, as you pass by, Look here and see where you must lie, For I lie here by God's Decree, My infant sister lies by me.* What killed them all, the young children? What terrible lives people led. Yet Phoebe often wished for the old times, the good times. "That was pleasure then," she'd say, talking of some grueling hardship or another.

She sat down on the warm grass, and straightened a pink plastic rose which had fallen by the stone of *Harriet, widow of Dexter Whelpley and Albion McGivney, in the 67th year of her age. Dearest friends weep not for me, Nor repine at Heaven's decree, That called me a little before, For soon we'll meet to part no more.* She found herself smiling, wondering whether it was Dexter or Albion from whom Harriet hoped to part no more. She lay back and gazed at the sky, the clouds drifting eternally by, and it struck her that these old people weren't kidding. They really did expect some reuniting, some warm green heaven, some lovely farm settlement in the sky. Or maybe not the sky. Maybe it's all around here right now, in another dimension, the fields and hearths and hardworking people, the animals, the children and dreams, New Jerusalem that was and still is, where the ghostly cowbells ring.

She raised up on one elbow; on the gravestone nearest, she made out the phrase, *There is a debt to nature due, which I have paid and so must you,* and the words gently filled her, not as a threat, but somehow, in this small country graveyard, as spiritual. Here in the woods, with bees buzzing, wild flowers growing, everything feeding the earth and bringing it forth again, people had lived with death as their daily view. She felt the old settlers' acceptance permeating her spirit, and it had nothing to do with the blistered white church or hymnals or preachers, but a pagan understanding hewn in stone. The stones were rough primal shapes, not polished marble of annihilating machine-wrought sameness, and these dark stones, each unique, together made a temple, a place of strong meaning, instead of a place that catered, even at the end, to commercial interests.

I'm having a religious experience, she thought in embarrassment. It isn't earth shattering, just elusive and tantalizing. And suddenly she understood what Phoebe wanted—not a picture of a graveyard, but a feeling—the lingering pagan assurance that all is one. This, to Phoebe, whose memories went back to the time when there was such a community here in close harmony with the earth, was the real New Jerusalem . . . not the run-down, forgotten, grown-over, abandoned ghost settlement it had become.

She returned to her canvas, and started to work with the feeling beside her, as an ally present gently in the mind, to look over her shoulder and see that it would be done right: She was bringing a message from Them to Phoebe.

■ ■ ■

"Looks jes like it too," remarked Phoebe accepting the painting, "don't it?"

Sara waited for more to be said, but the usual silence fell around them. The stove crackled, the sunlight danced through the mottled windows, Phoebe sighed. "Might as well have a cup of tea."

Is that all? wondered Sara. No recognition that the sacred trust was performed? *Has she gotten the message?*

They sipped their tea without speaking, until Sara could stand it no longer. "Are you going to hang it?"

Phoebe's eyes roved over the kitchen wall where the horse calendars hung, along with blurred horse snapshots. Sighing, she stood, and carried the painting into the living room.

Acknowledgment, thought Sara; the shrouded parlor, with its old prints and Perry's Nut House pillow was clearly the Grande Galerie. And when she saw Phoebe hold the painting up, in the place of honor, on the very same wall as *The Return of the Dog,* she knew it was truly appreciated.

"Think it goes good here?" asked Phoebe. "You hold it whilst I get a nail."

The canvas was hung, straightened, restraightened. Sara opened the curtains to give it light, and Phoebe closed them again.

They returned to the kitchen.

They stared out the pockmarked windows at the purple lilac bush, the big maple, the forest, and the hills. And Sara wanted more. Not a thank-you, but a summation, a statement indicating Phoebe understood.

Glumly she looked down at the linoleum floor and around at the calendar-peppered walls, at the gleaming woodstove and old backless chairs, the galvanized bucket of fresh cold spring water and racks of hot fragrant bread, the blackened pans, the sparse, clean, warm, unassuming plan, and that was her answer from Phoebe.

"Mornin," remarked Waldo, lathering his bald head with insect repellent.

"Been here long?" asked Daniel. Sometimes it was he and sometimes Waldo who arrived first in the morning; and sometimes Waldo didn't arrive at all; those were the difficult days when he had to reconcile his exalted image of Waldo the Master Carpenter with plain old Waldo the Lazy. But this morning, the holy head was being anointed, the birds were chirping, the air fresh and cool.

"Nail 'er," said Waldo, aligning a board, and Daniel nailed 'er, whacking the brads with his hammer, astonished at the beauty of the procedure, that the first-floor walls were already up, that a house was a very simple and logical thing to build. "Nail 'er," said Waldo, who'd built a hundred and never suspected that every moment on this job was filled with wonder for the man beside him.

From the other side of the brook, across the ridge, came the low moo of a chainsaw—Murvyle, Hilton, Anson; he knew their sounds, their routines, knew the five crows who cawed overhead, and the porcupine chewing the trees. "Nail 'er," said Waldo; both of them were running with sweat and insect repellent. The sun beat on the wood and on Waldo's red pate.

The rumblings of an old jalopy down the lane interrupted their work; villagers occasionally came by to see how the house was coming and to give advice, but this intruder, Daniel saw at a glance, was a Tempter; Tempters all had the same look round their eyes, as though they wore blinkers shutting out everything but their own wishes. This man, for instance, puffing heavily out of his broken-down car, was unable to see either Daniel or the house; he happened to see Waldo because Waldo was what he wanted.

"I got a small job, Waldo. Tain't much. Jes a wing I wanna put on my place. Mebbe you'd come over and look. Lemme explain . . ." and Waldo, listening, rolling a cigarette, answered, "Aye . . . aye . . ." as the man explained in interminable detail, while Daniel was footing the bill, a job which would mean the end of work on Daniel's own house for a month, and sadly Daniel watched Waldo the Wonderful, whose ability as a craftsman made every moment sacred, become Waldo the Vulnerable, tempted to bite off more than he could chew at the bait of *new* money.

Bad as losing a month to the man's wing might be, worse dangers lurked; another Tempter yesterday had suggested a whole new profession: "Listen here, Waldo, you and me could get a grant from the gov'ment if we was to start up a sawmill . . ."

"Aye . . . aye . . ."

Or the Tempter last night who'd wanted no more than the use of Waldo's big ton truck to haul some pig shit, but he needed it that very evening.

"Aye . . . aye . . ." And that evening, Waldo left work early, smiling blandly, no redder than usual, with no mention of pig shit, but this morning Daniel detected a strong smell clinging to Waldo's pants cuffs.

The Tempter rambled on until noon, the one hour which everyone agreed was sacrosanct, when Daniel and Waldo sat in the shade of the spruce and Waldo ponderously, reverently, impeccably ate a Thermos bowl of soup, half a dozen thick sandwiches, a cake, numerous cookies, a Thermos of tea, and a plug of tobacco. Renewed, he rose and announced, "Better get the missus. We're cuttin winders and we don't want her winders in the wrong place."

Daniel drove up the lane, across the ridge, and through the woods, a green rampant jungle steaming in the first heat of afternoon; the shack in the clearing had its windows and doors wide open. He whistled their private signal and walked in.

She glanced up, unseeing, from her work, then focused her romance-blinded eyes on reality.

"We're cutting windows."

"Shall I come?" She wore a towel wound round her head, indicating she'd given her hair its weekly olive oil treatment. He glanced down at the canvas of illicit passion among the mango trees, where a beautiful blonde swooned in the arms of a bare-chested slave, while lurking behind in the tropical vegetation was the cruel plantation master, with a startlingly familiar rotund shape and shining red pate.

Gathering her Scribbler Pad of house plans, she caught her reflection in the mirror. "I forgot my towel."

"Keep it on. Do you think Waldo cares? Look at his hair."

"Right, we don't want to give anyone time to steal Waldo." She swept out of the shack in her olive oil towel.

She had a way of climbing into their panel truck as if it were a sort of a joke, not her one and only means of conveyance, but perhaps her second or third vehicle, kept for roughing it in the Hamptons; it was these ways of hers, he was sure, that had started the local rumor about he and she being fabulously wealthy Americans; the fact that they lived in a shack swayed no one from this conviction. He drove through the steaming forest, thinking it must've been women like Sara who kept the tea-tinkling British traditions alive and starched in the jungle.

Waldo waved to them from the garden; he took a great interest in Sara's vegetable garden, particularly in the more exotic gourmet blooms; unfortunately, she hadn't written down what she'd planted where, and at this stage her guess was as good as Waldo's what the odd-looking growths might be.

"You got an awful yeller flower comin."

They examined the mysterious flower, which overnight had trumpeted open into a giant show of gold.

"Appears you'll have a great crop of them anyways," said Waldo.

He laid out his set of the house plans, on which he'd jotted notes. "Them big winders in the kitchen, you want them plumb facin each other?"

"I don't think I had them quite facing," she answered.

"No, you didn't."

". . . You think they should face?"

"Tain't my kitchen."

On this truism, they left the garden and strolled toward the house.

"If it were your kitchen?" she asked.

"I'd have them plumb facin."

"Why?"

He rubbed his head and stared at the skeleton of two-by-fours. He rubbed his head some more. "It'd look better is all."

"How much difference is there?"

"Eight inches."

She made some calculations on her paper. Eight inches was no small matter, Daniel knew; every stick of furniture had been prepurchased in her mind, arranged, and measured to fit the dimensions of the old foundation. "Okay," she said, "you can move the back windows."

All winter and spring, he'd watched her work on these blueprints, and now she made a major eight-inch change, based on no satisfactory explanation other than the length of time Waldo gave to rubbing his pate. It was an impressive display of her respect for the carpenter's ability, and though Daniel didn't care if the windows were upside-down or inside-out, he did care very much that she was with him on the matter of Waldo, because sometimes it seemed, especially when he had to defend Waldo's fishing trips, that she thought he was deluded by hero worship.

■ ■ ■

He stood on the ladder with his head and shoulders and arms in the sunlight, up above the completed first floor, up near the tops of the trees, pushing up into the clouds, and it hit him: I'm going to live in this house I've been building.

He supposed, of course, that had always been the idea; there was no reason for him to be amazed at this late date.

"Put the brads to 'er," said Waldo at his elbow, and he swung his hammer, feeling the nail push its way through the grain. He'd also learned to saw a board straight, because Waldo assumed he could, without criticizing or giving directions, and he suspected this new confidence he had in his own dexterity was the underlying basis of his great fondness for Waldo.

When he recalled how he'd come up with twenty-four volumes of torturously incomprehensible home handyman books, it seemed like some horrible nightmare of insecurity. Civilization, with its highly paid specialists, had intimidated him; he hadn't, he was gradually seeing, been born with a blank spot in his brain preventing him from ever understanding mechanical things.

"Nail 'er." He'd read that Eskimos were geniuses at fixing snowmobiles, though they'd never seen a motor before. He understood: An Eskimo couldn't afford to be intimidated by things that went wrong, or he'd die. When you had to catch your own food, make your own sled, candles, clothes, thread, and whalebone needle, getting a snowmobile running was nothing.

And hereabouts, people would try to fix anything, having the fundamental security that no one else was going to fix it for them.

■ ■ ■

They notched two long beams to look like the back of a brontosaurus, stood them up diagonally, and joined them to the vertical studs; starting from the bottom, they hammered in four-foot-wide treads; and in less than two hours, he knew the secret of stairs. Already he and Waldo were walking up them, down them, up them, from the cool fresh-pine kitchen to the wide-open second-floor stage set in the wilderness and bathed in sunlight like an Inca altar.

"Put the level on 'er," said Waldo, and while Daniel held the level, Waldo took a nail from his *Bound Brook Woodworking, Waldo Story, Proprietor* apron.

Waldo was not a fast worker. He was infinitely calm and infinitely bound to his own unflagging placid pace, and he never made mistakes, and he never had to redo anything. "Needs to be tipped a hair . . ." Waldo carefully adjusted the board under the level, while warm breezes blew the scent of roses up from the dooryard and swallows dove around them and Daniel wondered whether perhaps his books of Tibetan religion were discussing in a very complicated and poetic way something Waldo had mastered on his own.

At six, Waldo collected his tools and took off, and Daniel went to fetch Sara.

She was stretched, arms spread, on the bed, indulging in a crucifix of heat prostration.

"I've got something to show you."

She made a half-hearted attempt to rise.

"You'll love it," he promised; he cut up an orange for her as well as various other enticements, until she finally revived and climbed weakly into the truck.

"What is it?" she asked, as they drove up the hill.

"It's a miracle."

He steered down the lane, and parked; they stepped out onto the grass. He led her into the kitchen.

She looked around. "Well?"

He edged toward the stairs. She waited, expectantly.

He gestured significantly toward the stairs.

"Yes," she said, "that'll make things easier."

For the first time it dawned on him that she might not perceive the incredible stairs exactly as he did. Maybe you had to see stairs being built to fully appreciate them. "Would you lend me your hat?"

She lifted an eyebrow and handed over her straw sun hat.

In desperation, he began, winding his way up the stairs, singing in what might pass for a French accent, or at least Italian, or at the very worst Scandinavian, "*I'll build a stairway to pa-ra-dise* . . ."

He heard a clump-clump behind him, the sound of someone dancing up a stairway to paradise in thongs made in Taiwan. She emerged beside him on the wide open stage in the sky. And as they stood there together, in paradise, his thoughts turned to Waldo: The man had talent, imagination, and power. What else was there in life?

■ ■ ■

"Nail 'er," said Squealing Higgins in his cracked old voice. Squealing Higgins was the best he could get on short notice; or rather, no notice. One day, Waldo had simply succumbed. Or maybe it hadn't happened in one day, maybe he'd thought about it for many days, even weeks, but he hadn't shared his thoughts on the matter. One sunny Monday morning, he'd merely appeared for work twenty miles to the north, building cabinets for somebody else.

Squealing took out his pipe and filled it with tobacco, a unique aromatic whose dominant aroma seemed to be feet. "You can't depend on Waldo Story nohow. He does the same to all of them. He sells them the lumber and then he don't come back." The old man set down his pipe and coughed loosely into a handkerchief. "They tell me Waldo may open a sawmill. But it won't last. Same as that woodworking shop of his. Betimes he's there, betimes he ain't." The cough left Squealing shaken, and he leaned against a beam for a while. "Couldn't depend on Waldo Story's father neither. Nor his grandfather fer that matter."

The old man worked fairly steadily until noon, dined sparingly on sardines straight from the tin, and after smoking a bowlful of

foot-blend, looked suspiciously around the big empty room, until
he spotted a roll of fiber glass insulation tucked in the corner.
"Gimme a hand unrollin that, will you?"

They opened out the pink fluffy roll; fiber glass particles rose on
the air, filling Daniel's eyes with tears, exploding from his nose in a
series of sneezes, attacking his skin with instant itch, and when the
whole thing was spread out and the room filled with glass fiber, the
old man lay himself down inside and rolled it up around him like a
goose-down comforter. "Pour that last bit over me shoulder, will
you? Drafts at my age can kill a man." As the fog of pink fiber
glass settled around him, he fell into heavy breathing, sucking his
pipe.

Daniel stepped out into the sunlight. A half-ton truck was rattling down the lane.

"How you comin?" asked Murvyle, parking in front of the house.

"No work in the woods today?"

"The dukes wasn't feelin too good." The dukes, thought Daniel,
picturing Hilton and Anson vomiting in the oat bin, or perhaps
they hadn't yet gotten to that stage, but were still in the first fine
flower of Moosehead delirium, punching each other's eyes black,
careening ninety miles an hour over the highway, or snoring with
brotherly camaraderie in Anson's kitchen where soap operas flickered in front of them like lullabies.

Murvyle walked toward a shade tree, lurching like a short
stumpy sailor with two wooden legs. "How's Squealin?"

"Taking a nap."

"By rights," said Murvyle, rolling a cigarette between pitch-
blackened fingers, "Squealin Higgins should be dead."

"Is he as bad as all that?"

"He's nearly had the biscuit five or six dif'rent times. Doctors had
to open him and jump up and down on his heart. One time, they
even come round collectin fer his widder." Murvyle blew a puff of
smoke. "Appears you can't kill the bastard."

"I hope not," said Daniel.

Murvyle gave him a long look, his dark sunken eyes more expressionless than ever, the good one as well as the blind one. "Why
d'you think you got him so easy? A first-class carpenter in the middle of summer? Folks don't want him dead on their nice new front
doorstep."

"Maybe I ought to let him go."

"Suit yerself. He'll find another job somewheres else."
The sun played over their boots in the grass, and the cool shade
of the spruce enveloped their faces; Murvyle's weather-beaten skin
was swollen with insect bites, his wrinkled ears twice their usual
size. He swatted flies with his cap; the top of his head, unused to
being capless, was strangely pale against the leathery brown of his
brow; flies tormented his few wisps of hair. "Ever been out to the
choppins? That's where I first worked. Went through the woods before dawn with a stick and a lantern and chopped a path through
the ice fer the horses. Otherwise they'd cut up their legs when they
stepped through." He watched his smoke curl in the air. "The old
feller who showed me how was eighty. That was his job, showin
the young ones. Another old feller would gather sap. Or pick lice
off the beds. Or an old feller who couldn't walk a'tall, he'd sit
makin ax handles. With the grain right in them. Not these cross-
grained axes you get nowadays, turned on a lathe and break the
first time you use them."

A hummingbird quivered above a day lily; swallows chattered
on the electric wires.

"Then the unemployment come, and one winter I found meself
the only fool in the woods. No sir, only damned fools and horses
work, and the horse turns his back to it." He stubbed out his
cigarette and sprinkled tobacco over the earth. "That was the last
winter I ever worked." He got to his feet, brushing off his pants.
"One of these years I'll be lookin at the old age pension, and then I
cal'ate I'll jes curl up in back of the stove." He said it with sly satisfaction, as though he'd be pulling a fast one, but his one good eye
gazed sadly into Daniel's.

He slowly lurched to his truck and climbed in. Daniel turned
back to the house. Through the door frame, he saw Squealing Higgins stirring, and as the rattle of the truck faded off down the lane,
the old man stepped out of his bedding in a pink cloud of fiber
glass; grumbling sleepily, he staggered toward Daniel. "Dormers,"
accused Squealing. "You want dormers?"

Daniel took out Sara's house plans. She'd taken great pains with
her page of dormers, drawing them as if in late evening shadow,
evocative, exquisite, without a scrap of structural information.

Squealing eyed the drawing suspiciously. "What is she, some kind of arteest?"

"Yes," Daniel admitted.

Squealing stuffed his pipe with tobacco, studying the moody picture as if it were a plan for a bomb he was expected to drop on City Hall.

"Well . . ." Squealing started for the stairs.

Upstairs, he eyed Daniel's tools suspiciously; he eyed the two-by-fours suspiciously; he eyed Waldo's barrel of nails especially suspiciously. Suspiciously, he measured and cut and wheezed instructions, somehow penetrating the intricate puzzle of dormers, and little by little the inside of Sara's drawing appeared in three dimensions around them like a marvelous magic act, and the sun that streamed through the skeletal structure felt like the light of old Squealing himself.

"This the way you want her?"

"Squealing, what other way could there be?"

"I ain't sayin. I jes wanna know if it suits you."

■ ■ ■

"Who poured yer foundation?" asked Squealing, nailing a board.

"Uncle Burpee."

"I thought so." He felt in his pocket for his pipe. "Crookeder'n hell, ain't it?"

Daniel hammered the last board on the last of the dormers. Squealing had taken another dizzy spell this morning, but refused to go home, and Daniel'd finally resigned himself to accepting that if the old man died in his house, that's the way the old man wanted to die. Everything Squealing did was perfect; like Waldo Story, he'd had his training as a cabinetmaker. Only his style was different, being predominantly suspicious, but whether he was suspicious because Waldo, and not he, had masterminded the house, or whether he was suspiciously wondering exactly which aspect of the job would eventually kill him, was never clear.

"I seen a bunch of skunks one time," said Squealing, whose mind wandered freely over his long checkered life, "draggin one of their own who was dead."

Visions of the mythical elephants' graveyard passed before Daniel's eyes, miniaturized from gray to black and white, and he felt another profound mystery of the forest unfolding. "Did they bury him?"

"Ett him."

■ ■ ■

"Waldo Story drove over last night," said Daniel. "He's coming back to finish the house."

Squealing put down the pipe he was smoking preparatory to his twelve thirty nap. "Waldo's a good carpenter."

■ ■ ■

"Put the brads to 'er," said Waldo; they were closing in the house, standing high outside on a wide platform.

"Last stagin I worked on collapsed," remarked Waldo. "Didn't break nahthin much but me leg."

"I suppose this staging of ours is a lot stronger."

"You never can tell."

They climbed in and out through the unfinished spaces all afternoon, and exactly at six, they came out on the peak to hammer the last hole closed.

"Spike 'er."

"She's spiked," said Daniel, putting his hammer back in his holster, and surveying the finished roof from his straddled seat on its summit.

"A person could almost live here," beamed Waldo, and scuttled, baboonlike, across the smooth wood, until the red orb of his head disappeared over the side. Daniel scampered behind; as his boots touched the earth, a truck came rumbling down the lane.

"Roofed her, did you," said Murvyle laconically, stepping out and walking toward them.

"Anythin new?" asked Waldo.

"Nahthin much. I see where Squealin Higgins finally died."

"Left her, did he?" asked Waldo, packing his tools in his truck.

"About quittin time yesterday. He was buildin some cupboards." Murvyle chuckled. "Laid his head right in the cupboard."

"In a cupboard, eh?" chuckled Waldo, taking out a plug of tobacco.

Daniel stood between them, thinking he ought to strike a sorrow-
ful pose, demand reverence for Squealing, or at least silence, and
then say something fine. But they'd both known Squealing longer
than he had, knew better than he Squealing's good qualities; the
only thing they didn't know was the traditional city show of hypo-
critical woe; and Squealing wouldn't know that either.

■ ■ ■

The evening was damp, and he had to stop the truck several
times to avoid hitting frogs who were out eating worms in the road.
"Froggy evening."

She didn't reply.

"Like foggy evening," he explained, "except froggy."

She stared ahead through the windshield, as if deaf.

"It isn't Waldo's fault if he's gone fishing," he said. "Or even if
he's on another job. He can't help himself. Do you blame a squirrel
because he hoards more nuts than he needs?" He looked at her to
see how she was taking the analogy. "Waldo's a squirrel. He can't
stop himself from accepting more work than he needs. But it isn't a
moral issue."

"Waldo is not a squirrel."

"Maybe it's not a good analogy."

The light was on in the Bound Brook Woodworking shop. They
strode dourly toward it like a pair of deputy sheriffs: Okay, Waldo,
come out with your hammer up. "Don't be too hard on him," said
Daniel.

"What good would it do?"

Under the light bulb, the rosy dome of Waldo, sprinkled with
sawdust, turned around; he put down his saw and smiled—portly,
benign, utterly unabashed by the fact that he'd left their house
only three quarters finished.

"I see you're busy," apologized Daniel.

"Gotta get these winders turned."

"Will you be back on the job tomorrow?" asked Sara.

"I don't think it. Fact is I'm paintin the high school." He rubbed
his head, scattering sawdust. "Don't know how I'm gonna do it all.
School strikes up in a week."

"Want to hire some assistants?" she asked; Daniel was deeply impressed with the extent of her desire not to let Waldo out of her sight. "Two dollar the hour," said Waldo immediately.

■ ■ ■

The school perched high on a hill, spreading its clapboard grimness above the sleepy villages of Bound Brook, Marsh Creek, and Mugwash.

Waldo's truck was parked in the yard; they pulled up beside it, entered the lobby, and followed the odor of paint until they came to a large green room marked Home Economics, which seemed to be made up entirely of kitchens.

Waldo looked up from his green brushwork. "Glad you could make her."

"Is this the only room we have to paint?"

"We gotta paint the insides of her too."

Daniel pulled open the nearest drawer, gummed up with old parchment paper and stuffed with cake tins, greasy silverware, and recipes all thrown in together; he swung open the door of the cupboard above—more cake tins, mixing bowls, cookie sheets, pans, and a jumble of plates; the counters themselves were chaotically heaped with glasses and gadgets, teapots, spatulas, rolling pins, can openers, egg cups, sugar, enormous thermometers, salt, saucers, towels, toasters, and cans of shortening. "They call it home econ'ics," explained Waldo rubbing his pate. "Somethin new in cookin I guess."

Sara gave the offensive drawers and counters a delicate glance. "If you can find a big table somewhere and bring it in, I'll pile this shit out of our way."

"Open them winders too," said Waldo. "Gotta have plenty of air with this high-gloss enamel. One time I was paintin in town and three fellers closed themself up in the bathroom and all three of them had to be carted away. Only thing saved them was when one feller toppled over, he tipped his can of paint, and I seen it comin out under the doorway. Nother few minutes, they would've been dead. As twas, they was almost dead."

"Waldo, these windows don't open."

"No, they don't appear to."

The famous high-gloss fumes began to fill the room. The many nooks and crannies held it, intensified it, then poured it into the brain cells. Unsteadily, Daniel aimed his green brush up above him, going back and forth over the same dizzying square. He climbed down and went for more paint, passing Sara and Waldo who were wandering around with glazed eyes. Rambling half-finished sentences bounced around in his head, broke off, and reappeared later, slightly altered.

Sara's voice echoed hollowly from inside a drawer: "We all may end up like Squealing. Facedown in a cupboard."

Waldo's footsteps got heavier as he thumped back and forth, and the look in his eye began to be quite beyond Daniel's interpretation. He could see where his own mind was deteriorating, and knew Sara's was going through a similar jumble; he could follow her intoxication; but when he looked into Waldo's usually mild blue eyes, each now crazily gazing out in its own direction, when he saw the face of his guru off on the other side of the moon, reality itself turned to jelly.

Going to fetch more paint, he came upon Sara hanging over a table, sluggishly squeezing icing from the cake decorating kit; torpidly, she squirted colors with both hands, constructing a pink and blue maiden being ravished by a blob of green frosting. He got behind her and shook her. "You need some air."

He guided her through the hall and out of the building.

The late summer air was balmy with hallucinations. Four cows in the field below performed a stately minuet. He seemed to hear a car approach the school and pull up; a woman got out of the car and entered the school. The sweet smell of hay from the meadows wrapped him in stupor. Bound Brook broke its banks, flooding the valley. A bird suggested building an ark. Slowly the flood receded. The woman came back out and drove away. The cows bowed gravely to their partners.

He and Sara walked back into the high school.

On the floor of the home economics room, Waldo sat with his head in his hands. "She come in here and she said *yeller*."

"Who come in here?"

"The teacher." He looked up at them sorrowfully, looked around at the five green kitchens. "There go the profits." He lurched to his feet, reeling. "I'll give her yeller!" It was the first aggressive words Daniel'd ever heard from him. "I'll give her yeller," he repeated, opening one paint can after the other and wildly squeezing from the tubes.

They returned to their work, in yellow. Daniel mounted a counter.

"I'll give her yeller," cackled Waldo into a cupboard.

From the corner of his eye, Daniel saw Sara floating through kitchens. Kitchens, yellow kitchens, and then again kitchens. Surely, he thought, we've already painted them all. But the day had turned surreal. Each time you finished a kitchen, another appeared. Waldo's voice rose in disbelief. "I ain't never seen so many goddamn kitchens."

■ ■ ■

The varnished pine boards gleamed beneath their feet, and the plasterboard walls were flawlessly white, flooded with light which streamed through six mullioned windows downstairs, and patterned by the angles of the dormers in the three rooms above. You flicked switches and light bulbs went on; you turned faucets and water flowed. There was a woodshed, and a long-term plan for a veranda. In the cellar, stones divided large areas into vegetable bins. From cellar to second storey, he and Waldo surveyed it, and found nothing wanting. Waldo rubbed his gleaming head and remarked, "Appears we left out the chimbleys."

"You mean they're not supposed to go in last?" asked Daniel, unable to believe that his guru had made such a serious error.

"I ain't never seen them done that way. Course, I might be wrong, it could've happened to some others before us." He buffed his pate for what seemed a record-breaking length of time. "If that ain't enough to start old people fuckin."

"Will it be okay?" asked Daniel.

"Should be," replied Waldo with that ever-present effervescence which didn't quite commit him to either success or failure. "You go to town," he said, "and pick up a couple of chimbleys and I'll see if I can bore a hole through this place."

Daniel got into the truck, and drove to the camp, where Sara was deep in torrid passion among the aborigines of what looked like the Brooklyn Botanical Gardens, her hapless heroine erotically entangled with a half-breed orchid.

"Waldo needs you to show him where the chimneys should go."

"Be with you in a minute." She continued painting. "I was wondering when he'd get to the chimneys."

Perhaps, thought Daniel, in a flash of insight, it would be best to
say nothing about the normal order of putting a chimney in. He
drove her to the house, and continued on alone into town with
Waldo's shopping list: *Two chimbleys. Quick.*

■ ■ ■

She came out of the house to greet him, her contact lenses swimming in unshed tears. "Wait till you see."

He entered the kitchen; the once-gleaming pine floors were
covered with a chalky white film and rubble of broken-up plasterboard; a huge hole had been savagely slashed through the once-
pristine ceiling. He bolted up the stairs; in the once-beautiful
bedroom, sharp shards of steel roofing and jagged chunks of wood
were hurled all over, as well as bits of plaster, shredded black tarpaper, torn-up plastic vapor barrier, and blinding tufts of pink insulation. Through the fiber glass fog, Waldo beamed his greeting.
"Tweren't easy, but we did her." A round spot of sunlight shone
down through the circular hole in the roof, producing in its shaft
the illusion of a baby pink cyclone. It occurred to him that Sara
must realize this could not be the normal order of chimney inser-
tion.

"Let's see if them stacks fit," said Waldo. "Sure hope I didn't
make her too wide."

They went out to the van and looked at the stacks.

"Only one way to tell," said Waldo. "You go upstairs and I'll
climb on the roof with them."

Sara followed Daniel upstairs like a sunsuited ghost. They stood
and watched the hole in the roof and waited. After a while,
Waldo's portly form appeared above in shadow like Santa Claus on
Christmas eve . . . then the vivid red face . . . and the big stainless steel chimney glistening with sunlight.

"I'll pass her down."

Daniel extended his arms. If the stack was too big, they could always widen the hole, but if the hole was too big, they'd need a new
roof.

Slowly the shiny round cylinder moved over until it was centered, blocking the circle; slowly it moved until it filled the hole; and slowly it entered, with effort, tight on all sides, but coming, coming ever so slowly down.

From the roof, through the stainless steel cylinder, came Waldo's buoyant voice. "That's the cock fer Dolly."

■ ■ ■

He raced from the garden with his basket of corn; Sara had put it strongly: Every thirty seconds off the stalk, massive quantities of sugar were lost and turned to tasteless starch. He hurriedly locked the gate of the two-foot-buried six-foot-high barb-topped fence which he and Waldo had constructed the day after the Gourmet Society of Groundhogs held their convention in Sara's Imported Bush Romano Bean patch, precipitating the closest he'd ever seen her teeter toward total nervous collapse and cruelty to animals.

She was stirring the embers of the bonfire and waiting with the tinfoil; quickly they wrapped the ears and laid them on the coals, as Waldo climbed down from the roof where he'd been capping the chimneys; leisurely, he barreled toward the food, settling his bulk on the grass, ready for serious eating.

With a physical sense of well-being as sweet as the smell of the corn, Daniel breathed in the cool green evening, listened to the night birds, gazed at his castle complete with chimneys, and thought: At last I belong. I'm rooted in the earth, no longer just a wandering neurotic, a helpless city intellectual. Sara passed out the corn on trompe l'oeil corn plates with corn-shaped finger-saving push-pins, and he thought: Here I sit eating my very own starchless corn, in a real community where I know everyone else and they know me, where I've got my own grass to sit on, my own birds twittering, my own house, my own Waldo . . . Waldo was munching contentedly. "What're you gonna do now, Dan'l?"

"Plenty to do, I guess."

"Wanna build my next house with me?"

In his mind, he saw Waldo's question surrounded by a frame, behind glass, on parchment—*Diploma*, it said, *Carpenter's Apprentice, Plumber's Apprentice, Apprentice Jack of All Trades*—and it seemed the perfect answer to all he'd been feeling.

"Two dollar the hour," said Waldo.

And then he thought of the empty store he'd looked at in town—

the dingy, murky, dark, dreary, dusty, unhealthy place that he was considering for an antique shop. He thought of the antiques he meant to fill it with—horrible Victorian monstrosities, cobwebbed Early Canadiana, frumpy old costumes and campaign buttons which nobody wanted, moldy yellowed old books, the whole crack-brained collection of useless crap he used to surround himself with, and thought: Christ, I've missed all that. Here I've been out in the fresh air all summer long, from sunup to sundown, working at real work, swimming in a real brook, sleeping at night like a log, and I haven't spent any time with the dark, dreary, musty, dingy, old companions of my soul.

■ ■ ■

Antique store of my dreams, I have found you.

He stood in the midst of the gloom, which was so clearly everything he'd always wanted in terms of dinginess, darkness, lugubrious woodwork, mood, and sequence of rooms, plus a location in town that couldn't be beaten, in a narrow alley, with not another antique dealer for fifty miles.

"And the price," she said, "what a steal."

The local merchants clearly didn't know what they had in the old touches—oak counters and cupboards, a marble table, an antique scale and ball of string hanging from the ceiling; the fixtures alone were fabulous. So why do I feel terrible?

She drew him over to the grimy window to admire the view. Across the dark alley was an equally old fish market, and the quaint perfume of dead fish was another of the atmospheric touches that meant so much.

"It's damp," she admitted. "It could use a dehumidifier."

On the floor above was an office inhabited by a being purporting to be a barrister, but this you could tell only from the being's handwritten name plate, and never, in the times they'd looked at the place, had they heard any movement upstairs or had any barrister-seekers attempted the cobwebbed climb through the ten-watt-bulb-lit hallway past their lavatory; he had a fond idea that the office was actually occupied by Holmes's Red-Headed League, a suspicion he'd not yet divulged to Sara.

"We'll take it," he said.

They walked through the town to the landlord's office, where papers were signed, Sara got a promise of a dehumidifier, and he felt himself age twenty years.

■ ■ ■

"It's amazing in such a small town," she said, "to find such an excellent library."

They climbed the library stairs, and he beelined for Philosophy, Occult, and Religion. All things considered, what with the excellent library, the friendliness of the people, and the low rent on the store, it's quite the little place.

At the adjacent reading table, two men were arguing religion, the one a simple small-town Pentecostal, and the other a spectral figure with flowing hair and fiery eyes, who was spouting arcane Urantian lore about Christ, to which the poor Pentecostal could only reply in stutters and stammers about the Bible.

A town that even has messiahs, thought Daniel returning with redoubled pleasure to the books on Buddhism, Taoism, and clairvoyance. It wasn't that the selection here was as good as in New York, but in New York the good books were always on loan, whereas here, nobody but he, and perhaps the mad Urantian, took them out. He'd been given an Extended Loan Card, as a "serious researcher," which meant he could keep books literally for years. How did they perceive him as a serious researcher? That, he thought, is a question which pierces the very essence of what a small town is.

3

She gazed through the windshield at the dusty road, the parched stream, and the hill she'd climbed so many times to the building site, and she thought to herself: My troubles are over.

"We're going to miss that old camp," he said.

"I'm not." On her lap were piled electric kettle, electric iron, electric toaster, electric blanket, a Medusa's head of plugs. "I'm going to be plugged in again."

"There were a lot of nice things about the camp," he said, steering the truck round the corner; they rattled down the lane with their household.

"Whose Volkswagen is that?"

"Never saw it before."

They pulled up beside it. The car was empty, but a young woman stood in the dooryard, photographing the front of the house. *House Beautiful*, Sara realized. I wonder how they found out about it so quickly?

The woman stepped toward them as if emerging from the latest edition of *Vogue*, the one not yet on the newsstands, extending a small suntanned hand, so freshly manicured the nails looked still wet. "I'm Kim McKay."

Maybe it isn't *House Beautiful*, thought Sara, whose own hands were filled with electric appliances; there was something about the lady not homey enough for *House Beautiful*, and she tried to remember whether *Vogue* had an architectural editor, British edition; in an English accent, Kim was saying, "I had no idea you were just moving in. I'm on my way to Nova Scotia, and Carol and Judy insisted I stop off and give you their love."

"Carol and Judy?" asked Sara. "Are you a friend of Carol and Judy?"

"The closest of friends. We share the same primal therapist."

Carol and Judy have new friends, thought Sara, and some new kind of therapist. Life has passed me by.

"Come on in," said Daniel.

"I really shouldn't disturb you when you're moving in, though I am dead tired and I know Carol and Judy will never forgive me if I don't bring home some snapshots. It's such a dear little house. Did you really build it all by yourself? How clever you must be." Chattering gaily, admiring the house, smiling flirtatiously, and being endearingly frank all at once, she preceded Sara across her very own brand-new threshold, with Daniel hot at her elegant heels, pointed like a setter.

How could Carol and Judy have done such a thing? wondered Sara, trailing behind with blanket and kettle and toaster and iron. Surely Carol and Judy would never have done such a thing?

Kim filled the new kitchen with her charm, tripping here and there, exclaiming over this and that in the most complimentary tones to Daniel, who was lapping it up, not in any way you could see, of course, he was very clever about hiding his interest, but you could plainly intuit it . . . Sara realized that Carol and Judy would never have done such a thing. Carol and Judy are innocent.

But how else did this Kim find out how to get here?

Hydralike, she seemed able to examine the kitchen, reveal her best angles, subtly flatter Daniel, and talk about the most intelligent things simultaneously; Sara felt as if she and Daniel were two groundhogs peering out of their hole in the taciturn wilderness at some dazzling display of instant city cleverness and intimacy. ". . . Martin and I started primal together, but it's had a devastating effect on Martin, you give up all your defenses when you open yourself to your pain, and for a while there's nothing else there to replace your ordinary games, and you're just one vulnerable blubbering mass, anyway that's how poor Martin is, and, frankly, I can't stand it, so we're getting divorced."

A chic divorcée loose in the forest.

And Daniel seems to be interested. His phony indifference wouldn't take in a child. "Where shall I put this chair, Sara?" he asked, only his eyes peering out from between the rungs of the chair held upside-down over his head.

She'd let herself slip. In one short year, she'd become a dowdy country woman. Deep within herself, she felt the tremendous new effort she must make.

". . . I'm seriously considering doing just what you two have done, leaving the city and finding a place where I can be quiet and simply feel my pain."

In other words, she wants Daniel *and* my beautiful house. Note, she was coveting it with her camera before we got here.

"Do you want this table exactly in the middle?" asked Daniel.

". . . Such a refreshing place, so simple." Kim crossed her legs on the couch, and Sara noted with alarm that every one of her own skirts was utterly passé as to length, nor were her heels remotely high enough, and as far as eye makeup went, she might as well be dead. ". . . So thrilling to feel your pain, after being unfeeling for so long, to really get down into pain."

City chic. Talking deep. Immediate profundity. All I've talked about for a year is horse manure and pine boards.

Kim's coiffure, impeccably streaked, had a curly softness in direct opposition to last year's burnished sleek, and it was manifestly plain that lips were back. ". . . I feel this is the answer, what you two have here, this *real* life."

"Can I make you some tea?" asked Daniel.

There it was. He was attracted to her English accent. Not that he'd ever indicated a particular fondness for accents, but she strongly suspected . . . why else would he ask if she wanted tea?

"I shouldn't put you to the bother," Kim protested, "but I'm absolutely parched."

"Please," said Sara, plugging in her virgin kettle, with a sinking feeling. I've sunk my roots eight-feet deep in this out-of-touch place, topped by Uncle Burpee's footing course, and two more storeys, with dormers by Squealing Higgins.

". . . I'll bet you have a garden."

"Sara has a vegetable garden."

"Sara, darling, would you show it to me? I haven't seen a proper vegetable garden since I was a little girl in England."

She's forgotten her tea, thought Sara, amazed, then recognized the restlessness that used to be her own, in the city, when there were things going on every minute, all over town, to entertain you.

Kim bubbled up from the couch, somehow managing to turn her walk to the garden into a further display of personal elegance, charm, and exuberance, tripping gaily out of the house on her little high heels, exclaiming over the flowers in the field, whose million perfumes weren't as fresh as the very new, very fresh scent that helped to make her aura of fashion so up-to-the-minute. Sara hesitated to ask her the name of her perfume, asked instead, "Are Carol and Judy feeling their pain too?"

"Judy's simply marvelous. She cries all the time. She's totally open. I wish I could be half as open."

Sara opened the gate to her garden. "Is there a book you could recommend that tells about this stuff? We're a little bit out of touch, and I know I've got a lot of pain just waiting . . ."

"Marrows! You can imagine how long it's been since I've eaten a marrow."

"Take some with you."

"I couldn't take your marrows."

"Take a dozen, go ahead." Vegetable marrows had been the prodigious result of the mysterious big yellow flower admired by Waldo, and somehow Sara felt that if she could give Kim enough of them, it would produce the atmosphere of a going-away gift which, in turn, would produce the atmosphere of Kim going away.

"If you knew how this takes me back." Kim was gathering the fat phallic squashes with the zeal of a true marrow maven. "It's such a madly successful garden. It can't be your first?"

"There's my toad," said Sara, casually pointing to that warty horny animal.

"But he's darling!"

"And that's his house." There was no need to mention that he had never moved into his house. She had seen him in ditches, under loose stones, beneath an old piece of wagon, inside an old bone, but never once in Toad Hall.

"This is so inspiring."

"Are you really considering living in the country?"

"Especially after seeing *all this*."

The two small words struck the center of Sara's suspicions as an arrow strikes a bull's-eye. *All this* . . . the phrase shimmered with the thousand masks of Chic Divorcée Loose in Someone Else's Forest. "Of course *we* love it," she countered, "but it takes getting used to." She ended up carrying the marrows while Kim swept through the field gathering flowers to ornament her freshness.

They arranged the marrows in Kim's car, but Kim herself apparently had no intention of joining the marrows. Holding her bouquet prettily before her, she burst into the house, causing Daniel to look up from his furniture moving with startled setter eyes. The arrow of insecurity struck another bull's-eye in Sara's heart. At least, she thought, spying her wonderful Franklin fireplace, for which she'd scoured the countryside, I have the comfort of the hearth. "I think I'll light a fire."

"Too marvelous."

Just opening the doors of the splendid old stove helped her regain that *House Beautiful* feeling. She supposed, having made several hundred fires in the cabin, that she looked pretty professional in Kim's inexperienced city eyes, as she arranged paper, kindling, and logs, tilted the draft, struck a match, and lit the blaze. "Voilà."

Smoke billowed into the room.

"The draft," coughed Daniel. "Open the draft."

"It is open." The gusts of smoke rolling out of the stove intensified.

Kim's eye makeup was running badly, her breath was coming in gasps, she was deeply into her pain. Sara's own eyes felt as if they'd been hit by bricks, and much as she hated to leave Kim and Daniel alone together in an emergency, she raced upstairs to take out her lenses before her eyeballs melted.

She popped the lenses out into their case with unutterable relief, slipped on her glasses, and tiptoed toward the grate in the floor, where she crouched on her knees and peered down to see what was happening between the pair below.

Daniel, with remarkable coolness, was shutting the doors of the stove, which seemed to staunch the smoke storm to the point where life could be sustained.

Kim moved into the picture . . .

It was urgent to get downstairs, but not in her glasses. She flung them off and put on her sunglasses, rehearsing as she rushed down the stairs a casual remark about how the sun suddenly bursts into blinding brightness every day around this hour, in the country.

"Would you like," Daniel was asking politely, "to take your tea on the lawn?"

"I'm afraid I really have to rush off," said Kim, completely sincerely, blinking in the agonized manner of a contact lens wearer desperately trying to hold out until she's alone and can take out the discs that are torturing her. Her coiffure and clothes, Sara noted with satisfaction, will be smoked for a week.

She escorted her outside to the car, offering to pick more flowers for her, or for Carol and Judy, or to take a snapshot of her with her marrows. In a moment of pity she almost offered mirror and lens solution, but immediately realized that could result in a return to the house and reversal of plans.

"Good-bye, you wonderful people," said Kim, which was no doubt an overstatement of genuine feeling, but probably she hoped it would cover the fact that she was driving away in the midst of Sara's farewell.

Sara waved, watching the Volkswagen raise dust up the lane and disappear round the corner. Still listening, she heard the now-invisible car come to a stop, and could feel the relief of a sister sufferer popping her lenses.

She walked back in; Daniel was examining the smoldering Franklin. "There's nothing wrong with this stove as far as I can tell. And we put the chimney in with Waldo. It's got to be the draft, but I can't see where."

"Don't you think that was presumptuous of Carol and Judy?"

"You know how people give out addresses, never thinking anything will come of it . . . didn't you like her?"

How innocent. Didn't you like her? Wasn't she sweet? She dumped the undrunk tea in the sink.

"I'll wash those cups," he said, joining her at the sink. She busied herself placing the toaster and other new implements in the various nooks and spots she'd arranged for them.

"Sara," said Daniel quietly.

"What?"

He was gazing out the window over the sink, toward the opposite ridge. "I'm having a profound realization."

He's leaving me for Kim.

"We shouldn't have done it."

Oh God, she realized, we shouldn't have done it. We shouldn't have . . . "Done what?"

"Built the house. Left the camp. We were in paradise and didn't know it." His words were weighted with panic, the kind of panic that had a way of dragging her into its force. Sorrow and ruin, said his voice. "It's gone, all gone. We've lost our simplicity. Our privacy. Everything."

Everything, she thought, seeing immediately how right he was. And it's all my fault, me and my Scribbler Pads.

"The house burned for a reason," he said. "We were meant to live another kind of life. But we didn't understand. What a pair of fools we were. Blind bitter stumbling fools."

"Oh God," she said, sick with panic. "What're we going to do?"

"It's too late now."

"Maybe it's not! We can sell the house."

"Who would buy it, way out here?"

"Maybe Kim would buy it. She said she was looking for a house in the country."

Sorrow and ruin, said the walls. Sorrow and ruin, sighed the windows and the floors . . . sorrow and ruin . . . what a pair of fools.

"Christ," he said, "another visitor."

"Don't let them in."

"I've got to. It's Pike."

Daniel let him in through the shed; she heard Pike's voice; they entered her kitchen and she put on a brave smile.

Snarling, Pike slammed a carton of food on the table; wearing his red beret and warrior stance of being prepared for attack, he thrust a heavy piece of painted plywood into her hands. "Here's some kindlin fer yer fireplace."

Beneath Pike's glowering green sky was a scene so hideous in vision she could only think of Hieronymus Bosch, but the technique was pure Pike, and the details pure Atlantic Canada; the landscape was epic in scope, encompassing both farm and forest, with tiny stick figures going about their pastoral business of being tossed from plows and ground into hay, or caught like human logs in mechanical tree harvesters; a black bear pursued a man who was setting his shirt on fire; a barn was being put to the match by an oafish prankster; a bobcat ripped open a deer; a moose bayoneted a woman; in the air, birds of prey carried off a human infant, blood dripping; atrocities covered every inch of the plywood. "Where shall we hang it?" asked Daniel.

Where, in her beautiful house, in which the tiniest detail had been tastefully planned, was she going to have to put this aberrant portrait of Pike's mind? Then she remembered the house was no good, a tragic mistake, so what did it matter? She pointed to the spot of honor, the snowy pristine space above her antique butternut sideboard which she was saving for something truly exquisite, say a simple Zen calligraphy, or a school clock circa 1900.

They held a discussion of what height would show the painting off to best light, and Daniel whacked a nail in the flawless wall, and Pike's Inferno was hung; but we aren't going to live here anyway.

"Will you have some tea and a bite to eat?" she asked, examining the contents of his carton—Raggedy Ann peaches, Railroad Beans, Radio Peas, and sundry other Depression canned goods.

Pike's nostrils flared; he smelled Danger. "Somethin wrong with yer flue?"

"I'll have to climb up on the roof and look," said Daniel.

"Waldo Story."

"Waldo?"

"I wouldn't trust that bastard to sew a button on a shit house door."

"But, Pike," interrupted Sara, "it was you who recommended Waldo Story in the first place."

"I know I did," he replied cryptically, implying he had his own reasons. He took out a cigarette, lit it as if it were the fuse on a stick of TNT, and puffed furiously, glaring out the windows toward the road. "Anybody come around yet snoopin?" With no more than a glance, with a cursory flick of his ash, through the innocent drift of his cigarette smoke, he managed to paint a canvas of mad leering imbostyles and Depression hobos behind every bush, threatening her and Daniel by day and by night; and all these phantoms and specters, produced by Pike, could never be met aggressively enough, successfully enough by just her and Daniel; they could only be slain by the fierce rage of Pike, who would any minute finish his tea and leave.

He dragged on his cigarette, tossed an Oreo cookie down his throat, took a scalding swig of tea. "Ever seen a boar pig?" He flicked his ash significantly. "I knowed a boar pig once, out in the woods where I was workin. This black bear used to come round fer the feed, so a couple of us decided to get up a match between them."

"But a pig wouldn't stand a chance against a bear."

"This was quite the pig, he was one of them boar pigs. I say, he was one of them boar pigs. Great big vicious sons of bitches."

"What happened?" asked Daniel, deep into the adventure, and a faint light glimmered in Sara's heart, that perhaps his profound realization and seizure over house-versus-camp was but a thing of the moment if it could be forgotten in bear-versus-boar-pig; because, now that she thought about it, she didn't yearn with all her soul to return to outhouse and kerosene lanterns.

"Bear come up behind the boar pig at his feed trough and give him a judo chop." Pike's powerful hand stopped just short of flattening a tin of Radio Peas. "Knocked that boar pig out so fast he didn't have time to fart."

He stood to go, glaring hard out the window at invisible murderers. "When yer in the village, stop by," he said sinisterly. "I got somethin to show you."

Through the window, she watched him stealthily emerge from the shed and scan all directions to see that the coast was clear before he menacingly made for his car, stepped in, and roared away, raising a cloud of dust, in whose cumulus aftermath a truck appeared.

The truck doors opened; Murvyle and Phoebe descended, Murvyle holding a huge flowered bowl and Phoebe a huge flowered pitcher. Of all the treasures Phoebe kept untouched in her little back room, these were the two objects Sara greatly admired and had often wondered, when looking at them, how their graceful shapes and delicate glaze had managed to survive a century of children.

"Don't bother tellin anyone where you got them," muttered Phoebe furtively, as she entered the kitchen and laid her pitcher down on the table.

"Are you sure you shouldn't save them?" asked Sara, thinking of the children, the grandchildren . . .

Phoebe flushed. "You been awful good to me."

Murvyle turned away, grumbling loudly to Daniel about dust on the road, and Sara wondered guiltily in what possible way she'd been good to Phoebe. She placed the heirlooms on the butternut sideboard underneath Pike's painting.

"Would you like a cup of tea?" she asked, starting to feel like a human samovar, which must be, it occurred to her, how Phoebe feels most of the time.

"We jes ett," said Murvyle.

"Yes," sighed Phoebe, "we jes got done eatin."

"Still no rain," remarked Murvyle.

"Nor sign of it neither," said Phoebe.

They gazed out the windows. A peaceful silence fell, in which sorrow and ruin, getting into your pain, and primal tears seemed to fade like a dream, a dream she perceived as a troubled landscape, self-created and a thousand miles away.

Through the windows, they saw a big ton truck come down the lane and pull to a stop. Murvyle and Phoebe got to their feet.

"Must you go?"

"We jes stepped by fer a minute to make sure you got in all right."

They left through the shed, and the next visitation filed in past them, headed by Waldo Story, but a very formal Waldo Story, in a shirt that wasn't a work shirt and pants that weren't work pants and a wife and two chubby girls in Sunday dresses and a small chubby boy in a suit.

They stiffly took their seats on the couch which, not being a very large couch, jammed them together like a package of nitrite-red sausages.

"Well," said Mrs. Story brightly, "I see you moved in."

"Yes," said Sara brightly.

"This afternoon," offered Daniel.

"Zat so?" said Waldo, whom nothing had previously embarrassed, neither being caught fishing, nor taking on other jobs, nor forgetting a chimney, who'd been easy with them and they with him, until this evening when all three were profoundly embarrassed by the dreadful predicament of sociability.

Between Waldo and Mrs. Story, as between a large pair of bookends, the children sat unmoving, See-no-evil, Hear-no-evil, and Speak-no-evil; only the blue searchlights of their eyes rolled around the room, taking in what their father had built, and it occurred to Sara that Waldo's bringing his family to show them the house, when you thought about how many houses he'd done, was not all that much less than being mentioned in *House Beautiful*.

Daniel broke the pall. "The fireplace smokes."

"Smokes, does she?" asked Waldo. "I wonder what could be wrong."

Sara watched him rubbing his scalp, and cleared her throat. "I think," she said, "I must've designed it wrong. I read that a chimney has to extend two feet up from the roof, and I wanted to save

on chimney, so I put one at either corner where the roof is lowest
. . . but maybe what they meant was a chimney has to extend two
feet above the highest point of the roof."

Waldo's expression of blank incomprehension was crossed by a
gradual dawning; his puzzled eyes slowly grew round.

"That's it," she said glumly, "isn't it."

"That's an awful high roof up there."

"I know," she said glumly.

"That's a pile of chimbley we're talkin."

"Will it ruin the look of the house?"

"I never zactly seen no chimbley stuck up from the end quite so
far as yours'll be stickin."

"What else can we do?"

"Fireplace smokes bad, does she?"

"Smoked a woman to Nova Scotia," said Daniel.

"My!" said Mrs. Story.

"Afraid you'll have to," said Waldo.

They sank back into torpor, while Sara figured how many
lengths more they would need and how much it would cost and
that it would probably have to be braced in several places to keep
it from flying away like a long-necked stork.

"Anyways," said Mrs. Story brightly, "Waldo got yer house done.
I never did believe he would see it through, him havin to build
them winders up the railroad station and the vestry fer the church
and the porch onto the post office . . ." At the endless list, Waldo
rose. "Gotta finish off fifteen doors by mornin."

"Waldo's doin the doors fer the new nursin home."

Waldo's work, thought Sara, is the rock of Sisyphus; except
Sisyphus wasn't as serene as Waldo.

The children came to their feet in a body, and with one last
stone-faced goggle, filed out without having uttered a word,
brought up fore and aft by a parent.

■ ■ ■

The morning was sunny and cold. Climbing into the van, she
turned back to glance at the long shiny smokestacks adorning the
roof of her beautiful house, which now resembled a tugboat sailing
through the forest.

They drove down the lane, where curled yellow leaves scam-

pered like claws. Frozen apples clung to the trees of the derelict orchards, and the old gray birdhouses along the settlement road,
which had been joyous with birds during the summer, were now as
abandoned as the falling-down farms—but there was one old farmhouse which she'd lately discovered was not as abandoned as it appeared; approaching the wreckage of leaning gray lumber and sagging roof, Daniel slowed the van. "Looks like we're taking old Alf
in."

She glanced at the tree stump where Monsieur Alphonse had
hung out his hat, his signal that he wanted a ride.

Daniel leaned on the horn.

They waited, gazing at the bootlegger's hideout, which it was
rumored not even a dog would stay in, and it was true she couldn't
recall having seen Alf's puppy of summer for over a month.

"Good mornin, ma fran!" shouted Alf, striding out from the shed
in back where he kept his still. "Fine mornin, eh, ma fran?" He gestured with a ladies' umbrella as he wove his debonair way through
the debris of his estate, with his attaché case of home brew and
Duke of Windsor tie and fawn-colored raincoat, the most dapper
man in the forest, if not the county, and possibly the country.

"How're you doing?" asked Daniel, with a certain Duke of Argyll
flamboyance to match the nobility of his guest.

"I'm doin good, ma fran." Alf clapped his hat from tree stump to
head, completing his rakish toilette, and squeezed onto the seat beside her, filling the van with his bouquet of booze, tobacco, assorted powerful old Alf smells, and joie de vivre.

A monologue ensued, impossible for her to comprehend, delivered with sweeping flourishes of the hand, exuberant spray, and
accents continually rising to the challenge of life, which had treated
Monsieur Alphonse pretty well according to his own view of the
matter, though perhaps not one man in a thousand would think so.
She caught bits of plans for managing a chinchilla ranch . . . then
what sounded like a first-person account of the Boer War . . . followed by an invitation—and surely here she misunderstood—to
dive with him for pearls in the brook.

"I'd like to," said Daniel, "but I'm going to start a business."

"What kind business?"

"An antique store."

"Ah, de antique business. I use to be in dat business ma self . . ."
They left the dirt road behind, and hit the highway. "You play gui-

tarrr?" Alphonse's question fell like a lucid pearl from the unending string of his baffling harangue.

"A little," replied Daniel.

"You come by. I make ver good guitarrr. Straight neck. Not crooked. Everybody roun here use ma guitarrr. Fiddle. Ma snowshoe too . . ." He took off his hat and straightened the brim, fixed the crown, and snapped it back on. "You see dem donkey?"

They looked toward the right of the road where donkeys grazed.

"I sole dem people dem donkey . . . I shoe dem horse . . ."

She gazed at the winding river cutting through the valley like a taffeta ribbon, above whose surface shone the ceaseless flow of old Alf's words. ". . . Good faller dere," he remarked with a wave toward a tarpaper hut, in front of which sat an inebriated gentleman propped up by his cabin. "Fran of mine, mighty good faller." Good for what? she wondered vaguely, staring at the cadaverous figure who hadn't noticed Alf's greeting, being preoccupied with delirium tremens.

"Dat store dere." Alf pointed toward the tepee souvenir stand. "I use to own it. Now I jes make'm canoe. De best canoe in whole damn place. Take her down de big water. She never sink." He snapped his hat emphatically, while Sara tried to fathom the roots of his poetry: part French Acadian, part Indian, part crazy, and completely drunk. He opened his raincoat to search for tobacco; she noticed a pistol strapped to his chest. "You get yer apples in yet, ma fran? Mebbe I come over, help you pick some, give you good tips on pickin de apples." He gesticulated with his tobacco. "Dat lake over dere . . . I had chance to buy dat lake ten year ago. Should've buy it den. Look what's happenin now." The great happening, as far as she could tell, consisted of an iron fence. ". . . Faller drowned in dere. Was wanderin along dere, fell in, drowned. Mighty good faller." Perhaps, she thought, the good faller had some of Alf's brew in him when wandering . . . "Ma boy!" Alf's cigarette plunged past her face toward the gas station. "Ma boy workin in dere. Ma car in dere. He's fixin it good fer me."

"That's nice," said Sara, catching on; old Alf had no car; old Alf had no license. But everything he saw, he either had some hand in, or created completely out of the inexhaustible springs of his soul.

The truck bumped along the crowded slum road which led to the railroad tracks; outside the tumbledown shacks, small children of every race and shade played. "Some of ma grandchildren,"

Alphonse exclaimed, including the whole road in his wave, indicating that he'd populated the entire community. Every so often she grasped what he was saying, but most of the time she merely floated along on his nonstop oration; his accent was difficult to decipher but, more than that, the source of his thought was an inner reality so remote from the generally accepted one determined by physics, it was almost as if old Alf had the gift of tongues.

The slum road had a vacation aura, its white shacks pressed close together like a row of madcap beach houses; the general store owner, Ruby of RUBY'S ECT, a woman weak in spelling but strong of feature, lazily sat in the autumn sun, en masse, airing her formidable flesh, particularly the great girth of her thighs which were expansively spread, revealing gray garters and other monumental secrets. ". . . Ver good woman. Heart of gole. Let you run up a ver good bill. Give you plenty credit till pension check come . . ." Ruby's eyelids flickered; she glanced their way, and started to her slippered feet, flesh rolling in no uncertain terms, as old Alf quickly tipped his hat down over the side of his face. The truck struck a pothole and bounced forward, past festively clustered shacks, some set on stilts, some with porches precariously crumbling off; but one ambitious homeowner had gone way beyond his neighbors, by starting with a cellar instead of just stilts or four hunks of stone, then run out of money, roofed it, and moved into the hole in the ground with his family; smoke rose from their ground-level chimney like breath from a snorkel. "Ma daughter . . . best foundation in whole damn place."

As they neared the railroad, he suddenly shouted, "Hey! Hey!" and rolled down his window, calling out toward the little boxcar pumping over the tracks; the men in the boxcar halloed back. "Good fallers, dem . . ." She had a vision of the little boxcar pumping out in the night to the Hills of New Jerusalem, through the woods and the darkness for a blast of old Alf's home brew.

Rush hour traffic slowed them down; they maneuvered into the line of cars creeping over the narrow, rickety, rattling bridge into town.

". . . I tole dem about dis bridge. I went up to de parliament. I went up to ma good fran Marcel DuBocquet, premier of de whole damn province, you know Marcel DuBocquet?" Alf slapped his knee. "I say, *Marcel, dat bridge she gonna come down one of dese days.* I tole him what to do." He slapped his knee again. "Good faller, Marcel DuBocquet. One of dese days, she come right down."

A policeman waved traffic on into town, and Alf waved back, then turned to Daniel. "Openin an antique store, ma fran?"

Daniel nodded; they pulled up at the light.

"All right, ma fran, I get off now." Alf opened the door, struggling with his various encumbrances. "How much I owe you dere?"

"It's been our honor, my friend," replied Daniel.

The light stayed red; they watched him getting his bearings, pivoting jauntily on the sidewalk with hat, umbrella, attaché case—an ageless dandy, loose on the town, and ready for business.

They drove toward their new antique store in silence, accompanied by Alf's lingering aroma and the arcane echo of his rampage. Insane schemes flitted through her brain—for developing lake frontage, polishing pearls, packaging hooch, violin marketing—but as they parked, and stepped out into the crisp morning air, old Alf's fantastic ideas gradually dovetailed into her own commonsense plans and she felt her feet touch solid ground again.

"An indoor antique shop's fine for the winter," she began, "but come spring, wouldn't it be nice if we had a terrace where people could browse in a gardenlike setting?"

She unlocked the flimsy door which would be replaced by French doors come spring; the dingy grimness inside the empty shop took her aback after visions of terraces and greenery. "Paint. It's screaming for white paint."

She opened her handbag and took out her tape measure, a parting gift from *Bound Brook Woodworking, Waldo Story, Proprietor.*

Daniel took the other end, and they started to measure the rooms. He called out the figures, and she jotted them down, while pots of geraniums bloomed in her notebook margins—geraniums, pansies, fragrant splashes of color decorating the terrace. "And that," she said, pointing to the radiator corner, "is where the cat will sit."

"What cat is that?"

"I don't know, he'll come along. Windowsills, please . . ."

He took his end of the tape to the window.

"The other week," she said, "I noticed a cat by the library. A small odd-eyed white. He seemed to be quite homeless. I don't know if you noticed him . . ."

"I noticed him. He was eating a pigeon."

"Of course, the cat's the least of our worries." She jotted down the final dimensions.

"I don't want an antique shop," he said.

She stared at her notebook, the pots of geraniums and pansies. "But what are you going to do with your life?"

"Dive for pearls." He smiled, and she had a fleeting hope he was joking. Then their eyes met.

"I thought maybe after a while," she said, half to herself, "other nice shops might open up in the alley . . . boutiques and a little café with tables outside and maybe an art gallery . . ." She met his eyes again. "It was old Alf, wasn't it."

He didn't respond.

"Okay," she said. "So what now? Do we try and talk the landlord out of the lease?"

"I'll do it."

"Sure, and you'll offer him six months rent. We'll do it together," she said, realizing that her desire to make him suffer over her loss of geraniums and art galleries and café society and Greenwich-Village-moved-to-Atlantic-Canada would have to be swallowed in the more pressing problem of salvaging money.

She slowly closed her notebook and put it away.

They walked through the empty rooms.

He pushed open the door to the alley; outside, in the sunshine, a small odd-eyed white cat, slinking by, stopped and stared up at her.

■ ■ ■

"What a weight off my back."

"And your wallet," she added; they stepped out of the landlord's office, five hundred bucks in the red and free to dive for pearls.

He stopped to look at a window display of bridles and harnesses; she followed him into the store, dragging her feet.

He walked toward the back of the shop where the saddles and horse collars were kept, and she gravitated toward household things—bizarre rural items stocked from decades ago or still produced by some antiquated factory catering strictly to farm supply stores. There were speckled enamel pudding basins and chamber-pots and mottled Rockinghamware and butter churns and jelly bags and pot-bellied laundry stoves and cream separators. Maybe, she thought, he'd like to be a farmer. It's a respectable profession. He'd be outside in the fresh air, with animals and oats and alfalfa. It might be just the answer.

But why, she wondered, wandering through crank-mops and brooms and sump pumps and incubators, should I worry? It's his life, not mine. If he doesn't want a store, it's only less work for me.

Except here I am, looking at sump pumps.

She walked to the back room, where he was trying on cowboy hats.

"I'm going to the five and dime."

"What do you think of this hat?"

"Not much."

She gloomily made her exit, past a grocery whose genuine antique facade had once cruelly deceived her into thinking the province boasted a gourmet shop; on entering, she'd found the shelves to contain quart boxes of baking powder, gallon cans of jam, fifty-pound tins of shortening, hundred-pound sacks of animal feed, and other elephantine packages of grosse cuisine.

The five and dime, at least, had ladies' clothing, if mainly aprons and housecoats and flesh-colored lisle stockings and flesh-colored rayon drawers and similar flashy farm fashions. The walls were hung with decorations for the elegant rural home— Czechoslovakian tapestries of deformed bears and spastic rabbits stitched with Day-Glo thread on rayon velvet.

In a moment of suicidal moroseness, she purchased the flesh-colored drawers; they were too slippery to feel like a hair shirt, but the implication was close.

Falling deeper into depression, she made her way to the bank to straighten out their shaky finances. The bank also catered to farmers and lumberjacks, with dancing school type outlines of feet on the floor to direct the glassy-eyed patrons; flannel-shirted men and pillbox-hatted ladies stood in line with bovine patience, none of your city grumbling over time wasted; transactions were slow and personal, with drawling discussions of health and the weather. It was as foreign to her temperament as Mars, but here's where she was, trapped like a rat, without an antique store, and carrying a string-tied brown paper parcel of flesh-colored drawers.

Now glassy-eyed herself, with barely the energy to walk, she dragged her steps back to the bridle store. He hadn't missed her at all, was trading horse tales with a foul-smelling old country character.

"Here's the missus," said Daniel. "Guess I'll have to be going."

So it had finally happened; she'd been reduced to the status of the missus. She might as well hang a Czechoslovakian tapestry on her wall and be done with.

He led her through the one-horse street as if he'd been born there in his plaid flannel shirt, moronically cheerful, completely insensitive to her condition. "Let's have some chow at the Royal," he said, with an inane drawl.

The doors of the Royal opened upon the blast of a jukebox and a flannel-shirted panorama of stone-silent diners. Whether they were engrossed in the twangy ballad of the Nashville chanteuse, or in their muddy cups of coffee, or uniformly dull-witted, the ambiance was in shattering opposition to her morning vision of café society, art galleries, and Greenwich-Village-moved-to-Atlantic-Canada.

They found a booth with a view of the kitchen, where an inscrutable Chinaman went about his business of poisoning the barbarians. The waitress looked as if she needed to sleep for a week, but sleep alone would never restore her woman's spirit, nor youth, nor even her late middle years, which had beaten her to this ravaged state of sorrow, with pallid dangling skin, milked-over cornflower eyes, hopeless mechanical motions, and sad old lady's voice which bespoke a vanquished soul. Is this, wondered Sara, what the country will do to me?

"Terrific joint," said Daniel, on his way, she saw, to becoming a country person.

She sipped her strong tea, dunked her donuts, and as the sugar and caffeine clicked in, it occurred to her that these down-home people did have a certain something. You couldn't deny it. They were of the soil. They even smell like the soil. Silent, like a stand of trees. In a way, they're beautiful. In a way.

The song on the country jukebox concerned itself with love, infidelity, and drinking to forget. These were the human issues. And these people knew it.

The dour faces drooping over their cups of coffee, their laconic conversations, the worn-out plastic booths and tables, the Chinaman skulking in back, the naive little town with the great north forest all around it . . . it was the very essence . . . of something.

He got up to go.

She picked up her parcel of drawers.

They walked through the doorway, and the glory of autumn filled her soul.

And the good gentle people strolling down Main Street, the funny old farm things in the stores, the marvelous luncheonette they'd just left . . . She inhaled deeply, quickening her step and taking his arm. How awful it would have been to confine him to a life he hated.

Two donuts and some caffeine, she thought; amazing.

■ ■ ■

"Old Alf's a pretty good feller," said Murvyle from the lounge behind the stove.

"He is knacky," admitted Phoebe, but there was reservation in both voices.

Daniel and Hilton were outside with the dog, and she and Phoebe and Murvyle were chewing over the subject in the leisurely way of people who have few subjects. "Old Alf was quite the dude when he first come here."

"Still is," said Phoebe.

"Talk about clothes. You know that there white lampshade hangs over yer kitchen table?"

Sara nodded; she'd furnished her house with several Japanese paper lanterns, but the one over the table, being the largest size made, attracted quite a lot of admiration.

"When old Alf first come to Jerusalem, he wore one of them cowboy hats as big and white as that lampshade of yours."

" 'Tis true," said Phoebe earnestly.

"Two pistols," went on Murvyle, "with bullets strapped crosswise over his chest."

"Shiny boots," sighed Phoebe, "to his knees, and them puffy ridin breeches."

"He rode in on a horse?" asked Sara, beginning to form a mental image of a mad vaquero in bandoleers.

"He walked in, didn't he, Murvyle?"

"First time I seen old Alf, he was walkin round the bend by the churchyard. Never seen nahthin like it."

Phoebe shook her head in affirmation, at the memory of her own first sight of Alphonse, and it struck Sara that the old bootlegger had cut a romantic figure in Phoebe's life, and probably in the life of every woman for miles around. Because of low population and tight boundaries, it often seemed that country people fell into pairs without much choice; her introduction to Hilton's Frenchwoman had been the eye opener; Francine was not only rather pretty in a Piaf way, but coincidentally could strum three chords and belt out a song; yet there she was bending over her stove for a drunken, leering, caveman Hilton, her geographical field of men being so small.

And into this tiny world strode Alphonse, who would've been dashing in any arena.

"'Tis jes as clear as water," said Phoebe dreamily, "the stuff old Alf makes with rats' tails. Rich folks from town, women too, used to come out to buy his brew."

"He only uses female tails," winked Murvyle from in back of the stove.

"He never used Dolores too good," Phoebe admitted.

"Dolores was Alf's wife?" asked Sara.

"You know Dolores," said Phoebe, as if to a forgetful child.

Murvyle puffed on his cigarette. "She was dyin of the influenza one time, and old Alf wouldn't let her go to hospital cause he cal'ated she'd be more useful at home. But I had a couple of teams then, and I hitched them to the sled, and went fer Dolores after it got dark. I carried her out and wrapped her up, and jes about then old Alf appeared hootin and hollerin. As we drove away, he shouted, *Moorville* . . . he alluys called me Moorville . . . *Moorville*, he called, *I kill you son of a bitch*."

"Tsk, tsk," said Phoebe.

"Next mornin," continued Murvyle, "I was some perturbed, but I had to go to the woods and work, old Alf or no, so I hitched up the team, and started out. Only I had me ax beside me on the wagon seat."

"Coldest mornin we had in a whipstitch," said Phoebe.

"Cold? Icicles was formin off the breath of the horses. Is that cold enough fer you?"

"Twas cold," attested Phoebe.

"Then, I seen him comin. Walkin toward me with his high boots and both his guns and his five-gallon hat and a knit cap inside fer to keep him warm. He was only wearin the big one more'r less fer

the look. So I seen him comin, spurs jinglin—betimes he used to
wear spurs—and I was perturbed. I tightened me hand around me
ax. And Alf he kept comin, and he says to me nice as you please,
By Chri, she's a cold country, Moorville."

"That's all he said," agreed Phoebe.

Murvyle flicked his ash in the stove grate. "See why I say old
Alf's a pretty good feller?"

"And Dolores?"

"Dolores was a widder when old Alf come here. Richest woman
in the settlement, had five hundred of the very best acres and a big
house and only two young ones. One of the prettiest women you
ever seen, and Alf had that big hat." Murvyle chuckled.

"Twas her ruination is what twas," said Phoebe.

"Old Alf drunk away a hundred acres, gambled away another
few hundred, give her a baby every year, and beat her into the
bargain."

"All that's left is that shack he stays in, and he don't really own
that."

"But what of Dolores?"

"You know Dolores," Phoebe insisted. "She waits on tables down
to the Royal."

". . . *That's* Dolores?"

"Nice-lookin woman with reddish hair," said Murvyle helpfully.

"He still stays with her betimes, when he's sick and needs doctorin. She's got a little room somewheres at the end of town."

The murky haze surrounding the tale was gradually dimming
and the true facts fell into place in the clearing—the clearing at the
bend by the churchyard, where the ravaged old waitress from the
Royal was growing younger and younger, and plumper and love-
lier, with flaming red hair and amorous eyes; and striding toward
her, in shiny boots and bandoleers and a hat of unequaled white-
ness and size, was the young caballero Alphonse. It was summer;
Sara could see the sandy texture of the road by the churchyard,
could feel it forming under her paintbrush; all she had to do was
change the architecture of the church from clapboard to Moorish
and she'd have a full-fledged Spanish romance. I *must* get an as-
signment for a Latin Lover cover.

Then slowly, the cover changed: The fair red-haired beauty
started to age; her flesh was melting away, leaving hanging withered skin; her hair grew lusterless, mottled, and thin; her mouth

caved in; her amorous cornflower eyes were filled with pain; her shapely legs became bulged and veined; her hands shook as she set a teacup down in the Royal Café. And the young caballero was steadily shrinking into an elderly reprobate with ladies' umbrella and attaché case, ashes in his mustache and a house not even a puppy would stay in.

This is the part they don't tell you about in historical romances, thought Sara. Never had she painted a cover of a beauty older than twenty. What did all those femme fatales do with themselves after retirement? Probably they died of syphilis. She envisioned a whole new genre of covers—aging ladies in the romantic centuries before penicillin, with rashes, noseless, expiring amidst magnolias and crinolines, while around them, the men in their life went mad, crippled, and blind.

Phoebe sighed. "A person never can tell."

"That's right too," said Murvyle, lying down again in back of the stove. "She might've married one of her own and still done poorly."

"Tain't likely she'd have ever done quite so poorly as what she done with old Alf."

"'Tis hard to think how she could've," Murvyle admitted.

Unless, thought Sara, she was dinnamited.

"Dis ver good car you bought today, ma fran," said old Alf. "I know five, six people had dis car before, ver good car, dey all like her ver much."

Daniel steered his new second-hand Acadian convertible along the bank of the river. "You know five or six who had the same model?"

"De same damn car! De same scratch on de hood, de same dinge in de fender. Ver good car, ver good in de summer, you can ride her wid de top down."

Daniel glanced at Sara.

"Last summer," went on Alf, "I do some divin." He waved at one of his colleagues spread-eagled in front of a shack, and gestured expansively past Sara, toward Daniel's nose and the river. "I found ver rare pearl in dere. Almost swallow de goddamn ting. Faller offer me two, tree hundred dollar, but I hang onto it. Wort much more den two, tree hundred dollar, don' you tink, ma fran?"

"How big is it?" asked Daniel, steering onto the dirt road home.

"Is big, ver big, big red pearl."

Maybe I ought to buy it. Offer him three hundred and ten. Big red pearl. Put it on a chain. Give it to Sara. He drove up the Hills of New Jerusalem, knowing there was no big red pearl, at least not in Alf's possession, but liking the sound of it.

"Why," asked Sara, "did five or six people sell this car?"

"Ver good car. Top come down. She go to Vancouver and back many times," said Alf, with his instinct for exactly the words to strike anxiety into your heart. Daniel noticed that the odometer hadn't moved since he'd driven out of the lot, so apparently the figure of ninety-nine thousand miles couldn't be strictly depended upon.

They left Alf off at Château Rat-tail, and continued on alone. "I wonder," said Sara, "if that many people really owned this car."

"You know how Alf exaggerates," he said, turning at the schoolhouse; somewhere in the past year and a half, he'd discovered the futility of worry; you could worry over a dozen probabilities and then get clobbered in the dark by one you never thought of; but Sara hadn't yet caught on. "How many miles is a motor good for?" she asked.

"I don't know, but this motor sounds first rate."

"Why are we shimmying?"

"Road conditions." They shimmied down the lane, and she continued her inquisition, her voice getting more charged with worry and his answers proportionally wilder because he knew little more than she on the subject of cars, but since she depended upon his expertise to calm her, he heard himself discoursing learnedly as he parked axle deep in snow.

She took the groceries into the house, while he went to retrieve her portfolio from its hiding place in the woods, where he always put it when they went to town, so that whatever happened, fire, flood, or famine, she'd never again lose her life's work.

He tramped through the orchard into the thicket toward the overturned tree trunk. He bent down, reached in, and for some reason couldn't feel the portfolio. He must've hidden it more deeply; he scratched in the leaves . . . in the soil . . .

In the old comic books he used to sell in his shop, the world at such moments was rent by lightning; he felt the zigzag lines saw through his brain, and found himself covered in sweat.

Could I have hidden it someplace else? He scrambled to his feet, and looked around for other overturned trees. A few yards deeper in the woods was another, and he raced toward it, knowing full well he hadn't hidden the portfolio there.

He ran back to the original spot, the zigzag lightning bolts now slicing him as with a chainsaw. He crashed through the brush, branches scratching his face . . . and noticed the snow all around the roots had been scooped and tossed, the leaves scattered, the entire area violently disturbed. Sara's portfolio had been stolen.

Instantly, he knew who'd done it—the kids he'd put off the land during deer-hunting season, punks who shot up cabins, put sugar in gas tanks, and gang-raped their feeble-minded cousin. Obviously

our turn has come. Would it be easier to pay the kids a ransom or
intimidate them into returning the portfolio?

Suddenly, something odd struck his eye—a single very large
print in the snow.

It couldn't belong to the punks; aside from being just one solitary print, it was far too large, far too unshod, far too unlike a foot,
far too like an enormous . . . paw.

He felt the air all around him laughing and heard the voice of
the forest prankster—an overgrown gnome, giant elf, possibly a
large leprechaun—who'd played this joke to torment him.

He hurried up to the house.

There are no leprechauns in Canada. Or if there are, and perhaps there are, why would they leave a paw print? Paw prints are
generally left by animals. Isn't it therefore more likely that a paw
print, mathematically speaking, equals *animal*?

He flung open the door. His only hope was that he'd lost track of
the days and hadn't actually hidden her portfolio this morning. He
bolted up the stairs and asked as calmly as possible under the circumstances, "Is your portfolio in the studio?"

"No, you hid it this morning."

He ran back down the stairs in despair, thinking of all her paintings, all the snow scenes and farm scenes and woods scenes, all the
portraits of Phoebe and Murvyle, not to mention the book jacket
she was working on of a gay caballero wearing a five-gallon hat
and bandoleers, embracing a red-headed waitress whose Spanish
shawl was painted in intricate detail, at least an hour of Spanish
shawl; he raced to the woods, dove into the bushes, thrashed around
under the scrub, and raced back, up again to the house, feeling as
if he were caught in an old-time movie where the chase goes back
and forth in jerky frames; he burst open the door, and called up
the stairs:

"Sara, an animal took your portfolio."

From above in the studio came a long trembling wail.

She ran down the stairs, eyes bulged like a frog's, mouth set open
in a permanent *O,* and the chase resumed, the Keystone Kops,
rinky-tink music accompanying their race to the woods, along with
her trembling guilt-bestowing wail, which went on as if she'd risen
above the need for breath, or as if it were several wailers,
numerous wailers, an entire bereaved community of artists at the
wailing wall.

They staggered through the trees; insane with the need to shut up her guilt-factory wail, he said, "You see what I mean about worrying? Even if you worried about everything you could possibly think of, it would never occur to you that an animal might steal your portfolio."

His statement was greeted, first, by silence, then by a look which struck him keenly, and then by:

"What are you talking about! There's a year's work in that thing! And no animal took it. It was those kids!"

"But, Sara, the paw print . . ."

"They were impersonating an animal!"

His senses reeled; he recalled a Bugs Bunny cartoon of a character who went around with a fake paw attached to the end of a stick for making huge animal prints, exactly like this one.

The fine points were flashing by him too fast; it required a person who possessed a degree of woodsmanship beyond his own.

"I'm going for Murvyle," he said, and raced back to the car, jumped in, and pulled out of the yard, up the lane, to the schoolhouse, and down to the brook, feeling as if he spent his life tearing along country roads with everything out of control. Up the opposite ridge he sped, around the bend, to Murvyle's, and as he parked in the barnyard, the engine of his brand-new seventh-hand convertible went dead with a terrible explosion.

He leapt out of the car and tore across the snow-covered lawn, pursued by a barking Festus who'd caught his mood; he flung himself into the kitchen.

"Have a cup," said Phoebe.

"An animal stole Sara's portfolio!"

Phoebe blinked. "I jes made fresh biscuits . . ."

Murvyle slowly rose from his lounge in back of the stove, walked to the row of pegs on the wall, and took down his cap.

With a belch, Hilton followed, taking his plaid flannel overshirt.

"Did somethin happen to Sara?" asked Phoebe, agape, as they filed out, stuffing their pockets with biscuits.

"We can't use my car." Daniel ran in the lead toward the barnyard. "The engine conked out."

"That son of a whore," said Hilton. "Did you buy that son of a whore?"

"We'll take Hilton's car," said Murvyle, showing a rare understanding of the urgency of the predicament, that it warranted the Grand Prix driving of his eldest son.

Daniel climbed into Hilton's jalopy, beside the father and son, and babbled on about Sara's portfolio and animal prints in the snow, as the car jerked forward and the speedometer instantly rose to ninety; Murvyle touched his hand to his cap to keep it from flying off. The car careened around the bend by the schoolhouse, shot forward over the road, swerved at the lane, and they landed in the dooryard. A tremulous wailing from the forest indicated the portfolio had still not been found, and in the guilt-inducing echo of the sound, Daniel suddenly perceived his loss of her portfolio as a karmic judgment against himself for not opening the antique shop she wanted.

He ran down toward her wail; she was trotting aimlessly back and forth around the scene of the crime, crisscrossing the patches of snow, but the vital paw print was still visible.

Murvyle bent down and examined it.

"Bear."

Daniel turned to her. "Bear," he repeated, as if the case were solved. She let out a stifled sob. "But bears should be hibernating."

"I can smell him," said Murvyle.

"Then he ain't far off," said Hilton.

"Wait!" said Daniel. "I remember now, when I first got here, I heard a scuffling in the bushes." An image manifested before him— a huge lumbering creature cocking his ears and loping off through the woods with Sara's portfolio tucked neatly under his arm, executive fashion.

"But why?" she wailed. "Why would a bear want my portfolio?"

Father and son stood momentarily nonplussed, with their bearlike bellies and bearlike stances and bearlike shoulders sloping from bearlike necks. "A bear's a curious animal," remarked Murvyle. "The problem is it don't take a bear long to run to deep country, nor to get to the brook with a porflio and sink her, nor to tear her to shreds . . ." Each new hypothesis was greeted by a heart-rending whimper.

"We'd best get searching," he concluded. "Dan'l, you go up high ground. Hilton, you strike fer the ridge. Sara . . ." He furrowed his much-furrowed brow in her direction, harkened to her whimper, possibly realized she might attempt to wrestle the bear single-handed . . . "You come with me."

Hilton staggered off half-blind with booze and crashed slowly into the woods, sounding exactly like a bear with a portfolio. Daniel followed. With Murvyle on the job and his fifty years' tracking experience going for us, we'll track this bear three days if we have to. I'm ready. And he knew that Murvyle and Hilton were too . . . because, for one thing, it was something to do.

He sniffed the snow-covered ground, scenting something, hoping the animal was close, but not too close, and would, when confronted, sensibly listen to reason and kindly hand over the portfolio. From above, on the ridge, came drunken grunts and ineffable oaths. We're an unbeatable team, he thought, recognizing the bestial tones of his boon companion.

"Halloa!" called Hilton.

"Halloa!"

"What color was that there porflio?"

What color? thought Daniel, what color? his heart leaping with joy. "I'm coming!"

"I think I got a porflio here," yelled Hilton, "but I ain't sure it's the right porflio."

Daniel dove through the trees up toward where Hilton's plaid shirt made a bright red splash in the forest; before he knew what he was doing, he'd flung his arms around the barrellike figure.

They stepped back. Hilton was growling and sputtering, ". . . son of a whore . . . I seen this here porflio and I cal'ated . . ." The case had been torn open; the handle was off; one side was badly ripped, but Daniel could see the paintings were intact.

"Hilton found it!" he hollered.

Sara and Murvyle scrambled up through the woods, Murvyle in the lead, with bearish swagger and smile of beatific relief. "Don't it go to show? Didn't I tell Hilton to search up the ridge? Only time in his life he ever listened to me."

Sara was laughing maniacally, examining the dog-eared contents of her ruined portfolio.

"Appears to be the right porflio," said Hilton.

Daniel dug in his pocket, drew out all the bills he had, and pressed them on the hero.

"Don't want no money."

"Take it," advised Sara.

"Look at them there teeth marks." Murvyle pointed to the edge of the case. "He was carryin it along in his mouth."

Sara's laughter rose to a trill.

Murvyle glanced at her sharply. "We best all head home and have some tea."

They moved toward the clearing, Hilton muttering, Sara trilling, Murvyle explaining that ". . . a bear will take most anythin . . ."

Daniel helped Sara into the back of the car; she was caressing her torn-up portfolio and talking what seemed to be nonsense, her manic-depressive swing having approached its mad zenith. Hilton drove home at a leisurely eighty, and Daniel listened to the three simultaneous monologues and thought it was all right that he hadn't opened an antique store.

The sight of his stalled convertible in Murvyle's yard dampened his spirits somewhat. "Think you can fix it?" he asked Hilton.

"That son of a whore?" Hilton guffawed.

"Sure he can," said Murvyle, "he's fixed her plenty of times."

Festus bounded over, sniffing the portfolio with suspicion.

"Have a cup," said Phoebe automatically, as they entered in a chorus of voices and barks.

"Heat up them bodaders too," said Murvyle, expressing the general feeling that they were returning from many grueling hours of labor rather than three or four minutes of pushing through brush.

"I was walkin along," said Hilton, "and there twas, right in front of me . . ."

"I knowed soon as I seen that footstep," said Murvyle, "twas a mighty big bear, I'd say he went three, four hundred pound . . ."

Sara was showing her rescued paintings to whomever was interested, the most interested being Festus, crazed by the bear-scented artwork.

Phoebe tsk-tsked and nodded, serving the supper, but Daniel perceived a vacant something in her eyes, and wondered whether she comprehended what had transpired. If she didn't, he soon saw, she'd have ample opportunity to understand in future, because the adventure was being recounted from every possible angle, rechewed along with each mouthful of biscuit and bite of potato; it would be analyzed for days, weeks, months, generations. "Look here," said Murvyle, "'tis a wonder them pitchers wasn't scattered all over the hillside."

"Son of a whore might've carried that there porflio clear to Moncton."

"He must've dropped it when he first heard Dan'l comin . . . didn't you say you heard a sort of scufflin?"

"Two more minutes"—Sara shuddered with relish—"and it all would've been destroyed."

"Bears," said Murvyle. "Did I ever tell you the story about the bear and Maundy Wood's baby?"

"I think you did," said Phoebe.

"Twas gettin fer nighttime," began Murvyle. "Maundy Wood went to the field with her baby to wait fer her man to come back with the cows. Twas quite dark. She stood at the fence and waited with the baby in her arms, till old Wood come walkin toward her. He put out his arms fer the baby, so she handed it over the fence, and off he walked with it."

"Twasn't really Wood," explained Phoebe. "Twas the bear."

"What happened?" asked Sara.

"Nahthin. Never seen the baby again."

"But she would've known her own husband. Even in the dark."

"She might not've," said Daniel, wondering whether he'd know Murvyle or Hilton from a bear in the dark.

"But what did he want it for?" asked Sara.

"Likely he was hungry."

"Was this recently?"

"Oh, no, twas in the old days."

"So it might just be a story," said Sara.

"And what about yer porflio?" Murvyle's good eye twinkled. "Is that jes a story?"

"Listen here, Murvyle," said Phoebe, "you best not tell folks what happened today, or they'll be tearin Dan'l's woods to pieces lookin fer porflios and such."

"Tain't gonna be easy," said Murvyle, "not tellin such a good story."

"No, twon't," said Phoebe, "but you best keep it amongst yerselves."

"Cold nights," said Murvyle regretfully, "when a couple of fellers get talkin bear . . ."

Daniel saw how tough it was going to be for Murvyle to keep this bear tale under his cap. "They probably wouldn't believe it anyway," said Daniel.

"No," said Hilton, "them sons of whores wouldn't!"

"I don't suppose they would," said Phoebe.

"No." Murvyle sadly shook his head. "Fer who ever seen a bear with a porflio? Even in this country."

Wearing a red jacket to foil hunters, armed with a compass she couldn't quite read, hell bent on communing with nature, she cautiously moved through the forest.

Daniel had suggested that her sense of direction might actually be perfect, but she'd come into the world pointing wrong. As she walked, she recalled tales of bones found in the bog, of Phoebe's father who got so turned around he didn't recognize his own children or dooryard, of an old-timer who'd thrown his compass away in despair and staggered out of the forest permanently deranged.

Certain stumps and bushes had a way of looking like bear and moose; the illusion never lasted long, but while it did, it was disquieting. Occasionally a cozier class of mirage—giant cats and elephantine rabbits—loomed in the shadows.

Yesterday she'd met a teen-ager with a brace of grouse flopping at his belt. She'd seen what they got in the stew pot in exchange—a little bit of stringy gristle and giblets; but if you asked them not to hunt on your land, if you got between them and their stew pot, a few of your own feathers would fly, because their myth was that without this handful of gristle, they'd starve. Sometimes, she thought, I hate the country, where I have to wear red on my own property to keep from getting buckshot in my ass.

A crackling came through the underbrush, heavy feet . . . While she wondered which way to run, a native tom-tom started to beat, and only gradually did she recognize the sound as her heart's.

The underbrush parted, and a horse's head peeked through. Two big eyes blinked; the creature gave her a long-suffering look, drew back, and disappeared into the woods.

She followed its tracks in the snow, curious to see who'd newly moved in, and where, with their horse.

The trail came out in a grown-over orchard and a farm which had burned down many years before; only the ghost of a barn remained, and so many of its boards had fallen away that you could see through its gaping walls to the white fields stretching beyond. Through the shell of the barn, she saw the horse, standing alone on the other side.

Surely a horse doesn't move into a barn on its own. She approached the skeletal structure which separated her from the horse, entered, and saw it contained several bales of fresh hay.

Outside, the horse patiently watched her investigations, gazing down over his nose at her with large liquid eyes.

But where were his people?

There was no house. No camp. No trailer. No tepee.

I guess this is it, she thought. The new neighbor is a horse.

She sidled slowly toward him. He lifted his lip in the hideous semblance of a smile. His coat was brindled gray, coarse and scarred; his legs were scarred; his teeth were huge, yellow, dreadful.

She reached out a mittened hand and touched his neck. His breath was a warm enveloping vapor. Leisurely, he gave a snort, and sank his teeth into her jacket; leisurely, he chomped on her epaulet, and she thought how she wouldn't, under any circumstances, allow herself to fall in love, and the opened-up feeling inside her, like the big hole in the side of the barn, didn't necessarily mean she gave two hoots for this horse.

The big head rose and moved to her other shoulder, grazing her face with the steam of his breath; he lowered his teeth to the second epaulet.

She took off her mittens, and stroked him with her bare hands, feeling his lovely coarse warmth; touched his mane; decided to buy him some oats; decided to buy him.

■ ■ ■

"Horses . . ." said Murvyle, from behind the stove.

She waited.

"Horses . . ." he said again, more thoughtfully, and then: "We had a horse once back at the camps, dyin of the constipation . . ."

"Really dying of it?"

"Many the horse has died of the very same thing."

"You listen," Phoebe admonished Sara.

"Horse down, couldn't stand. So I got me a big box of Duz, dumped it into a bottle of water, and shook it good. Then I shoved that bottle into the horse's arse with me arm clear up to here." He indicated a point near his shoulder. "I took me finger off the top of the bottle and says to that horse, *It's shit or die*."

He paused to roll himself a cigarette, coughing comfortably at the fond memory. "That's all I could do, so I went to bed." The gloom of the canvas shifted; she saw his stumpy figure emerge from the barn; and then the focus widened; the sawed-off lumberjack, with his lantern held high, plodded through the dark to the bunkhouse, while shadowy Frenchmen watched in the background, the red points of their cigarettes glowing.

"Middle of the night, I hear them French fellers jibber-jabberin. I went to the barn with me lantern, and the horse was gettin to his feet. Then he let her go, soapsuds and shit, flyin in every direction."

"Tsk, tsk," said Phoebe, waking from her own dream on cue, having no doubt tsk-tsked at this climax numberless times.

"French fellers duckin left and right. Look here, that shit flew clear across the barn, must've flew fifty foot."

"Fifty foot?" asked Sara.

"Sixty foot."

Phoebe sighed deeply; Murvyle tapped ashes into his palm, having chopped off another story as abruptly as a branch; and an immense silence swallowed the canvas.

■ ■ ■

She sketched, wearing woolen gloves with the fingers cut out, and listened to the dripping of the rain on the stable, while outside, the horse stood placidly in the drizzle, munching a carrot. The lumber company who owned him, said Murvyle, wouldn't take him away to work until summer, so summer's when she would buy him; there was plenty of time between now and then before she need mention it to anybody.

She drew his face and his mane; she had several sketchpads filled with manes. How big his head is, she thought; he must be quite smart.

It was raining for miles, and she felt the rain as a great dispensation and saw the horse feeling it too, standing outside in the shower, experiencing it through his nose and mouth and skin and through his powerful anatomy which she'd studied so carefully. She'd watched him running across the field, his hooves thudding over the earth, merging with the day in a way that was staggering to see.

She listened to the fine drops on the roof and the soft rain hitting the straw at the end of the stable where the old roof had caved. A ripple passed over the horse's rough brindled coat, an involuntary expression of his pleasure; staring past him to the far horizon, she felt something inside herself lift and float out through the mist.

■ ■ ■

"Once," said Murvyle, rocking in back of the stove, "I had a horse that would not trot."

"No, he wouldn't," testified Phoebe.

"You could not get that bastard to trot, nor gallop, nor beat him, nor threaten him, nor kick him in the arse."

"Twas the night Hilton was born . . ." said Phoebe.

Hilton looked up from his chair in half-sober surprise to hear his name so mentioned; he'd been plunged up until this point in profound meditation on God knows what; now he lifted his ragged cigarette away from his mouth in a dignified gesture suggesting that he was about to give the latest quotes from Wall Street, kicked a stack of wood by the stove, and fell back into profound meditation.

"I ett onions that night," went on Phoebe. "And you know how Hilton will eat an onion sandwich to this day."

At the sound of his name again, Hilton glanced across the room at his mother, tilted his cap down over one ear, and spat in the stove.

"Phoebe says to me," continued Murvyle, *"Better get help.* So I knowed twas gonna be close. I went out in the snow to hook old Hazen to the sled and I says to him, *Well, Hazen, I suppose you'll take yer time.* Do you know, that horse run all the way? He didn't stop once. We went and got old lady Suttle, turned round, and Hazen he run all the way back. By Jesus, I thought we'd end up in the brook."

From his chair at the other end of the stove, Hilton shifted, burped, settled down.

Phoebe sighed, either at the memory of the horse that would not trot, or the memory of home-style labor and delivery, or perhaps at the thought of the wee baby born that night against the enigma of Hilton, and the ineffable turning of the world.

■ ■ ■

The moment of entry, when you walked through the lofty portals, into the sound of fifteen cash registers jingling and the smell of popcorn and pizza and the people with their paychecks and hopes, and you teetered on the edge of ebullience, while in the distance came the roar from the rest of the mall, this instant, she felt, was the quintessence of the K-mart experience.

They synchronized their watches

. . . exactly as they used to in New York, at the Metropolitan Museum of Art, after checking their jackets in the Great Hall, where to the left were the treasures of Greece, to the right the tombs of Egypt, and on the terrace above, the precious Ming Dynasty vases. Here, to the left was the pizza, to the right the great bargain bins, and above, the buzzing fluorescent lights which turned everyone worm-white.

As she'd come to know what Daniel's route would be in the Metropolitan Museum of Art, here she knew the steps of his pilgrimage through the K-mart; in the museum, he'd immerse himself first in antiquities, whereas here he'd start in hardware, followed by athletic equipment, toys, hamsters, and parakeets. Her own route was equally predictable; instead of circling through Rembrandt, Rubens, and Titian, she'd begin with last season's markdowns, the ones with the cigarette burns and broken zippers, followed by Taiwan Dynasty cookware, and conclude among Maybelline's chiaroscuro, the luscious blushing flesh tones of Max Factor, tints by Clairol, school of Cutex, and works attributed to Dura-Gloss.

A special exhibit caught her eye, of ritual drinking vessels whose handles were shaped like women with sacrificial upraised buttocks; alongside were ceramic ashtrays in the style of toilets, and cigarette lighters which, when turned upside-down, stripped the imprisoned homuncula of her nightgown. There were also battery-powered barmaids who shook their rubber tits and tassels—a utensil which seemed to her an artistic summation, symbolizing as it did so many of Atlantic Canada's deepest values, and was, in fact, being piled into the shopping carts as fast as the green-smocked stock girls could refill the bins.

Moving along, she found herself in audio equipment, assaulted simultaneously by three different soundtracks in a multidirectional tug-pull cacophony that created a middle-ear warp and upset her balance. The loudspeaker crackled . . . *"There will be a five-minute special in our jewelry department where all items of jewelry in the special tray will be marked down to fifty cents I repeat there will be a five-minute special . . ."* A secret surging, tidally controlled by the fifty-cent moon, drew her into its gravitational pull; she shuffled over with the rest of the group and buffaloed her city way to the tray.

It's not Bloomingdale's, she admitted, wandering through the familiar aisles, admiring the same old handbags from Korea, galoshes from Poland, plastic curtains from Hungary, but it's simple, it's nice.

Since she had extra time, she tried on some stiff plastic shoes, with only a fleeting second of disorientation that she, who used to wear shoes from Saks Fifth Avenue, I. Miller, and Bally of Switzerland, had lost her mind or was dreaming.

She stopped off at the perfume counter and sprayed herself with one of everything. Splashing on a generous helping of Saturday Night Cooling Cologne, she found herself experiencing a déjà vu of a warm April afternoon in the violet fresh ambiance of Bonwit's, standing at the esthetically soothing, luxuriously glittering perfume counter, purchasing a half ounce of L'Air du Temps in a Lalique crystal flacon.

She approached Daniel at the parakeet cages, her cloud of fragrance preceding her by twenty feet. He stepped back, eyes tearing. "Which do you like best?" she asked, helpfully offering a whiff of her right wrist, then left, right earlobe, and left, right inner elbow, left inner elbow . . .

"Maybe we could have some coffee," he suggested, "and an aspirin."

She accompanied him to the cafeteria, feeling rather buoyant over her fifty-cent necklace. She loved the K-mart Restauranteria; it was exactly like an outdoor café, except it was indoors, in the back of the store, and adjacent to the key machine, whose grinding metal scream tended to pierce through the nerves of your teeth.

Going straight to pies, she indulged in a protracted agony of which looked least inedible; it was an impossible decision, but she owed it to her plummeting blood sugar and, besides, something a little bit sickening was an essential treat of the trip.

A gentleman in a plaid flannel shirt with a goiter and missing thumb and a wife with severely bowed legs set down their trays at the hot food counter. Instantly, the sensitive ears of the hot-food lady perceived their presence, the swinging doors of the kitchen flew open, and out she rushed, her body curved toward the steam trays, elbows locked in position like a hot dog machine, slapping bun, dog, and fries on their plates, her neck and limbs unswervingly shaped to the effort, to service, eyes darting like a rabbit with one foot in a trap, her hair so hastily set it had emerged from her head in six giant curls protruding in six asymmetrical directions; having dished up the dogs, she frenziedly cleaned off the counter, then spotting a table which needed bussing, dashed out to take care of that too, bent at the waist.

At the end of the line, the cashier was, contrastingly, bovine; whereas most of the rural citizenry succumbed to a cowlike patience when standing in line, this young woman, being at the culmination of the line all day, had become the line itself. Her pelvic region had permanently fallen to evade the shooting-open cash register drawer; her shoulders and eyes had retreated beyond both life and the calculation of change; if the steam-tray lady was a steam-driven robot, the cash register woman, though still young, had already evolved to the zombie stage, awaiting ultimate metamorphosis into a French fry.

As Sara and Daniel searched for a place to sit down, they passed the long triple table taken up by the assistant managers on their perennial break; these important young men in suits and ties had the heavy task of supervising the harried steam-tray lady, the pelvic-fallen cashier, and all the other green-smocked stock girls of their harem, between sessions of supervising coffee to their lips.

How delightful, thought Sara, sitting down; how exactly like an outdoor café; she allowed her eyes to roam over the other eaters in hopes of spotting some interesting outdoor café people. There was, unfortunately, a prevalence of missing digits among the men who worked in the woods, as well as enlarged middles, the yellowish onset of cirrhosis, and here and there the stare of a mail-order glass eye; the women also showed severe deprivation in their haunted expressions, tumors, rampant rickets, tragic results of inbreeding and connubial beatings, lack of cosmetic surgery and dentistry, once-pretty faces collapsed every which way on a diet of molasses cookies and drippings; as they stuffed themselves with coconut plasticream pie, kept one eye on their offspring, and frequently the other out for erotic adventure, Sara realized with horror that many of these prematurely faded flowers of Atlantic Canada were a great deal younger than she was.

The grinding metal song of the key machine rose; she could almost see the jagged sound waves pass into the red ear of the elderly gentleman dining beside it; the elderly gentleman, however, continued gobbling his gravy and instant mashed potatoes without flinching, having, she supposed, gone deaf long before from the roar of his chainsaw.

As she glanced around at her fellow café habitués, Daniel was sharing a few Tibetan Buddhist insights with her, rambling on about yak-butter candles and dorjes. At the table behind her, two young country matrons were hashing over a truly remarkable incident:

"She wanted a new livin room suit, and he wouldn't get it fer her, but she's got these here relations who could use some furnipture. Up Bush Holler. I dunno if you know them, you know them? She says to them, *Come with the truck when Durwood's to work, and you can have our livin room suit.*"

". . . yantra . . ." Daniel was saying; she nodded, yantra.

"When Durwood comes home, what does he find? He finds her on the floor in the livin room without no furnipture."

". . . vadjra . . ." Daniel was saying, as she and he continued relating.

"Nat'ally, he had to buy her a new livin room suit. It's right here in the furnipture department, wanna see?"

Behind her, the two ladies got to their feet.

Sara rose.

Daniel looked up with surprise from his insight. "Where're you going?"

"Be back in a minute. Hold the yak butter."

■ ■ ■

She stroked the horse's rough coat; he coughed deeply. She wiped the corner of his eye. When he coughed, his big sides went in and out; he gently nuzzled her epaulets.

The atmosphere was heavy with spring, and around the barn a lot of the snow had melted, uncovering winter's manure piles. He offered his other runny eye to be wiped. But at least, she thought, he isn't constipated and I won't have to shove my arm up his ass.

She closed her sketchpad, and patted the horse's nose, promising to return tomorrow. They walked out of the barn together; she started through the orchard to the woods, and he followed.

She turned; he stopped.

She started again, and heard his slow tread, keeping its distance behind her.

In the woods, you could feel the streaming from the trees and moss; all the moisture suspended through the long winter was loose and flowing. Behind her, she heard the horse still following with his deep cough, and his lungs sounded moist like an underground stream.

He continued plodding behind her through the forest, coming no closer, but keeping the pace he'd set. When she came to the edge of the field, she felt a tightness in her throat. If he follows me out onto the field, I'm going to lead him to our barn. I'll buy him now. I won't wait until summer.

Halfway across the field, she turned around. He was standing in the little doorway of the woods, watching her.

■ ■ ■

"Sounds like heaves," said Murvyle, flicking his ash. "That feller's had the heaves before."

"Yes," she said, relieved. "That's just how he looked. He was heaving."

Murvyle leaned back behind the stove. "I'll let the company know."

"He's had it before?"

"That feller? I should say . . ." His voice trailed off in the dreamlike way that augured a story. "You can talk about yer horses," he began, "but lemme tell you 'bout the queerest rig fer pullin that I ever seen."

"Holyo-fuckeye," remarked Hilton, "look at them boots." His boots were a problematical issue; he'd had a run of bad luck with boots ever since she'd known him.

"Twas a little feller," went on Murvyle, " 'bout three foot high or so." He paused, puffing thoughtfully. "Can't seem to recollect his name."

"Oh, you know his name," said Phoebe.

"Yes, but I can't recollect it."

She pursed her lips, but apparently she couldn't recollect either. "He was some relation, but more onto old Burpee's side."

"But what was he?" asked Sara.

"One of them little fellers."

Hilton burped. "He was a goddamn dwarft is what he was."

"That's what he was," agreed Phoebe, "one of them dwarfts. Can't you recollect his name, Murvyle?"

"Lived up Bound Brook way," said Murvyle. "Worked in the woods." Sara saw it: a little dwarft, working in the woods, with a little ax and a brown tasseled cap, rather like the seven dwarfts in *Snow White.*

"Good worker too."

"Yes, he was," said Phoebe. "Jed . . . or Jud . . . or Jeb . . . wasn't it somethin like Jeb?"

Murvyle shook his head. "He had a little wagon fer his wood in summer and a little sled in the winter and a brown and white dog to haul it . . ."

"Look at this son of a whore of a boot. D'you know what I paid fer these boots? I paid forty-two dollar!"

"I told you to take them back when you first brought them home."

"Son of a whore of a goddamn rig . . ."

"And the dwarft?" prompted Sara.

"Take them back now," advised Phoebe. "Tain't too late. I'd take them back if they was mine."

"Y'know," said Murvyle, "I got satisfaction when I took them rubbers of mine back."

"Did he tell you about them rubbers?" asked Phoebe.

"Yes," said Sara.

"You and yer rubbers . . ." said Hilton, further attempts at a coherent retort getting lost in the cavities of his mind.

"Now, I had a pair of boots back in '33. Them boots was the best pair of boots, by Jesus, that man ever had. I walked through mud and water with them boots and never got wet. You remember them, Phoebe."

"They was good boots."

"Twas a young feller—young then, he's dead now," went on Murvyle, "would not get out of bed in the mornin. So one mornin I drug him out of the bunkhouse by his feet through the snow. Jes fer a joke. That afternoon, we was pilin wood, and he drove his pulp hook right through me boot, pinned me fair to the ground. *Let's see you pull me out of bed now,* he said. Laugh? I couldn't move. Twas all good fun anyways. But that was the end of me boot. Twas almost the end of me foot. Now, old Birdie Carlyle, he had a hell of a pair of boots one time. He was some proud of them boots . . ." With regret, Sara realized that the conversation had drifted irrevocably from the interesting, but apparently limited, subject of dwarft with sled to the seemingly boundless network of boot stories.

▪ ▪ ▪

The abandoned settlement was golden in the spring evening, its snow-covered fields catching the last hour of sunlight. They drove slowly home past old Alf's estate, where shards of junk glittered like jewels; Alf himself stood meditatively in the midst of his squalor, wearing an ancient Homburg, which he flourished toward their clunking convertible.

They turned right at the one-room schoolhouse; the road was shaded by woods and by high banks of snow which hadn't yet melted. Ahead, she could make out a truck, with a trailer backed up to a snowbank, and then she saw on top of the bank . . . her horse.

The scene grew sharper as she drew closer. Men were shouting at the animal and trying to pull him into the trailer. She saw his terrified eyes and the bit tearing his tender mouth. He drew back, kicking; he slipped, losing his footing; and she sat paralyzed in the clunking slow-rolling car.

"The company's come for their horse," remarked Daniel, in a voice that showed he had no idea they were seeing a violation. I should've told him months ago this was to be our horse, that I wanted to buy him.

The animal reared on his hind legs. His frustration was so intense, the conflict between the powerful horse and shouting men so palpable, that she felt herself slip into the creature's coarse rippling skin, felt a shrinking inside—a lunging—as the fearful ring of wood and steel echoed under the horse's huge hooves and he thundered into the trailer, defeated.

The convertible continued on down the lane; she felt she was living in a foreign police state where the SS had come in the night to take away her best friend, and she'd been too cowardly to do anything.

■ ■ ■

"It alluys pays to speak up," said Murvyle, "fer if you don't speak up, how they gonna know you ain't satisfied?"

"But I ain't satisfied," replied Hilton. "These boots ain't no better'n the others. Sons of whores don't turn back the water."

"Return them again," advised Phoebe. "Keep right on takin them back until yer satisfied."

Hilton looked up in disgust, rose unsteadily, walked to the washstand, and fell to contemplating his face in the mirror.

"Well," said Murvyle, after a pause during which they watched Hilton perform several ghastly operations on pimples, "I see where they took yer horse."

"I've been meaning to ask you, who'd be the one to talk to about him? Who'd have the right to sell him if someone wanted to buy him?"

"Elven Wood."

"Yes, that'd be Elven, all right."

"Guess I'll have a wash," muttered Hilton.

"Where's his house?" asked Sara.

Murvyle cogitated. "Y'know that there bridge on the way to Mugwash? Not the one by the church, nor the one near the dump, nor the one after that, nor the first one, nor the one where Royden Corey fell off . . ." She jotted down the salient negatives, knowing Murvyle's directions only seemed incomprehensible for the first fifteen minutes or so, but after he'd sputtered on long enough, he'd eventually hone in on the area.

"Why," said Phoebe, "that horse is at the cannery." Her words spread a cold silence around them, chilling the air in the kitchen. "Ain't he, Murvyle?"

Sara looked at Murvyle, waiting for him to correct Phoebe, pencil poised on the list of bridges.

"A horse like that," he said, "gettin the heaves so much. Ain't an awful lot you can do with a horse like that."

"I knowed I heard Elven sayin he went to the cannery," repeated Phoebe, satisfied. "Sometimes," she explained, "it's hard to understand Elven when he's talkin, but I knowed . . ." Sara felt the horse's soft muzzle, nuzzling her hand as he stood in the fragrant mist, ecstatically drinking the rain with his flesh, more alive than any of them; she saw his gentle sweetness, and his massive vitality as he ran across the field; and then she saw him cut up in cans, chopped and minced and divided and sauced with bits of carrots in gravy.

"I don't believe it."

The three faces stared at her dumbly.

"Surely they could've gotten a veterinarian for him. Surely they could've spent ten lousy dollars on such a young animal with so much life in him." She heard her voice shake with anger to keep from crying. After all, the fault is mine. If I hadn't told Murvyle about the horse being sick, he might've gotten over his heaves before the company found out. But I had to chit-chat, just for something to say, just to break the silence, small talk, babbling my worries, collecting opinions, looking for help, always calling on others; so I landed him in cans, when I could've saved him, the day they took him away, or the day he followed me, or anytime through the winter; how easy it would've been to lead him through the woods to our barn, get in touch with the company, tell them what I'd done, and pay. And never, if I shout myself blue in the face, will I convince Phoebe and Murvyle that what happened was horrible. To them it's an everyday thing; you don't waste ten dollars on a vet when you can get a dollar for a horse at the cannery. Where am I? she wondered, feeling her body lost in space, sitting in this strange foreign kitchen, living in this strange foreign place, with these strangers who stared at her as if she were crazy, a billion, trillion light years away.

"Lose yer peavey and you lose yer job," said the log boss curtly, handing Daniel a long stick with a hook at the end. Daniel stepped into the freezing stream, beside Murvyle and Hilton and Anson and a dozen others, none of whom seemed to notice that the temperature of the water was low enough for hypothermia and death.

The shock of the cold on his legs caused him to take a sort of dance step; the stones beneath were slippery with moss. "Watch you don't put that peavey up yer ass," shouted Hilton, his voice traveling out in the bright empty morning, out to the green sparkling hills and back to the brook, where the fresh smell of spruce filled the early air as the men steered ten thousand logs through the water.

"*We were drivin to Long River . . .*" sang one of the old-timers, but none of the young men picked up the song, and the old voice continued on its own, cracked and tuneless, the solo refrain sounding to Daniel like tradition's slow dying; it was the last year of the drive, they said; after this year there'd be only trucks on the highway, and the breaking up of the ice on the river would have no further significance.

The trick was to hook your peavey into a log to jockey it through, without letting the log take off with your peavey; it looked easy when the older men did it, and he supposed it would be for him too after a while, but now it seemed pretty chancy and of secondary importance to the problem of not getting his body crushed in the log flow.

A pool of small fish scattered before him; the salmon would soon be running up against the forceful current that swept the heavy logs along. Murvyle's voice joined the old man's, "*We were drivin to Long River . . .*" and the two old men croaked out the tune together, as they pushed the logs from Jerusalem Creek to Indian Stream, and stepped into the bigger water, deeper and warmer, where many more men already were wading forward, steering logs to Long River. He recognized a few of the faces—Pike, old Alf, chubby Phat Jarvis, goitered Toner Whelpley.

The river was covered with logs moving swiftly; ahead was the next landing, where a pulp truck was dumping four-foot lengths which tumbled heavily into the current. He leapt into the midst of the avalanche, scampering to separate the logs and get them moving, working without grace or skill, but with the will of a dozen.

"Ma fran, you get mashed like sardine," said Alf, moving his own peavey effortlessly among the thick logs.

On the bank, a second truck backed up with its load; the mountain across the road had a savage red scar, as flat as a ski slope, with nothing of last year's lush forest but a tangled carpet of dry limbs. Further along the once-green mountain, he saw the previous year's cuttings; the hill on the left had collapsed completely and was on its way to becoming a gravel pit.

A cheer rose from the ranks, and he turned round to see a mustachioed young man sail by on a log, his peavey jammed on the front like a rudder, his cap stylishly hung on the peavey; the acrobat balanced on the log's back end, waving.

"Dat's ma boy!" yelled old Alf, as the daredevil disappeared down river. Daniel managed to scramble up onto a log and sit for an instant, but couldn't get his footing; he would before the drive was over, he vowed; he would sail down the river with his L. L. Bean crusher hat on his peavey.

At lunchtime they fell into groups, taking possession of a warm pasture along the shore. The sun dried his clothes, and he lazily listened to talk of other times, other drives; he took a swig from old Alf's medicine bottle, whose label proclaimed it to be *Dr. Fowler's Strawberry Extract,* but the contents were as clear as only female rats' tails could make it and the fumes alone made his eyes water. "Ver good fer ma cough," explained Alf, "de Dr. Fowler, he know what he doin."

Laconic conversations crossed, boots as always a major subject. An ancient gentleman pointed a wizened finger at his own hip-high waders, then gestured to the whole dazzling display of his new yellow rainsuit. "I'm gonna be dry all the way to the mouth," he piped; it seemed a prudent course to Daniel; the frail little creature didn't look up to surviving a dip in cold water; in fact it was amazing the venerable gentleman had been allowed on the drive at all; now and then, the white-bearded figure lifted a small brown bottle to his dry lips, a bottle which on closer inspection bore the label *Vanilla.*

The groups were rising, trundling back to the river; Daniel woke Hilton with a jab of the elbow. The logs had piled during lunch, and the foreman shouted them forward to prevent a log jam.

"People's like trees," remarked Murvyle, following Daniel's gaze toward the barking foreman. "You seen them tall pines in the woods. Alluys a couple of big shots."

They waded forward, steering a hundred thousand logs; a hound dog ran along on the bank, following the drive.

"The devil," screamed Toner Whelpley, "he's got me!" He flailed his peavey, face twisted with horror, goiter bulging. As they rushed to his aid, he raised his leg from the dark flowing water, and for an instant Daniel believed him, because if it wasn't the devil, what was it? It looked like a great wriggling clarinet blowing Toner's leg, mind, and goiter, hanging onto his overalls by the mouthpiece, while its silvery buttons gleamed along its ebony side.

"Lamprey," somebody shouted.

"I kill de bastard," cried Alf, flourishing forth his enormous pearl-handled Wyatt Earp pistol, which he attempted to twirl on his finger; for a minute it seemed about to fly off into the water, but he dove and swerved to recapture it, managing in his maneuver to point it at everyone within a two-hundred-degree radius; one after the other, men fell in the water to evade him, after having tried to stay dry all day; Daniel, cowering behind him, felt relatively safe, though there was always the chance of ricochet.

"Don't shoot," screamed Toner, his life's blood being rapidly drained, while at the same time Hilton lunged with his peavey to stab the wriggling monster, slashing at Toner's leg and at the glittering silvery row of vestigial eyes; with a guillotine thrust from the peavey, the hideous body parted from its hideous head, and dropped like a nightmare into the water, just as the big gun fired.

The river exploded; its earthquake tremors passed around Daniel, who stood behind the old cowboy with enough of a view to see that the bullet went three feet wide of its mark; nevertheless, Toner folded his hands on his belly and sank into the stream, which proceeded to authenticate his hallucination of being shot by turning red with blood from both severed ends of the eel.

"I did it," shouted Hilton. "I killed the son of a whore."

The men emerged, one by one, dripping from under their logs, and Toner too came up, unsure whether he'd been shot through the belly.

"I shoot de bastard," declared Alf with satisfaction, blowing smoke off the end of his pistol.

"It's still on me," cried Toner, raising a trembling leg on which the bleeding bodiless head clung fast by its sucking mouth.

"Burn it off!"

The white-bearded little old man yanked up the top of his new yellow rainsuit and pulled forth several sheets of newspaper which were apparently part of his underclothing.

Murvyle snapped on his lighter; the paper took fire. They held it up to the terrible head, which sizzled grotesquely, then rolled into the water, as Toner's overalls burst into flames.

"Down, you bulb-necked moron," snapped Pike, and the pale shaking Toner once again subsided into the stream.

"Break it up over there," bellowed the log boss from his boat. "Keep her movin."

"I best go home," mumbled Toner, rising from the waves like a white baby seal.

"Best go to the doctor," advised Anson. "Ought to be good fer four weeks disability."

"Did you see me fightin that fuckin thing?" bellowed Hilton. "I cut him fair in two. Thought he'd get me when he reared up and struck, but I was too smart fer him." Hilton shook his head at his own courage, though what risk he'd run wasn't quite clear since the mouth-end had been fastened to Toner. He did risk getting shot, Daniel admitted.

"Bastard must've drained a quart of me blood," said Toner.

"I give you some medicine, ma fran. I got six, seven bottle of de stuff in ma lunch pail. I never go anywhere widdout de Dr. Fowler. She good fer everyting. Measle, mump, lamprey, spider bite, rusty nail . . ."

Toner took a medicinal mouthful, or two.

"Remember old Mushrat Bobkins," said Murvyle. "Lampreys killed him one time. Drained him dry."

"Twas the last year we was drivin them long logs," said the little old man in the bright yellow rainsuit, boosting his own health with a swig of vanilla.

"They killed him?" asked Daniel.

"Four, five lampreys latch on a feller, it don't take very long to empty him out."

"Specially a small feller like Mushrat," said Phat.

"What in hell's goin on down there?" boomed the log boss; reluctantly they got back to work, wading forward with the subject:

"Remember that lamprey back in '47? Bit Uncle Burpee in the shin? Sucked his blood so fast . . ."

"Toot'ache, gum-boil, snakebite, frostbite," continued old Alf, listing the merits of Dr. Fowler to Toner who, obligingly, kept drinking.

"Bastard seen me comin," said Hilton. "He was lookin at me with all them eyes, jes waitin fer a chance to gobble me down. Must've weighed fifty pound."

It was beginning to feel as if the Loch Ness Monster were accompanying the drive, and Daniel stepped lightly, furtively eyeing each passing stick, darting fish, and long floating weed; primeval elements lurked in the river, waiting to spring.

But gradually, there was no room to wade between logs; they kept coming and piling up, until they formed a corduroy highway you had to walk on top of; up ahead at the bend in the shallows, a couple of logs had gotten wedged crosswise, through which no timber could pass. He started to run out to the point, but Murvyle held him back. "Takes a real hand to trip a jam. I seen men killed who should've knowed better." It was Alf's daredevil son, who'd been weaving in and out all day on top of the logs with no apparent contribution to the drive other than keeping his feet dry, who danced forward across the log highway, his long black hair glinting, the drooping ends of his black mustache quivering, a circus dandy skating over the logs to the heart of the jam; he swooped down, gave a powerful thrust with his peavey, and twitched the cross-wedged log free. A mile of backed-up timber gave with a huge cracking noise, as the black-mustachioed figure disappeared in the avalanche that surged forward. A moment later, he was up again, twirling his peavey, and sailing away on a log down the river amidst the cataract.

"Ah, ma boy," cried Alf with pride, breaking open a new Dr.

Fowler for himself and Toner, whose blood had returned to his body, due to the miraculous curative powers of strawberry extract, out of old Alf's still.

"Remember that log jam in 1910," piped up the old white-bearded geezer, and although no one remembered, they fell to rehashing the details of the log jams of 1950, 1947, 1937 . . .

Listening, wading along, Daniel suddenly saw the answer to the question that had been bothering him all day: Why were these drunks, relics, and fuck-ups allowed on the log drive? Because, quite simply, everyone was allowed; if anybody couldn't handle it, he'd either be killed or fall by the wayside; it was an incredibly economical system of personnel selection, based firmly on Darwin; it also explained why he himself had been hired.

"Back in the camps, we was wet from one end of winter to t'other," said Murvyle. "Slept every night in wet clothes. Only ones ever caught cold was them smart fellers who took off their wet clothes. Worst thing a person can do."

On the shore, a herd of brown cows turned slow heads to study the drive. A farmer waved from his high yellow tractor; pigs sloshed in a nearby puddle; and the drive flowed forward, massive, unceasing. The afternoon rose, the sun hottest toward evening; shortly before quitting time, they came upon Alf's long lost son, playing cards by himself on the bank of the river.

"What do you think this is," yelled the log boss.

"My friend," said the young man, placing a card on the appropriate pile, "if not fer me trippin the jam, you'd still be up the river."

The boss snorted some unintelligible answer. At the next log landing, pickup trucks waited to carry them back to their villages.

Daniel's legs felt like numb logs, out of their element, on dry land; stumbling, he climbed onto the back of a truck, and let himself be propped up by his neighbors, who continued telling stories, reminiscing, complaining; two old men broke into their litany, "*We were drivin to Long River* . . ." and the truck started to roll, the wind lifting their voices with the smell of sweat and wet clothes, and he fell into sleep, the movement of the truck on the highway becoming immersed in the bright flow of the stream.

The logs were wet, dark, and shining, endlessly rolling, broken only when he woke to climb from one vehicle to another . . . and again when he stepped out at home . . . and again briefly when he got out of his clothes, protesting to Sara that he'd rather sleep wet, as changing would give him a cold; and then the river washed over and around him, and he felt its deep cool flow on his weary legs, and the men marched beside him; he saw the changing trees and fields of the bank, some pigs, a tractor, a dog, and the endless logs and the hot endless sun, and the tributaries streaming inevitably forward.

■ ■ ■

". . . Old cook at one camp," said Murvyle, "used to spit out the winder, right over the dough. Sometimes he give it one squirt of tobaccer, sometimes two. Give the buns a little dif'rent flavor . . ."

Voices were muffled. Mist wrapped the morning, thickly shrouding the river, and giving the work a slow-motion quality. He could see his own peavey and the immediate logs, but the banks were invisible, and the men beside him rose up in his vision like isolated wraiths and then disappeared, poling by, into the fog. A crow called, and its muted song seemed to come from nowhere.

". . . Them cooks was fussy 'bout their wood, needed jes the right heat. Bone-dry maple was donut wood . . ."

Gradually the fog burned off the hills, until only the river, the men, and the log drive moved along in a gray strip of mist, in an element of their own, different from the day beyond the banks; and then the warmth of the sun pierced their shroud too, which started to lift like steam off the stream, and Alf's pith helmet suddenly shone clear, and Murvyle's cockeyed cap, and Pike's red beret, and eyes and faces came clear, as the mist kept rising and the blue day lowered to meet it, and there were the men in their plaid shirts and rainsuits, poling their peaveys downward.

"Fine day," remarked Murvyle, his voice no longer muffled, the splashing now loud and clear, the last shred of mystery scattered in a wisp. The river again gleamed with logs, sunlight shone on the meadows and forest, and the valley wound ahead, distant and lonesome.

Daniel turned around to see how far they'd come, and saw a rider and log bearing toward him—the peavey again jammed on the front like a rudder, the jaunty cap cocked on the peavey, and Alf's son squatting on the back of the log with his jacket hiked up, trousers pulled down, ass bare to the wind, calmly taking a shit off the end of the log into the stream. Like a bizarre mirage, the acrobat sailed past, patently ignoring the cheers of his fans, but in the drooping mustache's quiver and in the nonchalant stare, Daniel recognized the real artist, bent on surpassing his own previous work.

As if the performance were a signal, the men stopped for their tea break; the old party in the bright yellow rainsuit, who'd been eyeing Daniel curiously all the previous day, elbowed over, exhaling a puff of vanilla; he reached into his waterproof pocket with senile glee, and handed Daniel a faded snapshot. "Old Perley Samson. Dead forty year now," cackled the relic, while Daniel stared at what seemed to be his own photograph. True, the late Perley Samson was a good deal older, with wild white hair sticking out in all directions from under the same soft-brimmed crusher hat, and the expression around the lips was a lot more cantankerous, and the eyes, though evidently of the same pale hue, appeared to reflect some advanced stage of psychosis. He gazed at his mad mirror image, and the ancient vanilla cracker chortled.

"You do," said Murvyle, "put a person in mind of old Perley Samson. Dif'rent times I remarked on it to Phoebe."

Is it possible, wondered Daniel, that someone wouldn't change his features at all from lifetime to lifetime? Not even his hat? The previous-lives seer at the Hotel Manhattan had told him he'd once lived in Canada, and he'd dismissed that incarnation in the glory of the more colorful ones, India, Tibet, you got three lifetimes for five dollars. But now he knew: Mad Perley Samson. His cantankerous look-alike answered his gaze from the wrinkled old snapshot: *Holyo-peena*, it seemed to say, *are we back here again?*

The white-bearded gentleman returned the photo to his waterproof jacket, and they returned to wading the stream.

"Old Perley was an arteest," offered Pike. "Built his winders out in a circle, lined his house with birch bark, and when she burnt, she went in ten minutes."

"Quite the frigger," agreed Phat Jarvis. "Alluys friggin with somethin. Frigged hisself a rig fer feedin his cows automatic, starved every last head of them."

"Apples too," said Murvyle. "Alluys breedin some new kind of apple. I could take you through Perley's orchard, and between the lot of us, we wouldn't find one apple fit fer eatin."

On the edge of the desolate landscape, they came to a new subdivision of heavily mortgaged split-level homes, clustered as closely as possible together, ignoring the vast rolling miles of unpopulated acreage on all sides of them. Wading through the cold river, Daniel felt that his leaky sneakers held more water than the television dream being built on the shore; and he accepted, with a pang, that it was not a beloved land; people stayed because they felt themselves stuck, then moved away from their farms as fast as they could, and built expensive media-image compounds to shut out the woods. Maybe it was because they hated the woods that they raped it so brutally.

A quavering cry interrupted his pathos; he looked up to see the ancient white beard, who'd vowed not to get wet, going under, but so waterproof was his brand-new bright-yellow outfit, that instead of sinking, the suit merely inflated, carrying the geezer quickly, as in a yellow balloon, to his doom down river. And there, thought Daniel, watching the beard bob away like hoar-bitten seaweed, goes old Perley Samson's picture, the only surviving evidence of my previous lifetime, other than a few sour apple trees.

It was the fleet-footed son of Alf who reached out with his peavey and hooked the yellow rainsuit high in the air; its frail inhabitant dangled irately, as the bright balloon around him deflated. Growling, he was set on his feet, demanding, apparently, his peavey, which was located and waved aloft upstream, then triumphantly passed from man to man, until it reached the infuriated old codger, who grabbed it without ceremony, and viciously set back to poling. By God, thought Daniel, I ought to try some vanilla.

■ ■ ■

"Where is everybody?"

"Oh," said Murvyle casually, "dif'rent excuses."

"But why all the same day?"

"Don't matter," said Pike, "the good ones is all here."

"Ah, ma fran," said old Alf, moved at being so described, along with the few select others who'd shown up for work. It seemed that most of the men who'd stayed on were in the pension bracket; not even Hilton had appeared.

Here we are, almost at the end, and four fifths of the men disappear. What's the matter with people, thought Daniel righteously, can't they see a job through? He breathed the crisp heroic air, and poled slowly into Cottonville, that oversize village of brick with its defunct mill and picturesque, decrepit, company-built row houses.

In three days they'd be at the great river, they had more wood than ever to steer, and where were the men? Just a handful of oldsters would see the job to its triumphant finish; how lacking in spirit, he thought still more righteously, breathing more deeply, and noticing a peculiar smell. Did one of the men have some trouble? he wondered, glancing around; no, it must've been that farm round the bend, farmer must've been spreading his field with pig shit.

He waded forward, enjoying the picturesque village with its jumble of brick and windows low to the ground. Christ, he thought wrinkling his nose, there must be a hundred acres of pig shit. "Big pig farm around here?" he asked Murvyle.

"Yer walkin in it."

He lowered his eyes: In among the logs, brown shapes merrily floated, and from under the bank, a huge sewer conduit grinned up at him, its mouth belching into the river. He gagged, sank to his knees, and realized sinking was the worst thing he could do; it was swirling all around him, a million turds liquified and much of it not yet liquified, but boiling hideously intact, around his dungarees, oozing through the fabric, like a major psychological dream—if only it were—but the sickening stench was clobberingly real. Why didn't they warn me?

"Ah, ma fran," said old Alf, "lot of piss under de bridge in dis life."

They should've given us typhoid injections! They should be paying us a hundred dollars an hour for this! They should be arrested for putting workers through this! As if on cue, the old men broke into their song, loud and ferocious, a pack of old dogs determined not to give in, working their peaveys, marching grandly through shit.

And for what? For some millionaire and his pulp mill?

"Breathe through yer mouth," advised Pike, who didn't deign to sing, but would never, knew Daniel, let himself be stopped by anything, least of all, shit.

I should climb out on the bank and go home, or to the hospital for injections, should burn my clothes; he figured how much it would cost to replace his sneakers and pants, subtracted from two dollars an hour.

"Here comes the big stuff," said Murvyle, as they rounded the bend at the railroad tracks, and Daniel didn't know if he referred to the turds, or the huge piling fields up above, stretching the whole width of the village, stacked with as much lumber as they already were hauling.

How can we steer this much wood? The day seemed a never-ending series of shocks. Ton after ton, the logs from the piling field were dumped into the river, splashing the feces high in the air and in their faces. A few of the Cottonville men now joined the drive, which should've been a relief because of the tremendous amount of wood to be moved, but by this time, embittered and wise, he suspected the Cottonville workers of being paid special hard-shit wages, double what he and the old men were getting.

"We're the fools," remarked Phat Jarvis, "and that's a fact."

"I ain't no fool," said Pike, "nor I ain't afeared of hard work."

"And what've you got fer it?" cackled the antique in the bright yellow rainsuit, his white beard besmeared and spattered. "Shit in yer boots."

"Won't need them boots no more anyhow," said Murvyle, "cause they're ain't gonna be no more log drives." This seemed to plunge them into moroseness, and again they burst into song. The essential thing, thought Daniel, is not wading shit alone.

■ ■ ■

A thin drizzle made everything gray; no one spoke of the shit anymore, and he, like the others, accepted the stench as normal. They waded past miles of black scraggly poles which had once been a forest, but had burned soon after being harvested of all healthy growth, leaving only sick and dead wood and tinder to catch in a dry summer season, fifteen years ago, and still nothing had sprung up, maybe nothing ever would, maybe the land had permanently accepted defeat. Having no root systems left to absorb the spring runoff, the whole burnt forest was now under water, its charred sticks protruding like the masts of old ships sunken by pirates. He could see the town in the distance and the mouth of Long River; booms and tugboats were taking over the job there, steering the logs to the ocean, to the pulp mill perched on the bay spewing its garbage into the sea, its poisons into the air, insatiably grinding the trees of the province until there'd be none left to grind and no more work for its people, all to make one rich man richer, and still, approaching Long River, wading through shit, he wished it weren't over, felt these hard weeks were his moment of glory.

4

". . . *This is Mortimer Astle, interviewing Brian Philbottom in charge of summer jobs for students in tourism. 'Tell me, Brian, what should a student do if he or she wants a summer job in tourism?'*

'*Well, he could go to one of the tourism offices and apply.*'

'*Thank you, Brian.*' *That was Brian Philbottom, in charge of summer jobs in tourism . . .*" The nasal voice petered out, and a recorded choir burst into song, *Back to the Bible, Back to the Bible . . .*

She strolled into Daniel's meditation room; it was exactly the right size for a baby; if things worked out, Daniel could meditate in their bedroom for a couple of years. The white garret walls formed half a dozen angles of roof line and dormer; the wide pine-board floors shone gold in the morning sunlight. She sat on his meditation cushion, and played with his toys—the brass altar gong, the Buddha, the many-armed Shiva, the sexy goddess from Tibet, Ganesh of the elephant face; and when the baby got older and needed more space, Daniel could move his religion out to the shed.

The minute hand of her watch had moved forward ten minutes, so she went back to the studio to check out the test tube over the mirror, but the particles in the test tube hadn't yet formed a pregnancy ring. She clicked off *Back to the Bible,* and walked downstairs, listening to her footsteps echo through the house; outside, everything was singing; in the city you heard it too, but in the city the song of spring was romance, and here, it was reproduction, reproduction, reproduction. From the window over the sink, she gazed out at the western field, where swallows swooped in and out of the barn with grass and twigs for nest building; butterflies flashed ecstatic powdery wings; in the distance, the brook moved through the valley, a murmuring counterpoint to the lovemaking.

A green hummingbird quivered at the mouth of a flower, drumming backward and forward through space with tiny shiny helicopter wings, while bumblebees droned as if bursting with nectar, their furry bodies vibrating with rapture; last night they'd been too glutted to go home to their hives and had fallen asleep hanging onto the blossoms like so many drunkards passed out on barstools. The buzzing of the bees and hummingbirds seemed to be swelling; she'd never heard them so loud before. It rose until it filled the whole sky, and over the treetops, she saw the droning approach of three World War Two fighter planes coming toward her in low-flying formation.

She hurried to shut the door and the windows; the planes were so close she could read the numbers on their wings, as three puffs of vapor came out of the fuselage, the deadly film floating free and spreading with the wind.

She tasted the poison on her tongue, and ran upstairs to close more windows, though she knew the spruce budworm spray would find its way down the chimney. The roar was so loud it sounded as if the planes were crashing in through the kitchen doorway.

Why did we ever rebuild here? We knew they sprayed each spring. How could we have done such an unthinking thing?

The planes skimmed the rooftop; through the studio's north window, she could see the obsolete fighters flying over the hollow, dropping their veil into the stream. Even the water we drink is now contaminated.

Standing at the window, she anxiously watched the low-flying aircraft move off in formation; the jets opened, closed, and opened once more, emitting three last puffs of poison, and slowly the three antiquated planes became three dots diminishing in the blue day.

I'm going to be sick, she thought, but her head hurt too much to think very clearly. And then she noticed the silence. No birds were singing. No squirrels chattered. No bees or butterflies danced through the glorious morning. Fumbling her way from the studio, she glanced at the test tube over the mirror, and saw the same deathly stillness reflected in the shape of a ring.

■　■　■

"Eatin much bakin powder?" asked Phoebe.
"Why would I eat baking powder?"

"I alluys did when I was that way. Straight from the tin by the spoonful. Couldn't stop meself." She paused from her work of rubbing blackening polish on her stovepipe. "You ain't supposed to eat bakin powder nor you ain't supposed to have none of yer teeth pulled. I got every last one of them pulled when I was that way with Anson. I jes set down in the dentist's chair and said *Yank 'em.*" She spat on her polishing cloth.

"I don't suppose you ever got sprayed by the spruce budworm planes when you were that way?" asked Sara, using Phoebe's euphemism; before she knew what *that way* meant, in the early days of their friendship, she'd wondered what in the world the woman was driving at when she said *that way:* homosexual? promiscuous? adulterous? feeble-minded? insane? maybe all of them?

"How old d'you think I am?" laughed Phoebe. "They only been sprayin fer twenty-odd years."

And in twenty-odd years, lots of normal healthy children have been born, and some of their mothers must've been sprayed. She wished she could find more specific statistics, but the government program was cloaked in Kafkaesque secrecy. "I got a reply from the Department of the Environment about my getting sick."

"What'd they say?"

"Thank you for your letter, you will be pleased to learn that no instances of illness have been reported from this year's spruce budworm spray program."

Phoebe knit her brows, apparently sensing something amiss in the logic, but her confidence stopped short at probing bureaucratic idiom. "Felt lots better afterward," she said, reverting to the subject of mass tooth extraction. At times Sara forgot how completely poverty colored life in the province; even now, when no one was as poor as they'd been in the past, tradition had cut so deep, people still didn't bother taking care of their teeth, assuming that dentures were an inevitable part of maturing. "I seen where Toner took an awful spell. Pretty near drowned in his own well house bendin down to take the scum from the spray planes off of the water."

"You don't suppose the spray got him dizzy?"

"More likely the bendin. I get dizzy meself when I bend." She stood back and admired her stovepipe. "Murvyle seen a lot of dead fish in the brook."

"Yes, the spray seems to kill them."

" 'Tis only nature," said Phoebe. Only nature, thought Sara; that's how the government gets away with its programs. Country people will accept any atrocity and figure it's nature. Besides, they've got so much wrong with them, between abscessed teeth and every other ache and pain of poverty, they wouldn't notice the symptoms of poison attack as anything different; what's new about dizzy spells or nausea or sniffles when you're used to being half-sick half the time anyway? She thought of all the congenital deformities and ailments she'd seen at the K-mart, and wondered whether they were a result of the twenty-odd-year spraying; such ideas tended to make her break out in a sweat, and she tried to think of pleasanter things. "How's your groundhog?"

They went to the window to see if Phoebe's groundhog was visible; she'd been denning under the barn since becoming *that way*. No groundhog, fat or thin, could be seen, just the big barn standing gray in the sunshine, topped by three white-balled lightning rods and a flock of swallows; every old barn in the country seemed a product of the same urban planner who'd arranged appropriate space for one groundhog family, one flock of swallows, a purple martin community, a few mice, a couple of chipmunk, and the odd porcupine, each at a level suitable for adequate privacy, maximum sharing of utilities, and a minimum tax load. Phoebe's barn also sheltered horses, but those two gentlemen were out on the job; the drone of a chainsaw drifted in from the woods.

"Dreamin, dreamin," sighed Phoebe. "I hate to dream. I keep dreamin I'm lost in the woods without no money."

The dream gave Sara pause. Here is a woman living the most Zen, the most simple, pure life imaginable, and quietly going crazy.

"How's yer garden comin?" asked Phoebe.

"Good. Why don't you put in a garden?"

"We alluys used to in the old days."

"What made you stop?"

"Now where would I put a garden?"

Sara gazed out the window at the rolling acres, the spacious field, the big pile of horse manure. Where could one *not* put a garden? In the midst of her puzzling, a chubby brown creature appeared, popping up from the earth by the side of the barn.

"Herself," said Phoebe, nodding toward the pregnant groundhog, "as big as billy-be-damned."

. . . wearing long black evening gloves, a hungry eye for dande-

lion greens, and—Sara particularly noticed—not a shred of maternal anxiety.

■ ■ ■

The yellow machine scudded forward, tearing a great chunk of
turf from the marsh; Waldo, perched high on the bulldozer's seat,
casually touched his red pate.

Now Daniel leapt into action, flushing unwary frogs and rodents
out of the way of the earth-eating monster, while Sara stood on the
slope, envisioning the finished pool, olympic sized and filled with
clear green water.

"Halloa!" came a voice from above; she turned to see Murvyle
and Hilton coming down past her washline, having sniffed out the
project two miles away. "Doin a little diggin?"

"We're making a pond."

Hilton rolled a cigarette. "Son of a whore of a small rig fer the
job."

"Do you think so?" she asked, her own worst worry confirmed.

"What's Dan'l doin there?" interrupted Murvyle.

"Warning the frogs."

Murvyle nodded, satisfied. "I knowed twas somethin funny."

"Halloa!" came a voice from above; Pike had sniffed out the
party from five miles distance; he approached with a suspicious air,
glancing toward the action and Waldo.

"Way I cal'ate it," said Murvyle, "they need a good high dam."

"Drainage pipes," countered Pike.

"Slope's all wrong," muttered Hilton.

"You wanna built it up high so the bank won't wash out."

"Oughtta sink a pipe clear through from one end of the bank out
t'other."

"That little pissmire of a tractor couldn't plow up a shit house."

"Ain't nahthin wrong with the tractor, it's the jackass on top it."

"First spring freshet'll wash her away." As they spoke, they
began to move down the slope, where all three were soon waving
conflicting instructions to Daniel and Waldo over the roar.

"Keep her comin," called Pike above the noise. "Yer perfectly
straight, if anythin a little to the left."

The bulldozer wavered, then turned toward the beckoning arms of the red-bereted director, as Sara realized: A little to the left is perfectly straight in this province. It went far to explain why almost every house was cockeyed and every man fearless; why hesitate to attempt any task when slightly wrong is perfect? It was a major realization to one trained in the tradition of the French academicians, who wouldn't put on their shoes without a plumb line.

At the moment, even Waldo, who usually respected plumb line and level, had given in to his native daemon, and was recklessly wheeling his tractor in the direction of whomever's voice caught his mood for the instant, randomly careening through the soft marsh while the other four shouted wildly, all drunk on destruction, though to the untrained eye—hers—nothing much, in the way of a pond, was manifesting.

Water was trickling into the pit, but it wasn't much, and a black oily scum was ominously rising to the surface.

"Oil," cried Pike. "We're rich!" With a mighty clank, the bulldozer ground to a standstill.

She ran down the hill to join the men converging on the scum.

Waldo climbed off his perch with unprecedented swiftness. "Don't smell like oil."

"Sure stinks like somethin," said Hilton.

Pike scooped up a handful of the disgusting black ooze. "Tain't oil after all."

"Uranium," suggested Sara.

"Manganese, that's what 'tis!"

They looked at each other dumbly.

"Most valuable thing there is," said Pike.

"Will it ruin the pond?"

"You've struck her rich," declared Pike. "I'd move to Hawaii."

"May as well," said Waldo. "Bulldozer's busted."

Immediately, the board of directors switched from wealth and manganese deposits to drive shaft, crankcase, broken treads, and ball bearings, as they slowly began to move the machine out of the mud, uphill toward level ground.

"But, Waldo," said Sara, trailing behind, "if you don't finish the pond today, it'll fill up with water and be too deep for the tractor."

He rubbed his head, flashing his cheerful smile. "They may jes be callin this Waldo's Folly."

■ ■ ■

The mockingbird who dominated the early airwaves had just woken up and was running through his midsummer repertoire, consisting mainly of swallow chatter with the occasional whippoor-will call, not at all like the tropical riffs he'd brought up from the South in the spring.

Seated in the convertible in her nightgown, she listened to the zany song, and pressed her bare foot to the gas pedal while Daniel, half hidden under the hood, performed some magic act with his screwdriver; after several minutes, the engine blasted to life, its rumble joining the bird tunes, and she slipped out of the car.

He slammed the hood, took his place at the driver's seat, and drove off to build houses with Waldo; she watched as the dust from the road flew up through the floorboards, forming a mushroom-shaped cloud round his head; the windshield wipers flashed in the sunlight; and, like the mockingbird, the gaudy convertible went through its ever-evolving exotic repertoire of tricks.

From behind the house, a small russet face peeked out, followed by a short brown body, and the tour of the groundhogs began, with mother in the lead and her four new pups tumbling behind. The fierce caravan made their way toward the old chicken coop where papa groundhog lived, and Sara followed, trailing her nightgown, but soon lost sight of the parade in the weeds. The warmth and luxuriant growth of the field enveloped her as if it were an extension of her own pregnant body.

A car started down their driveway, then stopped, halfway to the house, beside the raspberry bushes. A woman from the village stepped out, and Sara waved across the field; the woman had asked her about the raspberries and Sara had said, *Of course, you're welcome to come by and pick some.* The other side of the car opened, and two more ladies stepped out, ladies she barely knew by sight, but she waved to them anyway as they marched with their buckets into the berries.

At last we belong, she thought. It's funny it took us this long; it must be because everyone else is connected by blood, but now we will be too. She strolled through the apple orchard, with its gnarled arms bent like ancient people, and thought of the olden-day folk who'd planted these trees for their children, and she'd planted two apricot trees which might not bear for years, but future generations would pick the fruit. It was as if she'd been out of step from the day they'd come, and was finally one with the settlement, the flowering earth, and the species whose purpose was continuation.

Pale green lichen, no bigger than pins, with vivid red caps, grew on the old cedar snake fence, life resolutely springing from age; she touched her palm to the springy row of red caps, seeing them as so many gnomes protecting the place. Crickets sang in a round over the meadow; first the cricket at the end gave voice, then the next one picked up the song, continuing down the row until they all chirped at once, the song rippling backward and forward, everything a jubilation and growing.

A second car joined the first beside the berry bushes, and two more ladies stepped out with buckets. I wish I were dressed, she thought, uncomfortably aware of her flowing nightgown, but the ladies across the field didn't seem to notice her, plowing directly into the raspberry patch and setting to work in a no-nonsense manner.

She moved away from the orchard, out of view of the raspberry pickers, to the site of the old wagon house; the house itself had long rotted or been torn down, and only four wagon wheels were left, connected by iron axles; the bright paint had peeled, but the ghost of blue remained along the spokes radiating out from the centers and around the wooden rims; in the midst of the tall neglected grass, the four painted wheels stood as spirits of a gay farm life past, now about to start up again. She tried to get the frame rolling, but it was deeply embedded in earth, in the spot time had chosen, at the edge of the field facing west and the hills; and someday, she thought, Daniel and I will belong to the land like these wheels, and our grandchildren will play here. Above her thoughts, above the crickets' song, she heard *Back to the Bible* on the raspberry pickers' transistor radio.

■   ■   ■

After the fullness of day, evening resumed the empty quality of dawn, the cool time when voices travel; from beyond the open-hanging barn door, she could hear conversation and see the dis-

mantled tractor, jacked up on cinder blocks, with Waldo's huge
muddy boots sticking out beneath, beside the smaller boots of
Daniel.

No point in saying *hello;* the monster tractor had clearly claimed
the summer, as far as evenings went, and Waldo had become a
live-in cousin.

A nighthawk buzzed; a swallow shit on the tractor. Waldo's
grease-stained manual lay open on the hay, identifying the monster's nuts, bolts, rings, gaskets, and more recondite parts spread
out on the floor of the barn as meticulously as a Japanese garden,
inscrutable as a Chinese puzzle, all of it a ruse on Waldo's part, she
sometimes thought, so that he could refurbish his tractor with un-
paid help, but another part of her recognized Daniel's happier-
than-pig-in-shit state: In addition to his other bizarre north country
accomplishments, he would now know how to assemble a tractor.

Halfway up the lane, the last of the raspberry pickers' cars
pulled away, and she walked toward the bushes to see what they'd
left for her. The bushes themselves were a heartbreaking sight,
trampled down as if by elephants—the numerous village ladies
who'd been coming out every day for weeks, rampaging greedily
through *something for free.* In the fading light, she couldn't see one
berry remaining. The question was would the bushes ever recover
from the ladies' stampede?

Across the ridge, Hilton's drunken hoot was echoed by Festus's
bark, friendly music in the stillness of twilight.

She strolled down toward the marsh to look at the pond, a hideous unfinished trap of mud and manganese, a sample of which
was officially declared by the County Agricultural Station as worthless. At first sight of Waldo's Folly, she flinched and averted her
gaze, then noticed movement on the dark surface. She drew close
and knelt at the edge: A lone bullfrog tooled along through the
water looking vaguely like Waldo.

The moist heavy evening echoed with the bullfrog's croaking. In
the west, darkness was falling. She climbed back uphill toward the
house, and saw two figures emerge from the barn against the red
sunset, a huge bear and one slightly smaller. Has Daniel changed
his shape? she wondered, or is it just his movements that have
grown lumbering, the sturdy superstructure of a man who can tear
down and build up a tractor.

A car without a muffler raced by on the road; she heard the raucous cries of the village hooligans and the crash of tin against stone —empty Moosehead Beer cans being tossed from the window. For a moment her new mystical merger with the community reverted to paranoia: Are they going to come down the lane to terrorize us? But the drunken screaming faded, swallowed into the Canadian night.

The two bears stopped at Waldo's parked truck, the door slammed shut, the truck rolled up the lane, and the smaller bear stood alone in the darkness. A whippoorwill called; the bats began their skymouse squeaking; and suddenly above the trees, the yellow moon appeared, ten times bigger and brighter than any moon anywhere else in the world, she was sure; it seemed clasped in the quivering branches, so close she could reach it by ladder, so close she could see the yellow moonshine coming off it, beaming across the field, streaming over the lane and on Daniel, painting the lawn, and shining like floodlights against the front windows. At the magical moment, another stream also touched her, fifty-five tiny hot flies taking fifty-five bites out of her skin in their own epiphany of country living. Hurriedly, she slammed into the house, and made her way to the sink, by the glorious light of the moon, to plaster herself with baking soda.

■ ■ ■

I never noticed before what a great proportion of the population is pregnant. She found herself spotting big bellies as she'd spotted back-country roads the year they'd been farm hunting, or further back as she'd spotted stoned faces when she'd first smoked dope, and still further back satisfied faces when she'd discovered sex, and now it was bellies, of which there were many, three or four anyway before they got to the fairgrounds.

The music coming out of the carnival was a mixed-up blare of carousel tunes and the local radio station's Nashville sound amplified. To the right, as they walked in, was a hall marked ART. "We'll save that for dessert," she said.

The evening was cool; the ladies wore shawls and jackets. She and he flowed with the crowd, between stands of stuffed animals you hit with a ball, rows of dolls, and china prizes; the bingo-caller's voice crackled over the speakers, *G-four.* The bright lights on the booths made the night seem darker, and the air was thickly

scented with fried fish, chips, and foot-long hot dogs; cotton candy
waved by like a procession of flags; the carousel whirled, and the
whips, and the little cars that crashed into each other, and the
steep sliding chute down which children sailed on their bottoms,
one by one, after emerging above from a sort of tent in the sky; she
watched as the tent flap slowly opened and a child of about seven
ejected its infant sibling. Frozen in horror, Sara saw the baby
plummeting down alone, a tiny figure bundled in swaddling
clothes, too young even to crawl, still totally bald, even its fon-
tanelle still open; this last feature was painfully clear as the baby
was shooting down backwards, bouncing head first at a brain-shat-
tering speed. Sara rushed to the base of the chute to catch it, but
the mother got there first, casually turning away from her friend to
whom she'd been relaying some detail of scandal with the voice of
a macaw piercing through the carousel music, while simultaneously
eating jelly apple and cotton candy as if endowed with three
mouths and a syncromesh jaw; nonchalantly, she picked up the
still-intact infant and returned to her more interesting story, while
the baby, who by rights should've been traumatized for life, went
on beaming.

Dazed, Sara followed Daniel to the livestock show. The odor of
animals and hay floated over them as they entered the cavernous
hall with its long rows of stalls. Big pigs lay with piglets beside
them; sheep curled up with lambs; cows stood with their calves; it
was, she perceived, a huge maternity ward, and in the vast natural
bliss that suffused the whole place, the satisfied sounds of grunting
and snuffling, the unquestionable competence of the four-legged
mothers, she felt her confidence growing. If everyone else can handle the job so easily, so can I. Alone in a stall stood a chestnut
mare with her single pale colt, and through some accidental chink
in the wall a yellow shaft of evening shone in upon him like a spot-
light, turning his mane to gold; the mother, nuzzling, protective,
stood admiring her son and seemed to accept the gaze of the
viewers as suitable homage toward the golden colt.

"Maybe," said Daniel, "we'll get a pony for the baby."

On either side of the colt's stall, teams of workhorses were being
groomed and decorated, their coats polished and buffed, pom-pons
and bells woven into their manes, tails braided with bright strands
of wool and wound into colorful balls; magnificent metal-tooled
bridles hung on the walls of their stalls; and the forest workers and

farmers who groomed the godlike creatures seemed, if only for this single evening, to belong to the glorious time that was gone, when the province was filled with heroic men and beasts and trees, when the long masts were cut for the great sailing ships and settlements were carved from the vast wilderness, the time of Murvyle's stories, and the time before, of his hundred-year-old father who could tell you how they'd carried giant timbers a hundred miles to the ship-building center of North America, now just a seedy has-been backwater of a town, dominated no longer by the great sailing boats but a sulfur-spewing pulp mill.

The real fossils of the era, she saw, were seated next to the stalls, lined up on benches, old men with sunken cheeks and craggy faces, leaning on their canes and mumbling to each other of the animals, of bygone times, of God knows what; with rubber bands on their sleeves, thick suspenders, and antediluvian caps tipped forward, they didn't even acknowledge the new era; she half expected them, when the show was over, to pull out in their Model-T Fords and drive back into the past to disappear for another year. But the shaky old men still had neck muscles bulging like trunks, and you knew each one had chopped down thousands of trees; their eyes were sunk in everlasting suspicion and the sardonic smile on their gray lips said something like *taken again;* and still, there was a spirit in them from the old days, a spark of that distant sharing.

She trailed behind Daniel, past double-decker bunks scattered throughout the animal pens; some of the farm boys in charge of the feed were already asleep, others sat on their trunks and ate or played cards in the yellow beam of kerosene lanterns. In these children too, she felt that magic spark, if only a temporary thing; tucked in with the hay and the beasts, in the kerosene glow, they could've lived a hundred years ago.

"I have a feeling," she said, "that art show's going to be very worthwhile."

They moved on to the next exhibition hall, well lit, loud, and festive after the sleepy slurping scenes of the barnyard. The first booth offered oil-fired furnaces, the next featured ride-on lawn mowers, and a third sold insurance policies; some people were peering into a dishwasher as if it were a TV show.

She thought of the old men in the horse barn and wondered what it was from bygone days that satisfied their souls and hadn't produced in them this existential dilemma which could only be satisfied by more lawn mowers and furnaces, dishwashers, TV's, and insurance policies; she felt herself sucked up in the shuck, ogling the freezers; Daniel was staring open-mouthed at an army enlistment film of soldiers crossing a vine bridge.

She pulled his arm. "Let's go outside."

Amidst the games and the rides, gangs of high school kids walked by, dull-eyed, vacant, faintly menacing, drunk on beer and their mysterious small-town dream; it seemed to her the enchanted children in the bunks by the animals had been another species of human being, and she tried to figure out what was wrong, why this merger of old and new disturbed her, why this troubling shifting of eras seemed to encapsulate Atlantic Canada, the home she'd chosen, which was never quite what she wanted it to be.

"The folk art," she remembered, spirits rising.

They made their way to the art exhibit, and started the tour.

There were paste-on sparkle scenes, from kits; there were swirly pictures, also from kits; string art, from kits; and paint-on embroidery. The children's art consisted of coloring books, colored in; there were plastic model airplanes, from kits. The needlework was stitched onto printed patterns. The ceramics and greenware were cast from commercial molds. There were hours of labor, meticulous, carefully executed labor, and not a single thread-inch, blob, or stroke of self-expression; or rather, it was all the self-expression of the hobby companies' designers, but not of the people of the province. "And God knows," she said aloud, "they have a lot to express."

But Daniel had disappeared, and she was talking to herself, as she continued walking through aisles of kit-work with prize ribbons pasted on them. Decadence, she realized, has nothing to do with sophistication; it's a culture slipping to its greatest mediocrity without a grain of inspiration. And it isn't that the people are incapable; they're no less capable now than they were in the old days Murvyle spoke of when men in lumber camps whittled animals you'd almost think were real.

An old man with the smell of woodstoves and the forest clinging to his clothing brushed past her, reminding her of the woods all around them, the source that ought to bring out the best in everybody. Don't they see it? she wondered, staring at a paint-by-number scene. Or have they switched their focus, so that nature is now invisible, and all they can draw on is the hobby department of the K-mart?

■ ■ ■

"We was down to visit Father," remarked Murvyle from his lounge in back of the stove. "Tired? I'll say he was. Wouldn't rise from his bed all day. Claims he spent the whole night at the Exposition."

"Now you know," interrupted Phoebe, "Grampie Amos ain't been out of that dooryard fer seven years."

"Claims he was workin the horses," said Murvyle, "and got hisself all tuckered. Course, he jes dreamt it."

"Still," said Phoebe, "he was tired lookin."

"Jes a dream," repeated Murvyle. "He ain't been to no Exposition fer twenty years."

"No," admitted Phoebe, "but he did look awful peaked . . ." Sara could see that Phoebe felt there was something to it.

And maybe there is.

She couldn't help feeling that the old man's Exposition was a lot better than the one she'd just seen; and she would've rather been there, at the old remembered fair, than the real one of today.

The barn door creaked open, cracked, and fell off its hinges. Waldo rode out in triumph, high on his tractor.

"We want the pond wide," said Daniel, jogging beside him over the field, "but not so deep that it'll stir up the manganese."

"We don't wanna stir up no manganese," agreed Waldo from his mobile throne. They cut through the woods, where the leaves were turning orange, and roared down the slope to the half-hewn mud hole skulking in the sun.

"Think you'll ride high enough in the water?"

"Dunno till we try," replied Waldo placidly, as the great beast rolled forward. From the corner of his eye, Daniel spotted a team of advisors approaching downhill.

"I see you fixed her," remarked Murvyle.

"A tractor's a good rig," said Hilton, eyeing the miracle machine wading mud to its axles. "A feller could make some money with one."

Waldo'll make about a hundred, thought Daniel. And he's only spent five hundred in parts over the summer.

"Chew a little more out of that there bank," shouted Murvyle, pointing the bulldozer to the left.

"I'm gonna buy me a tractor," Hilton stated, staring challengingly from his father to Daniel and back, daring either of them to bring up the fact that he had no money to buy his next six-pack, having quit work early this year, in the middle of August.

From out of the woods appeared a sinister figure—tall, red-bereted, slinking suspiciously toward them. "What you want is some trout in there. Clear that water up faster'n a pipe will."

"Put in trout," countered Murvyle, "and a hawk'll only eat them."

"Tractor's runnin good, ain't she?" said Hilton. "I might jes buy me one of them rigs. Haul out some stumps with her."

Pike sneered and muttered, "Dumber'n a soldier bean," but the reference sailed past Hilton who wasn't tuned in on the insult level. If you didn't attack him outright, thought Daniel, your animosity wasn't substantial enough to penetrate his goodwill; basically, you had to blacken both his eyes, as often happened to him on Saturday nights, to make him perceive your intent as negative; anything short of knocking his head against the porcelain urinal in the Canadian Legion was too trivial for him to notice as insult.

"To the left," shouted Murvyle.

"To the right," hollered Pike.

The tractor veered, left, and right.

"Gonna be leeches in that son of a whore," predicted Hilton with gloomy certainty.

"All these mud holes draws leeches," said Murvyle. "Jes the kind of water they favor."

"They'll breed up fast in this one," added Pike, for once in agreement, while Daniel contemplated the perverse tendency of country people to paint the dreariest possible picture of an undertaking, before, during, and after, to ensure that no one would ask them why *they* didn't build a pond, the answer being leeches.

When Waldo finally rode out of the finished mud hole, sitting high on his tractor, roaring up the furrowed bank, black water lapping his treads, the only fly in Daniel's ointment was a vision of leeches slithering in on all sides, as if they'd lurked in the marsh for millennia, waiting for the pond to come along so they could ruin it.

"Anythin else you want plowed under?" asked Waldo.

"Can you cover the burned-out foundation?"

They started up toward the field, Waldo riding in the lead, Murvyle explaining to Pike how the banks of the pond would cave in by spring.

A lilac bush and a bed of tall golden glow stood at the edge of the ruined foundation. Waldo began pushing earth on top of the charred scar of the past.

"Feller don't wanna do this to a foundation," said Hilton ominously. "There's a lot of good stuff in there."

He's right, thought Daniel, what am I doing? There's a lot of good stuff in there. He looked down into the twisted wreckage of rusty furnace, stove, and bed springs, and thought of all the other old foundations in the settlement, superstitiously left uncovered to grow over with vines and turn into booby traps. "Plow her under."

"To the left," ordered Murvyle.

"Tumble them stones over there," said Pike.

Waldo plowed cheerfully forward.

"Sufferin fuck," shouted Hilton. "Hold that son of a whore!" He dove into the cinders. Jesus, thought Daniel, he's found Sara's jewels! Did Sara have jewels?

Hilton thrashed about below, while they stood in stunned silence, until he rose up out of the pit, holding an old porcelain doorknob. "Feller never knows when he might need a knob," he said slyly, sticking the precious piece of junk in his baggy back pocket, and clambering upward; as he scuttled over the top, the doorknob toppled out and Waldo resumed his plowing, burying the bit of porcelain ten feet under, but Hilton was still grinning as if he'd bested them all, getting a doorknob for nothing, oblivious of his empty back pocket.

It doesn't take long to burn a place, thought Daniel, or bury it; Waldo flattened out a neat mound of dirt, rolling back and forth on top of the invisible foundation to make it blend in with the surrounding terrain.

Then they backed the big truck against a mud bank, and with considerable hand-waving, shouts, and suggestions, the bulldozer was loaded, blocked in place, chained down, and ready to go for winter plowing; Waldo rode off, to turn thirty-six more window frames before supper. Pike remarked to the others, "That freckle-faced fucker took long enough to dig that pond, didn't he? I say, that freckle-faced fucker took long enough." He venomously glared after Waldo's dust.

"Bullshit and a gorby," announced Hilton with a loud belch.

"I guess," agreed Murvyle, moving toward his truck.

The vehicles slowly pulled away up the lane, while Daniel gazed in solitude over his estate, fully equipped with an olympic sized leechery.

In the wake of the trucks and jalopies, a Studebaker chugged down the lane; old man Suttle ponderously climbed out, fat belly shaking with mirth. "I see yer survivin."

"So far," answered Daniel, wondering what it was old Suttle always chuckled about; was he still laughing about the two Americans who'd bought his abandoned farm for twice as much as a Canadian would? "Do you want to pick some apples?" Daniel asked Mrs. Suttle, who'd emerged from the car with a bushel basket.

"If you've any extra," she said deferentially, though it was she who'd grafted many of the trees; she remarked on the autumn foliage and tiny changes in her former land as they walked toward the orchard, or rather as she danced, in sneakers and one of Suttle's overcoats and a man's peaked tweed cap inside of which she looked like an ancient tree elf.

They paused at the newly plowed earth which had once been their house, and Daniel found himself uncomfortably noticing that it looked like a fresh graveyard plot.

"I see you plowed her under," said Suttle, without chuckling, his eyes showing he was thinking that he too would soon be plowed under. But his wife was busy examining the bed of tall golden glow; for her, the valley had already come and gone; she'd delivered its babies, washed its corpses; nothing in nature was a stranger to her; as an ancient elf, she lived with the earth's fruits and flowers, and Daniel found himself wishing his own child could come into the world with this old midwife.

■ ■ ■

"Dr. Penn said there's no room for a father in delivery." Sara shuffled out of the medical clinic. "I told him you don't take up much room, but he wouldn't listen."

"Shall I speak to him next time?"

"I doubt if it will help."

He doubted it too; there didn't seem much room for him anywhere. He'd taken her to childbirth classes, but quickly escaped when he saw twenty fat women with pillows and no other men; from outside, he'd peeked through the classroom window and watched a childbirth film about corn kernels sprouting and horses running with colts to violin music, but how that would help anyone in labor he figured you had to be in labor to know.

They started up their convertible, he fiddling under the hood with a screwdriver and she pressing the gas; once in gear, they drove to the new shopping mall.

The interior of the giant complex was red like a womb, with soothing, gurgling, womblike Muzak and twinkling astral lights. Mock flagstones glistened; illuminated fountains were spritzing; on both sides of the long hallway, potted plants stood in profusion, bred by some horticultural genius exclusively for malls—though real, they managed to look like plastic.

"The new art gallery's open," she exclaimed, darting away from him, belly foremost, and he strolled on alone. It was lunch hour, and kids from the high school milled in groups; the planning fathers had constructed the mall adjacent to the high school so the kids could learn to be good, solid, daily consumers.

The sound of hard rock lured him toward a shoe store; he stood at the doorway, listening to the acid beat. Two prematurely aging ladies tottered in past him and immediately tottered back out, frail hands over their ears. ". . . I prefer the music at Pilkington's Dry Goods, it makes me wanna shop . . ."

New Orleans grillwork framed the art gallery, in which he spotted Sara's bulky form wandering among an assortment of clowns on velvet, art school matadors, Gypsy girls with cherries behind their ears, and vapid pastoral scenes. The paintings stood on fancy easels and hung in fancier frames, expensively priced, but none of them compared with Pike's cockeyed grostesqueries.

In the heart of the mall, the Mounties had their latest car displayed, with the newest in radar, sirens, lights, and Breathalyzer, so the good people coming out of the government store next door, with their twelve-packs of Moosehead, could pause to check out the equipment by which they would be stopped and convicted at some future date.

A baby wheeled past them in a stroller, and Sara made gurgling sounds toward the pink-bundled shape. Will we, Daniel wondered, be taking our kid through here too? Will we imprint our innocent baby with the Twice 's Nice dress shop and Casual Capers and pseudo flagstone? Yes. And it will continue for generations. Long after we're dead and gone, the mall will remain—an impregnable fortress of consumerism—the only hot spot in town.

"Daniel, they put in a real outdoor café! Just exactly what town always needed . . ." He followed her toward the answer to her prayers, and they sat down at the real imitation outdoor café, abutting the real imitation New Orleans grillwork, abutting the real imitation flagstone, on which strolled the gay boulevardiers of the temperature-controlled shopping mall. Across the corridor of the mall, for authentic ambiance, was the Singer sewing machine outlet, the eyeglass dispenser, and, for further ambiance, Household Finance; to their left, providing atmospheric sounds of squeaking shopping carts, was the Save Plenty Supermarket.

Sara ordered some real imitation cream pie, and asked excitedly, "You know what you'd pay for a pie like this in New York?"

"Six dollars."

"You would!"

He watched the shoppers zombiing along, in what seemed to be a province-wide epidemic of zombiism, and tried to view it through her elated eyes. A few feet down the hall, a photography booth was being set up, displaying portraits of happy people looking as though they were staring out from a poorly adjusted color TV set, and for five dollars more framed in distressed-walnut-grained plastic; or you could command an instant calendar picture of you and your loved one walking hand in hand down a simulated country lane, poorly color-adjusted; or a graduation shot to make you appear as if you had a glorious future as a K-mart management trainee, poorly adjusted.

"We'll have the baby photographed," she stated.

Is this the artist I married? he wondered, and glanced at her beaming upon it all, with her Paris street scene smile, her belly spreading a rainbow over the mall and turning it into the Champs-Élysées. Off in the distance, he spotted a genuine, living, breathing, vibrant boulevardier—old Alf himself—weaving rakishly along in fawn-colored raincoat and snap-brimmed hat, carrying his attaché case of fine rat-tail cognac, two hundred proof, guaranteed to temporarily blind and permanently disorient; he waved to the Mounties, "Ma frans . . ." His geniality echoed down the mall. The Mounties returned his greeting, evidently knowing him intimately from numerous arrests and prison sojourns, and Alf, his bloom untarnished, examined and gave advice on the new Breathalyzer, siren, and lights, and continued weaving along the hall.

"Ah, ma frans," he declaimed with a sweep of his hat, revealing that he'd recently painted his hair; he navigated the grillwork gate, and sat down at their table with élan and aplomb; for an instant Daniel felt himself truly at home, here on the Schnapps-Élysées in gay Acadie.

Alf ordered some ginger ale, to which he added a healthy dose of eye-watering Dr. Fowler. "Ver good fer de hole," he explained, pointing to his heart; he sipped, grimaced, shook his titian head, and waved with indiscriminate fondness at all passersby, including the two tottering ladies who patronized Pilkington's Dry Goods. "Ah, ma fran, she's a good location here. She get de crowd. She de best damn place in de whole damn town!" He lowered his voice confidentially. "De best spot of all is right across from de gov'ment store. Dat's where I'm gonna open ma shop."

"What kind of shop?" asked Sara.

"De antique shop. I got good frans in dat business. Ver good contact in de antique business . . ." He gestured vaguely with his paper cup, and Daniel realized old Alf had forgotten who his friends in the antique business had been, but the idea had seeded and taken root. "Dese frans of mine, dey know jes de kind of antique she'll go here in de province." He wiped off some spittle, grew munificent: "You want a good antique? You come and see me. Right down de hall, across from de gov'ment store. I'm gonna make big money in de antique business, and I give you good deal on an antique. Good antique too."

Sara nodded. "A good antique store's the one thing still lacking." Daniel saw she almost believed in Alf's store, no dream too far out for her now that the farthest out dream was her own.

"Ma frans," said Alphonse, glancing at his wrist, on which he wore no watch, "I gotta go now." He reached into his scruffy vest pocket and drew out an invisible fob-watch which apparently agreed with the one on his wrist. "Got ver important business deal," he confided.

Daniel watched in awe as Alf departed, a low-keyed sort of awe suitable to Atlantic Canada where no one gets too worked up over anything; old Alf, with his rampant delusions, somehow had life by the throat. The bootlegger weaved back and forth down the hall, pausing to look in the sewing machine shop, the eyeglass dispenser, the acid-rock shoe store, exhibiting his universal sense of curiosity and catholic taste. The man knows no defeat, thought Daniel, nor guilt; he's strewn dead cows and ruined women all over the county in the wake of his bonhomie and it's just a part of the day's work. He noticed Sara glancing in old Alf's direction with a smile on her face much like the bootlegger's own sublime expression, and it occurred to him that the secret of Alphonse's success was that the old man was perpetually pregnant—with mad schemes and imagination—and the fact that he never gave birth to anything real was irrelevant.

    ■ ■ ■

    Other cars were parked at the post office when he pulled up, and he tried to step out on the path with that native swagger, or stagger, or whatever it was that made a person belong. He could shuffle in humbly, or stride in with shoulders back, or proceed up the steps in his own unalterable manner, which was the way it always turned out anyhow. Climbing the stairs, he heard voices talking, but when he pushed open the door marked *King Cole Tea,* the thundering silence that fell would've gratified the greatest actor; Sir Laurence Olivier himself had never been blessed by a more attentive audience.

    Humbly striding, or proudly shuffling, to the counter, amidst the open-mouthed stares of the populace, he delivered his opening speech, "Good morning."

    His audience gazed at him with blank morbid curiosity, hanging lips and a haunted, cold, country look in their eyes. It wasn't that they were tactless, he'd decided, they simply didn't know the niceties of disguising one's inquisitiveness. The long gaping silence that bathed him was finally broken by the postmistress; in ringing tones, she inquired, "Makin a lot of money?"

    The ears of his audience twitched forward like those of dogs, with primeval attention; this was their burning question: How do these Americans do it, who live in the boondocks? Of course everyone knew he worked for Waldo, but somehow because of his attitude toward work—that he enjoyed it—they considered his job merely a hobby, masking the secret underground wealth about which he selfishly refused to talk.

    Never having figured out how to answer this question, he stood like an idiot, which made him seem richer and guiltier, in spite of the fact he was working, without vacation pay or unemployment, and was one of the very few in the community, besides the postmistress and Sara, who paid income tax.

    "Has Sara changed her mind about the baby shower?" asked the postmistress, for the seventh time.

    "I'm afraid she hasn't," he smiled, for the seventh time, and promised again to help change Sara's mind, though in truth he wouldn't dare mention a baby shower, whose subject had become such an issue at the post office that Sara refused to go for the mail anymore, leaving him to brave the scene alone every Saturday.

"All the ladies are so anxious . . ."

The ladies present gaped on in silence, which was, insisted Sara, the way it would be at her shower; it would be the Post Office Treatment magnified thirty times, with her at the center; and besides, she added, according to Phoebe, another girl got knocked up every other day, which meant she'd be involved in an endless round of baby showers for the rest of her life for people she didn't know, many of them fourteen years old.

"Could I have my mail?" asked Daniel humbly, after a suitable pause; for some reason, it never occurred to the postmistress that he came in on such an unsociable errand.

During the Ordeal of Mail Being Unearthed from the Jerusalem Drawer, an act of mind-boggling slowness, the King Cole Tea door banged open, and Murvyle made his entrance like the cavalry who rides onto the screen at the end of the movie with bugles blowing and flags waving to save the hero from the Indians.

All Murvyle actually said was "Mornin Minnie, mornin Dan'l, mornin Caleb, mornin Albion," etc., but Daniel was once again human, having been included by Murvyle as a fellow mortal, a friend, instead of an aardvark at the zoo. Gratefully, he hid behind Murvyle's lumberjack shirt, and managed to leave without further torture. Safely on the front porch, he realized he'd have to go to another store to pick up the food he could've bought at the post office but hadn't because he lacked the nerve to be stared at by a dozen curious eyes while making his purchase, as if his buying a bag of Robin Hood Oatmeal was more significant and suspicious than old Albion Wood buying the same bag of oatmeal.

He stepped into the convertible, which he'd left running as Sara wasn't present to help him restart it, nor did he wish to ask anyone else, because whenever he did he only unearthed another previous owner. ". . . I put eighty thousand mile on this wagon meself."

Thoughtfully, he drove to the fork in the road: Should I shop at Boudreau's where I have to shout my order into Boudreau's hearing aid, or should I go to Mulligan's Store, where Mulligan's pubescent daughters will overwhelm me with their burgeoning pulchritude?

Several trucks and cars were parked outside Boudreau's, so he braved the lovely daughters, who stood like a chattering chorus, too immersed in their own developing bodies and talk to pay attention to your order, but handed you whatever they grabbed off the shelf, which turned out to be typical native fare of Bisquick, canned spaghetti, Cheez Whiz, and potato chips. However, the girls also included his Robin Hood Oatmeal and Sara's all-important half gallon of milk, so he felt he'd done pretty well and was one of the family, if only a distant cousin.

Stowing his packages in the chortling convertible, he drove up the Hills of New Jerusalem, to the accompanying music of gunfire. Someone had shot the two baby deer who'd been born this year near Sara's clothesline. One day he and Sara had watched the mother suckling them, and the next afternoon both fawn were dead. Sara had been distraught; she was easily distraught these days, and identified with every species of mother.

He parked in the drive, and entered the kitchen, where she sat sketching in front of the fire. He handed her most of the mail; he rarely got any, other than envelopes marked *Private Confidential Information,* which inflamed the postmistress to a curious frazzle and contained nothing more interesting than mail-order occult advertisements; today's offered a fabulous buy on a personalized horoscope, which would tell him, perhaps, what significant conjunction of stars had landed him in Atlantic Canada.

". . . Judy and Carol are going to come up to help with the baby."

Maybe, he thought, reading the fabulous offer, I need a personalized horoscope, it does sound pretty indispensable.

". . . Did you ever hear of a jacket being discussed in a book review?"

He glanced up from the astrological offer, and tried to make the unfathomable journey from his mail to hers. "I'm not sure what you're talking about."

She silently handed him a newspaper clipping.

The headline read, TAWDRY COVER MARS NEAR MASTERPIECE.

Beneath was the title, *Eternal Fields,* which sounded vaguely familiar. He started to read . . . *Though it's wrong to judge a book by its cover, people do, and, unfortunately, in this instance, an outstanding book will suffer* . . . He put it down, still not comprehending completely. "Is this *your* cover?"

"Yes, it's my cover!"

"Which one?"

"The one I spent so much time on!"

"You mean of old Alf and the red-headed waitress?"

"Oh my God, what are the art directors going to think? Every art director in the business is going to see this. Who ever heard of a book jacket being reviewed?"

He picked up the clipping again. . . . *In a market flooded with books, when the discriminating reader has his choice of what looks like an interesting novel and what looks like trash of the tawdriest quality* . . . "This person really hated your cover. He says it looks like a Harlequin Romance."

"I've never done a Harlequin Romance!"

"If no one else will give you work anymore, you can always do Harlequin Romances." He said it jokingly, but the look on her face was of a mournful Harlequin heroine, after being told Lord Rothbert Cushbury didn't want her any longer for his file clerk.

"Philistines!" Her expression changed to that of Lord Rothbert. "What do they know? I worked my fingers to the bone painting that cover. It was a wonderful cover."

"It must've been. Even a bear tried to steal it."

She looked at him peculiarly; apparently his contribution hadn't helped. She snatched the clipping from his hand, and leaned toward the stove.

"Don't burn it!"

"Why not?" She flung it into the fire.

"Now we don't know where it was from. New York City or Shlubville."

"Wherever it was, they should be visited by famine. And plague."

"Well . . . don't worry about it."

"But I have a child to support!"

"I'll support the child."

"The point is," she said, "it's my career."

"Look . . ." he said calmly.

She looked, and waited for his solution.

Her career; he had no idea of a solution, but intuitively felt he ought to offer some nice, soothing, meaningless, supportive babble, the tone of which would be the important thing, since the content would be nonsense; he launched, listening to himself, wondering whether he could make money as a therapist. "These things are part of an artist's growth. You'll be stronger because you've been beaten and faced into it . . ." He droned on in that manner, his tone profoundly soporific, and gradually he felt her anger yielding; her gaze began to wander out through the window and over the snow-clad fields as an escape from the boredom of his therapeutic soliloquy.

He stopped.

She said nothing.

The crisis, he noted, has passed. There'll be weeks of sporadic doldrums and voodoo curses regarding plague and famine and the criminal waste of whole forests being cut down to print one Sunday newspaper containing scabrous reviews. But all in all, I have once again demonstrated, to myself and to her, that a good cliché is worth whatever you can get for it.

He took a tentative step toward the hook on which hung his L. L. Bean crusher hat and jacket, wondering whether it would be unforgivable in this moment of ebbing crisis to go for a walk in his beloved forest before it was devastated for a Sunday newspaper.

"Would it be all right if I went for a walk?"

"Go ahead."

"Sure you won't mind?"

"Why should I mind? My career is ruined."

"Okay, as long as you don't mind."

He tiptoed out of the house, leaving her rocking in lumpish benumbment.

The wind sang through the grand, hacked-out, scrubby, second-growth, marvelous forest, and it tasted like a perfect weekend. No one was around. His footprints fell on the thin white snow beside the tracks of moose and bear and trespassing hunters; he was sublimely united with trail and sky, and as he walked, he reflected on the difficult life of an artist.

In a way, Sara really had it hard. Though his was a heavy dirty job, building houses, painting houses, putting up four-by-eight plasterboard walls, spackling, and sanding, once it was done, at least he didn't have to deal with it again; it certainly wouldn't be reviewed in the *Daily Loyalist*.

Although, he thought, hiking down toward the stream, in every trade there are artists; for example, there are plaster masters who walk on stilts, whose ceilings need no sanding, who get each seam flawless with one wipe of a trowel, the edges perfectly feathered, so perfect that Michelangelo couldn't do better. He pictured the plastering job he'd finished yesterday up in Dry Creek, and one of the great plaster artists standing before it, looking at it critically, quietly commenting, "Tawdry spackling mars near masterpiece."

■ ■ ■

He walked into the doctor's office nervously, entering the exalted presence of the godlike being who had finally deigned, after delivering thirty thousand babies, to allow one lowly father to be present.

He supposed Dr. Penn's change of mind was a sign of the changing times, but he suspected it had much to do with Sara's technique of bearing down unrelentingly with hammer and anvil until you found it less painful to want what she wanted, even if you were a godlike being who'd delivered thirty thousand babies.

Dr. Penn offered a large hand in jovial greeting. "It'll be a first for both of us."

"Yessir," said Daniel, slightly awed by the old man's bulbous red nose, indicating advanced alcoholism.

"To tell you the truth," said the doctor, "most fathers couldn't care less. I've delivered seven kids for some men and never even seen them. Wouldn't you think they'd at least want to meet me?"

"You'd think so," said Daniel; it seemed the celebrated doctor had done a complete turnabout, under Sara's relentless brainwash, and was now the foremost champion of father-assisted childbirth in the country.

The old man's handshake, which continued as he spoke, was filled with strength and vigor, a confidence-inspiring handshake. Here was a man who could deliver babies drunk.

■ ■ ■

The Santa Claus at the shopping mall bore an uncanny resemblance to the man who was going to bring their baby into the world. It wasn't simply the twinkling eyes and bulbous red nose, the white hair and pear-shaped face, but also that he inspired you with the same confidence; small children mounted his lap as trustingly as lambs; in his long career, the kindly old geezer had probably held thirty thousand kids on his lap.

"Do you think he could be your gynecologist's brother?"

"Could be," said Sara distantly, watching the snow-suited urchins toddle up the red and gold throne.

"A tremendous spread can take place in these large rural families," said Daniel. "One happens to get a good education and another delirium tremens and a seasonal Santa Claus job."

She answered his remark with a flicker of her eyes, in front of which hung a familiar blanket of fog; whatever he said lately, she smiled, but he felt she was no longer actually hearing his witticisms.

The mall was frenzied with Christmas shoppers, and he and Sara moved through at her new slow pace, her placid expression changing only when they passed the bookstore, where he noticed her sneering at the tawdry display.

"I'll meet you in half an hour," she said. "And you're not to spend over ten dollars on a Christmas present for me."

He checked his watch, and walked down the hallway. The Parisian indoor-outdoor café had been dizzyingly short-lived. Now it was a bar, with no windows at all, boarded, stockaded, and draped like a hearse, as was the style in a small town where there was no discreet method of drinking away from your spouse, neighbors, and far-flung relations, short of total invisibility.

What should I buy her?

The level of gifts in the mall ranged from home appliances to bone china cups and saucers imprinted with your tartan; there were also some with shamrocks, and a presentation plate of the queen, but that cost ten ninety-eight.

It's the thought that counts, he said, but couldn't think of anything. He fingered maternity clothes, but she wouldn't be pregnant much longer. He looked at matching Orlon scarves and mittens, and in desperation turned his footsteps to the hobby store; tubes of paint were too practical, and she'd never do string craft, but perhaps there was something.

"A lot of people this Christmas," suggested the hobby saleslady, "are buying bottle cutters for presents."

"I don't think she'd like a bottle cutter."

"Macramé is always a welcome gift."

He shook his head.

But the more he examined the alternatives, the stronger seemed the appropriateness of a bottle cutter. It was practical, and hadn't they decided for once to be practical, limiting themselves to ten bucks apiece? It was also ecological; the dumps of the country were littered with bottles, a notorious waste, while people bought drinking glasses every day; with a bottle cutter you solved both problems at once. It was even artistic; she could cut colored bottles. She could cut bottles for glasses as gifts for other people in future Christmases; everyone appreciated handmade gifts. Birthdays too.

And think how much we'll save on glasses. I'm always breaking glasses. The baby will soon be breaking glasses. It's the perfect present. Funny I didn't think of it immediately.

The hobby lady gift-wrapped it for him. "I call this the year of the bottle cutter," she confided. "Last Christmas was the year of the rock polisher."

I'm right in style. Next year would be too late. Like buying a rock polisher this year. Passé.

Congratulating himself on his perfect choice of gift, he made his way to the cafeteria. At the gateway to the food line, hung a festive sign: *Senior Citizens' Tea Party, Every Wednesday from Two to Four, Free Tea to Everyone with a Senior Citizen Card.*

The long line of elderly people before him indicated the party had just started, though it wasn't literally a party in spite of the sign's evocation of paper hats and free cookies and cake and rollicking fun; it was simply a way to fill the cafeteria at what was usually the slowest two hours of the week, and with a crowd that would never come otherwise, since the old folks couldn't afford the overpriced plastic baked goods you had to buy with your free cup of tea; however, the old people in town, being of rural roots, couldn't pass up something for free, even if they had to pay for it.

He moved along the counter, amidst the venerable mob, and carried his tray to a table. A good number of the party-goers ate alone in stony silence, but a certain amount of festivity raged.

"I haven't sawed you in ages," screamed one old lady to another.

"You sawed me last week."

"Oh yeah, I forget."

A magician's act appeared in his mind, with the forgetful lady sundering her friend in two equal parts. The air was giddy with bludgeoned grammar, the old folks being better at this than the young, having grown up before compulsory education and television; and yet, he reflected, they all hail from England, Scotland,

and Ireland, and probably speak the purest Elizabethan English this side of Mrs. Malaprop.

The whalelike profile of Sara entered his view, marching unseeing past him, directly to nourishment. After spending a good time on line, she came bearing a rich assortment of pastries which she quickly explained were extremely healthful—one because it had a nut in it, another because it was made with a carrot, and so on down the line, until what looked to the untrained eye like simple crap-on-the-road was revealed in actuality to be up to the standards of *The Canadian Mother and Child* manual, provided free at her Thursday night maternity class.

She ate with intense concentration; the moment everything was thoroughly downed, she looked at her watch and announced, "Concert time."

His own watch showed they still had an hour, but he knew she didn't wish to be late to the major cultural event of the year in the province, an event she'd been looking forward to with excitement for months, a genuine afternoon chamber music recital.

They left the mall for the parking lot, and he noticed that her package was a lot larger than his, but he had confidence in his bottle cutter, which seemed by now a stroke of pure genius.

Sara just fit behind the wheel of the car to press the gas, while he did his thing under the hood, crossing starter motor with solenoid switch, and they drove downtown toward the Military Museum, which was hosting the major cultural event of the season.

"If yous'll wait till jes before the show," advised the old guard, "twon't cost you nahthin to get in."

But Sara wanted to make sure they got good seats, so they paid their buck, and climbed the spiral stairs winding precipitously through loyalist dungeons and military wine vaults. The concert was to be held in the Frog Room, whose main item of interest was a huge stuffed frog of doubtful authenticity, looking suspiciously like papier-mâché, purported to be the largest frog in the world, as indeed it must be, being every bit as big as a Bound Brook pig. All exhibits in the room except the room's namesake, namely the dubious frog, had been cleared away to make space for folding chairs and a rag rug indicating a stage.

Sara plumped herself down, first row center, in front of the rag rug.

He gazed at the frog.

They waited.

Thirty minutes or so of frog watching eventually gave way to watching four esthetic gentlemen carry in four chairs on their heads. After setting the chairs upon the rag rug, they disappeared and returned with appropriate instruments.

Sara squeezed his hand excitedly; the Frog Room was rapidly filling with the crème de la crème of local society, about a dozen college professors with their wives and a smattering of effeminate men whose life, Daniel imagined, was one of hellish fear and desolation in a town where the only blatant homosexual had been murdered in his furnished room by a popular brute who was applauded by a packed courtroom when the jury acquitted him; his wife and children led the applause, having evidently found nothing strange in their husband and father spending the night in his victim's room; he had, after all, defended his honor against the delicate fellow, a man of half his weight who had somehow forcefully propelled him across town to his bed and outraged him with a surprise suggestion, for which he was rewarded, at point-blank range, with a bullet in the head.

As the musicians tuned their instruments, a small girl wandered into the room. She carefully removed her snowsuit and sat down next to Sara, sensing the mother-love radiating from Sara's center, or maybe just wanting an unobstructed view.

The sheet music was in place. Throats were cleared. The great event began with Bartók; he saw Sara pass into heavenly trance; here was culture, as good as anything you got in New York; or maybe not, but could you get a first-row center seat in New York for fifty cents?

The lead violinist was clearly on the verge of a nervous breakdown from having served so many years in the boondocks, playing Mozart to the moo-cows; he rolled one eye and twitched as he fiddled. The second violinist was a Hungarian refugee who was so glad to be out of a Budapest prison that he didn't care where he played. The bass violin and cello were manned by two aspiring graduate students who hoped to fiddle their way, someday, out of Atlantic Canada. Thus, the chamber concert.

At exactly ten minutes to five, the child beside Sara suddenly realized that she was due home in ten minutes. In the middle of the lead violinist's crowning crescendo, whose brilliance was based upon borderline schizophrenia, the child rose to her first-row feet, directly in front of the cello, and began to assemble herself into her elaborate snow clothes.

Slowly and methodically, she donned first her overall snow pants, and that accomplished, her more difficult jacket. The near-mad violinist, to compensate for the loud nylon whisperings and zipperings, rose to greater heights of inspired madness, and as he musically flailed, she continued her meticulous dressing in perfect counterpoint.

Few, if any, were any longer watching or listening to the musicians, because now had come time for her galoshes, her hood, and finally both mittens, and fully clothed and ready to brave the wind, the star of the concert slowly and virtuously rustled her way past the four musicians, past the entire audience, past the frog, the elderly guard, and out the door, which slammed loudly behind her; by which time the lead violinist's face was ravaged by twitches; and even the Hungarian seemed to miss Budapest.

■ ■ ■

Mulligan's Store had cars outside, so he went to Boudreau's, having gone through, at the post office, about all the stares he could take for one day.

He left the car running, and stepped out, pausing on his way into Boudreau's to give a pat to a criminal-looking cat.

Boudreau, standing glumly behind his counter, nodded and switched on his hearing aid.

"Robin Hood Oatmeal!" shouted Daniel.

"Have to send out back fer it." Boudreau shouted to his wife in the back. "Bring in a bag of orange peel!"

"Oatmeal!" yelled Daniel.

After which there was a long silence, awaiting the orange peel, and Boudreau stood still more glumly.

"Nice cat!" shouted Daniel, in an attempt to be sociable.

"Which one?"

"The great big red one!"

"Somebody dumped him."

"Oh! Lucky for you!"

Boudreau snorted morosely. "I ain't gonna keep him. Got more goddamn cats round here than mice. All over the place," he muttered, adding more hopefully, "One of them young lads'll soon put a bullet in that cat's head."

The orange peel arrived, Daniel gazed at the candied pieces of fruitcake filling, and Boudreau repeated his hope that the cat would soon meet its end; apparently he was feeding the animal and, as stated, short on mice.

"Oatmeal!" yelled Daniel, but Boudreau had already switched off his hearing aid and was totaling the bill; Daniel departed.

The cat stared up at him with tough yellow eyes and a rough uncompromising face; he looked like the kind of cat who ought to have a bandage on the end of his tail.

Daniel made for his car, noticing as he did, a few of the local young blades swaggering over the bridge toward him, possibly the very lads Boudreau had in mind, who shot up people's camps and would, Daniel knew, shoot anything that moved; the cat edged closer to Daniel and gazed with shining eyes, mewing plaintively.

"Shit," replied Daniel.

The ruffian cat replied with a louder appeal.

This is no cat to have in a house with a baby.

Still staring woefully at him, the animal lifted a paw, and tapped the door of the convertible, just as the young men were upon them.

Daniel lifted the big red cat and dropped it into the car, where the unkempt beast immediately huddled between door and passenger seat, as if trying to become invisible to its approaching tormenters; it couldn't have looked more pathetic if it'd been choreographed. "Jesus Christ," said Daniel, which caused the cat to huddle still deeper.

Daniel re-entered Boudreau's, and shouted "Kitty litter!"

"Gonna take the red cat, are you?"

"I'm just going to try him out!" He also bought a box of cat food.

Driving home, eyeing the cat and the road, he thought: We're here, why not have a cat? His thoughts seesawed back and forth, until he arrived at the house, where Sara stood roundly in the doorway, wrapped in a shawl.

With trepidation, he emerged from the car, lifting the cat from its wedged hiding place; the cat, being the criminal stray he was, had no idea how a cat ought to be carried, but lay in an ungainly heap, four paws protruding north, south, west, and east.

"What's this?" asked Sara, opening the door.

"Just a cat I picked up," he said casually, walking in with his bristling bundle.

"What do you mean you picked him up?"

"At Boudreau's," he replied, indicating by his tone that he often purchased cats at Boudreau's, and furthermore he could've sworn he'd seen *cat* on her shopping list, between *oatmeal* and *orange peel;* why make such a fuss about it?

"My God," she said, "he's got orange balls."

Daniel took this as a compliment to his cat and his taste in cats; he set the cat down, and saw it did indeed have vivid orange balls, as it streaked under the couch, where it remained.

"He isn't very pretty," said Sara, "is he."

Not pretty, thought Daniel. I've brought her a monster. "But if he stays under the couch, you'll never see he's not pretty."

"Oh God," she said for the second time, but poured some milk into a saucer, in her maternal mood apparently unable to turn even a monster away. A face emerged from under the couch, and paused, framed in the blue-flowered dust ruffles, giving them a splendid view of what had been wrought: one ear chewed halfway off, scars decorating the ginger countenance in numerous places, jowls wide as a beaver's, thick neck, and suspicious country eyes, in yellow.

They were taking in the unsavory details slowly, accustoming themselves, when the flounce of the couch moved again to reveal a gigantic paw with more than its share of toes; the second paw presently followed, similarly overendowed; then came the body, muscles rippling under tiger skin; like his jungle cousin, he crept stealthily across the floor, flaunting his orange balls and a ring tail with a kink at the end, perhaps his variation on the bandage theme; he lapped the milk, and scudded back under the couch.

"See," said Daniel, "that cat's no trouble."

He brought in the groceries and set up the litter, but the beast remained behind the couch.

"He doesn't know about litter," said Sara ominously.

"I'll show him." Daniel crawled under the couch, hauled the cat out by his enormous front paws, set him in the box of litter, and explained the situation.

The cat replied by fleeing back under the couch.

"He's going to spray behind that couch," said Sara, "and ruin the house."

"Wait," said Daniel, hit by a flash of genius. He dove under the couch again, pulled forth the cowering animal, and carried it out of the house. Discreetly the cat crossed the lane to the orchard, swimming through the snow on short legs, and proceeded to relieve himself.

"What a cat," raved Daniel, lugging him back inside. "Did you see that? You don't even need litter with this cat."

While they ate supper, the cat crept out to eat from his dish, then zeroed back under the couch, from where he was tugged out again before bedtime.

"He sleeps on the shed," stated Sara.

"Right." Daniel carried the cat out to the woodshed.

"And," she added, "he's not coming upstairs. Ever. I don't want to worry about him smothering the baby."

"No upstairs. Never."

They went upstairs themselves, and tried to sleep. Sara had been taught a special position for sleeping, involving several pillows and strategic placement of belly, but he was kept awake by the noise on the shed; it sounded as if the cat were lifting lumber and flinging boards. With a sinking feeling, he realized there was a massacre going on.

What have I done?

He tiptoed into the meditation room, where he kept his *I Ching,* and rolled the coins for oracular guidance. There it was—the moving line—*His way of life is impeded.*

I've impeded the way of life of my mice.

He rushed back to the bedroom. "Sara," he blurted, "are you awake?"

"I'd just fallen asleep."

"I've impeded the way of our mice."

"Good."

"Good? That cat is out on the woodshed murdering our little friends."

"Yes," she said, "good," and rolled over, rubbing her belly.

He slipped in beside her, fighting his panic. He could take the cat back to Boudreau's, where it would be shot, or he could put the cat out into the cold night alone. He stifled a groan, and tried to contemplate the balances of nature.

■ ■ ■

"Good morning," she said excitedly.

He opened his eyes in the dark; every day lately, like an alarm clock, she woke him at five, she who'd always hated getting up early; it was as if now that the baby was due any minute, she was charged with the eagerness children have Christmas morning.

It really is Christmas, he realized, looking out through the window to see if it were still snowing as it had been all week. If they were stranded when the time came, he'd have to do the job himself, without even a horse and sled to get old lady Suttle and no one to boil the water.

She switched on the bedroom light, whose radiance extended only an inch or so beyond the window, where white flakes were softly falling; the rest of the world was dark; in a few hours the sun would be rising, but now it was all in abeyance, with the chilly house curtained by night. Climbing out of bed, he felt these predawn hours, with the lamps on and the sleeping stillness outside, were something extra, stolen, a way of sneaking time beyond your allotted life span by tacking it on in small pieces each morning.

They filed downstairs in pajamas, she cumbrously carrying her exercise blanket, which she spread out on the floor by the stove.

He started the fire, and opened the door to the blustery shed to let in a very cold Rumpus, who entered with kink-tail in air and hollow-bellied resonant purr of morning. Briefly, the cat circled Daniel, offering his cold fur for a pat, then marched across the kitchen floor to the blue woolly blanket, where he joined *The Cana--dian Mother and Child* exercise program, rubbing against Sara's arms and legs as she did her childbirth gymnastics. Maybe, thought Daniel, I can get Rumpus to boil the water. Nothing seemed beyond the cat's talents—he'd changed so much in the week he'd been aboard, from a scruffy paranoid outlaw to a gentleman of distinction—confident, poised, impeccably groomed, with just the panache of old war wounds to give his face that extra dash of worldliness.

On the kitchen table, Daniel noticed a large fancy-wrapped box; he hurried upstairs to where the bottle cutter was hidden, and brought it back down. Laying it on the table, he experienced a momentary wave of doubt: Would it have been better to get her a nightgown?

She was flat on her back with her knees in the air, and he joined the exercise class, lifting her arms and shoulders to help her push. It was strange, all this simulated pushing, the whole simulated dress rehearsal of labor, with the baby oblivious inside her, going about its business of growing and waiting its own good time.

He added more wood to the fire, she fixed breakfast, and they sat down to eat, ignoring the packages alongside them. A nightgown would never have compared with a bottle cutter; she could buy herself a nightgown any day of the week, but would she ever think to buy herself a bottle cutter?

Rumpus chewed loudly from his bowl. He had a way of sitting with three paws bunched and a single hind leg extended to the side like a ballet dancer's; it began bunched in with the others, then slowly inched out further and further, as if on its own secret reconnaissance of the area. "He's doing it again with his foot," said Sara critically, having maintained her position against the cat by discussing his charms as if they were vices.

Having eaten, cleaned the house, and gotten dressed, there was no longer any way of avoiding the presents; he poured himself a stiff cup of tea for the ordeal.

"I wonder what this can be," she said in a forced attempt at gaiety. The wrapping paper fell to both sides, and the bottle cutter's box was plainly revealed; she looked at it dully. Was she expecting something a bit more tender and in keeping with her position as mother-to-be? But what would that be? A bottle cutter was perfect.

Perhaps she doesn't know what a bottle cutter is?

"A bottle cutter!" she said; something, however, was missing in her voice, a certain measure of response. Where was that surge of excitement about cutting lots of bottles, glasses for everybody!

He moved in on the box, solicitously offering to help her open it; in her condition perhaps she'd lost the ability to open a small cardboard box. "Let me help. This is going to be lots of fun!" he exclaimed, trying to set the tone of the enthusiastic craftsman. Tone was everything. He unfolded the instructions. "First we need a bottle . . ."

"Don't you want to open your present?"

He sat down with his present, and saw her looking at him with the same anxiety he'd felt looking at her when she opened the bottle cutter; he found himself echoing her former forced gaiety: "What can this be!" It appeared to be a Chinese lumberjack shirt, in one of the three standard plaids that covered every back in the province. He already had the red and blue plaids and this was the green. "A shirt!" he exclaimed.

He had some difficulty getting the button closed at the neck, and finally left it open; it was also a little tight around the shoulders and a bit short in the sleeves. "It fits perfectly."

"You sure? It looks snug."

"Maybe a tad snug," he admitted.

"I can exchange it."

"Hell, no, I like it like this. Close to the skin. Warm."

"No," she said woefully, "I'll exchange it."

"What do you say we try this bottle cutter? I'll do it in my new shirt."

"No," came the woeful tone. "I'm going to exchange it." She was beginning to sound like a tape loop. From the floor, rose the crackling of wrapping paper; Rumpus, with red and green ribbon over his chewed-up ear, seemed to be the only one truly enthusiastic about it all; he sprawled in the shirt box without a trace of disappointment, anxiety, or guilt; it was a fine box, it fit perfectly.

"I'll get a bottle," said Daniel, going to the pantry and returning with a large green wine bottle. "This'll be great."

She ignored the directions, but stared at the bottle itself in mute incomprehension, as if lacking a deep abiding interest. He couldn't understand it; such a perfect gift; the most popular gift of the year; bottles, at this very moment, were being cut all over the province. He inserted the bottle into the cutting wheel. "Now what you have to do is turn it."

"Why don't you turn it?"

"It's your bottle cutter. You'll have to know how to turn it."

Lethargically, she turned it, round and round, round and round, bent over the table like an eighty-year-old hunchback watchmaker, her ordinarily nimble fingers dully fumbling. Their eyes met for an instant, and hers seemed to say, *I'm doing this only for you*, in a mixture of pity for him and personal defeat, based on its being Christmas and she obliged to be interested. He saw her regress before his eyes to a pale reflection of herself, a child who has to be instructed in cutting a bottle. "Now rub it with ice," he advised from the instruction sheet. Next, he made her pass it through the candle flame, until it cracked in two, with a saber-toothed edge, which she sanded, wearily, reluctantly; the finished product looked like something you'd break off in a barroom brawl to lacerate your opponent; as a drinking glass, it was the most deadly mouthed model in existence; only a carnival glass-eater would dare drink from it. "Isn't this wonderful," he said, "a free glass. This bottle would normally end up in the dump. What a waste. But here we are, recycling it." He launched on a major ecological speech, to which she listened despondently, as if under duress. Why, he wondered, can't she throw herself into this project wholeheartedly? Is it possible I really bought the bottle cutter for myself? Of course not, why would I want a bottle cutter? It's just extra work. Why would anyone want one?

She suddenly broke out of her moping. "Let's drop this present business. Let's never give each other presents again. Not for Christmas. Not for birthdays. Not ever." The sun broke through the clouds. The snowfall ceased. Down the lane came the roar of the snow plow. He felt himself fill with relief. "What a wonderful idea," he said, removing the Chinese plaid shirt in which he was choking.

"Isn't it a terrific idea?" she asked, once again eager, excited. Even Rumpus seemed to approve, tossing the ribbons from his ear, and stretching out of the shirt box, shaking his back leg behind him as if shaking off the whole bad business.

Behind the snow plow appeared Pike's fire-spitting jalopy; Pike, however, remained in the parked vehicle, unwilling to enter the house until Daniel went out to assure him by his manner that it was perfectly safe, no enemies lurking in the kitchen, no mines under the floorboards, no guerilla warfare on the woodshed.

Pike opened the trunk of his car and brought out a large plywood painting which might have been called *End of a Lumberjack;* nestled in the peaceful forest, beneath Pike's placid green sky, was a quaint Canadian sawmill, in front of which the stick figure of said lumberjack was breathing his last, or more specifically being sawed in half, the two blood-spurting portions of his body dropping off to either side of the great revolving blade. "I seen it meself," said Pike. "Twas back in '33. Young Gideon Whelpley

That Was, he called fer someone to throw him a tool, and when t'other feller throwed it, Gideon leaned forward and dropped fair into the blade." Pike gazed upon his work with satisfaction. "They closed the mill after that. Said they wasn't keepin the proper safety. Gov'ment boys." He spat.

Daniel examined the other stickmen standing around in the painting, gawking at their colleague's bisection; he thought he made out Murvyle's foreshortened shape, and Toner's bulbous neck, old Alf's fabled five-gallon hat, and Pike himself with snap-brim fedora and cigarette. "You don't often see that happen," said Pike. "It's a little dif'rent, ain't it? I brung it fer Christmas."

"Sara will love it."

They entered the house, where Pike drew himself up short, and suspiciously eyed the cat, who was washing himself on the sun-drenched couch. "Who's that?" asked Pike, narrowing his eyes.

"Rumpus."

"Rumpus, eh?" His sneering tone implied that he for one could not be fooled by a name.

Rumpus glanced up at the newcomer.

"I thought so," said Pike. " 'Tis that big red bastard I told you about."

"What big red bastard?"

"The same big red bastard put the run to every cat fer miles and a good many of the dogs. Would you look at that there awful bastard?"

They looked; Rumpus resumed his wash.

"Are you sure this is the cat you were telling us about?" asked Sara.

Pike snorted. "Was he dumped to Boudreau's?"

"Yes," she admitted.

"I ain't never seen such a change in an animal," said Pike, adjusting his red beret, as he sat down beside the beast on the couch. Puffing with pride, Daniel casually pointed out Rumpus's orange balls as a plus.

"Would you like some beer?" asked Sara.

"Give him the new glass."

Pike accepted the new glass, held it up to the light, filled it with Moosehead, and swigged it down. "Quite the weapon, ain't she. I say, she's quite the weapon."

Daniel showed him the new bottle cutter.

"We used to make glasses back in the woods," reminisced Pike, "without no bottle cutter a'tall, jes a bit of string, a nail, and some kerosene." He rose to his feet. "Got another bottle?"

Daniel brought another empty bottle from the pantry, a nail, and some string.

"First you scar her." Pike drew a circle around the bottle with a nail; it was a fairly shaky circle, but considering the way their own glass had come out they couldn't be critical; then he soaked the string in kerosene and tied it around the bottle at the circle. "We'd best go outside fer this next part."

They filed out to watch, Rumpus bringing up the rear.

Pike struck a match against the house and looked around over both shoulders, for approaching bears, wolves, whatever, before touching the flaming match to the string, which burst into flames.

"Hot," he cried, flinging the bottle into the snow. "Now you watch. Soon as I touch her, she'll crack clean as a whistle."

They stood waiting a suitable time, Sara hugging her shawl for warmth and Rumpus easing his hind leg out, until Pike picked up the bottle; it remained intact. He pounded it on the doorstep; nothing. "Got a hammer?"

Daniel went into the shed, and came out with a hammer.

Pike lifted the bottle in one hand, the hammer in the other and, winking significantly as if to say *Now you'll see*, he struck. The bottle smashed to smithereens.

There was silence, while they eyed the slivers of bottle and Rumpus rubbed his jowls appreciatively against Pike's trousers, clearly expressing that he knew another Bum With A Bandage On His Tail when he met him.

She switched on the lamp.

He blinked sleepily.

"We've got to go in," she said.

Across his tired face she read the tales she'd fed him of women going in with digestion cramps, false alarms, and contractions which went on for days. "Shouldn't we wait?" he asked.

She shook her head. Though the Thursday night class had been vague in the extreme about actual labor, on one point they'd been firm: If your water breaks, go in.

She stepped out of bed, water flowing, legs trembling; beyond the window, it was dark; she moved in slow motion, the whole world pinpointing into the moment.

He held her arm as she stumbled downstairs and into the bathroom; the shower curtain was sharply etched with a design of bamboo; the towels were neatly folded, red, white, and blue; freezing, trembling on the toilet, she thought, I'll never be more alive than I am now.

Something wrenched inside her, building in tension and power until it drove out her thoughts; then it gradually subsided; all her worries about the baby, her worries about everything, all seemed indulgent fantasy against this physical reality. Unsteadily, she walked upstairs, hung her wet pajamas on a chair, and put on the slacks and smock she'd worn to Dr. Penn's office—could that have been just this afternoon? She hung onto the bed as a second contraction swallowed her thoughts. *Raspberry leaf tea for easy delivery;* she'd drunk a cup a day, religiously.

He came up for her suitcase and pillows; she collected some books to read during labor. Looking around the bedroom, she thought: When we come back, there'll be three of us.

The car horn sounded; he's in a hurry; the snow must be coming down hard. She went downstairs, and he wrapped her blue exercise blanket around her, helping her through the snow to the car. She slid in with difficulty, and pressed her foot to the gas, while he fiddled with his screwdriver under the hood. She started to laugh at the absurdity, and her laugh was caught up in another contraction.

He got in beside her, and they drove through the settlement; up ahead, in the headlights' glow, the road and trees looked like one of those winter scenes where you shake up snowflakes inside a glass ball. From the depth of the glass a figure appeared at the edge of the road, swaying, knapsack on back, old Alf, undaunted by snowstorm, out on some mysterious nighttime quest, and another contraction took her.

■ ■ ■

"Dr. Dunbar will be delivering your baby."

"But my doctor's Dr. Penn."

"That's right," said the nurse, "but Dr. Dunbar's on duty for the weekend."

A contraction came before Sara could answer. "I'm supposed to call Dr. Penn," she said firmly.

"On the weekends, one doctor does all the deliveries," explained the nurse cheerfully. "This weekend, it's Dr. Dunbar."

"But Dr. Penn knows all about me."

"Friday night," said the nurse brightly. "No doctors are to be disturbed. Now be a good girl and let me prep you." She wielded her razor quickly and skillfully, stopping twice for contractions.

"I wonder where my husband is. He's supposed to be with me."

"Isn't that nice. A lot of the husbands are beginning to keep their wives company in the labor room."

"Dr. Penn said he could come into the delivery room too."

"That'll be up to Dr. Dunbar now, won't it."

Between contractions, Sara stumbled into the bathroom, as the nurse stood guard at the door in her impregnable sweetness. Sitting on the toilet, in the stark white hospital night, Sara marveled at how quickly she'd lost her volition in the face of authority. What could an ordinary person know from a handful of books? Staggering out of the bathroom and mounting the bed, she felt all she knew for sure were contractions, the wrenching waves that couldn't be altered by nurses or doctors or anything in the world.

"This is Dr. Dunbar," said the nurse, introducing the star of the hour. Through the mist of the wave, Sara caught a glimpse of a stocky young man in tan V-neck sweater, leaning over her bed. He lifted her gown and thrust a rubber-clad hand between her legs.

"A contraction has started," she said, and then when once again all was still, "Dr. Penn told my husband he could be with me at delivery."

The young man frowned. "I wouldn't ordinarily mind, except with a breech birth we have to use instruments. I don't think it'd be wise."

"The baby's upside-down?" she asked stupidly. But why didn't Dr. Penn mention it this afternoon?

The doctor left, and a nurse appeared offering sedation. "It's better to take it before you need it."

"No, really, thanks anyway."

The sedation nurse's place was taken by a young intern; he and the labor nurse spoke together in undertones, discussing the size of the dilation, but they didn't use the terminology of the childbirth manuals. "Could you tell me in centimeters?" asked Sara diffidently.

They told her, and she realized with shock she was already in transition. What had happened to the long first stages of labor? According to the books, the baby could be born in half an hour. Her confidence soared, and as the next contraction took her, she went into rapid transition breathing. The intern watched her curiously, and when the contraction was over, said ominously to the nurse, "She's hyperventilating."

Sara felt her mouth drop open. "That was just transition breathing . . . wasn't it?"

He didn't answer for a moment, then asked, "What method are you using?"

"You know . . . Lamaze," she replied, since every book she could find seemed, at heart, indebted to Lamaze.

"The doctors here take a dim view of Lamaze."

A dim view! Why didn't Dr. Penn tell me? Is Lamaze then no good? Is there some new important book I didn't find which contradicts all the others and alone is right? She felt her months of study and practice, the confidence she'd built, her tools for getting through without medication rendered useless. The next contraction came, and she refrained from transition breathing for fear of hyperventilating, whatever dreadful thing that might be. Helplessly, she rolled out on the waves. "What can I do?" she whispered.

"Just go back to doing whatever you were doing."

She tried, but it was too late to catch up with the wave.

He sat down at her side with pad and pen, and began to ask questions—how long she'd been pregnant, her age, history of illnesses, parents' names, and it dawned on her that Dr. Penn's files, which she'd imagined being dramatically whisked to the hospital by pony express at her all-important moment of entry, were safe and snug in Dr. Penn's filing cabinet.

When the questionnaire was completed, Daniel was led in, looking pale and anxious and excluded. He carried her bag of honey drops, washcloth, talcum, and the books she'd chosen to read with him during the long hours of the first stages of labor which had never been. She smiled, and put out her hand; everything was fine again; all the time she'd been alone with her contractions, it had seemed some kind of colossal mistake, the blunder of her life, to have gotten into this horrible state, but now she remembered: It's he and I and our child.

The next contraction came, and they breathed together.

"Isn't this thrilling," bubbled the nurse. "You must be terribly excited," she said, launching on a tirade of friendly questions, as though Daniel's entrance had turned it into a social occasion; the intern too grew gregarious, and the whole situation became strangely partylike, between the long tumultuous contractions.

Dr. Dunbar returned; Daniel was led from the room; and on the next contraction, the doctor asked her to push. For an instant she didn't know how, without Daniel lifting her shoulders, without her legs up on the couch, without her blue blanket, but when she started, the physical relief was overwhelming, not that the sensation of the contraction grew less intense, but she and it were now working together, pushing together with all their strength, and something in the joint effort was so old and deep and basic, so all demanding, so necessary, it seemed, within the pinpointed moment, the ultimate answer.

"Good," said the doctor to the nurse. "In two or three more contractions, you can let her begin."

He left the room, Daniel came back, and for the next two contractions, she fought the urge, but on the third, Daniel lifted her shoulders, and she pushed as hard as she could, harder than she'd ever done anything before, because always before, when lifting heavy things or whatever, she'd held herself back at the point where it felt something inside might break, but working with the strength of the contraction and the primal biological force, there was no withholding; if your head exploded, then it exploded. And she knew it couldn't go on very long; all the books were quite clear about this final effort being short; as soon as the baby's head showed as big as a coin—or in this case the baby's bottom—they'd wheel her into delivery for the final show; and the harder she could push, the faster it would happen.

"Where's Dr. Dunbar?"

"He's catching some sleep."

The other three beds in the labor room were empty; later they might be filled; she guessed the doctor considered himself lucky to catch sleep whenever he could, since he'd be in charge alone, around the clock, all weekend; it seemed a grueling system; it certainly hadn't been mentioned in any of the books.

The intern left, then the nurse, and she and Daniel were alone.

He lifted her shoulders and she pushed, as the contractions came in never-ending jagged waves; he cooled her forehead with water and dried her face, while the clock on the wall, by this time a friend, marched slowly forward, indicating she'd already been pushing much longer than the graphs in her books. It must be because the baby's backwards, she thought, that must be it.

The nurse returned, and the intern.

"Do you want to see your baby?" they asked Daniel.

He went to the foot of the bed, and gazed up between her legs. "The baby's pink," he said.

The baby's pink, she thought, the baby's here!

The party resumed, with the nurse and intern engaging them in small talk; they have a terrific bedside manner, she thought; she thought of the doctor too, who would be so busy over the weekend; it wouldn't be right to wake him one minute too early; he's like a pilot who needs his sleep; not that pilots work straight through a weekend; even truck drivers have to clock out after so many hours for safety reasons. It isn't at all like the books, she thought; in the books I'd be in the delivery room now that the baby is showing; but books are only a guide of averages; reality is always bound to be different.

The contractions took her; she pushed. The voices of the hospital night came and went. It seemed she'd lived in this green room forever, forever pushing, while Daniel gently cooled her forehead, and the clock on the wall slowly moved to two, then three, then four.

She closed her eyes and saw the women of the village, from old crones down to young girls, dancing in a circle, in a rite of fertility, and she alone was outside the circle.

"I think we can get Dr. Dunbar," said the intern finally.

The nurse disappeared, and returned with the doctor, who said she could be taken to the case room.

The procession rolled down the hall. Daniel touched her hand. "So long." As they wheeled her into the case room, she turned her head, and saw him standing alone.

But a few minutes later, while they were strapping her wrists to the delivery table, he was standing beside her, in pale blue coat and cap and mask, his pale eyes smiling down. "The doctor changed his mind."

"We'll have to cut you," said the intern.

The incision was made, and when she pushed with the next contraction, there was a dull sensation at the bottom of the wave's curve.

They checked the baby's heartbeat and found it strong. She thought she too was strong, but the next time she pushed, someone said, "She's getting weak." She tried to push harder to make up for this new weakness remarked on, while the doctor, reaching inside for the baby, pulled.

Suddenly, she saw a tiny foot. "Five toes," said the nurse in her playful voice. The second foot followed, and then a jet of urine rose up in the air, landing in a warm spray on her belly. A boy!

The forceps clamped inside her; she pushed as the doctor wrenched with force; it seemed a cruel tug-of-war.

With a great pop, the head broke free. The child was lifted into the air, pink and perfect and smeared with blood. "The cord," said the doctor sharply.

The cord was clipped; for an instant, the baby faced her, and she saw that he too had struggled, his expression fiercely determined, a warrior's face. The doctor turned him away so abruptly, she thought: He'll addle his brains! They disappeared beyond her range of vision, and Daniel left her side to join them.

"Now," said the intern brightly, "the afterbirth."

He sat staring and waiting, and Sara heard the doctor softly issuing orders she couldn't decipher. She giggled nervously, "Where's the baby?"

"The afterbirth's not coming," said the intern.

"I'll go in and get it," replied the doctor from where he'd disappeared with the baby.

She heard herself joking feebly, "Nothing wants to come out of me." And then she heard the baby, sighing deeply. "Is that the baby?"

Nobody answered. I didn't see him well, she thought, but he looked like a very sweet baby. "Was that the baby?"

"That was the respirator," said one of the nurses.

She strained her ears for the cry.

The doctor came to the foot of the table, inserted his hand inside her, and drew out the afterbirth. "You can sew her up."

The intern started to sew. "Does that hurt?"

"No," she said, listening for the baby. He was off to the right somewhere behind her, with the doctor, the nurses, and Daniel.

"Sure I'm not hurting you?" asked the intern.

"No."

She could make out the sounds of footsteps, of uniforms rustling, and within the mundane sounds, she heard a great blanket of stillness, stretching over the room and over the night and over all the years of her life, as if she'd always known it, that it was only to be she and Daniel.

"There," said the intern, cutting the thread.

From the corner of her eye, she saw Daniel walk to her side. He took the place he'd held before, and stood as if waiting to help her with the next contraction, and all the contractions, and she knew he would always help her, and she saw in his lonely eyes, between the cap and the mask, how much he would've liked the child.

The doctor pulled up a chair beside her table. He'd taken off his mask, and she could see him choosing his words, arranging his face, as she might arrange her hair, uncomfortably trying to set his mouth at the right angle between sorrow and smile, and she felt it wasn't right for this stranger to suffer for her.

"I know," she said, to make it easy for him, but her voice got caught in tears.

"It was too late by the time he came out. He was already gone. There was nothing we could do."

She nodded. "It wasn't your fault."

"There's no reason it should ever happen again . . ." he began, while the nurses moved in to end the scene, to give her a shot to dry up her breasts and get her back on the rolling bed and get the hospital routine back in crisp bustling order.

Wheeling her through the hall, with Daniel walking beside her, the nurse who'd been with them before resumed her professional cheeriness. "There's always a reason for these things, even if we don't understand why when they happen."

Sara supposed she was referring to God and His inscrutable ways, and searched for a suitable platitude in answer. "Yes, there's a reason for everything."

"I mean there was probably something wrong with him. You wouldn't want a baby who wasn't normal, would you?"

"I thought . . . he looked okay."

"He *looked* normal, but there must've been something wrong. There always is. Dr. Dunbar will find out what it was. We're very fortunate having Dr. Dunbar at a time like this. It's his special area of research, stillborn babies."

Stillborn, thought Sara, recalling the vast blanket of stillness. It seemed such a beautiful word for quiet babies.

■   ■   ■

"Let's see you smile," said the morning nurse.

Beyond the curtains, snow was still falling, and the room remained gray in daylight. The other bed was tautly sheeted, empty.

"Haven't you eaten? You've got to eat."

Her temperature was taken; she was given a bedpan and helped with her washing; her bottom was examined, lamented, and supplied with hemorrhoid ointment.

The nurse left with rollicking admonitions to eat, and made sure the door was left open so Sara couldn't hide . . . or maybe that wasn't the reason; she wished she could've held the baby for just one moment, or at least seen him for more than a second, but she didn't dare ask now for fear of encountering scandalized expressions; also, she knew they wouldn't allow it; it seemed the baby wasn't hers now that it had died, but had become classified property of the hospital; the best she could do was be inconspicuous as possible, and leave as soon as they let her; vaguely, she perceived she'd done something shameful, having a dead baby.

Outside, in the green corridor, she could hear Dr. Dunbar making the rounds with his entourage. There was a convivial aura around them, and she found herself quickly wiping her eyes, feeling hopeful, as if he could still make it come out all right, as if he might come in and say there'd been a mistake, the baby had come to life.

He walked in slowly, preceded by the head nurse with her clipboard, and followed by the intern.

"How are you feeling? Did you sleep?"

He instructed the nurse to dispense sleeping pills in the evening, and turned back to Sara. "I examined your baby. I couldn't find anything wrong with him. But when I examined the afterbirth, I found a tear where the umbilical cord was attached to the placenta. Usually the cord is attached at the strongest part, the center, but your baby's cord was attached at the edge. In labor, each time you push, the baby goes forward two steps and one step backward, so there's a lot of strain, but if the cord had been attached at the center, it would've held."

"But the heartbeat was strong until the last minute."

"It must've torn just before he came out. We knew something was wrong when we saw that limp foot."

". . . Did he suffocate?"

"He bled."

He was a small baby, he didn't have to bleed that much to die, and it must've happened quickly, between the last stethoscope reading and the foot, no more than a minute.

If we'd gotten to the delivery room a minute earlier, would he not have bled?

The doctor took out a pen and paper and drew a circle designating the placenta, and showed with a line how the baby's cord had been attached on the edge, not the center. "It's not anything we could've known in advance."

The entourage gravely left, and she felt their relief as they passed from her room; a moment later, she heard them joking next door with a successful mother. Sara wished she were gone and not marring the maternity wing with her sadness.

She shut her eyes, trying to sleep; something in her belly gave a roll, and for an instant she thought the child was still inside her, alive and moving. If old Dr. Penn had been there, she wondered, would he have allowed me to push for so long? Would the baby be alive now if old Dr. Penn had been there?

But the old doctor seemed only a dream; it was Dr. Dunbar who'd been there, asleep down the hall, Dr. Dunbar who'd delivered the baby and was tied to her grief.

She gazed at the doorway and the medicinal-green hall, where nurses and orderlies passed, and trolleys of food, and women going and coming from the baths; a girl in a long white nightgown, with a black pigtail hanging down her back, paced back and forth, in slow secret rhythm, holding her baby before her.

Two nurses paused near the door, discussing a young mother in one of the wards who wouldn't stop crying because she'd had a girl instead of a boy. In fantasy, Sara was given the unwanted child to nurse . . . to keep as her own . . . but even as she watched the dream, she knew it wouldn't happen.

Lunch was brought by the afternoon nurse who waved her cheerfulness at Sara as if it were a dustcloth. She cranked up the old-fashioned bed, and left it up, so Sara was stuck erect for the afternoon. Tomorrow, she thought, I'll be strong enough to crank the bed myself. Or maybe I'll be able to go home; she couldn't understand why she felt so weak.

The night nurse approached with a sheet of paper. "We've a little something for you to sign."

"What is it?"

"Permission for autopsy."

"Mine?"

"Your baby's."

Of course. It isn't I who've died. She felt gears slip somewhere inside her, and wondered if she'd died with the baby.

"Is autopsy necessary?"

"It's usual. You never know who might be helped in future."

Was there a chance of helping someone in future? She couldn't see how, but she signed.

"It's for you too," the nurse added, "to see if there was something wrong with your baby."

And would that help too? she wondered. Would everyone then feel vindicated?

■ ■ ■

"Did you sleep?"

It was a nurse she hadn't seen before, neither young and chipper, nor old and chipper, but sadly in the middle, with a memory of prettiness ravaged by something other than age. She didn't prattle as she made her examination, nor did she rush with that brisk efficiency which made you feel how very busy nurses were and how any extra second spent was charity.

"Do your stitches burn?"

She has unusual eyes, thought Sara, then perceived the only unusual thing about her eyes was they weren't hiding, weren't keeping their distance with that veneer of friendliness that pushed you further into isolation.

"Roll onto your stomach."

No bedside manner, thought Sara, thankful to escape the rollicking hospital optimism, the air that said: What happened was somehow all for the best.

"Haven't they given you hot baths? You should be soaking at least four times a day."

She doesn't make me feel like a failure, thought Sara, climbing into the tub. There isn't an impenetrable professional wall between us. She glanced at the nurse's sad face branded by some personal loss of her own, and the unusual eyes which didn't look on suffering as a sin.

■ ■ ■

"Now," said the gray-haired matron, sitting down with her clipboard, "what are your arrangements?"

"Arrangements?"

"For your baby."

". . . My baby died."

The matron tapped her pencil, but smiled. "I have to know which funeral home is handling the arrangements."

"None. They did an autopsy."

"You're still responsible for burying your baby. It was a full-term child, not a miscarriage."

"But they cut him up."

"They've sewn him back together. There's the Earl Pye Funeral Home and the James Llewellan Flagherty. Usually the Protestants use Pye and the Catholics favor James Llewellan Flagherty." The matron's voice was perfectly sexless, the system speaking, the ever-rolling system, and this was just the next step for factory rejects.

Flagherty. Pye. Sara turned the plastic identification bracelet around on her wrist; the admissions clerk had made it up from information given by Daniel; after her name was typed *Buddhist.*

The matron stared at it in perplexity. With pencil poised, she asked, "What was your father's nationality?"

They're going to get the rabbi after me and make us have a religious funeral. "German."

"And your husband's father's nationality?"

"Irish."

"Name of the baby?"

". . . He doesn't have one."

The system pursed its lips. "I have to fill in a name."

"We didn't name him."

Christian name: *Male,* wrote the system.

"Back to the funeral home problem. The disposal of the body is not the hospital's responsibility."

"We'll take the responsibility. We'll bury him ourselves."

The matron's face, for an instant, became individual, indignant. "I never heard of such a thing."

"But that," said Sara, "is because you've never had a Buddhist before." Do Buddhists, she wondered, bury people without funeral homes? She knew very little about Buddhists, but she knew she didn't want the baby involved in pomp and false sermons and any more professionalism. "I'm not trying to make trouble. It'd be different if there were a Buddhist monk in the area." She wasn't sure if *monk* was the right word, but she was quite sure the matron didn't know either, and the only Oriental in town was cooking chop suey on Royalton Street.

Buddhist or not, said the matron's eyes, this is the most ghoulish thing I ever heard. "Anyway, we can't keep him here."

"I'll be leaving in a few days."

"We can't keep him here a few days. We don't have the room."

"How much room can he take?" asked Sara, dismayed to find herself feeling rejected for the baby, that they were throwing him out, that they didn't want him here, the fierce little warrior.

■ ■ ■

"Poor Dr. Dunbar," said the night nurse, "he lost another baby this evening."
"Poor Dr. Dunbar."
"We all feel so sorry for him."
"Has he been on duty all weekend alone?"
"Yes, just his luck, a weekend like this."
"It's a murderous system, isn't it."
"Well, bottom's up for your heat lamp."

■ ■ ■

"Look what I did this morning." She opened her cosmetic case and took out the pieces of broken mirror.
"Oh, dear," said the sad-faced nurse.
"What more can happen?" smiled Sara. It wasn't much of a joke, but she was glad to have someone with whom she could share it; she wouldn't dare say such a thing to any of the others, couldn't admit to any of the others that something irrevocable had happened.

■ ■ ■

"Hope you'll be back again real soon," said the head nurse, a thin sparrowlike woman, helping Sara into her jacket. "The autopsy could find nothing wrong with your baby."
"Will he . . . look okay?"
"He'll look darling. I phoned downstairs and spoke to them myself. He's all clean and nice and ready. I wanted to send down a little jumpsuit and have them dress him, but they said they weren't allowed. You can dress him when you get home. I thought a jumpsuit would've looked cute."
The nurse helped her into a chair, and wheeled her to the elevator; they rode down to the lobby, where Daniel was waiting.
The nurse spoke to the clerk at admissions, asking that the baby

be brought. He'll look just like any baby, thought Sara, any baby going home from the hospital.

An orderly came out bearing a crisp white parcel.

A sound escaped Sara's throat.

The nurse handed the parcel to Daniel, who walked beside the wheelchair, carrying the baby to the door.

She hadn't realized until this moment how many times she'd imagined this procession, she and Daniel and the baby leaving the hospital together, exactly like this, a hundred times she'd imagined this moment; except the baby was wrapped in a neat, squarish, white parcel, rather like a long box of candy.

In the lot, the convertible was running. She wondered whom Daniel had gotten to help him start it these mornings; Hilton, she supposed.

The nurse helped her into the car, and left them. Daniel still held the baby. Will he hand him to me? she wondered. Will I carry him home as I always imagined?

"I brought the coffin."

It lay on the seat between them, a small wooden casket smelling of freshly sawed pine. He lifted the lid, and put the parcel in.

"You did a beautiful job on the box."

He smiled a forced smile. Would it have been easier on him, she wondered, if I'd gone along with the funeral parlor?

He drove from the lot, through town, and out toward the country; their hands met on the baby's box, and she felt how the three of them were united, even if one of them was dead.

The weather was warm; a lot of the snow had melted. He drove past woods and farmland, cars parked three deep in dooryards, families getting together for New Year's Day.

"I've been longing to see him," she said. "I'm glad we're taking him home."

Well as she knew the road, it seemed totally different from the last time she'd traveled it, in the storm, with the moon above and the child struggling inside her. Of course it was natural to feel empty; even successful new mothers felt physically empty; her maternity clothes hung against her like the skin of a deflated balloon.

She glanced at Daniel's profile; in a strange way it was as if they'd just met, the two of them so fundamentally alone again, like new lovers sharing what no one else can share, and what they shared was between them in the little pine box.

Everyone else was finally out of their lives, and they were free of the red tape, the system; it was back down to them, going home. He turned off the highway, onto the dirt road into the settlement, and immediately the snow became deeper because of the deep silent forest. She felt as if she were returning to herself, this most familiar experience, this background of stillness, this forest which was always there no matter what happened. They climbed the hills, and crested where the grain fields spread out with their distant white blanket, and she felt she was coming home from a carnival, a nightmarish circus of costumed people, strange machinery, and wheels of fortune. Here in the woods, death wasn't a failure or some kind of horror; it was part of nature; she felt grateful to the forest for showing that to her, here where the cycle was maintained and death familiar; she was glad to lay the baby in the forest and not in the city.

Smoke curled from old Alf's shack.

Up ahead was the derelict church and the graveyard she'd painted, with the tips of its old-fashioned stones sticking up through the snow.

He steered down their lane, and again, she perceived the intimate thing, the reunion with herself.

He helped her out of the car; the metal shell no longer protecting, she felt the warm smells and the mist of the day open and take her. The usually raucous blue jays were making the soft liquid call they gave when the weather turned soft, as if the melting world without was also within their hearts. She leaned on his arm, and let herself merge with the mist. The great moment we talked of so long, she thought, the three of us coming home. "I'll carry the box," he said.

They walked into the shed. The ginger tomcat appeared round the corner, returning no doubt from a stalk in the woods. I forgot all about him, she thought, patting his head.

"He's been a good friend," said Daniel.

They entered the house; the kitchen was bare of baby toys, rattles, rocking horse, all the things she'd spread about. It smelt of freshly sawed pine from the coffin, and in the echoing room, she tasted Daniel's lonely vigil.

■ ■ ■

It was dark out; the day had drawn in and turned cold. The cat had been fed and was out on the shed.

"Could we look at the baby?" she asked.

He walked to the table, opened the lid of the box, and carefully began the unwrapping. She turned her head away, stupidly afraid, of what she didn't know; she wanted to see him so badly, and at the same time felt like a criminal; people nowadays didn't handle dead bodies like this; only properly licensed morticians had a right to such things; morticians and murderers, and she felt like a murderer. All the ghost stories of childhood swarmed through her head —the one about the telltale heart that beats under the floorboards and tales of corpses turning rotten and green. What if he should be hideous? Wasn't death a hideous thing? If not, why had it become such a dreadful secret, the most taboo subject in the world; her heart pounded guiltily over this dreadful act, ghoulish, obscene, probably illegal, the hospital had never heard of such a thing.

But she had to see him, had to spend some time with the child she'd wanted all these years, the little boy who'd been born to her and Daniel, and it was tonight or never. From the corner of her eye, she watched the linen peeling away as from a mummy; suppose he's like a mummy, shriveled, decayed; I should've sent him to the funeral home and let them embalm him; surely there's a good reason why every corpse is embalmed, surely they wouldn't bother if it didn't prevent something hideous.

She half expected the police to burst into the house and arrest her and Daniel for vampirism; beneath the linen shroud, she saw from the corner of her eye a fabric less pristine, less crisp, rumpled cotton, bundled rather than wound. If they embalmed him, she thought, they'd have put a nice expression on his face, something suitable, acceptable; I should have let them embalm him. She found herself inhaling deeply, searching for the stench, the odor you come across sometimes in the woods, which is natural in the woods, but shameful in humans, sinful in humans, unforgivable and perverse in humans . . . or why else should we be so afraid of it? From the corner of her eye, she saw the cotton fall away; inside was dark green plastic.

"They bagged him," said Daniel softly. So that's how they do it, she thought, they put them in garbage bags—because of the smell; her body was trembling.

Tenderly, he turned down the top of the green plastic bag as if it were florist's paper holding a fragile bouquet; she glimpsed the paleness of flesh. He drew down the dark green drapes, the pale skin ended, and she saw a cavern of deep red.

"They left him open," he said.

She walked to the table.

The child's face was solemn, weary, and at peace, a terrible battle over. His lips were long and thin, like neither of theirs, and set in the resolute line of Daniel's bronze Buddha upstairs. "I'll cover his body," said Daniel, but she touched his hand to prevent him. The body was tiny and beautifully formed, and its gaping wound didn't matter; all the unmentionable fears of a moment ago, feelings of guilt and sin and disgust, had simply no relation to this quiet thing called death.

She lifted the child's fingers, stooping to kiss his cool round face, and noticed a plastic stick with a number on it floating in the cavern of blood like a cocktail stirrer.

She stroked the cold plump arm, which wore a hospital bracelet like her own with height and weight and time of birth and their name; she felt her tears flow that her son hadn't lived, and accepted her own culpability in trembling before authority, in trusting to others, when she'd known from all the books that the doctor should've been sent for the moment the baby showed between her lips; she felt how human beings had relinquished both birth and death, handing themselves over to the experts and allowing mystery to reign, veiling their beginning and end, and she saw these two taboos ruling everything, every troubling aspect of life, every warp of sex, every fear and aggression; and over it all, she saw the beauty of creation, and the awesome wonder of the child; and of death.

■ ■ ■

It was snowing lightly. From her couch at the window, she watched Daniel and Murvyle snowshoe off with their shovels and digging tools. Both wore the same plaid flannel shirt and tweed Murphy pants, and both lumbered over the snow-crusted field like clumsy bears.

She wiped the fog from the window; the clear glass framed Murvyle in the lead, trudging with his pickax over his shoulder and his back slightly bent, his ungainly gait embodying a lifetime of burials and deaths—of children and old people, of animals and the seasons; crossing the field with his pickax, he looked like the round of seasons itself, the patriarch of existence, and Daniel, from the distance, trudging behind, seemed, in spite of his relative youth, to wear a trace of the patriarch too, as if he weren't quite the buoyant young man any longer; there was a shadow of the world on his shoulders, along with his shovel and pickax. The two men turned at the barn with its gaping eyes where boards had fallen, and the barn stared upon them like a sentinel of time, the silent witness of generations passing.

She watched them disappear down into the woods, and unsteadily got to her feet and made her way out to the shed.

The coffin was balanced on two sawhorses; Daniel had hammered it shut at dawn, the sound of his hammer ringing out over the valley like a song the valley had heard countless times before. Gazing at the casket, shivering with cold, she suddenly felt very old, as if she too had seen countless homemade coffins; she felt like an old woman of the settlement, and realized her perspective was no longer of the twentieth century, and this older perspective felt more comfortable, more harmonious with her nature than the momentary adaptation which was modern life, that bubble of convenience which had burst upon the world so recently.

The ginger tomcat glided past her out into the snow, tiptoeing on ballet dancer paws; a few minutes later, he returned; she followed him back into the kitchen, and slowly let herself down on the couch by the window.

The air outside was gray, charged by the storm, whose flakes were sketched with fine precision, like a Hokusai painting. The cat curled against her, offering himself as a heating pad; several times during the night she'd awakened in tears on the couch, and encountered the vertical slits of his pupils watching her in the darkness. She saw the snow outside and the cat beside her now with extraordinary clarity, the strands of his fur standing out in a shimmering halo of sparks; it was as if, momentarily, she had the artistic perception she'd always wanted, and no desire to ever use it.

The cat tensed at the window, lifting his ears.

A tiny white ghost raced along the snow's crust, a streak of lightning with a black-tipped tail; the ermine paused for a second, its vitality so concentrated, its every fiber so intensely alive, it seemed to be showing her the secret of its existence. Long after the ermine was gone, she continued staring out at where it had been, until she saw, across the field, Daniel's red ski cap emerging from the thicket.

He was alone, without his shovel. Seeing her at the window, he waved a mittened hand in greeting, and lumbered toward the house.

He took his snowshoes off outside the shed, and entered the kitchen.

"Where's Murvyle?" she asked.

"In the woods. We found a nice place. It's high on the bank and you can hear the brook. It's the nicest spot on the land," he said, as if he were telling her good news, and she saw he was, that his choosing the right spot for the child and digging the grave had resolved something in him and given him a measure of peace.

He went back to the shed, and she watched through the window as he dragged out the sled and then came out again bearing the coffin. He roped the box firm to the toboggan, testing it to make sure it wouldn't slip. He strapped on his snowshoes, and started walking, pulling the sled behind him; his eyes met hers through the window, and he managed a smile.

He pulled more quickly. Suddenly, with his red cap and mittens, he looked young again, and festive; her heart filled with the good times they'd had, daydreaming together and planning, about what they'd do with the baby, and how they'd play in the snow and pull him on his own baby toboggan; and for an instant, through the haze of the storm, they looked like any father and his boy, with Daniel skimming along on his snowshoes, pulling his son behind him, pulling the coffin, pulling his little child; this, she thought, this is their toboggan ride!

■ ■ ■

She sat in Dr. Penn's waiting room. Dr. Dunbar had refused to do her postpartum checkup, saying her doctor was Penn; it was the rules of the game; the doctor you start with is your doctor forever.

Leafing through a three-year-old *House & Garden*, she thought it was strange how much the clinic had changed; just six weeks ago, it'd been the most delightful place, while today it was cold, poorly lit, dirty, smelly, and utterly depressing.

Her name was called; she put down her magazine, and walked the gray halls to the nurse's desk.

"You can go right in."

She changed into the paper shift provided, lay on the table, and after a while heard the old doctor's heavy footsteps.

"Good day," he said jovially, opening her folder. He rustled pages, coughed, and changed his voice, to the kindest voice in the world. "I hear you had a tough time."

The telephone rang.

"Excuse me a minute," he said, in the same comforting manner, then in his cheery business tone, "Hello . . . yes . . . yes . . . they found her where?"

At first, Sara didn't listen, but after a while the fragments of conversation began to tell a story; it was a call from the hospital about a woman they were holding; she was slightly feeble-minded and a part-time whore, had no known lodgings, had been dumped on the street by her latest boyfriend and taken, for want of anyplace better, to the hospital. Dr. Penn was authorizing them to keep her there. "At least," he said in his wise kindly way, "she'll be warm."

Sara—because something insubstantial inside her still hadn't healed—found herself crying a little for the feeble-minded girl . . . and also perhaps for her own stupidity in projecting so much filial faith onto Dr. Penn. You can't rely on anyone else, not even the wisest kindest old man in town; how could my baby have been more important to him than his weekend when he doesn't even know who I am without my folder?

The doctor hung up. "I delivered her," he said, gesturing toward the telephone. "Her mother's worse than she is." He turned back to Sara's folder. "I suggest you get pregnant again immediately."

"I thought it was better to wait awhile between pregnancies."

"If God wanted us to wait," he smiled, "He would've arranged things differently."

He examined her, and let her leave.

She stopped at the nurse's desk. "I got this bill in the mail from Dr. Penn. Do you know what it means?"

"Didn't we tell you about that before? The government insurance only pays the standard fee that family practitioners charge for delivery. But Dr. Penn is an obstetrician, a specialist."

"I see." Sara took out her checkbook.

At the clinic door, Daniel waited for her.

"They charged us extra."

"Why?"

She wanted to say, *because the baby died,* because that's how it felt, like another punishment the doctors were inflicting on her for being a bad troublesome patient who'd failed. But she realized that was just her oversensitive state. "They don't feel the government pays them enough."

They drove without speaking, through the familiar streets; town had lost its luster. The picturesque old houses were few and far between the ostentatious split-level subdivisions; men with ladders were sawing down the venerable elm trees; and the friendly, salt-of-the-earth, small-town faces wore a tissue of civilization a millimeter thin, unable to cover their xenophobia, anguish, and hate. She was dismayed to find herself suddenly a mind reader and shocked at the transparency of what had always been hidden.

Daniel parked in front of the bank; she went in, and waited as docilely as the other farmers and lumbermen. In one of the other lines was a mother with a new baby, the sight of which made her eyes well with stupid tears; this is absurd, she told herself, are you going to spend your life avoiding babies? As her turn came to present her passbook, she noticed a familiar face making a withdrawal at the next cage—the nurse who'd taught the Thursday night maternity class and had been so supportive of her desire to have Daniel with her at delivery; the nurse caught sight of Sara at exactly the same minute, hastily pocketed her money, and turned and hurried out of the building.

Sara dully presented her passbook, wiping the idiotic tears which had finally refused to stay in. Is this how a leper feels? she wondered, as she left the bank and got into the car.

"I met the nurse from my class, and she ran away from me."

"It's a natural reaction," he said gently. "You shouldn't take it personally. It's happened to me in the village . . ." He started the car. "It'll pass in time."

They drove to Sears to return the crib mattress, unopened in its clear plastic covering.

Daniel carried it into the store. The elderly saleslady in the nursery department recognized them, smiled, then noticed the mattress, and let her smile dangle.

"We'd like to return this," said Sara.

The woman nodded, momentarily not an employee but a human being who knew that something had gone wrong beyond the return of a mattress. Then the other identity crossed her face—the company person whose job it is to routinely make every return as com-

plex and difficult as possible in order to impress upon each customer, each time, that making a return is an unpleasant experience.
"I have to put down a reason."

Sara stared at the mattress, where pink and blue bunnies danced
behind the clear plastic covering. "The baby died."

The woman nodded, her own life returning to her face—weariness, tired feet, and empathy. *Not needed,* she wrote.

■ ■ ■

In the dream, it was the three of them again, as it had been for
nine months, the three of them together in bed, but when she
awoke, and reality filtered in on the moon, she saw it was he and
she, and the third was the cat.

Just the cat, she said, and her words, coming on the tail of the
dream, filled her with pity for the animal who was such a hopeless
substitute, wasn't even a substitute, but only a knocked-about beast
whom no one would give you a nickel for.

She saw his sides move in and out in the moonlight. For a month
she hadn't allowed him in their bedroom or the nursery, wouldn't
let him come upstairs to where her heart was locked; until one evening, she heard him softly pad up the steps, and saw his marma-
lade face, peering wide-eyed around the doorway, warily question-
ing.

He twitched on the bed in the moonlight. She found him peculiarly touching, this battered bum who expected nothing. It wasn't
his fault that he wasn't important, that he wasn't a child, but only a
sad awakening to a dream.

■ ■ ■

She snowshoed behind Daniel, and the cat came after, trotting
lightly along on top of their beat. He'd taken to following them everywhere, stopping to look at the view when they did, hurrying to
catch up when they took off again.

Their route cut through dense spruce forest, making a tightly
packed narrow path that wound between the tall trees like the
streets of a miniature village. Their goal was a ledge above the ravine, where you could hear the brook and see it far below, rushing
by with the ice breaking up on its surface. The spruce wore beards

of moss which swung in the wind, making the trees look like a circle of old men.

She sat on the snow, leaning her back against one of the trees; he sat against another, facing her; and the baby lay in the clearing between them, beneath the snow, beneath the ground, in an unmarked plot of earth.

The cat shared their stillness, as if he knew exactly what had happened, and was with them in silent intimacy no human being could share. Sometimes she imagined they were an Eskimo family, sitting with their snowshoes in immemorial tranquillity; often her face was wet with tears, but they no longer felt like stupid tears, nor as if they were coming from a hole in her chest. It's less terrifying to die in the forest, she thought, to merge with the source you came from; it's not so abrupt as dying in a city; in the city death has no place; when you die, the whole artificial world is left behind, lost, and you just topple off.

The cat broke out of their circle to sharpen his claws on a tree, then rejoined them, patient, glad to belong, if only to grief. A cracking sound echoed up through the forest as another section of ice broke off into the water.

She gazed out over the canyon. Snow clung to the trees. One day, she thought, and the thought held no sadness, Daniel and I will be buried here.

5

He knelt on the scaffold and hammered, gazing over the verdant valley at tiny houses and steeples plunging to railroad tracks and the river, a Currier & Ives print to which he was adding another tiny building. Summer's scents mixed with the perfume of freshly sawed planks; he stopped to reapply bug repellent, thinking that what made the scene so satisfying was wherever you stepped out of the print, off onto one of the miniature paths, you were in wild forest which rolled on for miles, uninhabited except for other tiny hamlets tucked here and there into the hillsides.

On the floor below, Waldo worked, and his son puttered about performing the easy chores a child can do; Waldo treated the boy with respect, they had an easy intimacy, and watching them, Daniel knew—with the authority of his own hammer coming down —that for good or ill, the dream of father and child, for him, was over. He felt it all the way down to his Kodiak boots, and the finality of knowing gave him a peculiar peace, as if a burden of joy were lifted. A decision had been made for him during the winter and spring; he hadn't come to it through thinking or will; a desire had simply left him. The things he'd wanted—the sharing of father and child, shaping his boy's future and watching him grow— seemed to have come and gone with the baby's brief life. He sometimes felt he'd aged in an instant, been a father who'd had a son, lived with him, seen him develop to adulthood, finally buried him, and come out on the other side with this strange feeling of having paid his dues to whatever it was that had driven him to wish to reproduce; the drive was over.

Kneeling on the scaffold, looking down at the blossoming valley, he realized this had been the first spring of his life he hadn't looked forward to anything.

"I hear tell," said Waldo, "there's one of them new-style communities goin up by the Tuner Bog. Quite a pack of Americans."

"Building homes?"

"Mighty queer homes too." Waldo rubbed his red pate. "I'd hoped to get some work on them houses meself, but by the Lord Jesus, I ain't never seen the shape of them there houses. Feller wouldn't wanna get too deep with a house like that, might find hisself onto a beam he couldn't get off of."

■ ■ ■

He parked at the edge of the clearing, near two half-begun shacks, a tepee, and a very small garden, consisting mostly of onions, with three huge piles of damp hay beside it. Allowing for rural exaggeration, it perfectly answered Waldo's description; the two half-begun shacks were clearly the pack of queer-shaped houses, one being roughly based on a geodesic dome and the other a bit like a tree house.

The only members of the commune visible were a small child and dog, who both approached warily, the child decked in mud and beads like Mowgli the Wolf Boy and the dog a rangy black beast who quickly discerned Daniel's hidden evil and barked hysterically, alerting the rest of the tribe that a vicious criminal was prowling.

No one responded to the dog's warning, but Daniel noticed smoke rising from the top of the tepee; he edged away from the dog toward the smoke. "Anybody home?"

There was a rustling, the wind flap parted, and a young man's head appeared, in pointed cap and beard like Robin Hood.

"I live down the road about twenty miles," said Daniel awkwardly, "and heard there were some other Americans here . . ."

He followed his host, on hands and knees, into the tepee, which was filled with smoke billowing upward from a small central fire in a manner the young man presumably considered natural, but which instantly clogged Daniel's sinuses, activated his dormant asthma, and caused his eyes to rain bitter tears. Through the acid clouds, he discerned two other tenants, crawling nude from a double sleeping bag.

"I hope I didn't wake you," he said, feeling prudishly overdressed in work shirt and pants.

"We were just getting up," said the girl, gleaming pink through the smoke; her silent partner ambled bare-ass around the fire.

"How're you getting along with your houses?" asked Daniel; his voice hung in the smoke.

The nude young man, evidently not having noticed Daniel, yawned. "What's up for the evening?"

"The summer solstice." The girl turned to Daniel. "Do you know Mark Sawyer?"

"I don't think so."

"It's over at his place."

Now that Daniel's vision was returning, he noticed two simple wooden guitars propped up against cushions. "I hear you make pretty good guitars."

"Do you play?"

"Only a little."

The two men lifted down the guitars, and began to dust them assiduously.

Having unsuccessfully struggled through Frederick Noad's *Solo Guitar for Beginners,* Daniel was uncomfortably anxious in the presence of people who could really play guitars, not to mention build them, and felt like an irreverent philistine who had not properly dusted his guitar and that's why he'd never mastered Frederick Noad.

They continued dusting, while the man with the Robin Hood hat explained how the art of making fine instruments by hand was virtually lost; Daniel knew he'd never be able to afford one of these museum-caliber instruments, but on the other hand, might it not make the tunes in Frederick Noad sound a thousand times more beautiful?

"I notice you don't keep them in cases. Do you feel the air is beneficial?"

"There's only one case I can recommend," said the craftsman, still dusting. "It runs about three hundred dollars, which may seem a little high for a case, but for a guitar like this . . ." He held the guitar out to Daniel.

Daniel took the precious instrument into his hands with reverence. "I don't really play well at all," he apologized, feeling the weight of hours that had gone into the instrument's making, not to mention its dusting. He hesitated before reverently plucking the strings. He stroked. The tone was astounding. Never had he heard such total deadness of sound. Not even his own seven-dollar guitar from Bill's Pawn Shop compared to this incredible instrument. He plucked again. It wasn't just nonresonant, but drastically askew in every department, and when he attempted to tune it, he soon perceived that persisting in such effort would lead to madness. ". . . Do you sell many of these?"

"All I need to sell is three a year. I'm not looking to be rich, only survive." A humble ambition, thought Daniel. He isn't piggish, just serving a tone-deaf few.

"It doesn't cost much to survive," explained the girl, "if you know how. Grow your own vegetables, tap maple trees, raise your own animals for meat."

"Have you been self-sufficient very long?"

"I haven't, but I know a lot of people who have. Malcolm Booth has been here almost a year. Do you know Malcolm?"

Daniel shook his head, realizing he knew no one of importance.

"I'm walking over to Malcolm's now," said Robin Hood, "if you want to come."

They crawled out of the tepee into the sunlight. The guitar-maker pointed toward the three mounds of steaming hay by his garden. "If you have to take a crap, I'd appreciate you doing it there. We don't have any animals yet, so we're using what fertilizer we can."

"Sure," said Daniel who had two locks on his own bathroom door. "That's a good idea."

The other residents emerged from the tepee, and made for the mounds; Daniel felt himself in a time machine plummeting back to the dark ages, as the girl squatted down, and a hissing stream added its nutrients to the hay.

The guitar-maker led him through the marshy thicket, along a jeep path where insects swarmed thickly around them. "The north woods are idyllic," said Daniel, "except for the black fly."

"Black flies are no problem. You just have to know how to get rid of them."

A faint hope sprung into his heart. "How?"

The guitar-maker had pulled down his Robin Hood bonnet so his ears and most of his face were impregnable; his voice came out muffled. "Build a couple of purple martin houses."

"Right, purple martins." He'd read the same pioneer manuals; he also had a barnful of purple martins, as well as other swallows, each of whom consumed something like a hundred thousand black flies a day, and made not a dent in the population. He figured it would take a billion purple martins working round the clock in shifts to tackle Tuner Bog.

Their path opened onto a grown-over field where a jeep was parked, in front of a dwelling which might've been lifted from his worst nightmare—the one in which he was a carpenter who didn't know what he was doing, and every cut of his saw, each blow of hammer, every placement of board was jinxed. The house's arms were spastically akimbo, its legs cow-hocked, and all its angles rakishly pitched. It had the look of an ancient structure that has heaved and settled over the centuries until no two lines are parallel, no door or window level; but the design had nothing antique about it, being inspired by the *Whole Earth Catalog*'s more experimental pages. The builder had used old nails, no doubt for environmental reasons, but hadn't sprayed them with rust preventative, so each board was streaked with red. He seemed to be a graduate of the Cock-Eyed School of Old Burpee, unhampered by Burpee's rural conservatism.

They knocked on the door, which swung to at their touch, and jammed mid-swing; they sidled in, onto a jagged plank floor which sloped decidedly downstream.

"Going to the summer solstice?" asked their host, glancing up from a comic book; he sat on the floor surrounded by hand-thrown ceramic bowls strategically placed under leaks to catch rainwater.

The guitar-maker introduced the potter as Malcolm, and explained how he'd built his house single-handed with no help from anyone. "I even built my own tools," said Malcolm, showing Daniel a homemade saw, plane, and chisel. "Of course, the place has heaved a bit with the frost." He pointed out his revolutionary insulation—instead of inner walls, the house was lined with bags of brown rice—an ecological solution to the problems of heat retention, pantry space, and nutrition all at once. Examining the sacks of grain, Daniel noticed numerous black kernels mixed in with the beige; as in any country shack, he realized, there were mice in the walls, but since the walls here happened to be rice, the mice lived unusually well, in a perfect ecosystem of give and take, the mice taking the grain, and giving back a generous lacing of mouse-piss and crap.

"I'm going to put this house on skids, and move it to where the others are living."

Daniel started to warn him that this was not the house for such an adventure; if one winter's frost had done what it had, the vibrations of an actual move would reduce it to brown rice and splinters. But how do you tell somebody he's built a Three Little Pigs Shack when he's smiling at you with smug complacency and speaking so knowledgeably it's obvious he has scorn for anyone who'd deign to find out the basics of putting up a four-square frame? Sure, I've built a few houses, thought Daniel, but only of the ordinary garden variety; maybe they don't leak, but they aren't ecological either, don't collect rainwater through the ceiling. Realizing his advice wasn't wanted, he turned to admiring the half-filled bowls, with their artistic underglaze and asymmetric hand-thrown shapes, reminiscent of comic whoopee glasses you buy in the magic store where the contents spill down your shirt-front.

"I guess," said Malcolm, "you've seen the work of most of the other potters in the province. Slick. Predictable. Each one of my tea bowls is different . . ." Daniel hadn't known there were other potters in the province; it sounded as if there were many of them, a veritable hotbed of craftsmen bringing art to the natives of Atlantic Canada. He envisioned Murvyle sitting down to tea with a hand-crafted bowl, searching round for the handle, looking for a side that wasn't swooped out, spilling hot tea on his venerable suspenders, and throwing it out the window.

I ought to get some for Sara. The work of one serious artist for another. "How much are you asking for these tea bowls? Let's say a set of eight with a teapot?"

The potter mentioned a figure which would be about a week's salary of hoisting beams and cutting steel roofing, a figure which could seriously mar Sara's appreciation of the whoopee bowls' artistry.

The woman and man from the tepee now joined them, and the four friends fell into discussion of what a crock of shit the American way of life is. As they spoke, Daniel felt more and more inferior to these idealists, in spite of the fact that he too had lived in a shack, that he and Sara grew virtually all their own food, and had survived on the land longer than any of them. "Hadn't we better get to the solstice celebration?" asked the woman.

Casually they wished Daniel good-bye; obviously he wasn't invited, wasn't—as he'd suspected—pure enough to share the coming of summer. He thanked them for their hospitality, and walked back alone through the path in the bush; the frogs began to croak their evensong in Tuner Bog.

■ ■ ■

He shelled peanuts for Festus and watched the dog eat, while he and Sara and Murvyle and Phoebe sat in silence. "I see," sighed Phoebe, "where the preacher's wife got a new set of teeth."

They absorbed the information without comment.

Phoebe poured more tea into their cups. "She sure does put me in mind of our Bertha. She must be a relation somewheres."

"Aye," agreed Murvyle.

"I paid thirty-five dollar fer my teeth," said Phoebe. "Up to Newcastle."

"Why don't you get out my lowers," Murvyle suggested.

Phoebe sighed to her feet, and came back from the pantry with Murvyle's lowers grinning up from their earthenware dish.

"Now these here teeth . . ." began Murvyle, like a professor of dentistry, but Daniel knew the tale would soon roam far from teeth, wandering over the hills and the years, with memories of old lumber camps and horses and dogs and kids and friends alive and dead, and Daniel listened to the old man's tales, gazing out the window at the forest and fields and the incomparable stillness over which the longest day was setting, as New Jerusalem celebrated the solstice.

■ ■ ■

The squeaking Ferris wheel turned in the sun, its steel girders crisscrossing those of the bridge beyond on the sparkling river. "It gives me great pleasure," said his Lordship the Mayor from the bandstand microphone, "to officially open this year's Native Indian Festival." The Indians on the lawn applauded politely; the Ferris wheel squeaked; a child cried, was comforted; his Lordship continued to ramble.

Daniel wandered away from the bandstand to a shady nook under some trees, where a silver-haired Indian was making furniture with a hand ax, curving ash boughs and swiftly hammering them together to form grotesquely beautiful bentwood tables and chairs; his prize pieces were a love seat of immense proportions, shellacked with maroon deck enamel, and the ubiquitous Atlantic Canada Victorian fern stand, taken to its ultimate conclusion of organic giantism. An aged Anglo-Saxon tippler emcee'd the demonstration, shouting "Nail 'em, Jim," and "Hit 'em, Jim," from a chair of serpentine monstrosity, an instrument of torture that only a lunatic, drunk, or cat could find comfortable.

A young man slipped Daniel a brochure entitled *Four things God wants you to know,* and invited him to enter his trailer. The sign on the trailer read *Missionaries to Lumbermen, Seamen, Indian Reserves, Prisons, Etc.*

"I am proud," said a new voice from the bandstand, "to be here on this important occasion, with his Lordship the Mayor and other honorable gentlemen. The tremendous turnout of crowds at this gathering . . ." Daniel looked around for the tremendous turnout, particularly for the Americans from Tuner Bog who lived in a tepee and were so deeply interested in Indian culture; but they were nowhere to be seen; nor were any of the college people; nor anyone who looked as if he might belong to the big group of potters, weavers, basket-makers, and other craftsmen he'd heard about; in fact, aside from the nobs on the bandstand welcoming each other, the Indian Festival seemed to consist solely of Indians and their poor white neighbors from the shanty road abutting the reservation. The photographer from the *Daily Loyalist,* who specialized in one angle no matter the subject or age of his sitters, crouched on the lawn to shoot up the little girls' dresses.

Daniel strolled toward the various crooked gambling booths set up to help the native population. One after another, the Indians paid to fling a ball into a toilet on a pedestal, the prize for which was a made-in-Japan doll of an Eskimo.

The voice from the bandstand continued. "The judges for the Princess Pageant are the honorable Member of Parliament Bertram Noyes, Fred Cowperthwaite of Cowpherthwaite's Photography, Mrs. Mercy MacLaughlin of the Horse and Bridle Club . . ." Daniel watched the beauty contestants being paraded, a dozen painfully awkward butter-tart teens, none of them remotely Indian; the princess of the festival would apparently be a WASP homecoming queen.

He was handed a second copy of *Four Things . . . Repent, Believe, Confess your sins . . .*

The canoe race began, the three-legged race, the ice-cream eating competition. The politicians and notables left as the afternoon wore on, and the festival relaxed, becoming what it was, a big neighborhood picnic put on for the kids. And now he heard people talking a tongue he'd never heard before, totally strange, intensely private; he'd assumed the Indian language had perished in another century, had been abandoned and forgotten ages ago; instead, just down the road from his home, it was being spoken as naturally as English, and as he listened, it began to sound familiar—the melody was the streams and brooks he'd gotten to know, the wind in the woods, the deep and musical sounds that surrounded him when he sat in the forest.

The Ferris wheel turned against the red sky, and the river moved quietly seaward as it had for many thousands of years when all the land belonged to the Indians, and the forest had not been this secondhand brush pile, but a Garden of Eden. The loud microphoned voice of the missionary came through the trees, inviting the people to the last showing of his "beautiful revival film inside the trailer."

■ ■ ■

He walked around to the back of a black-charred shack; a door stood open, leading into a shed which seemed all that was left unharmed from the fire that had burned the dwelling.

He stepped in; the place was stone silent, clearly abandoned, but for some reason he continued standing in the darkness, until gradually his eyes grew accustomed, and he perceived the red glimmering of a stove. Then directly in front of him, he saw an old Indian sitting in a chair, staring at him, with a kitten on his lap. Daniel drew back.

"I hurt my foot," said the Indian, as if they'd known each other for years and were merely picking up a lapsed conversation.

"How'd you do that?"

The old man shook his head. "This is my kitten."

Daniel approached, and examined the kitten in the dim glimmer. After a suitable admiration, he brought up the subject at hand. "They said at the festival you make baskets."

The Indian pointed. "You can have that one there." Around his words, the same silence seemed to prevail.

Daniel picked the indicated object up from the dirt floor—a large basket with thickly carved handle.

A shadow suddenly darkened his sight; he turned to see a tall shape in the doorway. A white shanty-road gentleman, smelling strongly of drink, entered and nodded to the Indian. He glanced at Daniel. "Buyin a basket?"

"Yes."

"These baskets are the best. You cannot break these here baskets. You watch . . ." He grabbed the basket from Daniel's hands, hurled it onto the floor on its side, and proceeded to leap on it with his steel-toed boots; he jumped up and down several times, and stepped off in triumph.

The old Indian quietly stared.

The kitten rolled under the stove.

The basket was perfectly intact. It was, Daniel realized, the most wonderful basket the world had ever seen. "How much?"

"Three dollars," said the Indian flatly.

Daniel looked around the floor of the shack; he didn't see any tools, only a bundle of ash strips, and tried to imagine what the man had to go through to produce a basket for three dollars. He took three bills out of his pocket, and handed them to the old basket-maker.

"You'll use that basket fer life," said the friend, who was now sitting motionless on the other side of the stove, as invisible as the Indian.

■ ■ ■

"Dreams," said Pike. "Used to be I'd dream of a deer somewheres, and next mornin I'd go to that spot with my rifle and find him."

Daniel's eyes roamed over Pike's kitchen; having run short of wall space for hanging his paintings, the artist now painted directly onto his doors; across the four kitchen cupboards strode a bestiary of dream animals in sundry acts of destruction. "I seen a wolverine t'other day," went on Pike. "Most vicious beast you will ever meet." It seemed he could scarcely leave his dooryard without confronting

a dangerous creature of the rarest variety not seen on the land
since it belonged to the Indians. Across the cupboards, he'd also
depicted several animals generally considered innocuous, here
shown in their less well-known aspect as fiends; there were saber-
toothed squirrels, rabbits kicking cats into trees, and giant owls
beheading lone travelers. "Could a man arm-wrestle better'n a bear
cub?" he asked suddenly.

"I would think so."

"No, he could not. We had a bear cub at a camp once arm-
wrestled down every man among us, includin them great big
Swedes." They spooned up their Radio peas, perusing the tragic
events on the cupboards. "Now there," said Pike, indicating the
corner of a panel, "was a funny thing. Did you ever see a crane in a
bear trap? I caught that there crane in a bear trap. Had the hell of
a time gettin close enough to set it free. And then, d'you know, that
son of a bitch follered me? Jes like a dog. Could not get rid of
him."

"He must've thought you saved him."

"I guess he kind of took to me." Pike opened the cupboard on
which the devoted crane was depicted, and took out a dark brown
bottle. They sipped rum with their peas. "Nother time," mused
Pike, "I was fishin down by the bridge, and one of them gannets
kept swoopin down over the fish. I dunno what got into me, but I
cast straight up the next time, and felled the damn thing."

"You caught a bird at the end of a fishing line?"

"I more or less lassooed the bastard." Pike downed his rum,
smacked his lips. "I set him free, and he spent the rest of the day
with me. Follered me all down the brook." The two tales seemed to
have identical endings, with Pike's feathered prey falling in love
with him. He lit a cigarette with fury, glaring at the painted cupboards. The air was redolent of rum and turpentine; the oil stove
roared with sympathetic rage. On the windowsill sat the lone potted plant he was growing in hope of harvesting his own opium
from seeds scattered over his fence by the poppies of the old lady
next door. He gestured with his cigarette toward the spindly
seedling. "I got some kinda crop comin up there." Alongside the
opium garden were empty cigarette boxes, molded-over jelly jars,
and a petrified donut. Pike flicked his ash into a torso ashtray decorated with bright red nipples. "I say, I got some kinda crop comin
up."

Outside, the trees were bare, the yard colorless and stark, waiting for the snows to fall and blanket everything; the chickadees and blue jays had come out of the barren woods to eat at the feeders; but much of the view was hidden behind Pike's cold-weather barricade of plywood. "Problem with this house is there ain't enough doors." Daniel looked again at the doors and cupboards; there was certainly no room for more art, every inch of wordwork already covered by some forest atrocity; it was inspiring to see a homeowner with such little monetary concern for his property. Pike leaned over, cigarette dangling from lips; he picked up a sledgehammer and thrust it at Daniel. "Anyone asks where you got it, tell them you found it by the side of the road."

■ ■ ■

"Used to bring the team along here," explained Murvyle, loping through brush and bramble, the ginger tomcat behind him, and Daniel bringing up the rear. "Course, you might miss the road if you didn't know it," conceded Murvyle, perhaps perceiving that the path was no longer the clearest; in fact, there was no visible sign whatever that human or animal had ever walked through. What are the traces, Daniel wondered, that Murvyle sees? Or is his body some kind of map with old trails drawn in its nerves?

Murvyle pointed to a mound of moss. "Lightnin struck that there tree in '37. Cracked her right off at the bottom." But how, wondered Daniel, does he know that bunch of moss was a tree, let alone a particular tree? The old man raised his boot high and stepped forward, sinking down between roots, a queer up-and-down dance which didn't impede his momentum; the cat, slipping under the creepers, had no problem either; only Daniel seemed to be attacked by branches grabbing his ankles and brambles tearing his clothes.

"Been a female moose passed through," remarked Murvyle, " 'bout five hours ago, with a little male yearlin." Daniel gazed down at the faint network of indentations pressed between brush, weeds, and dead leaves, and felt as Watson must've felt with Holmes.

They climbed over the rotted remains of a cedar snake fence, and stood at the edge of an enormous field. "By God, she's growed over," Murvyle admitted. "When old Odbur had her, he kept her as bald as me head." He removed his cap, and lovingly stroked his few wisps of hair as he gazed at the expanse of dry waving weeds. "He ruined her, Odbur did. He furrowed her, and then before he could smooth her, he upped and died." Daniel felt the petrified furrows under his boots, and the ghost of old Odbur anxiously hovering, wondering why no one had ever remedied the ruined surface, would they ever? Winter grasses whispered and crinkled under their feet, and not far from the edge of the meadow where the woods were creeping in, an old piece of farm machinery stood upended, its huge rusted parts in the air giving testimony to territorial rights, old Odbur's and the community that once had been.

"Over yonder a little piece lived old Caleb, and every night them two bachelors would get together and commence to argue politics, and old Odbur he'd hook old Caleb in the neck with his cane, and that's the way the evenin generally ended."

Daniel felt sure that both ghosts, if they could, would hook him round the neck with their canes.

"Many's the time," murmured Murvyle, "I helped plant this field, when the old fellers was up in their nineties, but them days is gone fer good." He took out tobacco and paper, and rolled a cigarette; two cantankerous ghosts floated by on his smoke, arguing politics.

"Lovely orchard up there," he said, and in amongst the poplars and brambles, Daniel made out the twisted shapes of old apple trees; grape vines had overgrown the foundation, whose great round stones, covered with vines and time, looked like the Buddhas of Angkor Wat; he caught the glint of a rusted stove in the ruins, and thought of the cheerful kitchen which once had been here, with an old bachelor rocking by the fire after a day's plowing, waiting for his crony to come by and be hooked in the neck.

"Nobody wants to work the land no more. Same as Hilton and Anson won't work no more in the woods with me. Anson's gettin the welfare and Hilton's gettin three-fifty the hour in town leanin on a shovel, why should they?" No reason at all, thought Daniel, gazing at the grown-over field which had once been productive and the settlement which had once been the human answer.

The cat nosed in the old foundation, while Murvyle stood as if planted; he always stood in a field as if planted, and Daniel looked at him enviously, knowing his own efforts to merge with field, forest, and stream in a mystical way were only roundabout second bests to having it born in your nerves.

And Murvyle doesn't give a shit. What he really wants is to win the lottery, buy a big car, and have a bungalow in the village with indoor bath. Which is, finally, why they all left. They didn't care for what they had—which I would give anything for—that instinctive ease with weather and wind and trees struck by lightning in '37.

"The trouble," explained Murvyle, "is we didn't happen onto old Odbur till a week after he took his spell. Old Caleb was already underground, and old Odbur was so goddamn independent and mean he didn't get too many other visitors. He was over a hundred by that time and we was never sure if he was eatin good, so I sent a couple of the kids up with some stew, and they come home and says old Odbur must've took a spell. He died anyways." There was a significant pause, while they mulled over another story without rhyme, reason, moral, or fanfare.

Murvyle tipped his cap. "Used to be a boilin spring over there somewheres." The wind sighed through the stiff grass as they walked, summer's flowering now a brown dying, and snow in the air. They hacked through a tangle of alders, the cat in the lead, and came out at a big clear spring.

The cat crouched down and tried to catch the darting trout; Murvyle lit himself another homemade cigarette. "If a feller was smart, he'd buy this here hundred acres, dig him out one hell of a trout pond, and put up cabins fer Americans . . ." Daniel listened serenely, recalling how a few years ago he would've panicked imagining his peace attacked by a tourist resort next door; but he knew by now it was just another backwoods pipe dream of wealth, that no one would put up cabins, or dig out the spring, or purchase this furrowed wreck of a field.

They stooped to drink, and crossed back toward the middle of the meadow, a long slow walk across a cleared immensity, a backbreaking job of stones and stumps long ago removed. "Woods has growed in some," remarked Murvyle. "Used to be cleared down to the brook."

Daniel's vision of back-breaking work multiplied itself by four. "Did those two old men clear it all?"

"Men worked hard in them days."

He imagined how it was, when all they needed or wanted to buy was kerosene, tea, and nails, and all they needed to sell was enough of their produce for those few things; it was a utopian dream, vanished into the wind. Overnight. In less than thirty years. A crow called overhead.

"Mr. Crow's still here," said Murvyle.

Phoebe sighed, pushing the newspaper toward Sara. A baby's face smiled up from the page. "Poor little feller."

Sara skimmed the article. The disease that killed the child was rare, everywhere except in areas sprayed for the budworm. This child had died a year after his home had been sprayed. Cattle and sheep had died too; ducks had been born crippled. Spray areas also boasted an alarming rate of human cancer, birth defects, and the highest stillborn figures in the country.

Will we ever have another child? she wondered. Each time she asked him, he answered *Not yet,* and she understood he was afraid of the same thing happening again; but maybe it was more than that; she'd mentioned adopting a baby, or an older child nobody wanted, and that suggestion too seemed to die in the wind.

"I dunno what's gonna be," sighed Phoebe, "pon my soul I don't." Sara examined the picture of the baby who'd died from Reye's syndrome. A Nova Scotia doctor had published findings linking the mysterious deaths to the spray; but government experts—the forestry management men—disagreed.

"Wanna see my rat-tail?" asked Phoebe.

They walked into the parlor, where the rat-tail plant, barren for thirty years, had finally flowered. Sara admired the late-blooming cactus, then glanced at her own painting of the old Jerusalem cemetery, now invisible behind family snapshots. At first when the grandchildren's faces began being stuck in the frame for embellishment, she'd been angry, but gradually as the new generation of grandchildren, horses, and dogs took over her portrait of the old generation, she perceived this was the painting's meaning—nature's cycle of death and new birth—and all these horses, dogs, and grandchildren would themselves end up in a graveyard. Murvyle's camera, a venerable box, produced pictures which were instant antiques—faded, unfocused, faintly nineteenth century. As far as the family was concerned, now that her painting was utterly obliterated by unfocused grandchildren, the work of art was complete.

"Cousin Tressa's comin home fer a visit," sighed Phoebe. "Last visit, she ett candy steady and scratched herself somethin terrible. One night, she went crazy and cut me winder shades off with a scissors. I says to her, *Tressa, what're them holes in yer arms?* And Tressa she says to me, *Does Sears tell Eaton's their secrets?*"

Sara turned her thoughts from death and babies to that middle-aged enigma of the family, Cousin Tressa; when Sara'd been introduced to the junkie cousin, Tressa's remark had been, *I'd take three drops of iodine right now if someone would give them to me.*

Outside, snow had drifted up to the windows, and another storm was predicted. "Some of them in the village got a letter from Noreen," said Phoebe. Sara recalled the woman who'd presented her husband's new girl friend with their three children, saying, *You took the stud, you may as well take the colts.* "Appears," went on Phoebe, "she done real good fer herself. Lives up to Ontario with a man who's got a car, a half-ton, and a color TV."

"Did she have any more news?"

"That's about all. Car, half-ton, and color TV."

Sara gestured toward the window. "You've got a dozen old half-tons right in your field."

"Nor I don't care fer color TV. Seems to make the faces orange or somethin."

They returned to the kitchen; Phoebe poured more tea. "Murvyle's out travelin the roads. He's jes like the Travelin Jew." She buttered a muffin. "Did you see Harley Rolland when he come back from Montreal? All doodled up with a tie and checkered jacket and paper bags. Was he ever some classy." How, wondered Sara, did paper bags add to his class? "He's a good-lookin shit," Phoebe admitted, then sighed. "I sent them Hush Puppies back to Sears. It's the fifth pair I sent back. Gettin kind of flustratin."

"You ought to try some stores in town."

"Ain't been to town fer two years."

I wish, thought Sara, I could stay out of town for two weeks.

"Our Bertha, she don't buy Hush Puppies. She buys Tender Tooties. But them Tender Tooties makes yer feet stink awful bad."

Why is Phoebe content to stay home year after year, while I'm like a child who needs constant stimulation? The furthest Phoebe's ever been from Jerusalem is fifty miles and she knows all a person needs to be satisfied. Phoebe gazed at the tea leaves in the bottom of her cup. "Puts you more in mind of a cage than it does anythin else."

"Read mine," said Sara, pushing her own cup forward, but Phoebe wouldn't read on demand, claimed not to divine tea leaves at all; you had to catch her unaware. She rose and stirred the embers in her stove.

"I seen where old Mrs. Partridge was arrested again up to the K-mart. I dunno why they do it. Whosoever you hear about, they never take nahthin good, jes bobby pins, foolish things." Phoebe sighed, adding logs to her fire. "They say she has the cancers. They must be catchin." A dry stick broke with a crack. "A lot of old people are dyin these days."

Sara gazed at the leaves in the bottom of her cup. If our baby had lived, he'd be over a year old by now.

■ ■ ■

"My little girl got sprayed," said the woman so softly you could hardly hear her, "and last year when the flu come around she got the Reye's syndrome. Only they didn't call it Reye's. They said she jes had a fever and would get better." The woman licked her pale lips. "Mr. Flagherty at the funeral home didn't believe twas my little girl, that's how much she changed . . ." The woman stammered on, describing her child's tremendously elongated body and other terrifying symptoms of the Syndrome.

There was silence, clucks of sympathy, then anger; the other women in the living room were college wives, and Sara felt very much at home with them in a way; in another way, she felt as estranged as the woman who'd just spoken, the country mouse now sitting expressionless, nervously twisting her hands in her cotton print lap.

Their hostess muttered over her coffee cup. "Those sons of bitches in their three-piece suits say, *If we thought there was one child who died, we'd stop the spray today.* And they believe it. Because it's still in their interests."

Sara sipped her own coffee, studying the almost-elegant living room and the faces of the almost-chic activists. "If they diagnose it in time," one of the college wives was saying, "they can take off the top of the skull and freeze it to minimize damage to the swelling brain. But doctors prefer not to diagnose Reye's syndrome because of the spray implications."

Sara didn't understand why she felt herself a separate animal from these educated women; it was as if her years with no other company than trees and country people had made her an anomaly, neither here nor there.

Their hostess shuffled some papers. "A woman researcher accidentally spilled a sample of the solution, and landed in the hospital with a case of acute pesticide poisoning. Now, whenever she gets run-down or loses weight, it flares up again, and she has to be rehospitalized . . ."

Sara leaned forward, listening intently; last month, she'd gone on a diet, and all the symptoms she'd had when being sprayed returned, multiplied; she'd gotten desperately ill and couldn't understand why; she'd dieted dozens of times before in New York with no side effects. "Surely," she interrupted, "the poison doesn't stay in your body forever?"

"It persists for a long time. But the fact that the researcher is still getting sick after several years shows it's no longer a question of persistence. Permanent damage was done to her nervous system."

"I see," said Sara, suddenly extremely depressed. Did I have to move to the pure, unpolluted, Canadian wilderness to lose my health? She glanced glumly around at the smooth faces of the college wives tucked safely in town; except for the country lady whose little girl had died, none of the women had actually been sprayed.

The hostess raised her cultivated voice, and shouted, "Lisa!"

"*I'm busy!*"

"I'll only need you for a minute!"

An angel of about seven presently appeared. "What?"

"I wanted my friends to see you."

The angel rolled her blue eyes and allowed herself to be looked at, then turned on her heels and marched out.

"They did blood tests on the kids in school," said her mother, "and found they had abnormal blood counts during each spray season. Some were worse than the others. And a few were abnormal all year long. Lisa was in this last group." On the coffee table along with the cups, mimeographed pamphlets were piled, and a petition with ten thousand names. Their hostess looked at her watch. "Shall we get over to City Hall and meet the face of evil? Paid researchers, paid doctors, paid journalists, paid politicians, paid by the chemical consortium to come down here and give false testimony."

The college wives hauled out their homemade signs. The country woman edged nervously toward Sara. "I can't go," she whispered.

"Why not?"

"My husband works fer the lumber company. He'd be awful mad if he knowed I told about our little girl, cause they'd fire him if they found out. But I had to come here. Only I can't go to City Hall." Her pale face, pinched by distress, reminded Sara of Phoebe's; what would it take to get Phoebe to come into town on her own to speak in front of a strange gathering, against Murvyle's wishes, risking Murvyle's livelihood? She couldn't conjure up even the fantasy; but this woman, out of some grief-stricken sense of right, had done it, like a miracle . . . or half a miracle . . . City Hall being the other half. They left the house with their signs, buttoning their coats, and the woman whose child had died hurried away from them with her head down like a person ashamed.

The girl Lisa came along with her own cockeyed sign, and as they walked through the icy streets, other women and children joined them, people from town, none from the forests which were sprayed, but all caught in the drift. They haphazardly proceeded toward the river and City Hall, where chartered buses were being unloaded; out of the buses piled country men and women dressed up as for a day at the fair, interspersed with organizers in three-piece suits, and the signs these country people carried couldn't have been lettered by one rural person in a thousand; in fact, Sara saw on closer inspection they were four-color professional printings.

"I am proud and gratified," said a voice on the loudspeakers, "to see such a popular groundswell of just ordinary folk coming out on their own to show they support my policy and the policy of this government."

"Popular groundswell my tit," said Lisa's mother. "They took them out of the pulp mills for the day and gave them a trip to town with their wives, with pay."

Sara looked at the people from the buses; they did have a holiday air, chatting and laughing as they waved their four-color signs;

but she couldn't find it in herself to blame them; they'd allowed themselves to be poisoned for twenty-five years without a peep because they believed the bosses who told them if the spray stopped they'd lose their trees, and they were more terrified of poverty than of all the viral enhancers, neurotoxins, mutation and cancer-causing agents in the world.

The political luminaries stood on the steps of City Hall, its dome shining gold in the sunlight against the river, on the other side of which were the slums, the Indian reservation, and the thousands of square miles of forest whose fate was being debated. "I have in my possession," said the Minister of the Environment, "a document which proves conclusively that the spray being used is absolutely safe and harmless . . ." A warm breeze blew in off the river; Sara opened her winter jacket; the mill workers and their wives smiled at the fine day it was turning into.

An elderly gentleman, heading a group of small-woodlot owners, took the microphone. "From time immemorial," he began, in sonorous cracker barrel tones, "the budworm built up and died down to the laws of nature. Like the rabbits. Like all God's creatures. Until the wonderful budworm spray come along. Wonderful, I say, fer the budworm." The holiday crowd from the buses broke into laughter, and were quickly hushed. "I say a boon to the budworm, because by killin out the worm's natural enemies among the birds, what started out as a natural and small infestation has growed until it covers this entire province. We have sacrificed our greatest renewable resource, the forest, to the mismanagement and short-term wealth of a few ignorant big shots." There was no more laughter; the elderly gentleman was allowed to rant a moment longer before being politely strong-armed off, "to allow equal time to our honored guests who have come from so far to share their knowledge with us here today."

The honored guest employed the hammer stroke style of repetition to bang his message home: "There has been no conclusive proof that the spray has been dangerous. There have been no cases of poisoning reported to environment or health officers. There has been no significant loss of game in the forest or streams. There has been no pollution of the watersheds. There has been no damage done to the dairy herds. There has, in short, been no evidence of an environmental problem." His voice swelled, blasted over the speakers. "So I want to know just what in hell these people are talking about!"

Cheers rose from the crowd, hypnotically primed by rhythm and tone. The feisty little leader of Sara's group angrily elbowed her way to the steps. "Fifteen Holsteins dropped dead in your own constituency. And you know damn well there've been sick people all over the province." She waved a sheaf of papers. "What in hell are you doing with these reports if you aren't reading them? Papering your walls? The evidence is in. If you're so convinced the spray is harmless, let's see you open a sample of it under your nose."

There was a murmur of approval from the crowd, the suggestion promising an interesting relief from speeches. The honored guest straightened his oversized lapels, and smiled condescendingly as if to say, *Little ladies will sometimes be naughty.* "I'm not afraid of your antics, Vivian."

"Good." She opened her purse, and whipped out a glass atomizer; the honored guest jumped back. "It's just perfume, André," she smiled, spraying herself behind both ears. She took the microphone from him: "I want to introduce two gentlemen who are suing for half a million dollars in crop loss due to the effects of the spruce budworm spray on bees required for pollination. These men have become known in the press as the Blueberry Brothers . . ."

The brothers shuffled up the stairs with their lawyer, and the crowd settled down. Sara gazed around at the faces and then at the sky; the sun was certainly out now to stay; the balmy wind lulled everyone nicely. The newspaper tomorrow would report that twice as many came out in favor of the spray as against; an editorial would be printed praising the democratic process; and, as sure as bees were needed for blueberries, she'd be sprayed again at the end of May.

■   ■   ■

She dreamt that Murvyle was carrying a small dead body; from where she stood, it looked like a grandchild, the youngest of the boys. She woke up, saw Daniel off to work, and tried to push the dream from her mind as she painted and listened to the radio.

"Former Prime Minister Don Huffenmucker gave his opinion

yesterday on our present troubles with the native population." The nasal drawl of the local announcer gave way to the senile irritability of the former prime minister:

"*There was no such problem in my administration. I always had a very good relationship with the Indians. You have to realize that the primitive mind thinks a certain way. And I know how these primitives think.*"

National news was followed by programs of more regional interest.

"*This is Mortimer Astle interviewing Bob Jaffles in charge of the provincial spring cleanup program. 'Tell me, Bob, would you say that the province is dirtier than last year?'*

'*Well, if we had a good snowstorm right now you wouldn't notice the dirt so much.'*

'*Thank you, Bob, and good luck with your cleanup program.' That was Bob Jaffles, in charge of the provincial spring cleanup . . .*"

The sound of a car came down the lane, and she went to the door.

Hilton leaned out, but he didn't approach. "Where's Dan'l?" he called.

"With Waldo." She walked over to the Oldsmobile. "Anything wrong?"

"Nope." He rolled himself a cigarette. "Grampie Amos went last night."

"Murvyle's father?"

"Died in his sleep. He ain't never done that before."

■ ■ ■

"Hello, I'm phoning to find out when the spray planes are due over my area . . . yes . . . yes . . . could you repeat that number please . . . thank you."

She replaced the receiver, and fished another dime from her purse; around her, the sounds of the shopping mall made a frenetic accompaniment.

"Hello, could someone in your office tell me when the spray planes will be coming over my area . . . you don't . . . you don't . . . is that a long-distance number . . . thank you."

She dug out several nickels, dimes, quarters, and dialed the operator for assistance.

The long-distance connection rang . . .

"Hello, I'd like to know when the spray planes are scheduled to fly over my area . . . you don't . . . yes . . . could you connect me with someone who does?"

She was put on hold; a gruff voice came on. *"Yeah?"*

"Can you tell me when the spray planes are due over my area?"

"Jessa minute."

She was put back on hold. Shoppers filed past her in the enormous droves that indicated the old-age pension checks had arrived this morning, the welfare checks, or both.

"Patterson here."

"I'm calling to find out when you'll be spraying the Hills of New Jerusalem."

There was a long pause, which even over long distance managed to convey coldness. *"We're extremely busy this time of year. And, in any case, we can't give out that kind of information."*

"Aren't you allowed to tell me when my own house is going to be sprayed?"

"We don't spray houses."

"What about the general area around my house?"

"Where do you live?"

"New Jerusalem. Look for Jerusalem Creek on your map."

"We do not spray brooks or waterways."

"Then can you tell me when you're going to spray the land on either side of Jerusalem Creek?"

"What is your name please?" he asked in a tone which was suddenly, unmistakably CIA. It was clear she'd be reported for subversive activity. Any decent Canadian patriot would *want* to be poisoned. She and Daniel would probably be deported. She gave him her name.

"Sorry, your three minutes are up. You will have to put in another . . ."

"Mr. Patterson, would you please hold? I've got to go to the hot dog stand and get change."

She dangled the receiver, and raced to the hot dogs. When she returned with her change, Mr. Patterson had hung up. She got the operator, and they started again.

"Hello, I was talking to Mr. Patterson."

"Mr. Patterson isn't here now."

"But I was just talking to him."

"I believe he's on another line."

"That's me. He's probably waiting for me to get back to him." Though why, she wondered, am I so anxious to get back to Patterson?

"Patterson here."

"Mr. Patterson, I'm sorry we got cut off. You were just going to tell me when the planes would spray the area around Jerusalem Creek."

"The spray maps of that area are presently not at our disposal. Furthermore, weather conditions are unstable and we have no idea . . ." His tone implied that she or her cohorts had stolen the relevant maps in the night, and furthermore were responsible for erratic weather conditions.

"I realize you can't predict exactly because of the weather, but maybe you have a general idea. They spray for six weeks. Is the Jerusalem Creek area supposed to be in the first week or the sixth?"

"As I've already told you, the maps of that area are presently not . . ."

"Could you tell me where they are? I'll call the office that's got them."

"I suggest you call the following number, five-five-five . . ."

She wrote down the number; it looked familiar. "I already called that number, Mr. Patterson . . . Mr. Patterson?"

■ ■ ■

"I can't go without my contact lenses."

"You don't have time to go back for your lenses." His voice came to her through the strafing drone of three fighter planes.

"They aren't even close."

He herded her out of the shed. "They're five miles close. If they were any closer, they'd be down the chimney."

"Do you think it's right to escape when other people are being poisoned?"

"How is your being poisoned going to help other people?"

"It doesn't feel right." If only he'd stop rushing her; she hated being rushed, especially in her glasses; she could feel the roar in her veins, but wasn't sure if her inability to go back for her lenses was due to being rushed or nerve damage. The planes were flying in a military pattern of squares, and she knew she was one of those squares, but how could she get away without driving through another square, since she didn't know the location of any of them?

Rumpus was struggling in Daniel's arms, mewing loudly. "You're torturing Rumpus."

"Sara," he said in strangled tones, "this stuff is giving me an asthma attack."

"Suppose while we're gone they burn our house down again?"

"Will you please get in the car," he replied, herding her over the lawn. Rumpus was flailing in terror against him, clawing his clothes; Daniel dumped the cat in the car, and threw their suitcase and her portfolio in back.

"It doesn't seem fair, us running off when Phoebe and Murvyle are still here." But she got into the car, because it looked as if he were going to drive off with the cat and leave her arguing with herself on the grass.

He started the car with a jolt, and raced it up the lane, while the three warplanes soared overhead, dropping their veil on the house, orchard, and road; she felt the familiar dizziness and congestion; Rumpus was frantically scratching at the inside of the door.

"At least we won't be here tomorrow or the next day," Daniel wheezed, as they swerved past the old schoolhouse, the abandoned church, and the graveyard.

She thought of the vegetable seeds she'd been going to plant today. "This is insane. I feel like a war refugee having to flee my own land." They drove past the hay fields and old Alf's shack. Shouldn't we give Alf a lift? But his hat isn't on the stump, and he has no intention of fleeing, and I'm not the evacuation officer.

"What was it you said," he asked, "about them burning our house down?"

"I was just talking."

"Do you think they purposely burned us out?"

"Never. Who would be cruel enough to burn two cats?" But as soon as she asked it, she thought of half a dozen people in the village who'd blasted their own pets with a shotgun the first time the pet became inconvenient. "You don't think they burned us out, do you?"

He was breathing with difficulty; Rumpus was calling piteously; the car bounced over springtime's ruts, with the forest rushing past and the drone of the three fighters above.

This is a profoundly mystical experience, he thought, working beneath the burning sun, cultivating the earth.

"I'm going crazy," she screamed, "I can't stand it!"

He continued hilling potatoes.

"These goddamn black flies!" she continued screaming. "No wonder Canada's unpopulated. Only a raving lunatic could bear it."

He continued working quietly, in a bee bonnet, long-sleeved turtleneck, and gauntlet gloves. "You're working yourself into a paranoid state."

"Paranoid? Do you know those Americans up in Tuner Bog got so desperate they were planning to set fire to their fields? Except the locals told them it wouldn't help. Have I suggested setting fire to the fields? Have I?"

"Why don't you take a break?"

"Breaks make it worse." She tore off her net bonnet. "I hate this!"

He gazed at a face streaked with despair. She tore off her gauntlets, followed by her turtleneck shirt, and bared her sweat-drenched prickly-heated breasts to the onslaught of the black flies.

"Aaaaaaaargggggghhhh!" she screamed, falling on her knees and drumming her head in the weeds, giving tongue to inhuman wails.

"Darling . . ."

"Aaaaaaaargggggghhhh!"

"Darling, there's a truck in the lane."

She lifted her head, and reversed the procedure, pulling on her turtleneck shirt in a frenzy of modesty equal to her former one of despair.

Murvyle and Phoebe stepped out and sauntered over to the garden. Murvyle had one eye stung shut and his swollen ears stuck out from his cap like a pair of red summer potatoes. "Nice day," he remarked.

"Kinda hot," said Phoebe, flapping a newspaper fan at her pink exposed flesh. "We thought we heard a fox barkin down here, didn't we, Murvyle."

"That was Sara," said Daniel. "She's finally gone buggy."

Sara picked up her basket and announced, "Phoebe and I are going inside."

The women walked off in two halos of black flies. Murvyle took off his cap to wipe his brow; his forehead was ringed with a maroon string of bites trickling blood.

"It doesn't look as if you've been using that bee bonnet I gave you," said Daniel.

"She was a pretty good rig till it come time fer spittin." In spite of welts, enlarged ears, bleeding, and half-shut eyes, the old man seemed to be immunized. He's never known any other kind of summer, thought Daniel, and never will. They walked toward the barn, and Daniel hung his own bonnet on the door; swarms attacked his face as he followed his mentor into the woods.

■ ■ ■

"This is the kinda car you want," said Hilton, as the speedometer on his Oldsmobile rose to eighty, "not that son of a whore of a convertible."

"I'd like something smaller," said Daniel, whose car had breathed its last, yesterday, between Poverty Hollow and Mosquitoville.

The foliage on either side of the highway was a blaze of autumn colors, but at the speed they were going, it was hard for Daniel to savor. "What you want," explained Hilton, "is a car with some room in back so you can have a little party there."

A party? What kind of a little party would I throw in the backseat of our car?

"Now you take t'other night." Hilton was cruising steadily at ninety, rolling a cigarette. "I was down in town, drivin along, and I seen this girl on the corner. Cunt shinin. She got into the car and I says to her, *You better give me some goddamn good fuckin.*"

It sounded one short step up from rape; but then Daniel had a mental flash of what kind of woman might hop into a car with Hilton—a poor, uneducated, backwoods woman, gross-featured from drink, loss of teeth, and being beaten around the face—to her this might be a perfectly acceptable approach, not overly romantic or suave, but well within her experience of the male animal. "Did she?"

"Yer goddamn right she did."

His mental flash now widened to encompass both the woman and Hilton in the backseat, with Hilton's drunken, sawed-off, gargantuan form bucking up and down.

Hilton leaned over confidentially, breathing Moosehead and speaking softly through jagged tooth stumps. "Course, the best fuckin there is is old women."

". . . How old?"

"Sixty anyways. You take a woman like that, she knows what fuckin is and she's glad to get it." The speedometer fell back to eighty. Hilton was musing with deep sentimentality. "You take t'other week. I walked out of the Legion. And there was an old woman leanin on me car. She says, *Let's go fuck.*"

This direct level of communicating one's needs made Daniel hark to an earlier freer era . . . or eon; his vision whipped quickly backward past turn-of-the-century Canada, on through medieval Europe, settling somewhere in ancient Rome. "But you gotta be careful in this town," warned Hilton. Daniel gazed ahead at the three avenues and a hilltop which made up the tiny city, and saw it suddenly as a strange seething pot of unexpected encounters with old women. ". . . I picked up a woman at the Society Saloon one time. Good-lookin. Goddamn good-lookin. Nice clothes on her. Money. Cigarettes. She took me back to her room over to the Cariboo Arms. Jesus Christ, I ain't never been so scared in me life."

"What happened?"

"She was a maferdike."

". . . A maferdike?"

"Son of a whore had a dick is what she had!" Hilton shook his head. "I cleared out of there some fast." He stared through the windshield at the dangerous streets, concluding, "You gotta watch out in this town." Daniel thought of the reckless closet queen who'd come near to having his head caved in by a terrified Etruscan country lad, and Hilton pulled into the used-car lot.

They both stepped out. At least this time, thought Daniel, with Hilton along, I'll get a car that's mechanically perfect. Sara had wanted to come, but with Sara's romantic notions they'd only end

up with another convertible, and he needed something practical
. . . and there it was, in the corner, the car he'd always wanted, a
little red sportscar, a British Rover, on sale for seven hundred dollars. He walked quickly toward it and peered in. The interior was
in A-1 condition; the interior was fabulous; Sara would love it. He
looked at the wheels, which would turn on a dime.

Hilton lumbered over, yanked open the hood, and made a face of
such disgust Daniel thought for an instant there was a dead porcupine in the engine in an advanced state of decomposition. "You
don't want this son of a whore." Hilton slammed the hood shut.
"Has two carburetors."

That's it, Daniel realized, like a calf with two heads, something
that's up in the barn you don't talk about. He hadn't the faintest
idea what was wrong with two carburetors, but wouldn't dare go
against the contempt of his mechanic.

Hilton strode away from the Rover, and sniffed around the other
specimens, mystically intuiting mechanical mysteries beyond Daniel's ken. "Here's the right cure," he said, stopping in front of an
enormous black Pontiac.

From the office, a rotund gentleman approached them, a jovial
farmer who'd donned a suit. He handed Daniel his card. *GMC
Award Winning Salesman—Grand Master.*

"She's a beauty," said the Grand Master. "Sixty thousand mile on
her, runs like new. Only had one owner, feller by the name of Job
MacLean, raises pigs over Nacadie, nice big pigs, mebbe you seen
them on the left goin through Nacadie."

"She's a good looker," agreed Hilton. The two seemed to have an
immediate and profound rapport. Do they, wondered Daniel, know
each other? Or do they share the same essential soul, a soul which
resonates to piston, valve, and transmission?

"Take her fer a spin down the highway," the Grand Master
suggested, "and let her out."

Hilton slipped into the driver's seat; Daniel got in the other side,
and they drove out of the lot. "She handles good," said Hilton.

Daniel gazed through the windshield out at the hood. "Isn't it a
bit big across the front?"

Hilton gunned the gas. "Hell, no. You want her big out there.
Helps you know where yer goin." But why would one need such a
mammoth reminder? Though perhaps when traveling blind-drunk,

every square foot you can get is of value to help remind you where you are, namely in a moving car.

"You like her?" asked Daniel.

"You'll get yer money's worth out of this car. We'll jew him down in price. Be a pretty good deal."

"You're sure it's not too big? I was hoping for a compact."

"Fuck, this one's smaller'n mine."

"I thought it was about the same size."

Hilton snorted and gunned it some more, while Daniel clutched the dashboard. "What you want," explained Hilton, "is a lot of room fer groceries. Now, you take and buy some groceries, you got someplace to put them."

They zoomed into the lot, and made a long stop; the Grand Master was waiting.

"Can't you do better than twelve hundred?" asked Hilton.

"Sorry, boys, I already took four hundred off when I give you the quote."

Daniel looked at Hilton.

Hilton rolled a cigarette. "What about takin off the sales tax?"

"I'd like to, boys, but I already went down more than I should."

Daniel looked at Hilton.

Hilton spat some tobacco off his tongue.

They entered the office, and Daniel wrote a check, after phoning the bank to make sure he had that much in the world. As he walked out, with the keys to his new car in hand, he noticed the Grand Master slip Hilton ten dollars.

■ ■ ■

He turned down his lane. Sara was waiting in the dooryard.

"What do you think of it?" he asked, stepping out.

"When you drive a car like that," she said, "you have to smoke a fat cigar and wear a diamond ring on your pinky."

As if a veil had fallen from his eyes, he suddenly visualized the Mafia bosses sitting inside; and then, the gangsters slowly transformed, and he realized what he bought the car for, as gradually the phantom of Hilton took shape, whooping it up in the roomy backseat, drinking and singing and bucking up and down on top of

a little old lady, her withered legs kicking the air, a bottle of
Moosehead in hand, her grandmotherly face creased in rapture.

■ ■ ■

"How long did they put him in jail for?"
"Ten days to two weeks," replied Murvyle.
"And how long will they suspend his license?"
"Six months, mebbe more."
The cat, in Daniel's lap, looked up with a conspiratorial contrac-
tion of his pupils.
"Tain't right, y'know," said Phoebe. "He couldn't have been
drinkin, cause that's the day him and you went in to buy the Pon-
tiac, and he didn't have but two dollars fer gasoline."
"But if he wasn't drinking," said Sara, "why'd he refuse the
Breathalyzer?"
"The dear knows," sighed Phoebe.
Daniel briefly flashed on the Grand Master slipping Hilton ten
dollars, but felt perhaps it should best remain a mystery, his private guilt pangs being sufficient. Rumpus's yellow eyes met his
squarely, plainly stating he too knew the truth, but wasn't about to
say anything either.
"Tain't him bein in jail so much," said Phoebe, "but when he
comes out and don't have no license and can't drive nowhere, it's
me who'll have him on the lounge fer six months."
"He's takin it pretty well," said Murvyle. "When I went down, he
was sittin in his cell, smokin with a few of t'other lads."
"Last time Hilton was in," said Phoebe, "twas afore they remod-
eled." Her statement floated on the air, somewhere outside the subject, while Daniel pictured poor Hilton, hulking on a board, thinking how his partying days with old women were over for six
months, mebbe more.
Phoebe sighed again; Rumpus shifted in Daniel's lap, and sighed
in sympathy. Murvyle turned to Phoebe. "Ain't you gonna tell them
about Hayward and Isabel?"
Phoebe's pink face grew pinker, her plump little hands fluttered.
"I dunno how to say it."
Daniel noticed Sara and Rumpus prick up their ears. Murvyle
rolled himself a cigarette. "It appears where Hayward was up to
see the doctor last week, fer one thing and t'other, and the doctor

says to him, *Hayward, how long is it since you had a bone on?*
Hayward, he thinks awhile, and answers, *Ten or eleven year.* So
the doctor, he gives Hayward an injection. Now, Phoebe, you tell
them what happened."

Phoebe pinkened more deeply and started to giggle. "The way
Isabel says it, the injection made him feel funny."

"To whom did Isabel say all this?" asked Daniel, in view of the
intimacy of the subject.

"Everybody, didn't she, Murvyle? She even told our Anson when
he was in to fix the leak in her shed. She was sure some excited."

Murvyle's eyes twinkled. "You can't blame the old girl, after ten,
eleven year."

"It made him feel funny," giggled Phoebe. "That's how she put
it."

Rumpus gazed at Daniel sadly, and Daniel returned the cat's
gaze, filled with compassion for Hayward, who was epileptic, dia-
betic, crippled, blind, and now feeling funny. In every kitchen for
miles around, the tale was doubtless being told, retold, and hashed
over, how Hayward finally got a bone on.

■ ■ ■

He looked up from splitting wood to see a very dented Oldsmobile coming down the lane.

The wrecked car came to a stop; the door opened, and Hilton
lumbered out, smiling broadly, breathing steam into the freezing
air.

"I thought they suspended your license."

"Hell," chortled Hilton, "I know when them Mountie bastards
are gonna drive out this way." It was a cherished belief of his, but
Daniel wondered why, if Hilton knew the activities of the Mounties so well, they were always arresting him.

The cat rubbed against Hilton's leg; he bent over and gave it a
scratch. "I told them fuckin Mounties, I told them, *If them stripes
up yer pants was down yer back, you'd be a skunk.* 'Tis the truth,
'tis the only dif'rence between them."

"How'd they like being told it?"

"They tried to give me the Breathalyzer. *No way,* I says, *am I
gonna take that son of a whore. I know me rights.* They take you

into town fer the test, and then who's gonna drive you back home? Tell me that if you will."

The cat furrowed his brow. Daniel set down his ax. "But when you refuse the Breathalyzer, doesn't that imply you have something to hide?"

"Christ, I wasn't drunk. Nor seein double. I fell off to sleep fer one little minute and this son of a whore of a Jeep drove into me road. Anytime I been in an accident I never had more'n two or three drinks, and the other parties they never had any. You know why them sober drivers go so slow? They're afeared to go fast cause they don't know how to drive. The only safe way to drive is fast. If they knowed what they was doin and hadn't been so slow, they could've got out of me road. Yessir, 'tis the sober ones cause all the accidents."

Daniel thought of them all, all the sober drivers of the province, driving carefully along, checking oncoming traffic and the traffic behind them, maintaining proper distance and speed, causing accidents by the score, while those on a spree, weaving back and forth up the highway, opening bear bottles with their teeth, swerving up embankments, driving ninety-five miles an hour on the wrong side of the road, cut a clear path of purity and safety through the countryside.

"I alluys like it in jail though. Warm. Plenty to eat. They really feed you better in jail than they do at home. Meat most every day of the week. Gravy. Mushruins." He paused as if pondering the delicacies he would miss now he was out, then shook his head. "But there's some bad pups in jail." If Hilton judges them bad pups, mused Daniel, what must they be?

"When will you get your license back?"

"That goddamn lawyer the Legal Aid give me. Son of a whore shufflin papers around. He should've got me off, the son of a whore . . ." Hilton's face suddenly brightened. "How's yer new Pontiac runnin?"

"I don't know, Hilton. It seems to have a miss in the motor."

"Shit, that ain't nahthin. Let's have a look at her."

They moved toward the black limousine; Hilton flung up the hood, and began tinkering. "Some fellers in jail, they keep them tied to a ball and chain . . ." His head was deep in the engine. "Some fellers set fire to the mattresses one evenin . . . Some fellers . . ." Daniel watched the investigations. When Hilton was bent over an engine, drunk or sober, he was meshed with his destiny and out of harm's way; only behind a wheel was he in danger.

"Heard about Hayward?" Hilton's voice was muffled in the carworks.

"Last I heard he was feeling funny."

"In hospital."

"What happened?"

"I cal'ate Isabel was too much fer him. She's a hot number, Isabel." There was a sound of smacking lips, and Daniel pictured the hot number, a grizzled grim-visaged matron who could neither walk nor talk straight, zonked out of her mind from popping the sundry drugs prescribed for her husband's numerous ailments.

But who's to say? he thought philosophically, in a world where the sober ones cause all the accidents.

6

" 'Well, Frank, we're interested in the weather.'

'I don't know, Mort . . .'

'Oh, take a stab. How d'you think it'll be?'

'Can't say exactly. We might have a few sunny periods on Saturday but for the most part the sunny day should be confined to Sunday.'

'Thanks, Frank.'

'That's all right, Mort.'

"That was Frank Plummador, our meteorologist . . ."

Sara smiled, having a soft spot for poor Frank, who was not only catatonic, but rightly modest about his weather predictions; for an accurate forecast, she had to rely on Phoebe, who could predict from the way her bread was rising.

"So that's our weekend forecast, folks," concluded Mortimer through his nose. She used to wonder why someone with such a dire vocal impediment had ever gravitated to broadcasting; one would think it'd be the last profession such a person would pick. But in Atlantic Canada, it seemed prerequisite for announcers to suffer severe vocal and mental handicaps; none of them could read fluently, string two logical sentences together, and all seemed to have palates bulging with adenoids.

She went down to the cellar, and crossed the soft dirt floor to the old fieldstone shelf for a jar of her chow-chow pickle, made of green garden tomatoes and onions and apples from an orchard as old as the foundation, from a recipe as old as the settlement, and she felt that click inside her, the meshing of her mind with the generations.

She walked upstairs with a basket of root vegetables and chow-chow. Outside, the roar of a snowmobile broke the stillness, then another, and another; occasionally they roared down the lane, shouted drunkenly, turned, and roared away, but it always sounded like vigilantes come to burn the house down.

She turned the radio back on:

". . . *When you get right down to it, this country has a lot going for it. With such a tiny fraction of the world's population, we have twenty-one percent of the world's usable uranium, twenty-four percent of the world's . . .*" She put on the carrots and pared the potatoes, hoping to speed Daniel's return from work by cooking his supper. ". . . *As the needs of other countries grow, there will be more and more pressure upon us. The day may not be far off when the rest of the world demands, physically or otherwise, their share of what Canada has. What we must face is the prospect to defend to the rest of the world our exclusive right to our disproportionate share of the world's resources.*"

She switched the radio off, and let the silent house engulf her. It was only at night that she felt how isolated they were. In a recent *MacLean's* magazine, there'd been an editorial by a woman who said she felt like throwing a hand grenade whenever she saw a U.S. license plate.

■ ■ ■

"Every time I look in the rearview mirror," said Daniel, "all I can see is Hilton partying with an old lady in the backseat."

She refrained from replying, *That's what you get for buying a car without me,* since the cars they'd bought together hadn't turned out much better. The Pontiac's engine made its characteristic death-agony sound as they rode into town, plowing across the narrow bridge in their oversize tank which forced lesser vehicles to cringe at the shoulder.

Though she looked forward to town all week, when they arrived, there were only the malls and the library, and if she was ruthlessly honest, the high point of the entire excursion was the slice of lemon meringue pie she would eat with her lunch. He parked, and they entered the library. As she wandered off through the stacks of books, she had the disturbing sensation that something major in her life was being deferred. It had nothing to do with her work, nor anything missing between her and Daniel, nor even with not having a child; it was something specifically connected to this town, this library, this moment, and was of towering importance.

She sat down in the reading room, arming herself with the latest *New Yorker* and *Vogue;* it was part of her work to keep in touch with civilization and stay up to date with changing fashions and moods, but turning the glossy pages, she admitted that magazines were always one step behind what was actually happening, which put her two steps behind.

At the table beside her, Daniel and the mad-eyed Urantian pored over their respective mystical tomes. The rest of the party consisted of several old people in coats, mufflers, and earflaps, seeking refuge from the cold.

She laid down *The New Yorker,* and went to choose the books that would keep her company for the week. She'd read her way through many stacks over the years—from architecture of country houses, through the care and feeding of horses, gardening, preserving, wildlife, childbirth, death and bereavement, pesticide poisoning, and lately she found herself gravitating toward the 940's—Fodor and Fielding, off-season and budget, by rail, by ship, by camper, boot, bike, and thumb around the world.

"I'm hungry," said Daniel, manifesting at her elbow precisely at noon, which was the hour he and Waldo ate lunch every day even if they had to leave a board half-cut or shimmy down a chimney to do it.

She checked out her travel books, and they walked through the blustery streets to the in-town mall, which boasted an overpriced cafeteria. Standing on the food line, she could remember when she'd found this ostentatious eatery perfectly charming, but somewhere over the years, the veneer had worn off, and since it hadn't worn off the cafeteria, whose red and gilt were polished each day, it must be she who had worn.

She selected a dietetic salad, and searched for the lemon meringue pie, but the wished-for pastry had not been baked today; twice she inquired to make sure, then walked to their table, devastated.

"How can you be so disappointed about a pie?" asked Daniel.

The procession of trays continued, all bearers looking pretty much the same, until one face appeared which did not immediately blend into the bland soup of Rent-A-Car managers . . . Irish tweed cap, pipe firmly clenched in teeth, a twinkle, a je ne sais quoi, a depth, a maturity, in short, worldliness. As his eyes met hers and Daniel's, there was that conspiratorial moment of *It's very crowded, may I join you?*, and as he came toward them, she felt, *Here is substance approaching;* for a second, she grew almost flustered at the lofty conversation in store.

"How're you doing, Harold," said Daniel. "Why don't you pull up a chair?"

The Local Author put down his tray and pipe and greeted them warmly, followed by Evan McNevin, the province's seventeen-year-old answer to Rimbaud. Sara felt her brain cells glowing.

"Haven't seen you for a while," said Harold. "You ought to drop by the house some time."

We really should, she thought; why stand on ceremony?

"I've got some excellent wine," he smiled. "I made it myself."

"Sounds divine," she said, as the cafeteria suddenly soared to the altitude of Montmartre, artistic ambiance rolling over her in dizzying waves—It's finally happening. "You must come out to our place too."

"We've got homemade sauerkraut," said Daniel.

"Ah, you folks in the wilderness have the answer." Harold turned to Sara. "Illustrated any good books lately?"

"The usual purple passion."

He chuckled. They chuckled. Evan McNevin chuckled loudly. She glanced at him, for the first time noting he was causing people to stare, owing to the decible level of his chuckles. Oh well, he's young, he's enthusiastic, he's excited by an older set; the thought was flattering.

"We're rounding out a really top-notch year at the U," said Harold. "My book has done rather well, perhaps you know. I was pleasantly surprised."

"Yes, it's . . ." She paused, her mind racing to come up with a compliment for a book she'd been unable to read beyond page two. ". . . a tour de force."

Harold puffed his pipe modestly; thank God she'd said the right thing. "I'm deep into numero two."

"Marvelous. What's it about?"

"My life," he replied, plunging into the tale, and gradually as he spoke, it became for her an experience very close to the one she'd had reading his first book; she found herself thinking of a hundred other things, while here she was undergoing the most stimulating conversation she'd had in years. Evan McNevin nodded, in close sympathy with every nuance of Harold's soliloquy. ". . . the sub-plot being . . ." Would he be offended, she wondered, if I slipped off for a minute to get a second piece of cake?

"Sounds pretty good," said Daniel.

Evan chuckled loudly. "*Pretty* good," he said, echoing Daniel. Is he being sarcastic? she wondered. Or just loud and stupid?

"I tell you," said Harold, relighting his pipe, "it's truly amazing what's been going on in the literary community here. The work I've done has been in many ways a result of the supportiveness of my colleagues and students . . ." It sounded to her vaguely like an acceptance speech. Has someone, she wondered, offered Harold the Nobel? ". . . Young men like Evan here, whose view is so fresh and at the same time so demanding of excellence, have put me on my toes in a way I never thought to be when I first arrived at the University . . ."

It was inevitable perhaps, but unfortunate, that his reference to Evan's work would remind her of the work itself, which had been inflicted on the local populace for years; in keeping with a national policy of fostering native talent, the kid's poetry had been pub-lished long before it was any more than it should be—the tedious twitterings of a still-wet embryo. "I always tell them, *Write about what you know,*" went on Harold; and Evan had done it ad nauseum, except what he knew was only what any sheltered, happy, middle-class, spoiled, applauded, small-town twirt of four-teen, fifteen, sixteen, and now seventeen would know—nothing. "*Don't tell it,*" said Harold, "*show it . . .*"

It isn't, she thought, that I want Evan to ruin his health with ab-sinthe and derange his senses and live with men and run slave boats out of Africa, but at least he might keep quiet until he has something to say. But no, she thought, as Evan himself began talk-ing, he insists on publishing locally struck pamphlets of abysmally free verse about his siblings and school and hockey and blueberry picking and Mother's cookies; in ashamed atonement for her un-charitable thoughts, she gave the voluble Evan an especially warm smile, which was received with protruding blind eyes that saw only himself. ". . . seems I've penetrated to a new level . . ." he contin-ued.

He doesn't care what I think, she perceived with mixed relief; he sees me as he sees everyone else, as an unthinking ear for his radio pronouncements. ". . . owing to my finally realizing," he was blaring over his built-in loudspeakers, "that Eliot simply isn't Yeats." Finally? she wondered. After what? After seventeen years of his mother's cookies? After one year of Harold's lectures? And finally, after thirty-two years, what am I doing listening to Evan McNevin? "Not that Yeats didn't have his blind spots . . ." Evan was saying in ringing tones which allowed many to benefit; wasn't he, after all, important in his own home? and in the classroom? and didn't Harold let him tag along? What, she wondered, is wrong with Harold?

"The unbelievable quality of writing coming out of this small Canadian town . . ." interrupted Harold, eyes twinkling. "But who would've ever thought Dublin in the Thirties?"

For a second she assumed he was kidding, then saw with his Irish tweed cap and pipe, he did look distinctly Dublinish. He gestured with his pipe stem as he spoke, and used the wafting smoke, the tinkle of glasses and lights to punctuate his monologue; she saw that to him this really was the Palace pub with Yeats and Joyce and Behan, and the reason she could feel the depth of his illusion was because she herself had been sustaining one in this very same room. Hers, she felt, had started to crumble when the quality of the lemon meringue pie had gone off.

"Absolutely true, Harold," said Evan. "I saw it in that piece Gordon Foxknot read in class only last week."

"Was that the piece about the meaning of Thanksgiving?"

"Yes, I wanted to tell him right then what I thought of it." Evan's voice, for him, grew low: "There's genius there."

She was flummoxed. I am, she realized, in the presence of not one, but two of the most pretentious conceited bores ever spored, the one from the other. And this is the intellectual highlight of my year. This is what my heart went pitter-patter about.

"I envy you two your pure life in the boonies," Harold twinkled at her and Daniel, "but how can I turn people down when they keep throwing more and more money at me?"

"That's the problem," agreed Evan, as if he shared Harold's dilemma of being a highly remunerated professor, which no doubt he one day would.

". . . The symbolism in the everyday act . . ." went on Harold, tamping his pipe with authority, while Sara nibbled her second-choice pastry and longed for Phoebe's laconic and fractured soliloquys on the effect of weather on the rising of bread. What differentiates Harold from the Rent-A-Car managers, she saw, isn't merely Art with a capital A, but the illusory status of University, an institution older than either Zeller's or Budget Rental; Harold's aura of maturity, substance, depth, and security boils down to tenure: Here is a man who can't be fired.

She glanced at Daniel, who'd finished his coffee and was listening serenely; he has, she thought, a very high tolerance for fools.

"In my small way," said Harold, "I try to instill a sense of values in life and art . . ." Even as he said it, a moment of high epiphany descended, in the shape of the Local Artist, bearing down with coffee and two bran muffins. I may not appreciate literature, thought Sara, but painting I know, and this mediocrity would be doing paste-ups and mechanicals in New York. The great man joined the party, and his smile in her direction managed to encompass a good deal—tenure, of course; the price his last painting sold for; contempt for her own crass field; and an interest in discussing, should by chance the occasion ever present itself, all of the above in bed.

But where, she wondered, as she put on her jacket, got to her feet, and left with Daniel, is the real meaning of life, if not here?

"Woolco?" asked Daniel.

The halls of the new mall were lined with gaping shoppers watching a group of poorly trained, gaudily costumed urchins performing a morris dance to a tape-recorded soundtrack over a profoundly deficient speaker. Standing with Daniel, watching the budding flowers of the community gustily tap up the middle of the mall, she wondered why parents would give their kids to a group of chain stores to help drum up business; something seemed out of balance.

Yet, entering Woolco itself, she admitted there was a perverse pleasure in knowing the stock from one end of the store to the other and a security in being familiar with every aisle. Looking at the book rack, she again had that feeling of deferment, as if she were only standing in Woolco looking at a book rack—or perfume or clothes or home furnishings—while waiting for something else to happen. Except she knew nothing else was going to happen.

They went to the supermarket, loaded the giant car, and started home; she felt like a junkie coming down, or a hungover drunk. She had new library books, socks, pencils, toothpaste, bananas, toilet paper, cake in her belly, a headache, had experienced another horrible day in town, and in two more days would be looking forward to their next weekly excursion.

"The morris dancers were cute," he said.

The highway was dark. He punched on the radio; the monotonous Nashville sound of Canada's airwaves had taken an electrifying slide into undreamt-of mediocrity with the most recent National Identity pronouncement that radio stations must play music of sixty percent Canadian content.

When at last the car turned off the highway onto the settlement road, he punched off the music, and they climbed the dark hills in silence. White snow canyons gleamed in the moonlight. The knot of the day seemed to loosen around her. Passing old Alf's shack, where woods gave way to fields, she caught sight of the stars, so bright they seemed strung from a clothesline over the trees. A cloud passed across the moon, making a fleeting pattern of leaves.

He drove down their lane and parked; he turned off the motor; they stepped out. "Why," he asked softly, "do we ever go to town?"

The air surrounded them with the crystal perfume of snowy forest; the stars and moon seemed as close as the chimney. Why, she wondered, do we ever run away from this magic?

The cat purred loudly, rubbing against them, and accompanied Daniel inside.

She saw the house light up, alone in the midst of the jeweled night and forest, and thought that if she ever came upon such a place, so utterly enchanted, she would give anything to own it, to live in it, and never leave it.

■ ■ ■

The electricity had been out for six hours, but a rumbling outside announced the snow plow, and then the power company truck.

The lights went on; the refrigerator motor kicked in. The man from the power company walked toward the house.

She left her work, and went to meet him. In the gray afternoon light, as the stranger came toward her, her heart skipped a beat; the man was devastatingly attractive.

"Evening," he said in a resonant voice brimming with charm and sophistication. He was gray at the temples, his features classic and chiseled. He moved with elegance and grace, and his gaze was penetrating. *Who* is this incredible vision?

He started talking to her, at first about roads and the weather, and it slowly became apparent that his intimate manner was because he knew her and he clearly assumed she knew him, but she couldn't for the life of her recall where she'd ever met this suave lineman.

". . . ax murderer . . ." he was saying, ". . . escaped convict . . ." The story sounded familiar, and gradually, imperceptibly, it began to come back to her, like the dissolve in *Dr. Jekyll and Mr. Hyde*, where the handsome stranger, frame by frame, takes the shape of the fang-toothed monster, the grotesque, beer-bellied, bumpkin tale-teller who'd tried to scare her out of her wits her first month in the country, years ago.

". . . buried his ax in her head . . ." said J. Nutting, Hydroman, as the dissolve flashed from the hillbilly liar to the sophisticated gent, and back again, ". . . turned the dogs out after him . . . mebbe you heard them barkin?"

She recalled the first time she saw him, when he'd looked to her like the creature from the lagoon, and his raspy rummy's voice, impeded by missing teeth, had given his fantasies an additional macabre ring. ". . . zactly the kind of place here a convict would 'scape to . . . nice old barn to hide in . . ." he went on, as she stood horror-struck in the doorway, watching the bizarre dissolves and perceiving in depth exactly how far her standards of male charm had fallen. I have, she realized, been in the country a long time.

"I got me license back," grinned Hilton, stepping out of his Oldsmobile. "All I gotta do now is fix her up."

"What does it need?" asked Daniel, gazing at the ruined car.

"Not much. I'll go to the junkyards. A couple hundred dollar." Daniel noted Hilton hadn't said what the car needed, but how much it would cost; a familiar opening. "I got five dollar to me name," he concluded.

"I'll get the checkbook," said Daniel, glancing down at the cat, who met his gaze with a yellow stare which said, *Sara is not going to like this.*

Quietly, he entered the house and tiptoed to the desk where the checkbook was kept. The balance was forty dollars. He wrote a note to the teller to transfer two hundred dollars from their savings account and honor the check for same presented by one Hilton McGivney.

He went outside, and handed the passbook, check, and note to Hilton. "Give this to the teller."

Hilton nodded. "I'll pay you back in two weeks. Mebbe four."

"Okay."

"Well . . ." Hilton pocketed the bankbook, anxious to leave, as he always was under such circumstances; the cat looked on disapprovingly.

"Four weeks." Hilton got into his Olds. "Mebbe six." He roared off in a spatter of mud.

Sara appeared at the door. "Who was that?"

"Hilton."

"He didn't stay very long."

"No, he just needed to borrow something."

■ ■ ■

"They'll put him away fer good this time," said Murvyle. "When he comes out he'll be whiter'n a badger."

He means an ermine, thought Daniel, but understood that Murvyle's mind was not functioning perfectly, stricken as it was with grief, just as his own was stricken with guilt. The cat gave him a long yellow look. *I told you not to lend him that two hundred dollars.*

Phoebe sighed deeply.

Sara poured tea.

"He shouldn't have took the Breathalyzer," said Phoebe.

"No," agreed Murvyle. "Twas that damn fool of a lawyer he had last time put it into his head tweren't no use to refuse it."

"Twas really *her* fault," said Phoebe, referring to the nameless hussy who'd prevailed upon Hilton to sully his innocent lips with spirits while driving down the wrong side of the road at ninety-five per.

"At least no one was hurt," said Daniel, deeply thankful that he hadn't been an accessory to murder, particularly of an old woman.

" 'Tis funny though," said Phoebe, "how he don't never get hurt. Ain't it? Not even that time he drove off the bridge. Nor twasn't right fer them to make him pay fer the railin. They had no business to put up a bridge railin if tweren't safe."

They munched their bread and sipped tea, pondering Hilton's invulnerability. The man was plainly immortal.

"Anythin new?" asked Murvyle presently.

"I guess you heard," said Phoebe, " 'bout the murder up to Murchville?"

Sara gave a slight gasp.

"Elvira Murch," said Murvyle. "One of her funny boys did it."

"Ice pick, weren't it, Murvyle?"

"Yes, I believe 'twere an ice pick. He come up behind her in the creamery and pierced her dead."

"Tsk, tsk."

"My God," murmured Sara.

"Poor Elvira. Not that anyone ever had a good word to say fer her, did they, Murvyle?"

Murvyle pondered and shook his head. "Can't recall where I ever heard a good word 'bout Elvira."

"I guess what they found in the house was really somethin," sighed Phoebe. She tsk-tsk'd some more. The tale seemed to be over.

"What did they find?" asked Daniel.

"Them poor funny children. She used them terrible. Had the little ones chained to their beds."

"What was funny about them?"

"You know. Funny." Phoebe pointed to her head.

"'Tarded," explained Murvyle. "She took in 'tarded foster children fer the money the gov'ment paid."

"Oh, she got rich on them children. Chained to beds. Locked in cupboards. An awful mess. Twas the one who took care of them who killed her. He did all the cleanin, cookin . . . he was really her slave is what he was more'n anythin else. He got the worst of, didn't he, Murvyle?"

"Seems to me Elvira got the worst of it," remarked Murvyle.

"How long did she have those children?"

"Long as I can recall," said Murvyle. "They was alluys dyin anyways."

"I wonder," mused Phoebe, "who'll get all the money? Elvira must've saved a passle."

"Husband, children . . . there'll be some scufflin fer Elvira's money, you can be sure with them Murches."

"You know them?"

"Know the Murches! I used to shoe Elvira's horse. Twenty year ago." Murvyle leaned back in the rocker. "The horse I alluys recall was quite a filly . . . nor never liked fer me to shoe her . . ."

Daniel leaned back in his own chair, knowing the details of the murder, the ice pick, and the funny children would have to wait, not only this visit, but perhaps many visits, until Murvyle had fully dredged and recounted every last aspect of every horse the Murches had ever owned, and, possibly, every horse in surrounding Murchville.

■ ■ ■

He closed his lunch pail, and pillowed his head against a pile of wood chips, breathing the intoxicating smell of the woodworking shop. Warm scents of spring wafted in through the open doorway. Waldo was still eating his second dessert, leisurely putting away three pieces of cake and a goodly assortment of cookies. "Appears I'm finally gonna start me that sawmill."

Daniel leaned up on one elbow. "When do you have time for a sawmill? We're fifty cabinets behind already and the house season's starting."

"I worked me last house season." Waldo wiped the crumbs off his round fáce, beaming. "The gov'ment boys was here and told me they'd back me to the hilt in a sawmill."

Daniel sat up. "You mean you're giving up carpentry to saw logs?"

"Interest free. I could've gone into pigs or logs, they'll pay fer either. Only pigs smell so damn bad. Course, turkeys smell worse."

"But you're a master carpenter."

"Did you ever see the gov'ment offer me dollar-one to build a cabinet?"

"But what do you need the government for? Everyone pays you for their cabinets."

"I got me a real good buy on some secondhanded machinery up to Poverty Holler. Feller there went bankrupt."

"What if you go bankrupt?"

"Tain't my money. Now how can you beat that fer speculatin?"

"But, Waldo, what about *puttin the brads to 'er?*" he asked emotionally, but even as he spoke, he felt the wall between them, six government figures high; Waldo'd struck the mother lode of government handouts: pigs and sawmills. Daniel's hand went to his head and he found himself rubbing his hair in the style of Waldo rubbing his pate.

"I'll need some good men like yerself," said Waldo.

"You're never going to build houses again?"

"Gov'ment don't pay me to build houses," said Waldo, downing his tea. "Wanna throw in with me?"

Daniel sat in the fragrant chips and the scents of spring, thinking how he'd always felt he'd throw in with Waldo anywhere because of Waldo's mastery and spirit; he could hardly believe it when he heard himself saying, "I guess I won't."

Waldo glanced up from his Thermos with benign interest. "What d'you cal'ate on doin?"

■ ■ ■

"What dat I see dere, ma fran, in de pan? She look yaller . . ." Daniel sifted the sand on through, and the yellow disappeared like sunlight on water.

"By Chri, we find gole soon," declared Alf, standing knee-deep in the brook, "I know she in dere." Daniel wasn't so sure, but the possibility, however faint, gave their days on the stream an interesting edge. He wore sneakers and rolled-up pants, pretty much his regular work clothes, but old Alf was fully costumed, in fishing waders, pith helmet, and bandoleers; two pistols hung at his hips in case he had to protect their strike. "What you say, ma fran, we sit down and have a smoke?"

They sat on the moss by the edge of the stream and leaned their backs against a big cedar; rest periods were frequent, far more frequent than work periods, but Daniel made allowances for his fellow-prospector being seventy; and what did it matter anyway; with the sparkling stream flowing past, the riches seemed to be the sun on the water and the conversation of his partner.

"Ah, de Dr. Fowler . . ." Alf screwed the cap on the bottle, wiped his mouth with the back of his hand, and rolled a cigarette. "She one beautiful day, eh, ma fran? Look at dem fish . . ." Daniel looked at the tiny trout skimming the brook, scales glistening with the treasure. "Dem de kind we eat bones and all, dem little ones, mighty good eatin."

The smoke from Alf's cigarette rose; the stream chattered over the stones; butterflies flew along above the middle of the brook, their golden wings fluttering. "I often wonder, ma fran, why dey never land in de water. You can watch dem butterfly all day long, up, down, never once dey fall in, you tell me why, look at him goin . . ." Gold and black monarchs flew around the bend of the river; birds chirped and dove for flies; skater bugs danced on the sparkling surface. "How 'bout dat, ma fran? How 'bout walkin along de water . . ."

Daniel settled himself against the warm moss, reflecting on old Alf's continual immersion in a world which was mythically animated; the old prospector knew neither boredom nor doubt; all was perfectly given to the gentleman in the pith helmet.

The helmet tipped forward, old Alf slept, and in the ensuing silence, Daniel noticed across the stream, camouflaged by leaves, a face peering out of the bushes at them; how long the spy had been watching, he didn't know, but its presence was clearly malevolent.

The beady eyes met his; the bushes parted.

Alf reached for both guns. A voice from the other shore called: "Freeze, you froggy-eyed fucker, or I'll blow you in the air."

"Ma fran, you give me a turn," replied Alf, as Pike stepped out of the thicket, carrying a shotgun in one hand and a kitchen strainer in the other.

"I'm joinin up with you," he said in a threatening voice.

"Ver good, ma fran, de more de merry. Lot of room on de stream. Plenty gole fer us all."

"Then let's get to work," snapped Pike, giving Daniel a glance that signified his interests would now be protected. Daniel looked at Alf's bandoleers and Pike's pockets bulging with shotgun shells, and felt he'd fallen into *The Treasure of the Sierra Madre*.

He and Alf worked with their pans, and Pike with his kitchen strainer. "I know there's gold in this brook," muttered Pike. "I knowed it fer years. A log come down the drive once with the head of it yeller. It must've drove into a vein of gold somewheres along the bank, and come out polluted with the stuff."

"I seen dat gole log too, ma fran." Old Alf nodded at the apocryphal memory. They panned with more purpose now, the vision of the gold-headed log shimmering before them; a squirrel scolded from a low-drooping branch.

"Squirrels are somethin," remarked Pike. "I say, squirrels are somethin."

"Dat's true, ma fran."

"I seen five, six squirrels one time eatin tree-moss, you know that stuff hangs down like beards? It appeared to get them drunk. They went crazy fer about an hour, then keeled over in the meadow and passed out. How did they know to do that? How?" Daniel couldn't answer, but the next time they passed under some spruce, he surreptitiously picked off a handful of tree-moss, and munched as they sifted for treasure.

Perhaps it was the moss, perhaps not, but as they walked on, the stream and he gradually began to unite; he felt it flow through his veins, and as the schools of tiny trout and spotted salmon prawn rushed before him, a quiver as of darting shining creatures passed through his body. They stopped at each inlet to pan, and he cooled his feet in the icy pools where runoffs came into the stream from the hills.

"Twas the log drive of '42," said Pike. "A dog come along the shore with a nugget of gold in his mouth as big as yer head." Maybe, thought Daniel, there really is gold in the river.

"I know dat story," vouched Alf. "She's a true story."

The river turned, opening onto a great tranquil landscape, a deep lake of still water held fast by a beaver dam. On either side, the woods had been timbered, making a ruined place, which the animals had transformed. Daniel stood quietly, inhaling the sacred quality of the restoration; perhaps if they all stood silent, they might catch a glimpse of the beaver by their lodge.

"I trap dese fellers Christmas mornin. Made a nice Christmas present fer me. Twenty-five dollar de pelt."

The lonely dam still held water, which spilled down the other side in a wide glistening waterfall. They crawled over the dam and continued until they came to the next likely spot. Alf dropped down to pan, and Pike dropped down beside him to get a jump on the claim; the two men were continually elbowing each other, hip to hip and gun to gun, ending up with identical panfuls of mud.

As they waded around the brook's turning, the foliage changed; it looked like the Amazon ahead; after a second Daniel realized it wasn't the terrain, but the exotic creature at the next bend: Tall and elegant, the pinkish apparition stood on one thin leg and bent its graceful neck to drink.

Pike and Alf stopped too, and stared at the crane, as if this was the treasure they were seeking.

"Hey, ma fran," called Alf, breaking the spell, splashing forward in his hip boots, always ready for conversation. The crane raised its head to look at them, slowly spread its long wings and flew away downstream.

"What in Christ did you do that fer?" demanded Pike. "We could've got him to throw in with us. Bird like that can be tamed to a man's hand." Throw in with us? wondered Daniel. On what basis would he throw in with us? He flashed on the four of them prospecting along, the three men and the bird, and it didn't actually seem much odder than it already was.

■ ■ ■

Fresh bear tracks crossed the stream, and Daniel half expected to hear the noise of a lumbering animal, but the only sound on the morning air was the babbling of water and his fellow prospectors.

". . . set yer shirt afire . . ."

". . . bear grease, ma fran, de ver best fer de boots . . ."

So that's it, thought Daniel, isolating one of the many perfumes surrounding old Alf amidst Dr. Fowler's fumes, tobacco, and woodsmoke . . . the heavy b.o. of bear oil. ". . . seen fourteen bear in ma field last night, fourteen ver hungry bear."

Pike concealed a sneer. "You wanna know about bear? I'll tell you the strangest goddamn bear story you'll ever hear."

They sat down on the bank, resting their backs against stumps; Alf pushed his pith helmet forward, took a swig of Dr. Fowler, and handed the bottle to Pike, then Daniel. From the forest, chickadees and gorbies flew down to the scene; a frog jumped out of the brook; Daniel perceived all the creatures of the woodland gathering, tiptoeing toward them to listen.

Pike viciously lit a cigarette and tossed his match in the water with a hiss. "One year, me old horse up and kicked the bucket. So I drug him down to the head of the field. That night I went back, and come upon more goddamn bear than any man ever seen. They was tearin the old horse to pieces, big fellers rearin up on their hind legs, swackin out chunks, blood drippin down their fangs, moonlight shinin . . ."

"I thought," interrupted Daniel, "bears were fruit-eaters."

"They eat what they can get, and if it's a dead horse that's a feast fer a bear. The hair was standin right up on the back of me neck, and I high-tailed her out of there. Didn't go back till the next mornin, and d'you know what I found? Twas the skin of that horse, all rolled up in the neatest little bundle you ever seen, with his head stuck on the end of the package like the bow on a ribbon."

Daniel looked around; every creature in the forest was silent; and downstream at the bend, staring up at them, was the crane.

■ ■ ■

"What a feller wants," said Pike, "is one of them Geiger counters."

They stood sifting in the shallows; the stream was warmer now, summer wearing on and the days growing shorter.

"We'll get one, ma fran. We'll get one in town. We'll search de whole damn stream wid it."

"First," said Daniel, "we'll have to search the whole damn town."

"You send fer them," said Pike. "I seen it in a magazine. Twenty-nine ninety-five."

"Not a bad price, ma fran. What you can find wid it?"

"Everythin there is."

"We get one tomorrow from de magazine." Alf was weaving along in the stream; mud flowed through their pans and strainer; little fish darted away from them.

Strawberries, raspberries, then blueberries had marked their prospecting progress, as well as the changing flowers and changing insect plagues, the fiercest of which had been two weeks of dog flies, and all they'd found so far was one bashed-in old Player's tobacco tin, which Pike claimed was worth plenty and which Daniel figured would bring them about three dollars, if they could find a serious collector; so for two months on the stream they'd earned a buck apiece. It wasn't much, but he felt comforted there wouldn't be any ultimate *Treasure of the Sierra Madre* showdown for it. He slipped his hand in his pocket and touched the valuable tin; they took turns carrying it and alternated guarding it nights.

"One time," began Pike, "I knowed a skunk . . ."

The stream grew silent. Birds fluttered around. Alf opened Dr. Fowler. And the forest waited for the three prospectors to take their seats in an inviting island of shade where green leaves hung over the bank.

"Dat dere tree," remarked Alf, settling in, "she ver good fer whistle dis time of year."

"Twas in a camp where I worked," went on Pike, while Alf took out his knife and proceeded to whittle bark away from the sapling reeds. "We'd open the floorboards at night, and old mother skunk would come up with her little ones fer supper."

"Ma fran, I got de skunk livin wid me right now, exact same place, under de goddamn floorboard." Daniel isolated yet another aroma from the pungent mélange of old Alf's bouquet. Alf squinted at his carving. "I tink she'll blow, ma fran."

He handed a crude whistle to each; Pike eyed his suspiciously; Daniel turned his over—the bark moved back and forth around the reed. Hesitantly, he lifted the flute to his lips, and the others followed. Three high-pitched sounds, as from three strange birds, floated over the forest.

They blew again, squatting by the shore, Pike in his beret, a red-crested bird of prey, and Alf with his head tilted back, pith helmet dangling. Through the woods, the eerie call resounded, and as they gathered confidence, the music grew more piercing and the woods turned into a jungle. Pike's cheeks moved in and out; he blew with a violence that made Daniel expect poison darts to eject from the end of his flute.

As suddenly as the symphony started, it ended. Red-faced, they put down their instruments.

From far downstream, echoing through the canyon, an inhuman howl answered, insistent, blood-curdling.

The three crazed explorers gazed at each other.

■ ■ ■

Pike skulked along the riverbank, ears cocked to his metal detector, Alf crouched behind him.

Beep. Beep. Beep.

"Ma fran, ma fran!"

"Step back! Out of me way!"

Daniel hurried forward with the shovel, and dug up the mud with a few swift strokes.

"Hubcap," explained Alf, wiping it off on his sleeve. "Nineteen-tirty-two Chev, wort plenty." He slipped it into his pack, and they got back in line on the bank, Pike hunched over the detector and old Alf hunched fast in his footsteps.

By evening, the detector had uncovered a bagful of rusty nails, several sardine tins, a bent fork, and a hobnailed boot.

"She's a good haul, ma fran, dis boot. Lot of life in her yet." Alf wiggled his foot into the muddy boot. "You got a good spare right here."

Daniel shined up the hubcap, which belonged with the tobacco tin and other valuable antiques to be divvied at the end. The end, he thought, looking down the river; there was a mile of stream ahead, and who knew what treasure lay beneath its rippling waters, what old wheel rims, beer cans, pieces of chain, shattered peaveys, and dreams.

■ ■ ■

He carefully sandpapered the corner of the cupboard where the rasp marks still showed. The air in his work shed was hazy blue with Murvyle's cigarette smoke.

"Too mean to buy a sheet of plywood?"

"What's that, Murvyle?"

"Why're you makin a cupboard out of such rotten old wood?"

"An idea I had." He put down the sandpaper, and switched to a finer grain.

The north light through the windows was fading; a few flakes of snow hesitantly fell.

"Why would anyone wanna go and make a brand-new piece of furnipture look old?" asked Murvyle. Daniel worked the cupboard door back and forth; it fit poorly as if it were warped. Murvyle added, "It looks older'n old Burpee."

Daniel searched in his toolbox for a ballpeen hammer, then struck it lightly along the edge of the shelves, making irregular pits in the soft discolored pine.

"Jes cause I said she looks older'n Burpee don't mean you gotta beat her."

"Want to set your cigarette down there on the corner, Murvyle."

Murvyle set down his glowing stub. They watched it smolder and die, scorching a small black circle on the wide stained surface.

Daniel reached into the corner, and brought out a half-empty plastic jug. Murvyle unscrewed the lid and sniffed. "Ammonier can kill a feller. Same as Javex killed old Birdie Carlyle."

Daniel sandpapered the dents he'd made with his ballpeen hammer, smoothing away any telltale edges.

"Now Birdie, he was quite the carpenter hisself. Had a horse with one crooked hoof. Never seen a horse walk so funny. Birdie alluys had to load his wagon leftwise fer to make up fer his horse pullin rightwise."

"Do you know where I can borrow a blowtorch?"

"Did you try Klinger's Esso?" Murvyle rolled a new cigarette. "Kicked the pig one time, did Birdie's horse. Sweet little pig he was. But that horse, havin one crooked foot, couldn't kick straight like other horses. Did you ever try and shoe a horse with a crooked foot? Yessir, he was quite the carpenter. Built more dingles onto his house than a little."

Daniel took a pinch of rotten wood, and blew it into the worm holes he'd made with an ice pick. "I never noticed any dingles on the Carlyle house."

"Not the house you seen. The one that burnt. Had a dingle in front, a dingle behind, two dingles on each side, and every shed had a couple more dingles. Till one night, old Birdie took a freak, fell onto the table, overturned the jug of molasses, slipped, made a grub fer the beam, took hold of his kerosene lamp instead, brung it down around him, set fire to the floor, burnt the socks off his feet, cooked the molasses, and commenced to burn the whole place down. Didn't they look pretty though? All them dingles burnin together."

Daniel sawed a narrow groove off-center across a nail head, making it look like an antique screw, then glued it into the wood so it couldn't be removed and only an X ray could determine the truth.

". . . We held a frolic fer to help him rebuild. But we'd be goddamned if we was gonna build all them dingles. Let him build them dingles hisself." Murvyle smoked in silent reflection. "He never did though. Appeared to have lost heart fer dingles."

The auction hall was rapidly filling, and she had to weave between other collectors to get near the antiques. A monstrous wooden object caught her eye, at least ten feet high, based by a short flight of steps, carved overall with gnarled vines, and topped by a thrashing bird; in front of it stood a man and his wife.

"*What is it?*" asked the woman.

"*I don't know,*" he replied.

"*I guess it's just some kind of piece of furniture,*" she concluded.

Sara gravitated to the trunks of old clothes, and rummaged through faded costumes for her nineteenth-century heroines. She opened an ostrich fan, whose dusty feathers flew in her face and settled on the surrounding objets d'art. What elegance, she thought, though the fan's glory was headed for baldness; I *must* have an ostrich fan on one of my covers.

Passing the doorway, she chanced to look out into the lot, where Daniel's counterfeit antique cupboard stood beside their Pontiac, surrounded by a small group of people.

She continued around the room, stopping at a table covered with little black boxes which opened to show old photographs of nineteenth-century lovelies. This is just what I need, she thought, swooping down. In the first of the frames, two young ladies held hands, and underneath, one of them had pasted the words *Truest Friends;* the young ladies wore black, and on their faces were expressions of the blackest unhappiness, each being obviously all the other had in a hard world. She turned to the next box; from one black frame after another, antique ladies gazed forth at her with a woe which was hell to behold. The young ones were painfully haunted; the middle-aged matrons were scowling squashes, having accepted their servile position in life and now determined to radiate their gloom to their homes, families, and the men who tyrannized them. She gazed into mean little eyes, born of enslavement. My heroines, she realized, aren't nineteenth-century women at all; they're twentieth-century bathing beauties yukking it up in Victorian outfits; I haven't begun to capture what it was like; but neither have the books themselves; because who wants to read about morose frigidity and lifelong misery?

A fashionable woman in leather pants with a tape measure around her neck and a friend in an antique white rabbit jacket embraced among the old clothes, exchanging greetings, compliments, and promises not to bid against each other. How marvelous, thought Sara, to be among people with style. As she went to the desk to get a bidding number, a slender gentleman who looked like Eugene O'Neill jostled past; she found herself quite overwhelmed by the civilized ambiance; and only three hundred miles from New Jerusalem.

The auction began; Daniel slipped into the seat beside her, wearing a smile which went far back in his past, a peculiar confidence she hadn't seen in years; this is his element, she thought, this used to be his world.

They listened to the auctioneer's musical spiel. "*Everything being sold as is, where is, till death do you part or longer . . . I have a pitcher right here, in the blue, hairline crack nothing more, may I have thirty dollars to start this rarity down the road . . .*"

A dour-faced gentleman who'd been hovering around the Pontiac separated himself from the crowd, strode over to where they were sitting, and muttered low in Daniel's ear. Daniel nodded without expression.

"*Magnificent slant-front spool cabinet, count them twenty-four drawers, burled walnut, raised panels, what do I have for this important piece . . .*" The elderly auctioneer spoke with the rising and falling inflections of T. S. Eliot. "*. . . I have a thousand in left field, fair warning at a thousand . . .*" Something about his venerable poet's manner or some magic inherent in auctions themselves produced a very strange effect on the objects offered; pieces which hadn't looked special when she'd examined them earlier, now when auctioned individually, became unique and desirable. "*. . . What am I bid for this little green whimsy, a dollar I have on this little green whimsy, a dollar fifty . . .*" She couldn't believe her ears; you couldn't get a little green whimsy in Woolco's for a buck fifty. "Two dollars," she shouted.

"*Two dollars I have, this is your last chance for happiness, two dollars takes the little green whimsy, number fifty-three.*" She looked at her bidding card: *fifty-three.* Quietly, she asked Daniel, "What's a whimsy?"

"Whatever you want it to be."

"But what's it supposed to be?"

"Just little shapes made from scrap glass."

". . . It must be worth two bucks. Don't you think?"

"At least," he replied, but she could see he wasn't keenly interested in the issue of her little green whimsy. An elderly woman who'd been among the group at the Pontiac made her way over and spoke softly in his ear. Sara noted the lady was heavily bedecked with antique jewelry; her bracelets alone were worth a hundred acres of rural Canada.

". . . *Stuffed bear on wheels, getting older every day, superb condition, will someone start us off at seventy-five . . .*" The lady talking to Daniel lifted her card to bid, as if hardly noticing what she did; after some further bidding, it was announced that she'd bought the bear on wheels, while she continued her murmured discussion with Daniel.

Listening to the lady and to others around her, Sara noticed certain intonations she hadn't heard in a very long time; she was startled to discern correct grammar and worldly references which, in Atlantic Canada, would've been greeted by the same blank stare you'd get if you were talking ancient Phoenician. She felt the sweep of sophistication in the room, an air that seemed to waft her away to Olympus. People, she thought, are wonderful.

The lady slipped off; the auction continued; Sara's eyes roved over faces which seemed, in their elegance and concentration, as old as the antiques being sold; it was a legacy of sensitivity as opposed to the legacy of wrestling and pig farms. With terrifying clarity, she saw the distance between these two world views, and how impossible it was to bridge the gap, much as she and Daniel thought they had. You can't be what you're not, she thought, and the struggle isn't worth it, to deny your cultural background for the sake of a half-felt notion about getting back to the land. Of course, this wasn't New York, it was only New England, and many in the audience had gotten back to the land just as she and Daniel had; but not so *far* back.

She rose to her feet, and slipped outside. In the glow of the parking lot lights, she saw the dour gentleman who'd spoken to Daniel, as well as a short man in a Cossack hat, and the bejeweled elderly lady, all gazing at Daniel's cupboard as at a sacred idol. With a shock she realized this was the granddaddy antique of the evening, momentarily forgetting that the rare holy object had been aged by ammonia, an ice pick, and Murvyle's cigarette butts.

She returned to watch the private auction Daniel was casually holding in his seat. At midnight, the auctioneer was hoarse, and both auctions finished together; as the last *Gone With the Wind* lamp was bidded for and claimed, the braceleted lady handed Daniel a two-thousand-dollar check for the cupboard.

Wearily, Daniel and Sara left the hall. Clutching her little green whimsy, Sara got into her side of the car, and he got into his. "I had a funny feeling," she said, as they drove out of the lot, "that she knew. Do you think she did?"

"Possibly. But she'll sell it for three thousand."

"And it isn't . . . illegal?"

"Did I lie to anybody?"

"I don't know. Did you?"

"I didn't have to." He hummed quietly, driving along the dark highway.

■ ■ ■

"*Some people were saying that spring had come. But I for one was not sure. I'd seen the odd robin, starling, and even some swallows, but still I was not quite convinced. Not until I was out in the yard with the old rake, looking up into the sky. And then I saw it . . .*" The nasal voice on the radio poised his listeners on tenterhooks . . . "*A flight of* Canadian *geese, heading north.*" His tone grew somberly patriotic. "*This sight is one of the finest experiences any man, woman, or child can ever have. This has been Mortimer Astle with comment.*"

The stuffed nose of Mortimer Astle was followed by the lilting *Back to the Bible.*

She put down her brush, and walked downstairs and out to the shed where Daniel was working. "Mortimer Asshole saw a goose," she announced. "We'd better make our plans for escaping the spray."

An old postcard projector set on a chair, projecting a museum photograph on the opposite wall, in full size, of a Shaker case of drawers; Daniel was tracing the projection onto paper pinned to the wall, and Rumpus skulked behind him, dodging his feet, as if to urge nothing but the highest standards of forgery.

"It's occurred to me"—Daniel studied his tracing—"that the best pieces I bought and sold in New York were fakes." His criminal proclivities had ceased to amaze her; his had become almost an above-board operation; each week, he ran an ad in the *Loyalist* offering cash for old furniture broken beyond repair, then used the antique wood for his new creations.

The familiar roar of Hilton's jalopy sounded in the lane; she went to the door to welcome him; he came toward her grinning broadly as if at some private joke between himself and the cat whom he stopped to pat or between himself and the beer he'd just drank; he burped a fragrant hello, and entered the workshop.

"How're you doing?" asked Daniel.

"Not too bad," he modestly admitted.

"Got any work lined up for spring?"

"A feller don't wanna rush into somethin he might think dif'rent of later on. Son of a whore might get a job shovelin shit somewheres. No sir, tain't gonna be easy fer them unemployment boys to get me a job this year," he said with what appeared to be high hopes. "I ain't allowed to drive cause they took me license, so I can't get into town, and there ain't nahthin much a feller can walk to."

"Nobody working back in the woods?"

"Problem with the woods is you gotta own a power saw."

"I thought you had three of them."

"Them's are all Dad's."

"Wouldn't he lend you one?"

"You never can tell about the old man. He might and then he might not." Hilton chewed it over thoughtfully. "Take Bob Skyert's chainsaw fer an example. I was standin with Bob t'other day watchin him work, and he run that chainsaw clear across his boot."

"Kodiaks?" inquired Daniel, stopping his work; she noticed he'd gradually succumbed to the local obsession with boots.

"Fifty-dollar Kodiaks. Bob Skyert he kept on workin, but he says

to me, *My foot is hurtin*. I says, *Let's take yer boot off and see if
there ain't some workman's compensation into her*. Son of a
whore'd sawed two of his toes off. Come right off in his sock. Pretty
near turned me stomach." He sank into torpid silence.

"Bob Skyert?" prompted Sara. "Could they do something for
him? Could they sew his toes back on?"

"We took them toes with us in the car, but son of a whore of a
car of Bob Skyert's, them floorboards are so cracked, the sock with
the toes must've fallen through. Course, a man will drink at a time
like that. I had to have one meself cause of me stomach." Sara
gazed at the stomach under discussion which would require, it appeared, enormous sympathies from nature owing to the size of it.
Hilton belched, wiped his mouth, gestured in a friendly way at the
cat, and took a stroll round the shed, examining Daniel's latest creations; sadly he shook his head. "Pretty crooked work yer doin,
ain't it."

"I guess it is," said Daniel.

"Couldn't you get no better boards than this? Looks like a
porc'pine been chewin on them fer a week."

"He has."

"Yeah, it looked like tooth marks to me. A porc'pine likes the salt
in old wood. Specially old outhouse wood. Took an awful fright
meself in the outhouse t'other night. Thought twas delushun trem-
bles."

"I guess I'll go back to work," said Sara, trying to catch Daniel's
eye, but he was turned to the wall and his tracing. She gave
Rumpus a long look instead: *Don't let him lend Hilton money*.

The cat replied: *It isn't going to be easy*.

■ ■ ■

"Come in fer a bun and a cup of tea," said Murvyle. "It's all
you'll get on a rainy day in life."

He and Phoebe made room at the table, and Sara and Daniel
pulled up two chairs. She glanced toward the lounge, where Hilton's form was imprinted on the empty cushions. "Where's the
duke?"

"Well sir," began Murvyle, about to launch on a lengthy tale;
Phoebe interrupted with a simpler rendition: "In again."

"Jail?"

Phoebe sighed. "I dunno where he got the money fer a spree. He didn't have a dime when he left here."

"Course," said Murvyle, "the lawyer's tellin it dif'rent. Appears Bob Skyert was up to the Legion all doped up on pain pills and Hilton he had to drive Bob's car home fer him. Bob Skyert he took a fit and grub hold of the wheel so Hilton he tried to straighten her out and the next thing you know the two of them was in two foot of water, trailin telephone wire."

"Cut the telephone pole clear in two," added Phoebe. "They say they're gonna make Hilton pay. I say they ain't got no right to make him pay fer a telephone pole."

Sara looked at Daniel, who was guiltily mouthing a biscuit. Murvyle took out tobacco and paper and sought solace in rolling a cigarette.

"I dunno," sighed Phoebe. "I wasn't there."

"Appears," said Murvyle, "nobody really seen zactly what happened."

"No," agreed Phoebe, "you can't tell what happened," the implication being, thought Sara, that perhaps there hadn't been an accident at all, or in any event it was far deeper than it sounded; perhaps Hilton had been framed again by his archenemies, the Mounties.

There was a general round of sighing, including a long one from the dog. "Yes," said Phoebe to Festus, "who's gonna bring yer wieners now?"

At the word *wieners*, Festus's ears cocked. "I suppose," replied Phoebe.

Murvyle tapped cigarette ash in his palm, a sign he was thinking deeply. "He was jes revivin hisself to go in fer a job."

"Can't work now he's in jail," explained Phoebe. Sara found herself picking up Phoebe's worries; she glanced across the table at Daniel and pictured him in a striped uniform, sitting in a cell next to Hilton, the drunk and the forger.

Murvyle rubbed cigarette ash in his boots. "Grampie Amos had a trout, put him in the well house fer to keep the water clean."

"Yes," said Phoebe, "and there's Hilton right now in jail." Sara's mind leapt to make the connection between Hilton and Grampie Amos's trout.

"One evenin," Murvyle continued, "I scooped up some water after dark, and poured it into the tank by the stove. In the middle of the night I woke up and says to meself, *What is that floppin out there in the stove?*"

"Twas the trout," explained Phoebe. "Warmed over."

"So I put him out to the well house again."

"Fed him by hand," said Phoebe. "Twas jes like a pet."

I wonder how long Hilton will be in for this time. Sara glanced at Daniel, who avoided her eyes.

"One time," said Murvyle, "the old man got to thinkin that his old trout might be lonesome, so he caught another trout and put him in the well too."

"The old trout ett him."

"Guess he didn't care much fer company."

"Don't know if he really even cared fer the old man."

"No, he might not've. One time Grampie Amos bent down to sip from the well hole, and got nipped on the lip."

■ ■ ■

"How do we always get trapped?" she wailed.

The spray planes were droning low overhead, their poison vapors falling across the western field.

"You get the suitcases," he wheezed. "I'll get Rumpus."

They raced into the kitchen; her head felt stuffed with cotton. She ran to the stairs where the valises were standing, grabbed them by the handles, and hurried to the door with the heavy bags. As she stumbled out, the cat fled past her, Daniel hard on his heels, and the two figures ran around to the back of the house through the raspberry canes.

She stowed the valises in the back of their truck, then hurried to the corner of the house to catch Rumpus when he emerged from the bushes; overhead, the fighters were circling back with a deafening roar. She crouched to catch the cat, but he darted off to the side, Daniel behind him, and the planes doused them all.

Daniel stopped, gasping for breath. The cat stopped too, eyes wide and wild; she lunged, and Rumpus leapt out of her grasp, tearing into the woods.

"He doesn't want to be moved," said Daniel. "There's nothing we can do."

"We can't leave him."

"The damage is already done."

"I could chase him through the woods."

"He's already been sprayed," wheezed Daniel. "Get into the truck."

"But what'll he eat?"

"Mice. It's what he likes best anyhow."

The planes were circling back a third time. Daniel lunged into the woodpile, and for an instant she thought he'd caught Rumpus, but instead he brought out his ax, which he whirled over his head and hurled at the planes; as if in a slow-motion dream, she watched the ax tumble down, turning and turning against the brilliant blue sky.

■　■　■

The auctioneer was a diminutive lady dressed to match her merchandise, in crisp Victorian shirtwaist with ruffled neckband and billowy skirt; she wore a mass of brooches and chains, and occasionally flirted a fan, as she jollied her audience into paying twice what Sara would expect the antiques were worth.

Sara found herself with sketchpad in lap, doing quick profiles of the lady; she wasn't young, and her honey hair was surely dyed, piled high and escaping in seductive ringlets and wisps, but she was an ageless femme fatale; as she gestured, here at a buxom rolltop desk, there at a swelling bombe dresser, she might have been selling curvaceous slave girls at an erotic carnival; then at times her voice and gestures became those of a revivalist, who could make you believe that Christ and his angels would pop out of the alleged Louis XV armoire, along with a flotilla of French demimondaines. Sara scribbled book jackets; the woman was perfect for period pieces, perfect in fact for half a dozen periods—one part Aimee Semple McPherson, one part Christ in the marketplace, one part actress, one part Gypsy, and one part moxie; she moved with restless energy, and her male assistants who brought out the antiques seemed to be her harem chorus, approaching from the four directions bearing desirable offerings.

A poker-faced dealer murmured in Daniel's ear; Daniel nodded; outside in the parking lot was their truckful of fresh antiquities, around which the pickers and dealers had circled with folded hands.

"*We're used to ball-and-claw pieces,*" the auctioneer was saying

drolly, *"but here's a grotesque little number with hands as well."*
She sat herself down in an antique chair with her own fingers
draped over the macabre oak fingers in such a way that it seemed
she had four hands; yet somehow her cynical mockery, instead of
diminishing the bizarre piece of furniture, made it seem doubly
unique. As the bidding on the chair got under way, Sara slipped
her sketchpad into her bag; entranced and curious as she was, she
felt overloaded with treasure; everything in the auction room was
rococo, gorgeous, ornate; she longed for simplicity, or at least a
breath of fresh air.

Quietly she stepped outside. The old inn, with its turrets and
towers, carried one back to a fabulous era; like a feudal castle on
the hillside, it dominated the rest of the pretty Maine village. She
strolled downhill; the tourist season hadn't begun; few of the shops
were open, and the town probably looked, at this moment in
spring, much as it had a century ago.

The narrow street she strolled on curved along the waterfront in
an arc of gray-weathered houses jutting onto the sun-dazzled bay.
Roses, blooming in profusion, covered the old doll-like gates, and
gray-and-white seagulls glided above the gray-and-white cottages,
filling the morning with their harsh call, the least beautiful of
birdsongs yet the one that most epitomized the eternal to her.

Nautical stores displayed heavy ropes, canvas, and brilliantly
polished brass navigation instruments; a quaint little tea shop was
juxtaposed against a little night spot promising disco madness beginning the Fourth of July; even the most modern boutiques,
selling soft sculpture or Scandinavian cookery, were set in carefully
preserved or restored old storefronts which tastefully blended with
the rest of the scene.

She entered a pink-washed brick building, once a bank and now
a bookstore; for an instant, she was shocked by the atmosphere of
intimacy, then realized the only bookshops she'd been in for years
had been the chain bookstores in malls, managed and staffed by
nonreaders, carrying a prepackaged selection of best sellers, tawdry
romances, and new releases; here, the books had been chosen not
by a sales figure–fed computer, but by a living, breathing, reading
human being. In the center of this intimate display of literate idio-
syncrasy, a great bank safe stood with its iron door open and its
safe-deposit boxes replaced by shelvesful of limited and first edi-
tions with rich leather and gold-tooled bindings; flanking the safe

were a pair of luxurious wing chairs. She sank down into one of them like her heroines erotically swooning, drinking in the culture of the village like ambrosia to her parched soul. Where, she heard herself ask, have I been all these years?

A few other people browsed through the store, men and women whose faces wore a veneer of education, taste, and a spark of something she missed terribly. Years, she realized, it's been years and years since we've spent two whole nights south of Mortimer Asshole with Comment.

Not having her heroine's ubiquitous smelling salts or vinegar, she pulled herself together by rising and walking out the door. But outside, the mystique of the town was equally devastating, from the crying gulls to the quaint narrow streets, the art galleries, the cultured faces, and on the corner—the coup de grâce—a French restaurant.

She threaded her way to the wharf, where a few yachts were moored, manned by worldly looking people in faded jeans. Further out was a fishing boat; and way out, on the horizon, a big freighter slowly moved in the sunlight. The grandeur of the sea combined with the special warmth of the village and its humanity to generate an overwhelming seductiveness.

Leaving the dock, she made her way around the cove, until she found a small isle of rocks sticking out in the foam. A warm wind stirred the air, and the surf lapped at her feet, its little white hands of water reaching up to her, while the the immense restless pulse of the ocean entered her bloodstream; the smell of seaweed flooded her nostrils; book jackets danced on the sunlit waves—*Bermuda Ecstasy, Purple Lagoon, Island Passion* . . . On the deck of one of the yachts a woman appeared, and behind her through the open doorway, Sara could see a cozy living room.

Do people actually live on these boats? Are there people who can change their environment with the lifting of an anchor?

■ ■ ■

She turned away from the disheartening panorama of rolling highway and green endless miles, and gazed at his profile. He might, she thought, look okay in a captain's hat. "Did you ever think about living on a boat?"

"I took sailing lessons once. After which I went out solo, nearly

killed two fishermen, almost sliced a seventy-thousand-dollar
cruiser in half, and ended up being towed in by the coast guard."

Still, the restless pounding of the surf and the little white wave-
hands reaching toward her persisted in her mind, a feeling she now
realized she'd harbored for some time, as if she'd long been
searching for a metaphysical answer, a magic environment.

Is Atlantic Canada my truth? she wondered.

She recalled how they'd circled the new Woolco mall for weeks,
awaiting the grand opening. Could I really have done such a
thing? I spend one day every week in malls, which adds up to fifty-
two days per annum, almost two months out of each year: *I spent
my summer vacation at the K-mart*. Everyplace, she thought,
weaves its web around you, and as if it were a distant temple
flashing in a dark night, she saw in her mind's eye the K-mart, and
perceived she'd been going to it as if it were a place of worship.

Fear passed through her limbs, not the heartbeat-racing kind,
but a bone-heavy dread of being imprisoned by something so subtle she couldn't quite grasp it. "You know that chic little town we
just came from," she asked, "how would you like to live near a
place like that?"

"I'd hate it."

"Why?"

"Because the forest's my teacher."

"Is it necessarily the only teacher?"

"Did you learn a lesson today?"

"All I know is I felt alive in a way I haven't for a long time. I
didn't feel like a Zeller's zombie."

There was silence for several minutes; finally he remarked, "People in that little town go shopping too. Does the type of store really
make a difference?"

"It's not the kind of stores. The stores only reflect the culture of a
place."

"So they keep their liquor in fancier cabinets, but they probably
get just as drunk as Hilton just as often."

She felt her dream turning to stone, her bones getting heavier.
He's permanently fixed.

It was getting toward night, and the dreaded hills were looming
into view, along with the endless, extended, impossibly boring
ranges of woods; she felt like Napoleon's army entering Russia (or

Hitler's, for that matter), marching into the frigid colossus, its vast spaces always retreating, defeating by dint of sheer coldness and size, without a shot being fired, until you bogged down in the mud of Stalingrad.

A truck rolled past, carrying a large load of pulp—a moving cultural exhibit of the province. My God, she thought with horror, I'm going back into it. After only one breath of civilization. "But it isn't enchanted here. It's dreary."

"It's filled with enchantments. You have to know how to see them." Exasperating as his attitude was, she had to admit his enchantments were as bone real for him as her disenchantment.

"What," he asked, "about women who live on communes? How do they make it?"

"They don't. You know perfectly well that those people who keep resettling the Tuner Bog stay on one year, get divorced in spring, and leave. Two years tops for the hardiest. Except for a handful of college teachers who can't get tenure anyplace else, no outsiders have stayed as long as we have. Only the natives can hack it."

"Then I guess I've become a native."

She could think of no answer. But staring at the green expanse of depression up ahead, she suddenly saw a tiny feeling leap out of it . . . a sort of quickening. What *is* it up there, she wondered, I can possibly be looking forward to? Slowly, the tiny leaping feeling took shape . . . the shape of a battered bum-faced orange cat with one leg out. She put her hand on Daniel's; in a gentler voice, she said, "Won't it be good to get home to Rumpus?"

■ ■ ■

"Aren't you going out, Rumpus?"

The cat lay in the rocking chair, his chin on his paws, staring at space.

"You've slept all day."

The cat closed his eyes.

She knelt on the floor. "How can you be so tired? You haven't even been out."

She looked at his untouched dinner. "Did you eat too many mice?"

Rumpus purred beneath her caresses.

"That's it, isn't it? An overdose of mice."

"An overdose of mice," said Daniel standing in the doorway, "doesn't last for a week."

"What else can it be?" she asked nervously.

■ ■ ■

They sat in the waiting room, a cardboard carton beside them, inside of which sat Rumpus with his chin on his paws.

"Who's next?"

Daniel picked up the carton, and she followed him into the examination room.

"What have we here?" asked the vet.

Daniel lifted the cat from the box and set him on the gleaming stainless table. Rumpus's legs slid apart on the smooth surface, and Sara pushed them back together.

"That's a sick cat," said the vet.

"He was caught in the budworm spray."

The doctor frowned, and gripped the cat's front legs; he yanked Rumpus's lower eyelid down. "This cat is anemic."

"I'm afraid he's been poisoned," said Daniel.

"Severe anemia." The vet filled a hypodermic needle with fluid, and jabbed the cat on the thigh. "Vitamin B_{12} and iron." Anemia, thought Sara, thank goodness that's all it is; doctors can cope with anemia.

Rumpus lay splayed and helpless on the slippery table, held down by the doctor's hands. "How old is this cat?"

"We don't know."

The vet pulled Rumpus's lower lip out and studied his teeth; Rumpus flailed his paws, but couldn't catch hold of the table. "Six, maybe seven years old." He pulled the lip down further. "You can see the gum color's poor, anemic gum color. I'd like to keep him here to give him injections of vitamins and antibiotics." He lifted one of Rumpus's paws and examined the pad, shook his head, then grasped the cat round the chest, and carried him through the doorway leading into the back rooms. Rumpus turned and faced them, writhing in the doctor's arms, moving his legs as though running through space.

■ ■ ■

The doctor emerged from the rooms in back, carrying an orange object. "It isn't anemia. I don't know what it is."

Sara stared at the limp little creature.

"He showed some interest in his food this morning," said the doctor.

"Did he eat?"

"No, but at least he showed interest."

"You think he's improved?" She looked at the inert animal; Rumpus met her eyes, and the doctor bustled among his medicines. "Give him a teaspoon of this every four hours." He grabbed the cat by the ruff, jerked his head back, and forced the liquid down his throat. "That's how you do it."

"I see."

"And you must get him to eat. Hand-feed him if necessary. I'm hoping his own environment will stimulate his appetite."

Sara took the bottle of medicine, and wrote a check. Daniel put the cat into the carton, and they carried him out, through the waiting room, onto the street.

They got into the truck, and drove toward home; there was no movement inside the carton.

"I'm not going to force-feed him," said Daniel suddenly. "I'm not going to torture him anymore."

"But Daniel, he'll die."

"Can't you see he's already dying?"

■ ■ ■

Dawn shone through the windows, and she started awake, looking toward the foot of the bed. The cat was still alive; he acknowledged her greeting with one eye. When she examined him closely, she saw the other eye had sunken in so far it was lost in shadow.

He dropped his chin to the floor, and breathed his heavy breathing, watching her with one golden eye as the day wore on. In the afternoon, he gazed toward the door, and they carried him out.

The fox was waiting. Rumpus looked at the big animal without fear, as if knowing how for millions of years this was always the way.

Sara chased the fox, but he didn't run; he walked slowly through the orchard, turning to taunt her with barking jeers. *This is my right*, he seemed to say; *your cat belongs to me now.*

■ ■ ■

She opened her eyes and sat up. In the moonlight, she saw the room was empty.

"Daniel," she called. There was no answer.

She hurried outside in her bathrobe.

His answer came from in back of the clothesline, from the hill going down to the pond. She fumbled her way through the raspberry canes out onto the moon-drenched clearing. Daniel stood looking at the ground, where Rumpus's form was crouched, hunched with his shoulder blades protruding; the cat lurched forward two steps, and paused in his hunched position to gather his strength; after four or five minutes, he plunged forward two more steps.

"What is he doing?" she whispered.

Rumpus rested, then plunged forward again, then rested, and continued inching down the hill in excruciating stages.

"Where is he going?"

He dragged himself along, concentrating on his goal, and she and Daniel followed behind. At the bank of the pond, the cat stopped and lifted his head to stare at the silver shimmering water and sky.

"He's saying good-bye to the night," murmured Daniel.

She didn't reply, but watched the cat gaze at the moon and the glittering stars.

Somewhere in the night, far away, the fox called.

Rumpus stared at the clouds drifting past the moon.

She turned her own face to the sky, and it seemed to be Rumpus's sky, and the pond seemed to be Rumpus, and the whole night.

He maneuvered himself around, and lifted his head toward Daniel. Daniel picked him up, and carried him back to the house.

She knelt down before him, but his sunken eyes gazed past her, and he dragged himself forward across the kitchen floor.

"Where is he going now?" she whispered.

He swung around and tried for the other end of the floor, then turned back in the original direction, getting nowhere; again he turned, torn between all directions, and a phrase glided through her mind, *his profound restlessness.* He collapsed, one haunch bent, and the other leg stretched out behind him. She stroked his back, hardly touching him with her hand as he lay in his awkward position.

Suddenly he straightened his ragged ears. She listened; it was starting to rain. "Just the rain," she murmured, smoothing the cat's head, "the rain on the roof, isn't it pretty?" Rumpus kept his ears up, listening. It's the last time he'll hear rain, she realized.

The cat snaked forward on his swollen belly, and let out a cry, then toppled to his side and repeated the sound. I'll kill him, she thought; I can't let it go on; I'll hit him over the head with something. The third cry was the longest, the cat putting forth all his strength, articulating his sorrow until it sounded like language. She whispered to him, but could tell he no longer heard; he stared unseeing before him, trembling with deep comatose breaths.

A loud rasping breath came from the little body and hit against her nostrils with the odor of poison; it's out of him now, she thought. Another of the breaths convulsed his frame. He lay perfectly still.

She touched his heart, but her own beat so loudly she couldn't tell if his had stopped.

Daniel tipped the cat's head up, and they stared into his eye, whose pupil had spread until it filled the whole eyeball with blackness, a blackness which seemed like the night itself, deep, and scary, and endless.

■　■　■

The grass was icy cold before sunrise, and heavy with dew; only a thin gray light filtered down through the leaves, and she trusted her footsteps to guide her . . . not that there was anyplace to go or any reason to be out before dawn, but she found herself moving through the woods every morning, and every night, and it was somehow connected to the cat, who seemed to move beside her, during his favorite twilight hours, and along his haunts.

Against the raspberry leaves, something sparkled in the sunrise, a pattern of lace flung over the greenery like the finest of cloths; crouching, she examined the dazzling web, newly completed, its perfection unbroken by any passing wind or insect; from each angle the sun's rays made it different, and from certain angles the entire elegant trap was fatally invisible.

With the sun, came the heat and mosquitoes. She heard the flap of wings in the air and the whooshing of feathers; looking up, she saw a black crow flying over the trees, then out above the ravine, floating in empty space, and she felt her mind, like a black crow, hover over the valley. High in the stillness, they floated, she and the crow, the whole vast world within the grasp of their wings and the wind, and as she watched she felt a mouth open in her stomach and swallow the experience and store up the forest at dawn.

A tree with a certain peculiar U-shaped twist to its trunk made her aware that the baby's grave was near; she followed the crow's path to the ledge above the ravine, where in the small spruce clearing, two stones now faced each other.

She sat down on the damp moss, recalling the first year after the child died when she'd been grieving and had walked here each day with Daniel, and Rumpus had come with them. Leaning her back against the rough bark of the tree, she gazed at the stones and listened to the silence and accepted that this was her home, this forest which, finally, mysteriously, she'd come to feel connected with viscerally, perhaps because of the peculiar hours of her stalking, the inhuman eerie quality of nighttime and dawn; and I suppose, she thought, this is how Daniel always feels.

A crashing sound from the ravine brought her scrambling to her feet. She looked across, and saw a huge creature emerge through the brush on the opposite shore and then, behind the giant, a smaller splindlier version; it took a moment before she realized they were moose. The mother's movements radiated physical power and thoughtfulness; she led her calf through the forest with absolute understanding, as if it were the most familiar aisle of the K-mart and she and the calf were munching the day's choice bargains.

Except, thought Sara, they don't have to carry the bargains home. Their entire scene moves with them—house, land, plumbing, stove; all they own is their naked bodies, and they wander unencumbered wherever they want, with no home to get back to or get away from; the entire immense forest is theirs, and they know it better than any lumberjack or biologist; their woodland knowledge is so refined, if they were human, they'd be considered great minds.

With massive aplomb, the two animals splashed into the stream, bent their huge necks, and drank. The sun, rising gold in the east, touched their chestnut flanks, and she felt the little mouth in her stomach opening and closing over the awkward calf and its mother.

■ ■ ■

"Aye," said Murvyle, rolling a cigarette, "put you or me out in the woods, we'd either starve to death or freeze or eat poison, whichsoever took us first."

"An animal knows," agreed Phoebe, in that tone that made you wonder what incredible marvels she'd witnessed which you'd never find out about.

From behind the stove on the lounge came a muttered "son of a whore," from Hilton, who'd gotten out of jail that morning.

■ ■ ■

The moon . . . the nighthawk's Bronx cheer . . . and then something weird; the nighthawk landed quite close in a tree, and sat there staring at her. He was a plump-faced individual with what appeared to be a set of whiskers, and he stared at her curiously, sitting comfortably on the branch above her, with the moon beyond his shoulder like a reading lamp.

She moved a few steps down the hill; the bird rose in the air and followed, settling on the next branch to continue his investigations. He definitely had whiskers—tiny bristles around his beak—and was definitely, in his own peculiar dimension, taking mental notes. In a funny way, the oddball nighthawk was a comfort; one didn't feel so desperately alone as a human being when there were other creatures around with curiosities similar to one's own. She eyed the nighthawk; the nighthawk eyed her; and eventually the bird stared her down. She pulled away, and walked down to the pond, where the yellow moonlight spilling on the clearing made the circle of water shine like a flying saucer, a magic disc gleaming in the field.

The calls of the frogs, which had stopped when she first appeared, as the conversations of gossips stop when you enter a room, soon resumed, a *ga-lunk* on one side, then on the other, and third from the middle, question, answer, and comment.

The moonlight's yellow sheen on the water, like a beautiful mir-

ror, and the frogs cooling themselves in the weeds . . . surely, she
thought, since they live inside this thing, frogs must be aware of its
extraordinary quality; more aware than we.

Ga-lunk, ga-lunk.

She recalled one dawn seeing a frog in labor, a labor which continued for hours, with the frog panting, almost expiring, a web of
her own secretions stretched from legs to ears like some strange
chamber of pain, and as the frog labored on the bank, inside the
pond another frog swam steadily back and forth in front of her;
was it curiosity, Sara wondered, coincidence, concern, connubial
love? Another dawn, she'd seen a frog being eaten by a snake, and
after a certain point, when the frog's skin was pierced, whether he
was poisoned or drugged, he stopped his struggling, and a look of
acceptance crossed his face, remaining there hour after hour, as his
body was slowly, terribly ingested, a fraction of an inch at a time,
becoming food for another, as luckless dragonflies had been food
for him; and the frog's look of acceptance was like that of Rumpus
when he hadn't fled the fox whom he'd outrun so often in the past,
once he saw death was his destiny.

It seemed, as she stood in the moonlight, listening to the conversation of frogs, that she was emerging from a pit of ignorance and
pride, a sort of blindness, and that had been her restlessness.

■ ■ ■

The stars shone through the glass; night's sounds came in
through the screen; she sat in her chair at the screen door, staring
out and listening, experiencing it all through the veil of the house.

But the magic lure was gone.

Something was still out there, speaking, beautiful . . . the
crickets passed their message down the line from one to the other;
she felt the message come closer, felt it being picked up by a
nearer cricket, felt it get to her, and stop; she didn't pick it up. She
didn't go out. A nighthawk called, and she didn't answer.

Daniel glanced up from his reading. "Not going out tonight?"

"No."

It was over. Its motivating force had been spent, and she felt
regret, but what was the use? You can't control a frame of mind.
She saw—now that it was fading—the state of grace she'd been in
was a gift of the wild which Rumpus had given her when he died,

an animal present of appreciation and perception, a present of a certain duration and size, which she'd used up.

So now I'm on my own again. And I simply don't have the desire to go out in the night; nor to walk before sunrise; yet when it was going on, I thought it would continue for the rest of my life.

7

"Tea," declared Murvyle, "is the stem of life."

Daniel drew up his chair and accepted a cup; Hilton gazed at his father with an expression which said, *The old man's into his stories again,* hiccuped, and lay down on the cot in back of the stove.

". . . We thought," said Murvyle, "we seen the tail-end of Uncle Burpee. We carried him to the ambulance, him moanin and cryin *Why me? Why me?,* and I cal'ate the Powers That Be, hearin Burpee pose the question, got to wonderin the selfsame thing. What in hell, they must've wondered, do we want with this no-good old bastard?"

"Yes," said Phoebe, "and since then, Uncle Burpee's buried wife and six children, but it surely seems he ain't never gonna die hisself."

Daniel munched bread and peanut butter. "How old exactly is Uncle Burpee?"

"All I can tell you is he was the first man in the county to draw the pension, and likely he'll be the last. Since old Burpee made his pact with the Powers, he appears to keep growin stronger."

"Twas really that doctor's fault," said Phoebe, "perscribin beer fer Burpee's cons'tution."

"Before his stroke," explained Murvyle, "Burpee didn't drink no beer, bein the most religious person fer miles, but once he got the medical seal, it give him a new lease on life."

Phoebe sighed. "Aside from makin him piss his bed and hastenin poor Aunt Edwitha to her grave."

"He's still the most religious person fer quite a distance," Murvyle admitted, "but there's been spirits added to his religion."

"Son of a whore's too contrary to die is all," came a voice from the lounge.

"Did you ever hear tell of a person stoppin the clock?" asked Murvyle. "Old Burpee's stopped two or three clocks. That's why he wears so goddamn many watches. They'd go fine on anyone else, but they won't go more'n an hour on Burpee, so he wears three and if two run down, he can reset from t'other. But he has to be fast on his feet in order to catch them before they all stop."

Daniel set down his cup, knowing he'd just heard a parable on life which he couldn't understand. He looked across the table at Murvyle; Murvyle gummed a molasses cookie. "Yup," he said, glancing at Daniel like a bright-eyed old bird who knows a secret he isn't going to fully share, because the secret is too twisted and ineffable to be defined by a sound more specific than the gumming of a cookie.

The long thoughtful silence was broken by the sound of the lounge springs and Hilton rising laboriously to upright position. "Christly fuckin liquor strike," he said with feeling.

Phoebe sighed. "They say it'll last all summer and through to Thanksgivin."

Hilton smiled slyly. "I ain't goin dry."

"No, Hilton ain't goin dry," said Murvyle, rolling a cigarette. " 'Cept he's payin ten dollar fer a six-pack of beer."

"Better than drinkin some goddamn shoe polish."

"Shoe polish?" inquired Daniel.

"Yer right, shoe polish. Son of a whore at work today fell off the scaffold from shoe polish. Fell off drunk and singin both. Catch me up on no Jesus scaffold!" Hilton stared at the three of them as if daring them to say different; Daniel well recalled the traumatic winter Hilton fell off the roof shoveling ice, the result being he hadn't climbed anything higher than the lounge since.

"Old Burpee was alluys drummin up work fer hisself," said Murvyle, picking up the thread which had been dangling in his brain. "He'd say the school needed a new set of steps, or a new footin course, or chimbley repair, or whatsoever . . ."

"You know what I'll do they try and make me go up onto that fuckin scaffold?"

"Burpee alluys worked slow, but even so, the time did come where there wasn't nahthin more he could drum up fer the schoolhouse. It had a new door. New winders. New sidin. New footin course. Rebricked chimbley. Painted inside and out. His and Hers outhouse. So at the next school meetin, Burpee give a little speech,

sayin the trouble with the children was they daydreamed out of
them winders. Then he suggested if they could hire somebody to
take out them winders and board them in good and tight, the children would commence to learn."

"I'll tell them I won't do it." Hilton jerked his head several times
to reinforce his surprisingly mild position.

"The other members got perturbed cause they jes got done payin
fer them new winders, but Burpee argued till they fell asleep and
then he voted hisself the job, and that is how we come to be the
only settlement you'll ever see with a schoolhouse ain't got no
winders."

"And," asked Daniel, "did the children commence to learn?"

"That has never been proved. Twas the very next year the
gov'ment closed all them old one-room schools as part of the Equal
'Tunity Act. Which was okay with Burpee, because by that time
they'd started the old-age pension." Murvyle puffed his cigarette.
"That's how life fits together. The Equal 'Tunity Act, old Burpee's
pension, and his last job onto the schoolhouse."

Phoebe sighed. "The settlement did have quite a hard time sellin
it though, due to lack of winders."

"In the end, some poor family paid fifty dollar. But they could
not abide the air inside." Murvyle stubbed out his butt. "So there
she stands. Empty on the corner. More or less a testament to the
old days."

■ ■ ■

The sunset followed him into the village, shedding its rosy rays
on picture-postcard houses nestled in hollyhocks, perennial borders,
potato blossoms, and burpless cucumber vines. In the midst of the
slumbering scene, one building stood out, one structure raged
against the pastel hollyhocks and protested against the burpless cu-
cumbers struggling to grow at its base; this monstrous facade was
the front of Pike's white clapboard farmhouse, colorfully covered
by a mural of mind-jelling violence.

Daniel turned his truck into the driveway, parking in the shadow
of the great work, which was creeping menacingly around the side
of the porch like the paws of a vast hulking creature, in a horrific
triptych of beast against man, man against beast, machine against
man, and all three against women and children.

Daniel knocked on the kitchen door; within, the lights went out, and a shadowy figure moved with suspicion from window to window.

"Come in, come in," muttered Pike conspiratorially, quickly closing the door behind them.

The light went up on an interior in which every square inch of wall space, each flat surface of furniture, and all available implements were vividly painted with portraits of carnage. "Better have some tea," warned the artist.

"How've you been?"

Pike replied with a mysterious sideways movement of the jaw, indicating there was plenty to tell, but first there were defenses which had to be tightened; teapot and two chipped mugs were slammed on the table.

Safely seated opposite Daniel, drinking tea so strong it made Daniel's eyes water, Pike tilted his red beret, narrowed his eyes, and asked, "How's that new family moved in up Jerusalem?" He gazed at Daniel as at an innocent lamb in a den of wolves, and Daniel felt the beginnings of anxiety. Clearly the arrival of the new family in Jerusalem was endangering his life; he wasn't yet sure how, but that made it only the more threatening.

With a sudden upward motion, Pike struck a match on his cardigan zipper, giving the illusion of pulling flames of wrath from his heart. "Oily black Cheekoslovakian bastard."

"Are the Glinkos Cheekoslovakian? I thought they were Gypsies."

"Whatever in hell they are, they're no good."

"But what have they done?"

"I'll tell you what they done. Number one, who took all the tools out of that there bullnozer parked up on the hill? Number two, one of them old camps was busted into and they didn't take nahthin but bullets. If they're lookin fer a fight, by Jesus, they'll get one from me. Number three, who took the battery out of yer half-ton?"

"Glinko?"

"Yer goddamn right Glinko. You better watch yer step out there. Take a rifle along with you this evenin. Take a bear trap too. Set it right at the head of yer lane."

Daniel lifted his head from his bitter tea, and met, on Pike's walls, several human figures captured in just such arrangements—suspicious swarthy strangers thrashing their life away in bear traps laid in Pike's picture-postcard lands of horror. "Have you sold any paintings lately?"

"A Jew from town come here. Offered me fifty dollar. He says he'll be back fer more," Pike added, in a tone implying that what he and the imaginary Jew were trafficking in wasn't art, but some illegal unnamable substance, possibly to be used in a plot to overthrow the government. Pike's racial slurs were not always denigrating; on the contrary, he identified strongly with the Israeli army, whom he admired for their aggression in the midst of outnumbering hostile forces, a situation he believed to be identical to his own. "All the same, don't you go trustin no Glinko. That lad would steal the teeth off a dog."

"Which lad is the bad one?"

"Ain't none of them any fuckin good. Old man's supposed to be a bricklayer, only thing he ever laid was his hat on a chair. Whole family's a bunch of goddamn criminals and they ought to be persecuted." He means prosecuted, thought Daniel; at least I hope so.

■   ■   ■

The alcove in the trees gave him clear range of vision up and down the stream without allowing him to be seen. There were a lot of fish in this pool and sometimes one fish in particular with whom he felt a special affinity; often he'd wait for hours, wondering why he wasted his time, but it was always faintly thrilling to catch sight of the enormous trout—the venerable citizen of the stream who'd managed to escape so many years of Sunday fishermen.

He turned, and saw a swarthy figure fishing his way downstream. Daniel smiled at his own invisibility; if he'd set a bear trap, he'd have Glinko thrashing in the water right now. The lad in question looked up; his eyes found Daniel with only a flicker of surprise, as if he'd been expecting ambush as a matter of course. He continued casting downstream, and then walked over to where Daniel was hiding.

"Nice spot here," said Daniel.

Glinko set his creel on the bank and sat down beside it. "It's a lot better than jail."

"Been in recently?"

"Out a couple of months," said the lad, with the faintest trace of another sort of accent mixed in with his Provincialese. "Spent a whole year in the fuckin place."

"What were you in for?"

"Weed."

Glinko began the ritual of rolling a cigarette, while Daniel found himself pondering what it would be like to turn on with Glinko, and the vision made him sense the wide gulf between them which no amount of weed would close, would in fact make yawningly wider; meeting Glinko's eyes, he felt to his core that here was a friend you couldn't trust, and yet this same aspect, Glinko's fugitive quality, made him feel in fundamental rapport with the Gypsy.

"First thing I done when I got out," said Glinko, "was go over to the cafeteria and score a bag of grass. Ten minutes after I got out of jail. Then I went up to the gov'ment store and bought a case of Moosehead. Comin out of the store, I see a cop car with the constable that arrested me and the bastard who runs the fuckin jail. I give them a big wave. They smile back and say, *Glinko, where're you goin?* I says, *I'm goin to the woods to get drunk.* They laugh and say, *What've you got in the paper bag? Pound of grass,* I say, and walked on by them."

Looking from Glinko's face to the passing stream flowing so freely, Daniel wondered whether Glinko actually felt he belonged in jail, or simply took little care to cover his tracks because he knew that when his time came to go in again, he would go, no matter what he had in his paper bag; either way, Glinko's demeanor was fatalistic in the extreme, and lent a gravity to his presence not found in other country people, who didn't usually perceive themselves as hunted. Glinko leaned back in the grass, tossing his match into the water. "I likes peace and quiet much as the next feller. You take that party I gave when I had my own room in town. One of the fellers was actin the fool, so I shot him in the leg. That shut him up in a hurry. Oh, I likes peace and quiet."

Daniel made an effort to maintain peace and quiet. Then to solidify his position: "I'm the same way myself."

"My brother now," said Glinko, "he's crazier'n hell. Tetched in the head. Liable to shoot anybody."

Daniel peered peacefully and quietly upstream. "Where's your brother today?"

"In town. Buyin us a suitcase full of weed."

"That's a lot of weed."

"I'll deal any amount of weed." He puffed on his cigarette, coughing a blue stream into the sky. "But I won't deal chemical. The chemical in this town's no fuckin good. I seen a man pretty near die from the chemical in this town." It crossed Daniel's mind that perhaps he should buy some weed from Glinko seeing as he was shortly going to have a suitcase full of it. But do I, he asked himself, want to enter into a business relationship with the Family Glinko? Do I want a Glinko, perhaps, knocking at my door when I'm not home? And how would Sara take to the Brothers Glinko? He knew immediately what would ensue; their swarthy criminal faces would begin to appear on book jackets, threatening the chastity of timorous maidens in billowing gowns. Do I want this? Do I want the Glinkos posing in Sara's studio, stoned, drunk, tetched, and shooting up the plaster?

Glinko glanced at him with a friendly smile. "You need any work done on that half-ton of yours, you tell me." Daniel reflected that if Pike's story were true, Glinko had already done some work on the half-ton, having removed battery of same. "Fer I have the tool," said Glinko, "I got seven-hundred-fifty-dollar worth of tool," naming the exact value of tools recently stolen from the bullnozer on the hill. "Yessir, I got tool."

"Where'd you get the tool?" asked Daniel.

"Been buyin them one at a time over the years." He gave Daniel a look of curiosity as if wondering how much his neighbor by the stream would believe. "A little bit out of each paycheck."

"That's the way to do it," said Daniel, peacefully and quietly, "a little bit at a time."

Glinko flipped his cigarette butt into the brook. "They won't take me the next time."

"Who won't take you the next time?"

"The Mounties. Fer I have ammunition up at the house," and he named the precise caliber of bullets stolen from the camp. "I got a sawed-off shotgun too. And I'll blow a Mountie's fuckin head off if he comes in the door after me, cause I'm a three-time loser, and if I go to jail one more time, I'll be in the rest of me life." He spoke softly, staring at the stream as if perceiving there the inevitable flow of events which would carry him back to jail.

"You should be very careful what you do."

"If it ain't one thing it's another," said Glinko. "Did you say you wanted to buy some weed?"

". . . No, I'm trying to stay away from weed. And chemical too."

"I don't deal no chemical," said Glinko quickly.

"Maybe you shouldn't deal weed either."

"I can't get no other work." He shifted his weight comfortably. "What I like to do most is fish this stream. That's what I like to do most in the whole world. I been all the way to the mouth of this brook. I know every inch of her."

They sat in silence, staring at the water and the big rock in the center of it. Daniel saw the huge old trout peek out and dart around the rock; Glinko quietly picked up his pole, and cast lightly into the pool. "One of these days I'm gonna catch that feller."

■ ■ ■

"Wanna see somethin pretty?" called Murvyle from his car. "Come down to the house and bring Sara." He started to drive away. "Festus caught a young fox in the dooryard."

"I hope this isn't going to be gruesome," said Sara, as she climbed into the truck.

"It didn't sound gruesome." But he knew what she meant. Often on the road between the two houses, he'd pass a dead porcupine and the marks of Hilton's tires, swerving, obviously having gone out of the way to run down the animal. Even Murvyle's tales sometimes smacked of brutality, like the one about the time he ran out of bullets and hacked a deer to death with his ax. Daniel secretly knew his admiration for country people was supported by some harmless myth-making on his part; he viewed them through the kind of lens used to photograph aging movie queens, gently smeared with Vaseline to hide the wrinkles.

They bounced along over the dusty road; in the back of the truck, some chains, a few logs, and assorted broken furniture parts rattled around. He turned at the top of Murvyle's hill, and made for the old farm; Murvyle, Hilton, and Phoebe were gathered in front of the house; Daniel parked at the barn and stepped down.

"Festus caught hisself a fox," bellowed Phoebe, in her hog-calling voice which always had such a shattering effect coming from that dainty lady.

Festus was chained to the woodshed, where he strained to get free, ears up, mouth slavering; a wee timorous beastie was cowering in the dooryard.

"Why doesn't he run away?"

"Festus bit his back leg."

"Still, you'd think he could limp off," said Phoebe, while the little fox sat by the corner of the house, burrowing himself into the grass and looking sad.

"We was jes eatin supper," said Hilton.

Festus let out a howl, pulling against his leash. The fox replied with a small woofing sound.

"Head fer the woods," Murvyle advised the young fox.

Hilton disappeared into the shed, and reappeared with a snow shovel, with which he tried to shovel the fox like a chunk of wet snow; but the animal wouldn't let the shovel get between his bottom and the earth; he bared small needlelike teeth. Hilton jumped drunkenly back. "Son of a whore tried to bite me!"

Sara went into the shed, and came out with the rake. It looked to Daniel like an interesting idea, but the fox refused to be raked.

Phoebe brought a buttered bun from the kitchen, and Hilton brought out what was apparently his interrupted supper, which he flung at the animal with a volley of oaths; the fox sat on the grass, bun on one side, meat on the other, and woofed.

"I never seen such cowards," said Murvyle, approaching the beast with a burlap sack.

"You ain't gonna put him in that?" shouted Hilton. "Did you see the son of a whore's fuckin teeth?"

Murvyle hesitated with his sack; Daniel could see the old man's courage vying with his assessment of the situation. "Wait a minute, Murvyle," said Daniel. "Phoebe, have you got a washpan?"

"You can use me old one."

He went into the shed and took the washbasin off the wall. Quietly he approached the quivering creature, who crouched further into its corner; Daniel crept toward him with the overturned basin, leaned forward, reached swiftly out, and dropped it lightly over the animal.

"I said me *old* washpan." Pheobe's voice was woeful. "That's me new one." Within the overturned galvanized chamber, the young fox, for the moment, was speechless.

"Look at his tail," said Sara; the tail stuck out from under like a twitching red-and-white plume. "Broom it in," Murvyle advised. Hilton swept the tail under the washpan with a surprisingly expert stroke for a man three sheets to the wind on vanilla extract, aftershave, shoe polish, and whatever else was giving comfort this long, dry, liquor-strike summer.

Murvyle sawed off a piece of plywood about washbasin size, and slid it under the pan; the fox inside scurried away from the oncoming board, but each time he lifted his paws, the board had space to slide further, until the creature was firmly boxed; then Murvyle tied the package with rope. "As nice as if he come from Sears," said Phoebe.

The three men carried the package to Daniel's truck, the washpan reverberating with fox protests, while Festus gazed reproachfully at the disappearance of his rightful dessert of fox liver.

Daniel drove the truck up the road, heading toward a grown-over trail which he hoped was out of the dog's roaming range. "Not yet," said Murvyle. They bounced further along through logging roads. "Stop here," said the old man, rubbing his head and scratching his ass, a keen indication he was giving the cream of his wits to the matter.

They stepped out of the truck, and took the fox package down from the back. "Over that there knoll"—Murvyle pointed—"used t'be a creek. An animal oughtta be near water when he's doctorin." Hilton guffawed enigmatically, perhaps thinking an animal in any condition ought to be near something stronger than water. He and Daniel each lifted an end of the plywood, bearing the fox through the woods in its upside-down washpan as if the animal were an emperor in a glass-enclosed palanquin. "Son of a whore don't weigh much, do he."

"Set her down here," said Murvyle, at a place with moss and trees and hollow logs for a fox to hide in a dozen yards above the creek. They set down the tub, Murvyle untied the twine and lifted the lid; the little fox snarled up at them.

Then he looked around, saw he was safe in the woods, nowhere near Festus, and limped down the path to the creek as if he'd always lived there; he turned only once to give a last menacing woof of bravado, and for an instant his small slanting face looked exactly like Glinko's.

■ ■ ■

"I like to talk to people," said Orvis, who'd been talking straight all the way to the meeting. "That's what I alluys look fer in town, people I know, so I can talk to them."

Murvyle steered up the drive to the meetinghouse.

Orvis said, "I'll talk to anyone. I'll talk to perfect strangers in town, if I don't run into someone I know."

"What," asked Daniel, "do you talk to strangers about?"

"The weather. I might say *Nice day.* Then they'll say *Nice day.* Then you'll talk back and forth and pretty soon you'll have somethin in common."

Murvyle parked, and they got out of the car.

"Course," said Orvis, "there are some people will turn their head away."

They brushed the snow off their boots with a broom, and entered the meetinghouse.

"Howdy, Murvyle," wheezed a rheumy old party.

"Howdy, Judge."

"Howdy, Orvis."

Daniel'd always thought of the Christmas Tree Growers' Association as Murvyle's club, much as one might think of an Englishman's club, and had therefore been quite honored to receive a mimeographed invitation in the mail, personally addressed to him as a substantial woodlot owner.

"Howdy, Orvis."

"Howdy, Virgil."

"Hello, Murvyle."

"Evenin, Royden."

"Howdy, Hickey."

"Howdy, Edsel."

"Howdy, Lucius."

"Evenin, Hiram."

"Evenin, Culver."

"Howdy, Pious."

"Evenin, Elroy."

"Howdy, Nackles."

In comradely fashion, the members of the Christmas Tree Growers' Association greeted one another and shuffled into their seats. Daniel was pleased to see that Murvyle's club consisted of a rare collection of gnarled old codgers, most of whom looked like venerable Christmas trees themselves.

The big room smelled of tobacco and pine and old tweed Murphy pants, a pleasant if strong ambrosia. He took his seat beside Murvyle and Orvis, and the members settled in, rolling themselves cigarettes and lighting up for business.

The president moved to the front of the room, a big unhurried gentleman with cap tilted back, jacket patched in wild abandon, hands in pockets, and belly hanging over split-open waistband. "Well, boys," he began; and those were the last two words Daniel caught of the speech, because, after that, old Edsel appeared to mutter in another language, or as if his mouth were stuffed with pine cones. The other members seemed to understand him perfectly; they chuckled at the occasional incomprehensible joke, along with Edsel himself; and finally Daniel began to wonder if perhaps the business jargon of Christmas trees wasn't too recondite for the ordinary layman; or was it just that Edsel wasn't wearing his uppers.

The room grew chilly. Edsel went over to feed the stove, showing the clubmen his broad back as he flung in a huge chunk of wood. He had the true countryman's touch with a fire; the stick he hurled into the stove was so green you could see sap running, but in Edsel's hand, the green stick exploded like napalm.

"That there's an Indian fire," one of the other old codgers remarked. "All smoke and no flame." If that, thought Daniel, is all smoke and no flame, what kind of conflagration must *he* have in *his* parlor stove?

The room began to warm appreciably, and as it did, Daniel noticed that Orvis was beginning to bloom with the bouquet of pig shit. As the room rose another five degrees to a cozy seventy, the pig farmer's clothes began to put forth an aroma of such intensity that Daniel's nose started to run. And, he wondered, if the noxious qualities are so potent to someone alongside Orvis, what must they be to Orvis himself, who's not just sitting in the middle of it but oozing it from his very pores. Glancing at his fellow clubman, Daniel perceived for the first time that Orvis's fat pink face looked like nothing so much as that of a friendly pig, obliviously smiling at old Edsel's garbled bon mots about Christmas trees.

Daniel glanced at Murvyle, whose head was cricked far to the right, upwind of Orvis. Daniel raised his hand across his own face, trying to casually block his nose and breathe through his mouth, but this merely opened the door to the taste of pig shit, which if anything was worse than the smell.

What must life be like in Orvis's home, he wondered, where everything tastes of pig shit, smells of pig shit, and the wallpaper and rugs themselves are imbued with it?

In the front of the room, Edsel continued to mumble, and hurled another stick of green wood in the fire, which swelled the fumes to mustard gas proportions. What if I have an asthma attack? wondered Daniel fearfully, but knew he couldn't show signs of weakness in the presence of all these backwoodsmen.

In his incomprehensible monologue, Edsel must've mentioned something about a break, because the members of the Christmas Tree Growers' Association, en masse, filed to the back of the room with their dinner pails and proceeded to eat and tell stories. After which, they all returned to their seats, but not their original ones. To a man, every club member went and sat on the opposite side of the room from Orvis.

Daniel looked at Murvyle. Murvyle alone assumed his seat beside Orvis, and Daniel knew he couldn't desert his friends. With a sickening feeling, he took his place beside the pig farmer, who was still smiling fatly, pinkly, beatifically.

∎ ∎ ∎

"That smell'll be in this car fer two weeks," said Murvyle, after dropping Orvis off at his home-cum-piggery.

"It was pretty strong," agreed Daniel, rolling down the window.

"Cruel is what twas."

"How does Orvis's family live with it?"

"Tain't easy. Now you take Orvis's wife. She used to work in town, had a nice job in an office. But after them pigs come, they fired her. Didn't wanna. She was a good worker. But them other girls couldn't take it. *Gimme another chance,* she told them. *I'll get some new clothes.* And she did. But inside of one day . . ."

"Not one day," Daniel protested.

"Inside of one day," reemphasized Murvyle, "them new clothes stunk the same as pig shit. Twas in her hair. Twas in the bark of her skin. Appeared to cling to her anyways."

"You wonder whether it's worth it."

"They pay good money, them pigs." From Murvyle's tone of voice, Daniel realized that Murvyle, and probably every countryman in the province, had considered a government-supported piggery, stink or no, wife or no.

She could tell it was well below zero because her teeth were snapping, a kind of pop around the dog teeth; her nostrils had contracted and she had to breathe through her mouth; if you stood still for more than a couple of minutes, you'd be preserved in ice like Walt Disney.

This, she thought in anguish, is normal weather up here. Slugging along the narrow sidewalk, among the uncomplaining, long-suffering, numb-with-cold citizenry, bundled with mufflers up to gray-blue lips, which exuded steam as if each person were a small machine puffing up or down Main Street, she wondered why she put up with it. Was it for such consolations as the art store on the corner whose main business was potato-fermenting equipment? Or was it for the colorful street experience of mingling with the living dead, who shuffled apathetically from one consumer nightmare to the next, with no apparent interest in anything; even consumerism seemed just a dull opiate that bored them. Trudging past the art-brewery shop, her restlessness came on full tilt again.

A fashionable-length coat and a pair of boots she hadn't seen in the local Woolco moved into her line of vision. Her eyes traveled up from the stylish boots past the fashionable-length coat to the face of a woman who was staring back at her with a look Sara had gotten to know well, a gaze of despairing hope. *Could it be?* asked the woman's eyes. *Is it really another emigré from culture?*

They passed on the cold blustery street, Sara knowing it was hopeless; for one thing there was no place to meet, no facade to reflect an artistic soul, no spot where you weren't bludgeoned under by five-and-dime store loudspeakers or bustled along by the herds of Neanderthals. She felt sorry for the woman, one of those rare beings in the area with some yearning to share and grow.

But what about me? Didn't I used to have the same pathetic look in my eyes?

She knew that the woman in the fashionable-length coat simply hadn't been in the province very long; that was why the woman still had some faint hope left to break the mind-paralyzing loneliness.

Sara's wind-embattled trudge got heavier. The dreadful thing was you knew the place would never blossom. Geography, climate, and history were against it. The lethargy was too heavy, and that, not any imperfection of genes, was what gave the Neanderthal cast to the people.

It will never blossom, never change . . . She knew she'd already penetrated all the unknowns of the place; there was nothing left, and there never would be anything. Daniel kept telling her the unknown is everywhere, but she had to accept the fact that she wasn't a mystic; she needed stimulation on less subtle planes.

At times, she thought, plowing past the farmers' bank with the feet painted on the floor, it seemed as if the people were under a spell, like so many iron filings being pulled in a stolid stream through the doors of Zeller's. She felt the curse in herself too, the cold lethargy. I'm middle-aged, I'm not doing anything, I'm not seeing anything, I'm not learning anything, I'm not growing. This place has turned my husband into a criminal, and I'm rapidly deteriorating into a soggy, heavy, indigestible country donut.

At the thought of the donut she would soon eat, her spirits lifted. As she walked through the doorway into the cultural center of the city, as she moved through the heat of K-mart goods and goods-buying zombies, toward the back of the store and the Fiesta Restauranteria, she felt that same old little high. And to compound the horror, it didn't feel merely oral, but spiritual as well. A transcendental piece of K-mart pie, I must be out of my mind, she thought, as she got on the cafeteria line, alongside the showcase of baloneys.

Behind the steam trays, the girls met the world with a gross stare, flinging French fries, stirring canned peas; not only didn't they care what they dumped on your plate, but they didn't to all appearances care about anything. Sara longed for the fierce hostility of New York waitresses, because at least it was alive, it said, *I'm being used, go fuck yourself.* But these girls had been so bludgeoned by the dullness of their environment that their eyes were utterly cowlike, without the lovely velvety contentment of cows, only the blank heaviness. A twinge of fear cut through her numbness; one of her art directors had been recently fired and replaced by a total question mark who might never give her another strong-willed-but-a-slave-to-her-senses historical romance again. I may wind up working at a K-mart steam tray.

I believe I'm undergoing a nervous breakdown.

She took her pie to the table.

From a nearby table, conversation drifted her way.

"*You know how wonderful Mum is. I mean I can't help missing Mum. Mum is so special . . .*" Mum, Mum, Mum, thought Sara, seeing a mental picture of a jar of Mum's deodorant. That, she thought, is definitely crazy. Who would miss a jar of deodorant? I must be delirious with boredom to think such a thing. In fact, she realized, seeing the deodorant jar again in her mind as the woman at the next table continued her eulogy to Mum, I'm hallucinating.

The Mum jar gradually faded, but now she found herself blinking at the Restauranteria wallpaper, whose design consisted of a completely innocent geometric sprinkling of tiny teapots. But there was something about those teapots . . . maybe it was the vomit-toned color combination, or perhaps the inane and frenetic spottiness of the pattern. The deeper she looked, the tauter she felt her brain stretch, to the point where it would explode; and the tiny teapot wallpaper which was so torturing her wasn't merely hideous in design and color scheme, but symbolized, epitomized, the unendurable fact that she was stranded hundreds of miles away from anything the least bit tasteful.

Simultaneously with this sickening realization, a second trauma washed over her—the disappointment of the truly shitty plastic pie and polyfoam tea.

In gut-desperation, she got to her feet and, for the first time in her life, left a piece of pastry uneaten. She fled the Fiesta Restauranteria, bumbled her way up the Aisle of Values, out through the doorway, onto the tooth-snapping agony of Main Street.

■ ■ ■

"It's been three days now," said Murvyle, "since Hilton come home to change into his good brown pants and teensy little shoes."

"We asked," said Phoebe, "but nobody knows. Cause nobody

ain't seen him. They ain't seen him up to the Legion. They ain't seen him down to the village. They ain't heard him talkin over the CB." Sara's gaze went to Hilton's photograph on the wall—the dazed drunken leer, shirt buttons burst, fly safety pinned. "He'll freeze his ass off," predicted Phoebe, "in them thin pants and them thin teensy shoes."

"If I thought this time he'd get shackled up fer good"—Murvyle winked—"I'd buy him a new pair of boots and her a new pair too."

The woodstove crackled; Sara felt the familiar security of this welcoming kitchen, of Murvyle and Phoebe's warmth; the exciting news about Hilton slowly soothed her K-mart–frazzled nerve endings. Wouldn't it be wonderful if Hilton found love?

"Betimes," sighed Phoebe, "a person gives up hope. Bachelors run strong in the McGivneys."

"Old maids too," agreed Murvyle. "Take old Aunt Amasa McGivney, who fell off the stool at Woolco and sued fer ten thousand dollar. That's quite a pile of money too."

"And Theoda McGivney," said Phoebe. "You recall how they tried to pin Theoda's baby on Hilton that time? But Hilton wasn't takin no blame. After all, there was a dozen more had her the same night as Hilton, even if Hilton is her cousin, besides which most of the others was family too."

Outside, through Phoebe's window, a gentle snow was falling and a pure white stillness hung over the forest; the sky was open and free; chickadees were feeding on seed; the snow was covered with the elegant tracks of birds and animals; and as the endless family saga unfolded, whose details and genealogy Sara knew for a hundred years back, she felt her ordinary mind returning, and with it the sense of reality that the K-mart had taken away from her.

"Where we cal'ate he is"—Murvyle rolled a cigarette—"is down the Poor Farm Road. More little back lanes and shacks down to Poor Farm than a person can count."

Phoebe sighed. "Anytime he's away this long, a body don't know if he'll come home with another tooth gone, or his nose twisted in t'other direction, or eyes black and blue . . ."

"Still," said Murvyle, lighting his smoke, "three days is longer than he ever stayed in a ditch."

"No," said Phoebe, "you can tell by the way he's failed, it's a woman."

"He has been failing lately," Sara agreed; he'd lost at least a quarter of his giant beer belly. What a book cover it would make, the dashing reprobate transformed by a good and beautiful woman.

"Way he looks"—Murvyle puffed on his cigarette—"puts you in mind of Festus the week after he was off with the bitch who come into heat over the ridge. Why that dog was but a shadow of hisself, limpin into the dooryard, burrs in his fur, couldn't eat if he wanted, and the same sheepish grin on his face as Hilton lately."

They gazed at Festus hacked out in front of the stove; hearing himself under discussion, the dog flapped his shaggy tail. "Land," said Phoebe, "if we could count the times Hilton has got our hopes up."

"T'other year," said Murvyle, "you recall twas the Frenchwoman. The only dif'rence bein they didn't get on so good. Each weekend she'd get bossier and Hilton he'd get uglier and one Monday mornin she stood out in the road, mad as a hornet, and thumbed her way back up north."

"And when she finally come back," concluded Phoebe, "twasn't to Hilton, but to young Cuthbert Wood, and now there they are with a shack of their own, all paid fer, a dog, and d'you know that dog speaks French as good as he does English?"

Through the window, Sara watched the falling crystals of snow, each facet of which seemed another glistening aspect of Hilton's courting. "What about the girl who knit him those socks last Christmas?"

"She was nice enough," said Phoebe, "but as I alluys say, a twelve-year-old woman hasn't really had much chance to 'sperience life yet, even if she is old enough fer the bellyache."

■ ■ ■

"There's been some tall developments," said Murvyle, marching into the kitchen.

"Seein is believin," added Phoebe mysteriously.

Sara put on the kettle.

"Well sir," began Murvyle, "Hilton finally let it out of the bag as to who he's been seein."

"Who?" asked Sara and Daniel simultaneously.

"Appears to be one of them Gruber women down the Poor Farm Road."

"I says to Hilton," said Phoebe, "*I recall hearin how one of them Gruber women lost her husband recently,* me thinkin that might be the one. *Nope,* says he, *this is a difrent Gruber woman.*"

"So then," said Murvyle, "Phoebe asks, *Has she got any family?* And Hilton says, *Mebbe two or three children.*"

"Then," took up Phoebe, "he let it out of the bag how the woman's 'bout the same age he is, though whether she ever been married he didn't mention, and bein as Poor Farm has changed so much," she sighed, "I really dunno any of them Gruber women."

"I says to Phoebe we mustn't get our hopes up, but I'll tell you twas buzzin out at Bertha's house when we visited yesterday, fer Hilton had been by to try on Tom's plaided jacket."

"Not only that," said Phoebe, "but young Tammy swears he was into the Sears book lookin at rings. And young Leroy swears . . ."

"Leroy *is* a liar," Murvyle noted.

"Young Leroy swears he's been asked to do the honors of holdin the bride's dress up."

Sara gazed out the window, at the chickadees clustered around the feeder; and because it was a soft, streaming, false spring, the chickadees were chasing each other in courtship, driven to love in the middle of winter by the force of the melting snow, a force of nature stronger than even a confirmed McGivney bachelor; and she hoped Hilton's wasn't just another false courtship.

"Yessir," said Murvyle, "I'm ready to make a small down payment."

"Now Murvyle," protested Phoebe, "there's many a slip in the twixt."

"I dunno," said Murvyle. "Bertha cal'ates he means it this time. Tom, who ain't no talker, merely pointed to his plaided jacket."

"And I'm thinkin," said Phoebe, "how will it be fer me, with no more worryin and wonderin whether he be sleepin in a ditch, and no more lunch pails to get ready five o'clock in the mornin times he's workin, and no more fightin, and scenes, and scrubbin clothes, 'cept fer Murvyle who's pretty clean, and mebbe even more grandchildren, though land knows we got enough, and I says to Murvyle," she sighed heavily, "twon't hurt *my* feelin's none."

■ ■ ■

The rainbow lights flickered; a young couple walked into the jewelry store; country music blared from the hi-fi shop; and in the window of the camera store stood a selection of telescopes for viewing the mall on the moon. Dragging her feet, she admitted she was incurable; after all her resolutions, after a single week, she had to come back in and get her fix.

She paused at the impersonal, illiterate chain bookstore and saw Daniel collecting a pile of books which he wouldn't finish reading, as he wouldn't play his new tapes and records more than once; he too was caught in the maze.

She continued wandering, into one of the newer gift shops, which featured a wall of Bible greeting cards and another wall of inspirational books on Christian life and love. In the middle of this insipid display, set as if in her own plastic bouquet, an elderly saleslady beamed at the world.

"Go ahead and browse," she chirped cheerfully. "Enjoy yourself. We have so many wonderful things here." Her tone was slightly hysterical, a little bit nutty, but genuinely alive.

Sara lingered among the garish centerpiece candles, listening to the saleswoman's ceaseless happy chatter to all and sundry.

". . . Can I gift-wrap this for you?"

"No," replied the customer, "it's for myself."

"What a wonderful thing to buy for yourself! So extravagant! So gifty!"

"I deserve it," replied the young woman matter-of-factly.

"You're so right," cried the saleslady, from the bottom of her matronly heart. "Treat yourself like a friend! For forty years I never bought one present for myself, but now I'm out in the world and enjoying every minute of it!" She went on, babbling gaily, and Sara picked out catch phrases, women's lib lingo, clichés made original through the sincerity of the speaker. Has the feminist movement, wondered Sara, reached this deep into the heartlands?

Stunned, she continued listening. When she and Daniel had left New York, women's lib had just been born. Perhaps the movement had trickled past a few working women, but it certainly hadn't hit nice sixty-year-old provincial ladies. Fingering some fancy tea tins from New Jersey, listening to the happy, slightly nutty monologue, it came over her like swamp water from New Jersey that she had missed the Seventies.

What, she wondered, has been the Seventies experience?

She felt like Rip Van Winkle, who'd slept twenty years and returned to find a different world. Except, unlike Rip Van Winkle, I haven't returned. True, I've scanned magazines. I've listened faithfully to the news interpreted by Mortimer Asshole. But hearing about a thing isn't the same as experiencing it. I have, she repeated, missed the Seventies. It seemed a rather significant thing to have missed.

He rubbed his back against a tree; Murvyle always said spring was coming when your back started itching. At times, Daniel suspected that truth was a rabbit, sitting white and still as a statue in the snow.

He slid down the embankment, stopping to admire the caves in the ledges which formed a high-rise apartment complex with porcupine droppings set like name plates in front of each doorstop. He walked the river's edge, noting the tracks of animals who'd used the frozen stream as a highway through the forest—round-clawed bobcat tracks, slender hoof prints of deer, and rabbit tracks which looked like a head with two long ears. He noticed a tiny space in the middle of the ice where water was flowing, and decided to drink before he went home, and take the benediction of the stream; it doesn't do, he mused, to go to a place and turn right around and go back like a pedestrian, without performing a sacred act.

With reverence, he started down the bank toward the little hole in the middle of the frozen stream, and as his foot crashed through the ice and everything cracked at once, he had the fleeting impression the brook was laughing at his sentimentality. But such thoughts didn't persist, because he was chest-deep in the coldest water he'd ever felt, with ice blocks rushing and banging around him and snow slides tumbling behind him.

He broke across the stream to the side that was still holding, and tried to claw his way up the bank; it collapsed on top of him. He grabbed further downstream and the bank there too fell away, enormous piles of snow sliding onto his head. With a desperate lunge, he flung himself onto what remained of the bank, willing it to hold him, and with one foothold of ice and a handhold of snow, he yanked himself up.

Hurrying to the road, he suddenly felt the pain of the cold he'd been dipped in. His clothes had turned to ice and ice had penetrated, he felt sure, to his bones. There was even a chance, he suspected, that his blood was jelling with cold.

Rigidly, moving his aching limbs with effort, he started up the hill to Murvyle's, then stopped. Murvyle must never know what happened. *If he finds out, the story will spread through the Christmas Tree Growers' Association and every gentleman in my club will know how the greenhorn went under.*

Returning across the bridge, he noticed the enormous hole he'd broken in the stream; where a quiet white blanket had lain before, there was now a huge swirling abyss of black water, and the snake of the river deity seemed to be saying, *Don't tread on me.*

He began to jog homeward, his blood once again circulating as he reached the hill; in half a mile, he could feel the bone-freezing cold abating. He mounted the crest, turned at the windowless schoolhouse, and jogged the last sweet lap, down the lane, with his boots squishing water at each step; it sounded like a pair of plungers coming across the yard. He flung open the door, jogged into the shed, took off his watery boots, gathered an armload of wood, and burst into the kitchen.

Sara's footsteps came down the stairs as he was jamming more wood into the stove urging the fire to a flame hot enough to thaw his frozen being.

"What happened to you?"

"I fell in the stream." He'd taken off his Murphy pants, which stood on their own stiffness in the middle of the room; his jacket stood on top of them, arms stiffly out, an instant scarecrow.

"How did that happen?"

Naked in front of the fire, rubbing his deeply chilled person, he explained, "I was paying homage to Jerusalem Creek in a very sentimental way, and apparently it doesn't like sentimentality. It gave me the worst dunking I ever had, up to my chest in ice water."

"But why didn't you go straight to Phoebe's and get warm there? She would've given you a pair of dry pants . . ."

"And listen to Murvyle cackle at me for the next ten years about how I fell in the brook after all his warnings?" He faced her sternly. "We've got to keep completely quiet about this or I'll be the laughing stock of my club."

His pants and jacket suddenly collapsed like someone in Pike's paintings who'd been karate-chopped behind the head, and what looked like a pool of blood was rapidly hemorrhaging around the clothes on the floor.

Sara went for the mop. He continued rubbing his naked bones at the stove. "I'm lucky I didn't drown. I'm lucky I'm alive."

She nodded, mopping.

"You probably can't appreciate the enormity of what I've been through," he said. "I'll have to take you there and show you the hole."

She raised a quizzical eyebrow; he perceived he had her curiosity aroused.

"I'll just be a second," he said, "I've got to put on dry clothes . . ." He padded upstairs, and put on fresh clothes, slowly, luxuriously, reveling in their dry warmth. Renewed, he returned downstairs to find her waiting in her winter wonderland suit—an enormous outfit that made her look like a pair of bears; her feelings about winter were that when outside one should be inside as much clothing as possible; she subscribed strongly to the "layering theory," and inside these layers, she was hard-pressed to get out through the doorway; her face, within the great furry mass, gave the impression of a little creature peering out of a hairy monster; her après-ski boots were as wide around as wastebaskets.

"Better go back for your camera," he said on the shed. "You'll want to have a picture of the hole."

She took off her five pair of mittens, and removed her wastebasket boots, which was no easy matter in her unbendable snowman of clothes, then lumbered back into the house, returned with her camera, and labored to reboot herself; puffing, she tried to bend over and get visibility, came to an impasse, groped around blindly, and finally jammed her feet into the wastebaskets; lurching, she righted herself and stuffed on her mittens.

"Sara, if you ever went through the ice with the amount of clothing you're wearing, you'd sink like a stone."

She smiled smugly. "I don't go on the ice when Murvyle tells me not to."

He drove up the lane and along the road to the school, turned, and headed down the hill, where he pointed out the jogging track the wet woodsman had left. At the bridge, they stepped out of the truck.

"There," he said.

"Goodness. Did you do all that?"

"I was thrashing for my life."

"It's certainly a big hole."

"The water there's chest-deep."

"So you said."

"I was never so cold in my life. Better take a photograph."

She peeled her mittens down to the pair with three fingers, and aimed at the hole.

"Take another. Take a few. This is one for the scrapbook."

"What scrapbook?"

"This'll be the first page. *Winter breakup. Spring thaw.*"

She took some pictures, and they got back into the truck. He slammed the door. "Remember. Mum's the word."

■ ■ ■

"Young Glinko come by," Murvyle was saying. "Told me to lock up Festus cause the Glinko's she-dog's in heat. I answered in a nice friendly way I wasn't gonna lock up me dog fer no bitch. *If yer dog comes round,* says Glinko, *I'll take the gun to him.* Says I, *If you do, there'll be black blood on the Hills of Jerusalem.*"

"I seen them from the winder," Phoebe attested. "Murvyle picked young Glinko up by the scruff of his neck and throwed him out in the road."

"You can do anythin you want to me," said Murvyle mildly. "But don't step on me little toe."

Daniel glanced toward the toe in question—Festus—who flapped his tail in reply.

Murvyle sipped his tea. "I notice you took a swim in the brook, Dan'l."

Daniel looked up, mouth open around a biscuit; the biscuit fell out onto his plate.

"You dropped yer uppers," said Phoebe.

He threw a swift look at Sara, but detected no sign of betrayal; she was as astonished as he at Murvyle's revelation.

"Yessir, and then you come out and started up the hill to visit me, and then decided mebbe you wouldn't. Though yer alluys welcome here, dry or soakin."

"Yes," agreed Phoebe. "You could've hung yer clothes on the stove, and I would've given you a pair of Hilton's conversations."

Daniel gazed at Murvyle keenly. "How did you know?"

Murvyle gummed his biscuit. "Then you went home and come back in the truck to show Sara the big hole you made."

Sara gazed at Murvyle too. "Can you recognize my tracks?"

"Course I can. Ain't I seen them enough times?"

Phoebe covered her mouth and started to giggle.

"What's so funny?" asked Sara.

Murvyle's eyes were twinkling. "You had yer boots on the wrong feet."

On the front page of the newspaper was a hazy picture of four deer who'd appeared on Main Street, fleeing the black flies in the woods.

"You can't blame the deer," said Phoebe. "Twould drive anyone crazy."

"No," agreed Sara, raising her hand to her head, touching the permanent bumps and welts the black flies had raised, wondering how many more would be added this year; a phrenologist, if he examined the people of Atlantic Canada, would think we had the most complex destiny he'd ever seen.

"Twouldn't wonder if they get moose and bear on Main Street too. A person's safer out here in Jerusalem than they are in town . . ."

Sara glanced from Phoebe to Ms. Gruber, the newcomer in the McGivney kitchen, the mysterious woman whom Hilton had been courting, now at last revealed, sitting on a lone backless chair, staring out the window as if wondering what she was doing here at the ass end of nowhere; she was clearly a country kicker who'd kicked around enough towns to find life in the country insufferably boring.

A few feet away from Ms. Gruber, Hilton lay in his place on the lounge, mooning at his beloved, who was, Sara noticed, a woman of some experience. She wasn't the same age as Hilton, as had originally been thought, but several years older, and it was plain that part of Hilton's appeal was based on the fact that not too many men, at this date, were breaking down her door.

Hilton, in his clumsy bearlike fashion, offered her all he could. "Have some more to eat, Jeffer." He gestured to buns, preserves, cigarette papers, whatever the lady might desire. Is her name

Jeffer? wondered Sara, or is that a nickname? Since introductions were not de rigueur, she'd have to find out from Phoebe.

The lady expertly rolled herself a cigarette and lit it with the grace of a dyed-in-the-wool boondocker. A woman, thought Sara, who can take care of herself under any circumstances . . . but prefers to have a little help. Her hair was henna'd and her teeth were similar to Hilton's; Sara wondered whether Ms. Gruber and Hilton opened beer bottles together with their incisors.

"I hear you're thinking of moving to New Jerusalem?" offered Sara vivaciously.

"Yeah," said Ms. Gruber dryly, "I'll give it a try." Unlike Hilton's voice, hers betrayed no emotion; on the contrary, it seemed to say Hilton was just the luck of the draw for the year. Puffing her homemade cigarette, she crossed her muscular legs, looking like the sort of woman who was very much at home on a barstool at the Legion.

"How's your job, Hilton?" asked Sara.

He snorted. "Quit the son of a whore. Goddamn fuckin work was too hard."

"Perhaps you'll get something better."

"Sons of whores at the unemployment ain't got nahthin. Offer me five dollar the hour to work in the fuckin woods. Five dollar the hour." He laughed scornfully.

Phoebe sighed. "Goin to the village picnic?"

"I don't know," said Sara. "Are you?"

"We might," said Phoebe; Sara knew it would take a forest fire to get Phoebe out of Jerusalem, but still she always went through the drama of considering each invitation carefully. "Gonna have a lot of good things there. Greased pig. Worm pull. Hamburg eatin contest fer the dogs." Festus looked up with interest.

"What's a worm pull?" asked Sara.

"You don't know what a worm pull is!" said Hilton, guffawing in disbelief at her cultural ignorance.

"See who can pull their worm the longest without snappin in two," explained Phoebe. "If yer worm snaps in two, they disallow it."

Sara glanced again at Ms. Gruber staring out through the window. Though the lady wasn't a great talker, nor obviously terribly excited about Hilton, nor about being in the bosom of Hilton's family, nor about anything else for that matter, she had a pleasant manner, without the overtly cruel, defensive hostility of many country women. She seemed tolerant and uncritical, as if all she wanted in a man was a little peace and quiet and if Hilton behaved himself, she'd be nice to him.

Hilton groaned to his feet. "We best be headin down the Christus road."

"Plenty of time," said Phoebe automatically.

Hilton muttered; Ms. Gruber, as if not caring particularly whether she stayed or left, murmured good-bye and proceeded out the door with her Knight of the Oath.

Phoebe and Sara went to the window, and watched in dead silence as the lovers got into their car and departed.

Dust rose up in the road behind the vehicle.

Phoebe sighed back into her seat.

". . . Is her name Jeffer?" asked Sara.

"I dunno what her name is zactly. The way Hilton says it, sounds like Jeffer."

"Where do her children live?"

"The dear knows." Phoebe shook her head, and Sara got the feeling Ms. Gruber's children were spread all over Canada.

"The problem," explained Phoebe, "is they need to find a shack with two bedrooms. Cause of her bein on welfare. Them welfare people ain't supposed to think her and Hilton live together."

"What are they supposed to think?"

"That Hilton's the lodger." Phoebe paused. "If you was welfare, would you believe Hilton was the lodger?"

Sara thought of the happy couple, with Hilton mooning continually at his landlady. *The Lodger*—It was a perfect title for a romance about a retired English colonel who lodges at the chalet of the lovely redhead who turns out to be, ultimately, a woman of courage and fiber. The cover took shape . . . Hilton in monocle and waistcoat, white gloves and spats . . . but she couldn't make the image quite solidify; certain features kept getting in the way.

"I wouldn't," sighed Phoebe.

■ ■ ■

"Is that short enough?" asked Sara.

Phoebe reached her hand up over her plastic-bag cape and felt around her head. "Mebbe a bit more off back. It's so hot out."

Sara snipped a bit more off back, stood away and examined her work, then went to the wall and took down the mirror. "What do you think?"

Phoebe examined her mirror reflection without expression, devoid of vanity or even interest; she had Sara trim her hair every few weeks just as she had Murvyle trim the grass, to keep disorder and the black flies at bay. "I guess it'll do," she sighed, turning away from the mirror, and taking off her plastic-bag cape. "Feels cooler anyways."

Sara swept off Phoebe's neck and the floor; she went to the stove and put on the kettle.

"I cal'ate," said Phoebe, "you heard about the little boy . . ."

"Which little boy?"

"The one in the K-mart."

"No, I didn't."

Phoebe shook her head, pursing her lips. "Bertha told me 'bout it yesterday." She looked around, lowered her voice. "They cut his business off."

A shudder of horror passed through Sara. "They cut his . . . business . . . off?"

"Right in the restrooms."

"But who would do such a thing?"

"Bertha says must've been drugs."

"It must've been a madman."

"Murvyle says twas a perkvert."

The kettle was steaming. Sara found her hands were shaking as she poured water for tea. "Is he dead?"

"I don't see how he could live."

"But what did Bertha say?"

"They took him to hospital." Phoebe wiped her brow. "Poor child is really better off dead, ain't he?"

Sara nodded, and it suddenly struck her: Could it have been the K-mart wallpaper that drove the perkvert crazy? She could see him staring at those vomit-toned teapots, then grabbing up a serrated plastic Restauranteria knife, and slicing some poor kid's balls off. ". . . What exactly did he cut off?"

"The whole works, I guess."

Thrills of horror went through Sara.

Phoebe tsk-tsk'd. "I dunno what this world is comin to, pon my

soul I don't. A person's afeared to go into town." She really looked
afeared, sitting there like a scalped chicken. I didn't, thought Sara
sadly, give her a very good haircut.

They sipped their tea.

"Anyways," said Phoebe, "Hilton and Jeffer are takin an apartment in Mosquitoville."

"Did Hilton get another job?"

"No, he took a freak about it. Says he won't work fer no seven
dollar an hour. Claims he can make almost as much on the unemployment."

"Won't his unemployment eventually run out?"

"Likely he'll go onto the welfare when it does." They returned to
their tea and biscuit. Phoebe studied the leaves in her cup. "It gets
them all after a while."

■ ■ ■

Wood crackled in the stove; the temperature of Phoebe's kitchen
was close to a hundred; Sara sat in the breeze of the window thinking: This is the ebb and flow of my social life, from having tea
with Phoebe at my house to having tea with Phoebe at her house,
talking about Castration at the K-mart.

". . . Course, Hilton says twasn't the K-mart a'tall. Twas the
men's room at McDonald's."

"Did you find it in the *Loyalist*? I can't seem to find it."

"Oh, them newspapers is keepin it quiet, cause they're right in
the midst of Dollar Daze. But after Dollar Daze is over, then it'll
all come out."

"Is the child still alive?"

"Hilton says he's in hospital in his own private room and nobody
ain't allowed to know which room 'tis."

"Does anyone know the family?"

"Murvyle thinks he does."

"He does?"

"He's pretty sure he knows them. But they're protectin the family
till Dollar Daze is done."

They sipped their tea and chewed it over; it seemed to have endless possibilities for gory discussion and investigation; and, after all,
this *is* my social life.

■ ■ ■

"... *Mortimer Astle with today's headlines* ... *In the Provincial Legislature today, octogenarian Minister-Without-Portfolio Rufus MacLeash suggested that some alcoholics should be forcibly confined to institutions and furthermore half the members of Parliament who voted for the decriminalization of marijuana don't know what they're talking about, they dunno the first thing about marijuana* ..."

She switched the radio off, and turned angrily on Daniel. "I don't understand why they don't come out and tell about the little boy who was castrated."

Daniel glanced up from his book. "Because it's bullshit from start to finish."

"... It is?"

"It has all the earmarks of a collective delusion. Quietest town in the world suddenly struck by Chinese eunuch maker. It's summer madness."

"You seem to know all about it."

"I know a myth when I hear one."

"But what about all the details?"

"Exactly. Was it the K-mart? Was it McDonald's? Was it the men's room? Was it the stockroom? And in a town where everybody knows everybody else, how is it that this set of parents are able to hide the most incredible event of the century."

"But Daniel, Murvyle knows the family."

"Murvyle knows every family for fifty miles, so it's safe for him to assume he knows this family. But has he named them? Like everyone else in this province, he has nothing to do but sit behind the stove and figure out whose son got his balls cut off."

"Not just his balls ..."

"I'll tell you what it means." He closed his book. "It refers to the whole province. The lumber companies have castrated the forests, the lumber companies and politicians have castrated the people, and half the population's on welfare."

She frowned. She didn't admit it out loud, but she knew he was right. And she realized she too would've seen the story was bunkum at any other time of her life. Except starved as I am for excitement and feeling perhaps a little castrated myself, I swallowed it hook, line, and sinker. "Well," she said finally, "I'm glad it never happened."

"It has happened."

"I mean to the little boy."

"When did the Glinkos take off?" he asked.

"Last weekend," answered Murvyle.

"Where'd they go?"

"Some say over Mugwash."

They were walking toward the Glinkos' ex-dwelling; even from a distance it looked sadly abandoned. Of the three giant trees which had graced the broad lawn in front of the farmhouse, nothing was left but three raw stumps with sawdust scattered around them.

"Orvis told them they could take firewood from the forest, not two-hundred-year-old shade trees," said Murvyle, shaking his head; he led the way to the house, through the spindly, weedy garden patch the Glinkos had fed from.

"Didn't there used to be flowers?" asked Daniel.

"Aye. Glinko took them too. Lilacs, phlox, bleedin heart . . ." The farmhouse looked naked, like some poor old woman who'd been put up against the wall and violated.

They moved forward and gazed in through the parlor window. "Holyo-peena," said Murvyle, "they took the furnipture."

The kitchen door was gone. "Hinges'n all." Murvyle flicked his cigarette at the door frame as they entered. "Old Aunt Effie's stove too." Aunt Effie's stovepipe dangled from the ceiling like a broken arm.

They strolled into the front parlor. "Took the oilcloth right off the floor," remarked Murvyle with what almost sounded like admiration at the thoroughness old man Glinko and his family had shown. A great pallid square on the hardwood floor revealed for how many generations the linoleum had lain, pre-Glinko. "What I can't cal'ate," Murvyle continued, "is why they left the stovepipe."

"Why did Orvis rent to the Glinkos?"

"Who else would stay way out here in Jerusalem?"

The cellar door was open. Murvyle stepped toward it. "Wonder what would be worth takin from down there?"

They proceeded down the dimly lit stairs, to a stone-walled dirt-floored basement. Hovering over the chamber was a multiarmed monster of air ducts, converging on nothingness. "That's it," said Murvyle with satisfaction, as if conclusively solving the last piece of a puzzle, "they took Orvis's furnace."

■   ■   ■

He stumbled out of the woods onto a mist-covered field, a meadow he'd been in often, but he'd gotten so turned around by the thick blanket of fog and there were so many derelict fields in the settlement that he couldn't place it.

Stalking further into the mysterious field, he found himself in a cumulus soup of mist; the landscape remained a dream.

A sound close by made him freeze . . .

He stared ahead where the noise seemed to come from, but his eyes couldn't penetrate the fog's thickness.

Suddenly, out of the soup, an image took shape . . . of an old gray house in a meadow, with two ancient figures, like a nineteenth-century painting of Gypsies. The two painted Gypsies were emerging from the gray house, carrying stovepipes under their arms. They piled the pipes with a loud clanking noise into a jeep. And then, as suddenly as it had appeared, the entire scene faded back into the mist.

■   ■   ■

"Have you often done this?" he asked.

"Aye."

"With a roll of tarpaper?"

"Aye." Murvyle slapped the roll against his leg and marched through the thicket like a bandy little Canadian colonel with riding crop. Daniel carried Sara's camera, though he knew there'd be nothing to shoot; Murvyle had as much chance of calling out a moose with a roll of tarpaper as he, old Alf, and Pike had of striking gold. There must be something intrinsic in the children of the forest, thought Daniel, that gives them this crazy blind confidence.

"You'll see," muttered Murvyle; no silent Indian, he loudly struck brush out of his way as he lurched through the trees, footsteps sinking into the ground as if he were some old tree himself, who'd sprung from the earth, the embodiment of the soil stomping around. He'll never do it, thought Daniel, with the racket he makes and his roll of tarpaper; but he's such a contrary old codger that here we are, marching off to summon a moose.

Murvyle's stubborn back, his patched plaid shirt, his crooked cap, the tube of tarpaper, all seemed to express the ferocious nature of the dying race of backwoodsmen, who'd had to cope with the climate and wilderness and knew how to use it, eat it, blast it away, and hack it to pieces.

The overgrown logging trail was lined with pulp piles; Murvyle continued crashing along in his rough intimacy with the woods, and Daniel followed with painful respect—painful because he couldn't begin to talk to Murvyle about it or get behind the meaning of the act; they were simply out there and would blow a roll of tarpaper. In spite of Murvyle's thumping steps and sometimes-loquaciousness, he was, in his way, silent as a bear, because like a bear he couldn't give voice to what was in his soul . . . except, thought Daniel, with a roll of tarpaper.

The old man stopped by a big pine tree which had been shattered by lightning. The woods around were stark and bleak, clear-cut to brush, with only the charred pine tree standing; it was so empty and forlorn, you couldn't imagine a less likely place for a moose to appear.

Murvyle braced himself against the tree and, with a warning glance toward Daniel, warmed up with a few birdcalls, which sounded absurd, but Murvyle was so awesomely sincere that you couldn't look on the sounds he made as silly. Then the old man lifted the tarpaper roll to his lips, digging his boots deep into the earth like a demented substitute cheerleader.

Daniel readied himself with Sara's camera, feeling the raw primitivity of the moment, as a bloodcurdling cry issued from the end of the tarpaper.

Daniel staggered backward, steadying the camera, and Murvyle let loose with a series of coughing grunts reminiscent of the deranged wrestlers Daniel'd seen on Murvyle's television. Murvyle motioned him to sit. They sat down and waited.

The only sound they could hear was the far-off scurrying of animals, all apparently racing in the opposite direction from the horrendous call, in order to take refuge in deep forest seclusion.

■ ■ ■

Opening his eyes, he heard what sounded like heavy crunching outside; he fumbled his way to the stairs in the dark, and went down to the kitchen.

The sound seemed to come from the raspberry bushes; he crept to the back window, and looked out at the big harvest moon casting its pale silver rays on the amorphous foliage of the raspberries. As he watched, half of the bush-mass separated itself and stepped out. For a moment, the shadow was indefinable in its frightening grandeur; but then he saw, in the light of the moon, the seven-pointed double crown of Murvyle's bull moose.

"This is Mortimer Astle with headlines. In the Provincial Legisla-
ture today, octogenarian Minister-Without-Portfolio Rufus Mac-
Leash stated that the high rate of working mothers is causing the
high incidence of alcoholism and drug addiction in their children
and furthermore that women were born to have children . . ."

Gently, she clicked off Mortimer Asshole, and stared out the window at the interminable snow interminably falling. She switched
on the lamp, and the snow outside was a veil across her reflection
in the dark window.

Turning away from her snow-powdered face, she gazed around
the studio walls, where her canvases of bucolic Jerusalem had
gradually been replaced by passionately painted seascapes and
dreamscapes—the blue-green of the Caribbean, the Arizona desert,
the mountains and canyons and Badlands of the West; she'd done
pastel drawings too, of crowded Piccadilly, Paris cafés and roof-
tops, the temples of Kyoto . . .

With something of a Phoebe-sigh, she cleared her drawing board
of the day's work, and drew toward her a stack of library books—
*Great Museums of the World, The Indian Art of Central America,
Lost Civilizations of Peru,* and *Irish Horse-Drawn Caravans.* Opening a pad, she resumed taking notes from *France on Fifteen Dollars;* at the same time, she slipped a Living Language cassette into
the tape recorder and let the mellifluous sentences wash around her
while she jotted names of hotels, amenities, and mentally repeated,
Ou se trouve le téléphone?

From downstairs, Daniel's hammer rang out on the shed, where
his forgeries were taking shape.

Wistfully, she opened a folder in which were filed the stubs of chances she'd taken on free-giveaway trips. On top, in the place of honor, was the Gillette Vacation for Life. If you won first prize, they'd send you away every year as long as you lived.

Would one fabulous trip per annum carry me through from year to year in New Jerusalem?

The folder was thick with the perforated halves of coupons she'd sent in, and there they set, waiting for the results; and there she sat, waiting to be contacted, like a medium.

Going through the coupon halves, she sadly eliminated two which were so far out of date she knew she'd never be contacted.

And then came the nagging worry: How will they contact me? Will my lack of telephone disqualify me? She was sure it wouldn't. Or would it? When they discover I don't have a phone and am hard to contact, will they ignore the fact that I've been selected and choose an alternate winner?

She reread the words at the bottom, which were always the same, burning out from the coupon at her: *Winner must answer a timed, skill-testing question.*

Do I have the skill to handle it?

Or will I win a vacation for life only to have it snatched away because I'm too stupid to answer the skill-testing question?

But surely they couldn't only give prizes to geniuses. It's undemocratic.

Then why the skill-testing question?

Perhaps they don't want the responsibility of shlepping a retarded person through Europe. Could that be it? What else could it be? Surely I'm not retarded. I ought to be able to answer a simple, timed, skill-testing question.

Unless I get rattled.

What is the skill-testing question?

It all seemed to rest on that variable.

She examined a couple of contests which were coming up for draw very soon. Green Giant Corn Niblets; *send in three wrappers and win your own valley.* Her own valley wasn't as good as a vacation for life, but at least it would be a change from the valley she was in. And maybe bouncing back and forth between valleys would alleviate the boredom of both of them.

Beneath the Corn Niblets, she'd filed the *Reader's Digest* Dream House contest; they could build the Dream House in her jolly green valley. She switched off the Living Language tape, and quickly sketched a blueprint of her dream house, then rapidly landscaped the valley, leaving the minor details for when she had more time.

. . . Cheese Dream Sweepstakes, from Kraft: *You will take the plane on February 7th to Frankfurt, and no substitute date will be permitted. There you will pick up your prize Volkswagen, and without stopping, you will proceed to the Black Forest* . . . She hoped Nazis didn't come with the Volkswagen.

She turned to her Catelli Spaghetti Rome-Paris Itinerary, and her spirits lifted. It wasn't a long vacation, but the quality was outstanding. A chauffeur-driven limousine would meet you at the airport, and for six unforgettable days you would attend the grand couture openings in these two top fashion cities. She roughly sketched a few of her own ensembles, and then all around her, on the gilt chairs, the other chic and beautiful people. Catelli Spaghetti only gave you five hundred in cash to spend on clothes, which wouldn't, it was true, pay for a couture sock, but, after all, she wasn't going to shop. She was going to soak up ambiance, and for soaking up ambiance there was no one more desperately suited.

At the bottom of the pile were the dribbly little contests, which she leafed through with only a modicum of interest; still, they weren't to be sniffed at, not even the Kotex Tampons Cash-for-the-New-Year Giveaway, which gave you about enough cash to keep you in tampons for eighteen months, if you menstruated lightly.

■ ■ ■

The crowds were tremendous, almost as big as for wrestling, at the event of the century, the visit of an International Star to the province. They entered the Hockey Arena and took their seats on folding chairs which had been set up by the thousands on top of the carpeted ice.

"It's kind of chilly on the feet," said Daniel.

"Who cares," she shivered, wrapping her jacket more tightly around her, and beating her cold hands for the opening acts—a ventriloquist with a dummy, the band, and the shapely Rayettes—performing on a platform set up at one end of the ice field.

The audience applauded with patience, freezing, waiting, until

from out of one of the dugouts leading into the arena, leaning on
the arm of his manager, the Star appeared, smiling blindly, shaking
his body to the music, climbing the stairs in an aura of such palpable ecstasy that Sara, along with the rest of the audience, starved
for this electricity, rose to her feet and roared; here was the big
time; life lived with a vengeance; here, at last, was something happening. Probably, thought Sara, gazing at Ray Charles's ecstatic
form, he's stoned beyond my wildest dreams, but at his core is an
urbane blasé man who knows the score; she continued clapping
with the others, an audience delirious with appreciation for the
Star who'd come to this last outpost of lethargy to revive it.

Charles played a few opening bars, and the musicians behind
him joined in, professional performers functioning as a smooth
polished unit; Sara couldn't help thinking of the acts which usually
came to the ice rink—Stompin' Stanley Stibbers, hockey games
which ended in brawls, and the wrestling dwarfs. Charles looked
up from his piano. "Goddamn, it's cold in here. Before the show,
my manager said to me, *Ray, there's ice out there.* I said *You're
jivin me, man.*"

The audience clapped wildly; even his mentioning the ice was
recognition—of the ice, their ice. His face broke into a grin. "You
know, I might move here."

Sara found herself cheering with the others; though he was
clearly making fun of the place, at least he was touching it, a place
nobody had touched on any level above Stompin' Stanley since
1882 when by some incredible quirk of a delirious fate, Oscar
Wilde, on his American tour, had read poetry to the local lumberjacks, and been arrested two days later.

Charles sang, while Sara let herself dissolve in memories of Manhattan, memories of life at the center of the world, memories of intensity, of things she hadn't felt in years, and at the height of her
ecstasy, the pedals fell off the piano.

Charles stopped, gazing blindly down toward his feet. In the
stunned silence, one of the other musicians walked over, stooped
under the piano, and came up holding the entire trio of piano
pedals. Only in Atlantic Canada, thought Sara, would they give
Ray Charles a piano that's falling apart. The Star held the pedals in
his hands, disbelieving for a second, then handed them back to the

other musician. "Put it over by the drums," he said. "Maybe it'll learn to read music."

■   ■   ■

She clung to Daniel's arm as they threaded their way out through the crowd; her feet were numb from the ice and she was trembling from the emotional changes of the last two hours, hearing forgotten tunes of a life which had once been hers.

From the corner of her eye she caught sight of a familiar figure vivaciously herding a couple of old men and another elderly woman, and Sara recognized the daffy saleslady from the gift shop, dressed to the teeth, in a long taffeta gown, rhinestone tiara, elbow-length gloves, and radiating as much as Ray Charles. Noticing Sara looking at her as she swept by, the saleslady stretched one gracious arm out in a magnanimous gesture of her liberation, and asked grandly, "And did *you* enjoy it?"

Sara smiled back at the bedazzling lady, envying her liberated state; though it was daffy, though it was relative, it was quite beyond the aching feeling the music had brought up in her own soul —of grinding limitation in this cold and barren outpost. Leaving the Hockey Arena, she realized with inevitable clarity—Charles will get on his plane tonight, and within twenty-four hours the energy level will sink back down to the nasal rambling of Mortimer Asshole.

■   ■   ■

". . . *Mortimer Astle with today's headlines . . . Octogenarian Minister-Without-Portfolio Rufus MacLeash has been asked to resign from the Provincial Legislature for saying that the high rate of working mothers is causing the high incidence of alcoholism and drug addiction in their children and furthermore that women were born to have children . . .*"

8

The current raced him along, as he steered with his one aluminum oar, wearing his Allagash Waterway hat, going down Jerusalem Creek's white waters, navigating the terrible spring freshet, perhaps the only white man ever to do it, solo, in an inflatable tub from the K-mart.

Branches leaned out over the water, slapping his hat as he zipped past the green shoreline; he came to a bend across which several trees had fallen, and his injured craft ground to a stop. Climbing out on shore, he pulled the flopping boat after him, and examined the damage done to it. He attached the foot pump, pumped in more air, then carried the craft around the fallen logs, and launched it again. It wobbled beneath him, the current was strong, and he and his boat were off.

The water spun him to the left, to the right, and he straightened the raft with his oar through the churning foam. Roots dangled out at him, giant claws from the stone cliff, a passage through an enchanted forest.

The raft emerged in a place of still water, the stream widening and deepening. From the cliff above, the child's gravestone gazed down, a face which had merged with the forest.

He floated through slowly, touching ancestral layers at the center of his nature, while the spirit watched with its face of stone, and neither owed the other any sadness, because the truth was shrouded in mystery.

He glided on, the feeling following, knowing its way through the channel as surely as the water, and then everything was just motion and sunlight all mixed together; a quiver of pain went through him, and still he knew he was happy, as happy as he'd ever been, and his happiness was a tangible thing.

The stream quickened again; he was swept out of his thought into the excitement of guiding the rubber raft. The shore flashed by, foam sprayed over the bow, the tub began to sag with leaking air . . . but the bridge was ahead, and he steered toward the landing beside it, and stepped out just below the road.

Above him the clear open sky held a single crow flying silently on the wind, and beside him the stream continued on its way through the spruce. He stood on the shore with his sagging boat. God, what a life!

And Sara is going bananas.

■ ■ ■

"We'll travel," he said. "Six months. Maybe a year. As long as you need."

She sat across from him at the kitchen table, surrounded by travel books and pamphlets. "But who'll watch the house?"

"We'll rent it."

■ ■ ■

The real estate lady shook her head. "You don't want to rent. I've seen it happen too often, somebody rents their beautiful home, and comes back to find it ruined."

"But we can't leave it empty."

"I'm only saying, golly, I wouldn't want the responsibility. I'd have to be out there all the time to check on it for you and make sure they aren't hacking your walls up for the copper wiring, stealing your storm windows, selling your bathroom fixtures . . . and how could I stop them?" She gazed with wide-eyed sincerity. "The only people you'll get to rent way out there would be on welfare. Gosh, the lovely homes I've seen torn to shreds. Just worthless. I could tell you some stories . . ." she began, and as she told them, Daniel vividly pictured the Family Glinko, hacking up his antiques, chopping down his shade trees for firewood, prying off his perfect plasterboard walls for the copper wiring, wrenching out the chimneys—all the limbs and organs of his beloved house, which Sara had designed and he and Waldo had so lovingly built, their house mutilated, massacred, destroyed . . . "And when they came home," she concluded, "they just sat down on the plywood underfloor and cried."

"What," asked Daniel, "if we hired a caretaker?"

"Caretakers are worse, here today, gone tomorrow. Why, you'd be up here every other month trying to find a new one. And they wouldn't even bother telling you they'd gone."

"But," said Sara, "we want to travel."

"If it were me, I'd sell."

"Never," they answered as one.

"It'd be worth quite a lot," she said, naming a figure that set his head spinning; was it possible his little house in the woods was worth so much?

He met Sara's eyes and turned away. He saw her longing for freedom. And in a way, the figure the agent had mentioned changed everything. Or did it?

"We do want to travel," said Sara, with that look of longing that cut through him.

"Well there," said the agent. "You'll have plenty of money to travel and you won't have to worry about the house."

He sat and listened, without speaking, as the forces of the two women merged, and gradually became a current as powerful as Jerusalem Creek in spring, sweeping him along in its wake; he knew he couldn't fight it any more than he could turn his raft around and go upstream. He felt the strength of Sara's determination to be free; her determination was the boat he was floating in, the boat which automatically joins with the water; and he was just a passenger.

■ ■ ■

They sat in his workshed, each on a sawhorse.

"If I had the guts," said Murvyle, "I'd do it meself."

Daniel knew Murvyle was only talking about moving five miles out to the village, but to the old woodsman that in itself was going to another world.

"Yessir," said Murvyle. A heaviness settled between them that they knew to be a decision; the old man would never try to hold him. "Sure," said Murvyle, "everybody leaves Jerusalem sooner or later. I'm the only one too dumb to get out."

They looked at each other across the top of the pseudo-antique dry sink, Murvyle tapping his cigarette ashes onto the wood and rubbing them in as he'd been trained.

"I'm going to miss this place," said Daniel in spite of himself.

"Hell, there ain't nahthin here."

Daniel turned and gazed out the window toward the endless expanse of forest, whose inner reaches he knew with an intimacy that sometimes made him feel it really was his, every blistered clear-cut mile of it.

"No sir, ain't nahthin but a bunch of brush. Worst tangle a man can get hisself into is the woods. I know, I been in them all me life. Yer lucky to be goin." He looked across the false antique into Daniel's eyes.

They fell again into heavy silence.

"You'll come back to visit," said Murvyle, "and won't recognize the place, there'll be so much brush. All them old trails'll be growed up. Tell me"—Murvyle leaned toward him over the dry sink—"you want me to keep an eye out fer busted old furnipture? I could store them fer you in me wagon house."

"Okay." Daniel nodded, feeling he could safely agree, the scheme being so vague, and like other schemes he and Murvyle had cherished, would result in nothing more than Murvyle taking his usual piss in the wagon house through a crack in the floorboards. Sitting there with the old man, he felt a weariness he couldn't explain; any bit of restlessness he'd ever had in the country seemed totally drained from him.

Murvyle stubbed his butt on the table. "Let's go in and see what the women are hatchin."

They lumbered to the door, and entered the kitchen, where the women were sharing a pot of tea. Phoebe looked thunderstruck and Sara was babbling hollowly about how they'd still see each other often, and it sounded, in the clear light of Jerusalem, like the feeblest of dreams.

Phoebe's pretty pink flesh had never looked more naked to Daniel; it was as if he could see through her skin to a fine network of roots, which had along the way allowed themselves to grow intertwined with Sara's, and now the entire structure was being tugged.

"Some tea, Murvyle?" asked Sara.

They sat down for tea, and he glanced again at Phoebe; behind that strange transparency he saw her rummaging for something to speak of outside her feelings, anything . . . "Well," she blurted, "I see where they're tryin to put old Johnny Trout out of his house."

"Aye," replied Murvyle, "and 'tis a shame too."

"Why are they trying to put him out?"

"Not a reason in the world. 'Cept his house is three foot wide, four foot long, and six foot high."

Phoebe sighed. "It's on skids too, ain't it, Murvyle?"

"That's to move her around. Old Johnny gets tired of her in one place, he hauls over to another. But the gov'ment wants to put him in them-there new senior citizen apartments. They say he ain't got a winder nor a facility in his shack."

"Didn't they say in the *Loyalist*, Murvyle, twas a fringement of his civil liverties?"

" 'Tis too. Man can't have his shack where he wants her, when he wants her."

Daniel emerged from shock to inquire, "His house is three feet wide by four feet long by six feet high?"

"Yer right. 'Bout the same size as our well house."

"How does he lie down?"

"He sorta curls up. Cozy."

"And there are no windows?"

"He can reach his head outside the door easier than strainin his back on a winder."

"Many's the time," said Phoebe, "Murvyle helped old Johnny haul that house with the horses."

"Yessir, we'd take her over hill and dale till he'd find the view that suited him. I'd say, *Does this suit you, Johnny?* He'd say, *Aye,* and we'd put on a pot of tea right there."

"He has a stove?"

"Oh," said Phoebe, "he's got everythin in there . . ."

Daniel looked at the pair of them, each in a rocker, rocking and chewing over the contents of old Johnny's abode and the adventures of the old boy's travels in said abode, and he knew how much he'd miss these aimless conversations about people he didn't know and heroes he would never meet.

■ ■ ■

THE MAGIC OF MULTIPLE LISTING has already started working for you. A photo of your home has been taken and within forty-eight hours . . . Nervously, he laid down the booklet which had come in the mail, and looked at his watch. "Do they mean forty-eight hours from right now or from the hour they mailed it?"

"I imagine from right now."

Which gives us, he thought, forty-eight hours to change our mind.

She beamed at him over the travel folders which had also arrived in the mail. "I feel as if the weight of the world is off my back." A veil seemed to have fallen from her face, which in the rosy light of evening streaming through the western windows looked to him as young as when they'd first met, glowing with the unknown. Her depression had definitively lifted, and in its place was an excitement which was totally charming; I have, he realized, been looking at her through a very dark cloud for an awfully long time. He reached across the table of mail and took her hand. She seemed to float on Pan Am folders into his arms and, without exchanging a word, they found themselves drifting upstairs, pieces of clothing marking their progress like the crumbs in *Hansel and Gretel*. A warm breeze came through the bedroom windows with the scents of spring, and the fragrance of fields and forest seemed to emanate from her skin. She was already on the adventure; her kisses spoke of distant places, and she moved languidly beneath his caresses, as if they were journeying far together, through other sultry evenings, mysterious, endless . . .

"Do you hear something?" she suddenly asked.

They stiffened to upright positions, their radars clicking to what was undeniably a car in the driveway. "Could it be the magic of multiple listing, forty-eight hours early?"

"I'd thought"—her voice was regretful—"it'd be the magic of multiple orgasm."

He jumped out of bed and scuttled to the window, gathering up shirt and pants as he went. "Strange car parked outside."

"I'll straighten the bed," she said, hurrying into her clothes. "You let them in."

The pounding on the door was growing impatient. Quickly, he scurried down to the kitchen, his boot laces trailing. Through the front windows he saw a woman with a clipboard followed by a middle-aged couple, and all three were staring back in at him. For an instant he imagined he was naked; the attack on his and Sara's intimacy was so pronounced, he almost felt the three people out-side were watching them make love. He opened the door.

"I'm Linda Bowen from Highland Realty," smiled the lady with the clipboard, leading her charge into the kitchen, "and this is Mr. and Mrs. Avery."

"Glad to meet you," said Daniel.

"Same here," said Mr. Avery, heartily offering his hand; as Daniel shook it he realized his own was covered with K-Y Jelly. He moved to the kitchen sink and turned on the tap, then realized it must seem he was washing off Mr. Avery's handshake; he gazed at his hands in the running water, wondering what move to make, and caught the agent staring at him. Smiling lamely, he grabbed a towel and turned back to the crowd, hoping Mr. Avery didn't, in passing, sniff his own hand.

They filed upstairs, Mrs. Avery pausing to admire the shelves of books lining the stairwell.

"Do the books come with the house?" asked Mr. Avery.

"I'm not sure what we're doing with the books." What *are* we doing with the books? What are we going to do with everything? At the top of the stairs, Sara manifested like the ghost who defends the upper regions; as she ushered them into the bedroom, he no-ticed the bed had been hurriedly made with a large lump at the bottom. Could that be my underwear? Wrapped around the K-Y Jelly?

"What beautiful antiques," said Mrs. Avery.

"Do the antiques come with the house?" asked Mr. Avery.

Daniel opened the door to his meditation chamber, and everyone crowded into the candlelit room with its altar of Buddhas, many-armed Shivas, and erotic Dakinis; from the walls, mad-eyed yogis with matted beards, loincloths, and caved-in bellies stared at the trespassers, while wrathful Tibetan deities drank blood from human skulls; incense wafted around them.

"Reminds me of the war," remarked Mr. Avery, standing firmly on the meditation cushion. "Place I had in Germany. Smallest darn bedroom you ever saw." He chuckled at the memory.

They filed downstairs. "Shall we look at that pond?" asked Mr. Avery. "What I've got in mind is a beef farm, with a little aquacul-ture project on the side."

Daniel led him outside, behind the clothesline, down along the path he and Sara had beaten over the years; the heavy unfamiliar footsteps behind him belonged to someone who'd dropped into their life like a parachutist. Above the pond, the sun was setting, the water streaked with red, a favorite hour now shared with someone who was going to turn the place into a fish factory; he hoped Mr. Avery felt it was suitable for aquaculture, and at the same time he felt a shadow falling across the peaceful body of water.

"I've inquired at the Agricultural Station and I've got all the specifications. I daresay there'll have to be some changes made in the overflow."

They walked back up to the house, where the three women were chatting. "We were just saying," said Mrs. Avery, "that we could come through the wall over there and make another bedroom out of the combined workshop and woodshed." Daniel felt walls crashing down around him; he suddenly saw the house in its skeletal form—he and Waldo hammering the studs of that particular wall on a summer's day a lifetime ago. The voices chattering around him grew distant, like a time that hadn't yet come, and it was just he and Waldo hammering nails in the hot pine-fragrant sun, and then he returned to the present and plans for tearing the wall down.

"We'd better be going," said Mr. Avery; they stepped outside, waved good-bye, and their car took off in a cloud which settled slowly, the last rays of sunset coming through the screen of dust.

Daniel listened to the sound fade up the road. He and she went back into the house.

"The Averys'll never take it," she said. "The bathroom's too small, the meditation room's too small . . ."

"What do you mean? It reminded him of his room in Germany."

"The wall needs to be knocked down between the workshop and woodshed . . ." That's right, he thought. Maybe I should knock it down myself before it discourages other people.

Half-heartedly, he asked, "Do you want to go upstairs?"

"No."

The magic of multiple listing, he knew, had struck its first blow.

■ ■ ■

"But I luv her so much," sobbed Hilton.

Daniel patted his back, hesitantly, a bit stunned by the big man's emotion.

"D'you think she'll come back to me?"

"I don't know, Hilton. What made her walk out?"

"Twas that fuckin whore upstairs from us, tellin her stories about me gettin drunk and sayin things . . . son a fuckin whore-suck . . ." His words were lost in sobs.

Daniel shifted his weight uncomfortably. In all the years he'd lived in the country, he'd never heard anyone speak of love; they joked of sex as naturally as they joked about excretory functions, but the only talk of love he'd ever heard was on Phoebe's soap opera and the radio's endless twanging ballads from Canadian Nashville. He pictured the lethargic middle-aged woman he'd met, and wondered what it was about her that inspired this earthquake of passion in Hilton, who was hanging onto the stable door, sobbing loudly, while the horse within stamped his hooves in embarrassment; or had Hilton forgotten to feed the beast in his anguish? Festus too was hanging around, gnawing a dead beaver he'd caught and dragged in from the stream; he glanced up from his feast to look askance at the unprecedented floodtide of emotion.

"I luv that fuckin bitch so much," wept Hilton. "You think she'll come back, Dan'l?"

Daniel gazed at his friend; a more pitiful sight he'd never seen than the giant bear moaning at the stable door. "I'm gonna put a pitchfork up that old whore's ass," Hilton sobbed, driving the pitchfork deep into the manure and flinging shit wildly in the air above their heads.

Straw and fragrant seed and angle worms fell around Daniel's shoulders. "Don't cry, Hilton. She'll come back."

"How d'we know?" Hilton sobbed. "That no-good whore," he whimpered, staggering toward the shit maw; he stuck his head through into the stable, and the horse let out a neigh. "You shut up," Hilton yelled at the animal, "you fucker . . ." He looked like a man with his head in the stocks, and Daniel wondered whether Ms. Gruber was suffering comparably, but as soon as he wondered, he knew: She was apathetically rolling a cigarette, staring out some window, and not suffering from anything but her usual boredom.

Hilton's head reappeared from the shit maw, his bloodshot eyes sending dirty streaks of tears down his puffy cheeks. "I ain't never luved nobody like I luv her." Spittle and tears dribbled off his lips, slobbering onto and extinguishing his cigarette. His eyes rolled drunkenly, the corners of his mouth turning down in an anguished cry. "Jeffer! Jeffer!" So primeval was the force behind the love call,

Daniel feared a moose might come charging out of the woods. Hilton thrashed his arms in the air, calling across the valley at the top of his lungs, "Jeffer . . ." and fell backward, into the manure pile.

The laughter of a crow echoed down into the valley. But Hilton was asleep, in deep relief from his misery.

Quietly Daniel walked to the house.

Murvyle and Phoebe looked up from their tea.

"Anythin new?" asked Murvyle casually.

"Hilton's in the manure pile."

"Tsk, tsk," said Phoebe. "I dunno what's gonna be with him, pon my soul I don't."

Daniel pulled up a chair, and accepted a cookie. "He's taking it pretty hard."

"It come to him too late in life," explained Phoebe. "That's why it took him like this."

"Never too late," said Murvyle optimistically, undoubtedly hoping, once more, to have Hilton out of his hair, home, and manure pile.

Phoebe sighed, shaking her head. "He says he loves her."

"Aye," replied Murvyle.

Hilton's distant wail filled the air, followed by retching sounds.

Phoebe glanced across the table at Murvyle. "You ain't never said you loved me."

Murvyle puffed at his cigarette thoughtfully. "No, I don't recall that I ever did."

■　■　■

"If I sell me 'ouse in town, I can buy this place with money to spare." The cockney's eyes were bright with excitement, his ginger mustache trembled, and Daniel reflected that he probably lived in the suburb of Militaryville, a hotbed of Englishmen, with the only drugstore in the province that sold mustache wax.

They sat around the table, the enthusiastic cockney, the low-keyed agent, he, and Sara, wondering when it could all be accomplished and the Englishman move in and they move out. "By the end of summer anyway," guessed the agent.

Daniel looked at Sara; she nodded. "The end of summer's perfect."

"Me life'll be one long 'oliday. It's cheap at the price."

"We priced it to sell," said Sara, who'd picked up numerous real estate expressions in the course of the past few weeks.

The Englishman nodded sympathetically. "Must break your 'earts to leave the place."

"It does," said Daniel.

"Eight years," murmured Sara vaguely.

"I feel it in me bones!" he exclaimed. "This is where I'm meant to be. I've loved the woods all me life. Just to walk among the trees and 'ear the buzzin and the twitterin . . ." His eyes grew glassy with emotion, his ginger mustache went on trembling, and Daniel felt like putting his arms around this man who was such a blood brother. *It'll almost be as if I'm not leaving, selling to a person who's so much like me.*

The Englishman got up and strode to the window, gazed at the endless procession of ridges, and laughed aloud with happiness, a man dying of thirst who'd found water, a great bubbling spring, the fountainhead of pleasure. "I'll be back tomorrow evening with the old bag."

■ ■ ■

A man who would bury a mustache of such magnitude in the forest has to be a great nature lover.

Daniel glanced at his watch, as he heard the tires turn down the lane; the car came into sight, with the ginger mustache at the wheel.

Daniel got up and walked toward it.

The Englishman parked, climbed out, and opened the other door for his wife, who came rollicking forth in a cloud of hair spray and perfume, with merrily jangling jewelry and a bust meant for balancing tankards of ale. "'Ello, ducks," she said to Daniel with a wink, stepping onto the grass, followed by the passionate lover of nature, who—Daniel realized with a sinking feeling—had been kidding himself; the closest to nature the Englishman would ever get was wiggling across the lawn right now, and having chosen that piece of nature as his primary object in life, he was going to have to live with her, where she wanted to be, which was certainly not in the boondocks, with no one to appreciate her but one eccentric whippoorwill, a mad mockingbird, and two tame gorbies.

"Cute!" she said. "Oooh, 'tis cute, but like I said to Charlie 'e couldn't expect a girl to live so far out, specially without any telephone, and I never learned 'ow to drive . . ."

"But I'm going to teach you 'ow to drive," said Charlie. "And I'm going to 'ave the telephone brought out. 'Tis cute, isn't it? You do like it, don't you?"

"Oooh, you silly old cock-doodle, I'd perish of loneliness."

"Let me show you the 'ouse," said Charlie. "Let's show 'er the 'ouse," he muttered to Daniel.

"Right," said Daniel. "Won't you come in?"

She bounced in before them, balancing her invisible tankards of ale and filling the kitchen with her cozy good cheer.

"Hello," said Sara, stepping forward. The two women eyed each other slowly. "Dearie," said the Englishwoman with compassion, "'ow did you ever stand it for eight years!"

"Nice kitchen," began Charlie. "See, plenty of windows. I could build on a veranda for you . . . She likes a veranda, she does . . . I'll build verandas all round," he added desperately.

"Funny old rooster. It doesn't need verandas. It's cute as can be." She turned to Daniel. "Poor old rooster doesn't understand. I work as a commercial traveler, and me boss picks me up in his Caddy. Now, can you see Hizzy coming out 'ere?"

"No," admitted Daniel.

"Just one minute," said Charlie. "*I* can see Hizzy coming out 'ere."

"Would you like to go upstairs?" asked Sara.

"Deed I would. I love seeing other people's 'ouses." She wiggled up the stairs before Sara, and Charlie gazed at Daniel with infinite sadness. They followed the two women up.

"Dearie, don't tell me you're going to let these antiques go with the 'ouse. I'd put them straight away out of sight. Take down that Victorian light fixture this very minute before anybody sees it, and tack something cheap up instead, it won't get you one more cent on your price. And you ought to 'ide that china cupboard standing downstairs, I noticed it right off, everybody's going to want it, and they'll want it included for free. Oh, now!" she exclaimed, sashaying into the studio. "A real arteest! We used to know a lot of arteests . . ."

Daniel tried to comfort Charlie. "The furniture's going over big anyway."

"What difference does that make? She won't let me buy the

place." He lowered his voice. "Ever since I was a boy, I've always loved the fields and woods, the trees and the birds . . ."

The women clattered out of the studio, and trooped to the part of the show Daniel'd come to dread most—his meditation room. "This . . ." began Sara, opening the door.

"A box room! Isn't this 'omely. Every 'ouse 'as a box room in England. Remember our box room, Charlie?" she asked with a wink.

"I 'ad to give it a try," apologized Charlie, as they walked down the stairs.

"Don't mention it," said Daniel.

"Why don't you visit us in town," his wife was saying warmly to Sara. "You must be perishing out 'ere with no one to talk to."

They strolled through the garden, admiring the flowers.

"I love it 'ere," repeated Charlie sorrowfully. "Just the kind of place I do like. Peaceful and quiet. I see you 'ave a mockingbird."

"And these," he heard Sara explaining, "are my rugosa roses. They aren't as pretty or fragrant as the others, but they have extra big hips and they're good for tea."

"I've got big 'ips too," came the answer, "but I'm no good for tea."

Charlie gazed at his wife's form, then turned back to Daniel. "I'm the boss," he said. "When she's not around, like."

■ ■ ■

"Sara," he said, "do you have to keep ringing that cowbell?"

"I have to make sure the bears know I'm coming. Pike said the only time bears will attack is if you get between them and their cubs, or accidentally surprise them."

"And if someone comes to look at the house, are you going to explain why you're walking around with a cowbell?"

"If someone comes to look at the house and runs into a bear, do you think they're going to buy the place?" She gave her bell an extra loud ring, as they marched across the field. "I've never seen the bears so thick as this summer."

He opened the gate, and they entered the garden, he with his fork and she with basket and cowbell.

He dug into the soft earth, and began hilling beans, raising the soil like a collar around the neck of each plant. "Do you think we'll ever have another garden?" he asked.

"Someday," she murmured, "we'll have a pied à terre, a little retreat that's not too far from everything . . ."

A car turned down the lane, and drove toward the house.

"I can show the house myself," she offered, "if you want to keep
on gardening."

She left her basket and cowbell, and walked toward the house,
while he continued hilling beans.

After a while, he saw the car pull away; it stopped near the head
of the lane; a man stepped out, walked around to the back of the
car, and bent down; a woman stepped out the other side.

Daniel put down his digging fork, and left the garden; he
strolled across the meadow to the disabled car.

"Had a flat?"

"Afraid so," said the man.

"Hope it isn't an omen," said Daniel lightly.

The woman's face clouded over. "You don't really think it could
be?"

"Only if you believe in omens," he smiled.

"I do," she said with a worried look.

"Then you know how they are," said Daniel, helping the man
jack up the back of the car. "The problem's always interpretation."

"That's just it," she said.

"I've been trying to interpret omens for years," Daniel continued,
warming to the subject. "Sometimes they're obvious. Clear-cut.
Other times you simply don't know."

"Exactly, Jan," said the man, replacing the tire, "there are always
two sides to a coin."

"But a flat tire. Oh, dear." She looked genuinely distressed. "I
hadn't thought of it as an omen . . ."

"I'm overly superstitious," Daniel admitted.

"So am I."

The man extended his hand to Daniel. "Thanks for the help.
We'll be seeing you again real soon."

"Have a nice day," he replied.

They got into their car.

The woman waved as they pulled away, with a worried expression on her face, and Daniel heard the man saying, "Now, Jan . . ."

Nice people, he thought, walking back down the lane. The door
to the house flung open, and Sara came running toward him.

"Did they tell you?" she asked.

"They had a flat."

"Darling, they're going to buy it!"

"They are?"

"They want to pay cash and move in the middle of August. They loved it! Wasn't it lucky we were home? Goodness, we'd better get a move on if we're going to leave the middle of August."

". . . No need to get prematurely excited."

"Are you kidding? Cash."

"You know how people say things on the spur of the moment."

"These aren't people. They're Ian and Jan, and I'm telling you they loved it."

"Maybe," he said hesitantly, "I shouldn't have mentioned the omen."

"Exactly what omen did you mention?" she inquired icily.

"You know, the one about the flat tire. I didn't interpret it for them. But they had a flat tire leaving our driveway, and it seemed significant to me. And to Jan."

"Oh my God. I don't believe this. They're offering cash, and you're offering omens. What are you, a soothsayer? When did you ever understand omens? When did any of your omens ever come true?"

"Sometimes they do," he said lamely.

"Omens," she repeated, putting her face in her hands, and staring through her fingers up the lane where the dust was settling ominously.

She removed her hands from her face; he saw her pull herself together. "Why am I getting excited?" she asked rhetorically. "They were sane people. They won't take it seriously. People who talk cash don't let omens stand in their way."

■ ■ ■

"I can't understand it," she said listlessly.

He guiltily put down his book. "You know how people are, they indulge in fantasies and then have second thoughts."

"I know about people's fantasies," she said pointedly. "But Ian and Jan seemed so in love with the place . . ."

There was a knock on the door, and Orvis entered smiling. "I heard you was sellin, so I come to say *good-bye.*" He settled his bulk down on the couch, with vapors of pig shit wafting around him as attar wafts from a rose bush.

Daniel noticed Sara's eyes grow wide with alarm: *What,* they asked, *if a prospective buyer walks in, with the house smelling like a piggery?*

My friend, thought Daniel warmly, my fellow clubman.

"Talk about movin . . ." said Orvis.

Daniel agreed. "Talk about movin."

"Talk about movin," repeated Orvis, apparently waiting for the phrase to inspire him. ". . . Did you ever hear tell of Tabitha Weed?"

"Can't say that I ever did," replied Daniel, attempting to unobtrusively lean away from the fumes; he heard Sara's rocker working backward over the floorboards.

"Tabitha Weed growed up in Jerusalem, but soon she left fer to shack up with one man and t'other in pretty poor conditions. But they was city conditions, see?"

Daniel nodded, eyes smarting, sinuses draining, wondering whether the tale of Tabitha Weed who'd gone off to the city would be a long one.

"So, she come back t'other year to see us." Orvis's pink face took on a pursy quality; his voice rose to a snooty falsetto: *"How can you get oil back in here?* she asked. *And how can you go to an outhouse? I know I couldn't survive without no bath!"*

Daniel heard Sara's rocker back into the stove; her last retreat from the smell was to get up, which she did, her face the same antique apple green as the porcelain of her stove.

Orvis's cheeks bobbled up and down as he laughed at his story; his snout wrinkled in amusement; and Daniel felt, in many ways, it did seem as if a pig were paying a visit, a very pleasant jovial pig from his club; and the story *was* a long one. "How'd she survive twenty years in Jerusalem?" asked Orvis. "Tell me that?"

"Dunno," said Sara hoarsely.

Orvis pursed his lips and resumed his falsetto: *"Our kitchen at home is so much bigger than this!"* His voice now lowered considerably: "She knowed we'd never get to see it out to Alberta so she cal'ated she could say anythin, but her husband he tripped her up. *It's two foot bigger,* he said. You should've seen her! She looked like a gander gazin cross-eyed through the gates of hell fer a roast bodader that wasn't there . . ."

"You must be hot," blurted Sara, switching on the electric fan, which only served to stir up the vapors.

"Tabitha's husband was honest as the sun, but tighter'n the bark to a tree. Wore the same pair of shoes ever since I first knowed him, must be fifty year."

The crickets started singing; Orvis looked at his watch . . . paused. "Did you ever hear tell of a person curin a rupture without no operation? Use to be an old feller in the settlement name of Dunstan Feathers, set in his rocker without gettin up fer seventy-five year, and d'you know that rupture mended itself together?"

Daniel noticed that Sara was sitting on the steps, as close as she could be to going upstairs without actually departing the company; her knees were up, arms crossed, head down, nose muffled in her sleeves, and only two green eyes peeked over her wrists.

"How does it go now?" mused Orvis. "You take a big pitcher and fill it partway with water . . ." He scratched his head to recall. "What else is there? Part vinegar . . . part sugar . . ." He smiled kindly. "Would you care fer me to make some up fer you? Coolest drink there is. I see Sara there looks kinda bedraggled. Now, Sara, you come here and watch how I do it."

The great bulk lifted itself from the couch, and moved toward the counter, while Sara assembled the ingredients; Daniel saw her hands trembling, but he had to admit he felt in need of a drink.

Orvis poured, stirred, measured, stirred some more, filled the big pitcher to the brim, and sat down with it.

"She's right tasty, ain't she?"

Daniel took a sip; liquid pig shit.

"Jes the right 'portions." Orvis smacked his lips. ". . . Yessir, the most despisable man who ever lived, even if he was me own uncle . . ."

A car horn shattered the reminiscence.

"That's jes Becky, settin in the truck."

"She's been out there all this time?"

"Yup." He pondered. "Mebbe I ought to see what's itchin her."

"Tell her to come in."

"No, I think it's prob'ly time to get back, tuck them hogs in."

Daniel stood and said good-bye to his clubmate and friend;

Orvis left; Daniel contemplated the country style of visiting—man visits, wife sits in truck in the dark for an hour. He looked to the door . . . and saw, through the glass, Orvis's face reappear in the night like an apparition. "She jes seen a bear. Scared her fer a minute." He lumbered back in and sat down on the couch. "Talkin bear . . ." resumed Orvis.

"Think they'll stay together this time?" asked Sara, pouring tea for her guest.

"No tellin," sighed Phoebe. "Twas really that woman livin upstairs from them made all the trouble."

"They won't have anyone upstairs from them in the Glinkos' old house except porcupines."

"Nor they won't have to pay no rent. Orvis give it to them fer to keep the Glinkos from comin back."

"It's a big house to heat."

"That 'tis, but they gotta have more than one bedroom so welfare will think Hilton's the lodger."

"Doesn't it seem welfare would wonder why her lodger keeps moving around with her?"

"Beats me. Jes the same, they have put up some curtains." Phoebe's head snapped round to the window. "Car."

Sara looked out the window; around the bend in the lane came a white Lincoln Continental.

The door of the car opened, and what had to be one of the province's foremost pimps got out; he came to the door, knocked, and entered.

"Hi, there. I'm Doug Dettol of the Happy Home Agency."

"Help yourself." Sara gestured toward the stairs, having gotten so blasé about the whole thing, she no longer bothered to get out of her chair.

Doug Dettol climbed the stairs, and disappeared out of sight.

"Some snazzy shit, ain't he?" asked Phoebe.

"Sure is."

"See them fancy little shoes?" Phoebe shook her head. "Tsk, tsk." Overhead, came the sound of Doug Dettol heavily stomping in said fancy little shoes. "Don't you hate them snoopin round like that? I know I couldn't abide it."

"I hate it."

"If they want it," said Phoebe, "let them buy it outright. Why do they have to snoop around?"

"I hope you never have to go through this."

"Not likely I'll go through it," sighed Phoebe. "Couldn't get Murvyle out of Jerusalem with dinnamite."

The footsteps returned to the stairs, and Doug Dettol came down, puffing a cigar and smiling with an insincerity that made the honest Phoebe shudder perceptibly.

"I understand there's a swimming pool?"

"There's a pond," said Sara. "Go back under the clothesline and keep following the trail. It's not far."

Doug Dettol walked out, leaving the kitchen filled with cigar smoke.

"Awful smile," said Phoebe, shaking her head. "Makes a body think they're in a nightmare. Puts you in mind of that feller burned the gas station down fer the insurance, snazzy-lookin shit too. Some kind of an A-rab."

"Syrian," said Sara, who'd used the snazzy-lookin shit in question on several bedouin romances.

"I hear tell he's carryin on with Greta Samson's oldest girl."

"Isn't his wife carrying a child?"

"That's prob'ly what 'counts fer it. You ever seen the jewelry onto him? Shiny? And his pants is shiny too."

The door pushed open, and Doug Dettol returned; Sara noticed that his pants shined, as did his eyes. "All you need for that pond," he said, "is some geese. And there's your Christmas roast goose."

"Is there anything else I can show you?"

"I think I've seen enough," he murmured seductively, flashing the smile that again made Phoebe shudder. "We'll be discussing financing."

"Fine," agreed Sara.

She and Phoebe watched through the window as he departed.

"He must be gonna buy it," said Phoebe. "Talkin finance."

"I'll believe it when I see it."

The long Lincoln drove off, but before the dust had settled, a rusty jalopy came chugging down the lane and parked in its place.

The mismatched doors of the jalopy opened up, and disgorged—

as from the little car in the circus—a huge country family—father, mother, grandmother, grandfather, children, and grandchildren; gawking, they lumbered splay-legged to the door.

"Come in," called Sara.

"I declare," whispered Phoebe.

Father, mother, grandparents, and children trooped in, silent, boggle-eyed.

"Have a look," said Sara. "Don't be shy."

". . . Is there water in?" asked the matriarch of the group.

"Kitchen and bath," said Sara, pointing to the kitchen sink.

"Oh," they breathed, and tiptoed up the stairs.

Sara and Phoebe listened to the tiptoeing over the ceiling. Phoebe shook her head, repeating her complaint: "If they want it, why can't they jes buy it?"

Presently, the troop tiptoed back down, and filed toward the door. The matriarch turned. "There's water in too?" she asked.

"Hot and cold," said Sara.

They nodded, tiptoed out, and hobbled splay-legged back into their jalopy.

With much coughing of motor, the rusted car pulled out, and in the cloud of dust behind it, a small foreign auto appeared.

"Pon my soul," said Phoebe, touching her hair, having now encountered more strangers than she would've in an entire year's normal traffic out to Jerusalem.

A man stepped out, followed by a little girl who wrapped her arms around him; thus entwined, the couple approached, and entered.

"Hello. Can we look around?"

"Feel at home," said Sara.

Tightly embraced, the pair climbed the stairs. Phoebe's eyes met Sara's. "Is that his girl friend?" she whispered.

"It must be his daughter. She couldn't be more than ten."

"I dunno. You seen the way they was walkin? He might fancy them ten," she added sagely, accustomed to the most precocious country belles. "What's more," she whispered, "there was young Elva Weed, took up with her own father when she was eight."

Hand in hand, the team came down, and departed.

Sara and Phoebe watched through the window as they walked

toward their car, arms wound tight round each other. What a book jacket, thought Sara.

"Sure does put you in mind of young Elva."

■ ■ ■

"Back again," announced Linda Bowen of Highland Realty. "You remember Mrs. Avery, and these are her three lovely daughters."

"Surprised to see us?" twinkled Mrs. Avery.

"Why . . . no." It was the woman who'd come the first evening, whose husband's hand Daniel had shaken with K-Y Jelly; it seemed a very long time ago.

Mrs. Avery took out a typewritten sheet of paper. "My husband wanted me to ask you a couple of things. Would you consider selling us the china cupboard, the lamps, the round oak table, the antique bowl and pitcher, the storage bed, the wicker chairs . . ." She finished her list, and turned to her daughters. "Look around, girls."

The agent beckoned to Sara; they walked together to the shed. "Mr. Avery is a very thorough man. He takes his time, he investigates, but when he makes a decision . . ."

"He investigated?"

"He went to the Forestry Service and found out the worth of the timber on the property. He also found out how much it would cost to bring in a phone . . . Mrs. Avery, may I help you?"

"Would you help me with my measuring?" Mrs. Avery giggled gaily. "It's amazing what a memory my husband has for things."

The agent went in with Mrs. Avery, and Sara stepped outside. The teen-age girls approached her ominously.

"Where are the boys around here?"

"Boys?"

They nodded in unison.

There's Hilton, thought Sara. But no, I can't lie to them. "There aren't any boys."

"Where are they?"

"The closest are five miles away, and there aren't a lot of them there either . . . did you see the nice swimming pond?" But the girls were walking away.

The agent came out of the house, fanning herself. "Mrs. Avery has a few more things to check off. Mr. Avery's memory really is amazing."

"The girls asked me where the boys were, and I told them there weren't any."

"Don't worry, Mr. Avery makes all the decisions, and he's decided he wants this property. He's a very strong-willed man. Will you come into my office on Monday, both of you?"

"Are you that sure?"

"If you knew Mr. Avery as I do . . ."

■ ■ ■

"That's all right," said Daniel. "We had to come into town anyway."

Sara sipped the coffee the agent had offered. It was a very feminine office, with toile de jouy on the walls and French provincial furniture.

"It was the daughters," explained the agent.

"You know," said Sara, "we had the impression it was going to be easy to sell our place. It isn't overpriced, is it?"

"I think it's dirt cheap." The agent opened an enormous looseleaf book on her desk. "This is your problem. I've got a thousand homes for sale right here in town, never mind the country."

"You mean," asked Daniel, "a quarter of the town is for sale?"

"And most people would rather build new houses in subdivisions."

Sara reached for a second donut.

"On the other hand," said the agent, "your place is unique. On the other hand, people get put off by that telephone thing. They fall apart when they hear the phone company's quote. Of course, anybody with brains could get the company to put the goddamn thing in for free. All you have to do is raise a little hell."

Sara examined the agent more closely. "Are you, by any chance, American?"

"You didn't think I was a native, did you?"

■ ■ ■

They were just sitting down to dinner, when a car pulled up. "I don't know about you," she said, "but *I'm* eating."

"You can't be rude to people."

"Why is it rude?"

But he was up, and opening the shed door to what was starting to seem to her the eternal trio—vivacious agent and wary couple. This particular agent was Cookie Norton, who'd helped them make their decision to sell, and the wary couple consisted of a fat shifty-eyed man of about thirty and a mousy wife who had already decided she would never live this far out in the country.

"Golly," said Cookie, "I hope we aren't disturbing your supper."

"Not at all," said Daniel. "Come in."

The man walked ponderously around the room, jingling coins in his pocket, swinging one pudgy fist, grunting, and peering behind pieces of furniture; still grunting, still punching, he stopped jingling coins in order to free one hand to open up all the cupboards and examine each item of food, container, utensil . . . while his wife moseyed behind him with the apathy of a wind-up mouse.

"Shall we go upstairs?" blurted Cookie, when the couple began circling the room for the fourth time, with every indication that their compulsive tour would continue indefinitely.

Daniel followed them up, and Sara settled herself deep in her rocker, feeling more invaded than usual by the inquisitive punching man and his wind-up wife; their elephantine steps thudded overhead, along with more grunting, and she envisioned the couple examining every cranny of her studio and bedroom and the bedside drawer where the K-Y Jelly was kept. The footsteps paused, as always, at Daniel's meditation room; she heard conversation, and wondered whether the punching man was standing on Daniel's cushion. And then the elephantine procession came down again.

Cookie examined her clipboard, turning to Sara. "One of the other agents asked me to find out a couple of things for some clients who've already been out here . . . the Powells . . . do you recall the Powells? They want to know if any of the furniture comes with the house."

The heads of the man and wife snapped round with interest; it was the first sign of life the woman had shown since her arrival.

"The storage bed," dictated Sara, "both woodstoves, all major appliances, all fixtures . . . and fifty dollars worth of birdseed."

". . . *fifty dollars worth of birdseed,*" repeated Cookie, completing her notes; Sara'd said it as a joke, but immediately perceived that fifty dollars worth of free anything could be the decisive factor.

The man thrust his punching hand toward Daniel, who shook it. "I'll be back," said the man; it was just three little words, but somehow he managed to invest them with a solipsistic weight, and Daniel answered with equal earnestness. "I know you will."

As the door closed behind the trio, Sara plunged her fork into a cold dinner.

"He'll be back," said Daniel.

"So sit down and eat."

"He's different from the others. He had a firm handshake. And clear eyes."

"Clear eyes?" she asked in amazement. "Those were the shiftiest pig eyes I've seen in a week."

"Anyway, he was the only one who understood my meditation room. That's got to be an omen."

She looked at him cuttingly.

"All right," he said, "not an omen. Cross out omen. An indication."

"Are you going to eat?"

"Do you know he studied to be a priest?"

"I've always wanted to meet a defrocked priest."

"Not defrocked. He never took his final vows. But there's a sincerity in the guy. A certain depth. I can tell these things."

■   ■   ■

"I told you I'd be back," declared the defrocked priest, standing at the door with his mousy wife and an embarrassed young giant whom he introduced as his brother.

It was drizzling, and Sara asked them in with more friendliness than was called for, in atonement for having thought he would never come back and for still thinking he had shifty pig eyes.

"This is the kitchen," he explained bombastically to his brother, who hadn't inherited the family forwardness, who was, in fact, introverted to the point of deaf mutism. The wife maintained her wind-up indifference. As the tour continued, Sara slipped next door to Daniel's workshop.

"Pierre Petite is here."

"Did I tell you?" asked Daniel.

"You told me."

"He was able to sense the spiritual atmosphere of the place."

"He brought his brother."

"We'll go for a walk in the woods."

"It's raining."

"That won't bother us."

There was a knock on the workshop door, and the defrocked priest entered, grabbing Daniel's hand and pumping it with enthusiasm. "I want you to meet my brother. He's going to live here with us."

At the attention he was getting, the brother recoiled more deeply into his painful mutism; Sara wondered if, perhaps, he weren't what Phoebe referred to as *funny*.

"Maurice is going to live out here on the shed," explained Pierre. "He's examining the structure to see if he can combine the workshop and woodshed." They watched the brother examining the structure; he must know a lot about carpentry, thought Sara, since the examination seemed to require nothing more than mute gaping.

"Ready for the woods?" asked Daniel.

"That's what we came for."

The three men and the wife trooped out, and Sara returned to her baking.

After a while, through the windows, she saw the caravan return sopping wet; instead of entering their car, the Petite family entered the kitchen with Daniel, dripping puddles.

"I'll make a fire," said Daniel, throwing open the doors of the Franklin, "to dry you off before you go home."

The Petites gathered round the fire in the chairs Daniel pulled up. He put some tea on the stove, and took Sara's cookies as they came out of the oven.

The dripping Petites dug in, with healthy appetites, and Sara supposed Daniel was trying to show them how nice it could be, living here, with the fire, the tea, her cookies.

Fortified, the defrocked priest launched into a sermon; the brother stared dumbly into the fire; the wife, Sara noted, when wet, with nylon jacket plastered against her, and hair over face like a naiad, lost a great deal of her mousiness. As Pierre's rambling washed around them, Sara found herself dwelling more and more on the ménage à trois situation; what part will strong silent Maurice play when Pierre goes away on his long business trips, during which he doesn't wish to leave his wife alone with anyone but his dull-witted brother in his dripping, size fifteen shoes? "The thing that's wrong with the Church . . ." rambled Pierre, while book jackets swirled in Sara's head: *My Brother's Wife, A Backwoods Saga of Betrayal and Murder,* involving a sensitive, if boring, priest, his funny brother, and the sometimes-mousy but not-so-when-sopping-wet woman caught between them. Sara gazed at the tableau round the fire, as Daniel encouraged the group with his warmth and hospitality to feel the happy home that could be theirs.

All her cookies were gone, and she wished the Petites too were gone, but Pierre, with his pants wet up to his knees, sprawled over his chair and rocked in front of the fire, gesturing with his pudgy fingers as if he were their host. "A socialist community isn't something you can plan," he declared. "It just happens . . ." describing for them the band of Petites who would flock to this haven of his. Sara could see the far-flung relations dancing *Le Grand Chapeau* in the orchard, and she found herself combating her boredom by trying to remember all the numerous verses of that local ditty while Pierre explained the fall of Western democracy.

Like that other great French revolutionary, Marat, he seemed to have the ability to philosophize immersed in water; the rain from his clothes sloshed in his chair as he rocked, making a sucking accompaniment to his all-encompassing critique of the immoral, capitalistic, materialistic clique that had ruined the twentieth century.

At long last, he sloshed to his feet. "I guess it's no secret we're in love with the place." Sara thought it was certainly a secret as far as his wife and brother went since they'd said scarcely a word, but like many great men, when Pierre spoke, he spoke the mind of a larger group. "Now," he concluded, "it's just up to the bank."

Sara glanced at the not-so-mousy woman, wondering how in love *she* was. "Do you," asked Sara, "want to live here too?"

"Yes," said the woman with surprising authority. "I've wanted to from the first."

They shook hands firmly all around, which seemed to cause endless anguish to the retiring brother, and with vows of undying love for the place, the Petites squished out. Her last image of Pierre was of a shifty-eyed toad, squatly squelching his way across the marsh of her kitchen floor.

She got out the mop.

Daniel turned to her. "Was I right?"

"I guess so."

"Aren't they the greatest?"

"They are," she said, following his policy of only speaking the highest of pivotal people, so as not to put bad vibrations into the air; had he not trained her so well in this superstition, she would've loved discussing the ménage à trois and getting his opinion; instead, she stifled her instincts and said brightly, "A socialist community."

"Yes," he said, helping her wipe the floor. "Once again, New Jerusalem will be a settlement. Families will multiply from one abandoned farm to the next . . ."

"With gay melodies floating on the summer air, fiddlers' reels, dancing in the orchard . . ."

"I'm glad it's the French."

"I am too," she agreed, understanding his feeling for the downtrodden minority of the province; it was almost as if the land were being returned to its rightful owners; not that the French were any more the rightful owners of the land than any other white conqueror; but it had a ring, and they rang it; it had a storybook symmetry, and was possibly the opening of an immortal family saga with its humble beginnings as a moronic ménage à trois spreading to generations; so they talked on, praising what would be, as they mopped the floor, and the rain came down, bringing with it the gray curtain of twilight.

■ ■ ■

"I'm back," announced the defrocked priest. It was a hot dry day; his last visit had also been the last rain and seemed to have ushered in drought.

"Glad to see you," she lied, having left a painting mid-inspiration.

"I know we're not supposed to come in the morning," apologized the intruder with an expression which said he knew the rule couldn't possibly apply to him. His companion wore a clip-on tie and carried a spade.

"Is it all right if I look at the soil?" asked the clip-on man.

"Of course," she replied, and a second later saw him plunge his spade into her flower bed.

She hurried into the workshop to tell Daniel that Pierre Petite was here with a man digging up her flowers.

Daniel came out to greet them.

"Soil somewhat alkaline," sniffed the man with the spade.

"I've got it all settled," said Pierre. "I'm going to get a mobile phone; Celeste calls her parents a lot; and I can call home when I'm on the road and check in with her and Maurice. I have all the prices . . ."

"Mind if I go off in the woods and dig there?" asked the spade man.

"Go right ahead," she said, wondering whether she could save the blooms he'd tossed up if she quickly reburied their roots.

"You've lived in New York?" asked Pierre. "I was there myself once. I was offered a novitiate in Brooklyn, but of course I couldn't live in such a dangerous place. I'd be crazy after one week. A ground-floor apartment too. Can you imagine living in a ground-floor apartment in Brooklyn?"

"Easily," she said. "I grew up in one."

"A person would have to be crazy. What a place. That was it for me," he said, sweating profusely at the remembrance. If, she thought, he was terrified of Brooklyn, is it any wonder that before he moves to New Jerusalem he wants to make sure he's surrounded by his brother, a mobile phone, a soil expert, and eventually an entire community? She saw her home through Pierre's darting eyes, and the prospect was fraught with dangers—not just bears and being miles from neighbors, but everything about country life. Why would he even consider living in the wilderness?

"Was that why you left the priesthood?" asked Daniel.

"That was the last straw," said Pierre, nervously punching his fist and jingling the coins in his pocket. "Boy, it's nice here."

"You know," said Daniel gently, "I had a lot of doubts before we came out. I worried about a lot of things . . . telephones, the soil . . . but once you're living here, all your doubts fade away. The peace of the place takes you over." He continued speaking soothingly until the gentleman with the spade returned and announced the soil in the woods was a bit acidic.

"I guess this is it," said Pierre, as if the soil testing had been the clincher. "I'll tell the agency it's okay."

"You won't be sorry," said Daniel.

They watched the car drive away.

"You don't think," she asked, "that Pierre's a little indecisive, do you?"

"Because he's being thorough? I know how he feels."

"That business about leaving the priesthood?"

"That's all in his favor."

"It is?"

"You weren't brought up Catholic. I was. You don't understand these things."

"No, but I was brought up in Brooklyn, in a ground-floor apartment."

"He's a simple country priest. New York scared him. I know he's going to be very happy here."

■ ■ ■

"I came to look at the fuse box," said Pierre.

"Sure," she smiled. "Come on in."

"I brought my friend Wayne," he said, introducing a simian-browed individual with a severe overbite.

"Glad to meet you," she said, wondering if Pierre had an endless supply of pseudo-expert friends. "It's right down past that door-way."

The two men went down to the cellar, and she walked through to Daniel's workshop. "It's Pierre Petite again. With a friend to look at the fuse box."

"I showed him the fuse box. In fact, I showed it to him twice."

"He had a concerned look on his face."

"I'll go down and explain it to him in more detail."

They went back into the house; Pierre and friend were coming up from the basement, Pierre wearing a reassured expression; he jingled the coins in his pocket and punched his chubby fist in the air. "Boy, it's nice here. Is it okay if I show Wayne over the house?"

"Absolutely," said Daniel. "I'll go with you and answer any questions Wayne may have."

They went upstairs; she stayed in the kitchen, staring out through the window. The flower garden hadn't been doing too well ever since it had been dug up by the spade man and declared alkaline; also, it still hadn't rained, and according to Mortimer

Asshole, if the drought continued, there'd be "a widespread boden-tial of forest fires."

■ ■ ■

"Me again," said Pierre. "Is Daniel here?"

"I'll get him for you." She excused herself, knocked at the door of Daniel's workshop, and slipped inside. "Pierre Petite. Looking worried again."

Daniel put down the wood he was sanding, and walked out to the yard. "Good to see you, Pierre. What can I do for you today?"

"I forgot where the well was."

"Right here by the ivy. If you want, we can pace it off from the house."

She watched them pacing it off. "There are two or three old fellows around here," said Daniel, "who know where everything is better than I do. I'll introduce you to them, so if you ever have any problems, there'll be someone who can help. They've known the place for years, probably dug the well themselves . . ."

"And the septic system?"

The two men walked behind the house to discuss, for the third or fourth time, the location and working of the cesspool. She strolled across the drive to the orchard, and took an apple; in spite of the drought, the summer apples were ripening nicely.

"Want a yellow transparent?" she asked Pierre, when the men reappeared from in back of the house.

"I'll just take one."

"Let me give you a bagful," said Daniel.

She saw a sneaky look cross the fat man's eyes, making them shiftier than ever; his untrustworthiness seemed for an instant troubled by guilt as if he knew in advance he was going to do something underhanded and perhaps shouldn't take a whole bagful of apples; but then across the piggy eyes, more fundamental feelings passed. "I could use a couple of bags," he replied.

■ ■ ■

"Hi, there," said Cookie Norton, getting out of her car, with an elderly gentleman who had obviously spent his life chopping trees. "I've got an offer for you," she said.

Sara looked at the gentleman questioningly.

"Not Thurston," laughed Cookie. "He just came to keep me company. I brought out the Petites' offer."

Daniel turned to Sara. "Your troubles are over."

"Shall we go in and talk?" asked Cookie.

Sara gazed at the sky. "Do you see any chance of rain?"

"Nope," said Thurston decisively. "Wells is goin dry all over the province."

"I've been so worried about our well. It never went dry before, but the pump's been working so hard . . ."

"Want me to take a look at her fer you?" asked Thurston.

"Would you?" she asked inanely, knowing she was clutching at straws, that Daniel knew as much about their water system as anyone, since he'd installed it, and that Thurston was only, as the locals would say, "an old frigger," having gained a certain amount of expertise tinkering with things because he was too cheap, or poor, to hire professionals. She led him down the stairs to the pump.

"Lovely cellar," he said. "Them old fellers could put up a wall."

"Yes, it's all flat-faced fieldstone . . . but listen . . . do you hear that pump laboring?"

"Aye. Tain't nahthin wrong with that pump."

"Are you sure?"

"Sure as shittin."

"You hear how long it took to fill up?"

"I bet this old cellar's awful good fer bodaders."

"Oh dear, I wish it would rain."

"Good fer apples too," he surmised, as they climbed back upstairs.

"Shall we sit down?" asked Cookie.

"I'll jes take a walk through the woods," offered Thurston discreetly.

"You can't," said Sara. "All the woods are closed because of forest fires. I heard it on Mortimer Asshole this morning."

"I won't set no fires," winked the old frigger, shutting the door behind him.

"He really shouldn't go in the woods," she said.

"Please stop worrying," said Daniel.

"Now," said Cookie, spreading out papers. "The Petites hired the bank assessor to come out here one day last week. I believe you were in town when he came."

"The bank assessor?" asked Sara.

"Will you please calm down?" said Daniel.

"And," continued Cookie, "the bank assessor put the value a little below where we priced it."

"He did?" asked Sara, growing ashen.

"Just a few thousand."

"A few thousand dollars?"

"Five or seven thousand. He said he wouldn't care to live so far out himself. No neighbors or street lights or anything. But the Petites have a substantial down payment, so they won't have a bit of trouble getting a mortgage."

"Five or seven thousand . . ." said Sara.

"The Petites' offer," said Cookie, "is a tiny bit lower," and she named a figure so small that even placid Daniel stood up from the table. "Sorry, Cookie. If it comes to that we're not selling. I'd rather rent to the Glinkos."

"Golly," said Cookie, "I know how you feel, but it's an awful bad time for real estate. And some of the other agents said . . . I don't know if you met Doug Dettol . . . he said you'd be lucky to get half what you're asking."

"But Cookie, *you* set the price."

"I know." She shook her head. "But Doug Dettol said he went over in a plane and that's what he told me."

Sara had an image of Doug Dettol's shining trousers, and his teeth, and recalled how Phoebe, who was surely clairvoyant, shuddered twice.

"I'm afraid we're not selling," said Daniel.

"Now this figure of the Petites'," said Cookie soothingly, "is only an offer. We'll make a counteroffer."

Only an offer, thought Sara. It doesn't mean anything. "How much can we counteroffer?"

"We can go up one or two thousand."

"But that's still far less than it's assessed at."

"I don't know," said Cookie. "Doug Dettol said you'd be lucky to get anything."

Lucky to get anything, thought Sara. Lucky not to have to pay somebody to take it away. She gazed at Daniel and saw it in his eyes: The forces of Atlantic Canada had joined and were buffeting them; it was she and Daniel sinking, with the province pushing their heads under the mud. The people had rendered their judgment, with airplanes, assessors, soil testers, and found against the two of them. Even their agent had found against them.

"We'll counter two thousand more," said Daniel, "and that's it. If they don't come up two thousand dollars, we're quits."

"I'm sure they will," said Cookie, pushing forward the offer to be countered and signed.

"What's this?" asked Sara, reading the addenda. "We have to include all major appliances, both stoves, all fixtures, and fifty dollars worth of birdseed?"

"Yes, the Petites wrote that in."

"We were going to include it all anyway," said Daniel.

"Not at this price," said Sara.

"No," agreed Cookie, "it's too bad they heard about it. I wouldn't leave them a nail at this price, but what can we do? Sign right here . . ."

"What," asked Sara, "is this *hundred dollars subject to financing?*"

"That's the Petites' deposit."

"Didn't we," asked Daniel, "have to give you a thousand-dollar deposit when we bought the place?"

"Subject to nothing," added Sara.

"Gosh," said Cookie, "I'm lucky I got a hundred from them. Pierre only wanted to give a dollar. He said his lawyer told him that's all he's legally bound to give is one dollar. I really had to fight for that hundred."

"I never trusted those little pig eyes of his."

"I'd count on moving in a month," said Cookie.

Sara gazed through the window toward the forest, where one of the trees appeared to disentangle itself from the others. It was, she saw, the old frigger, gnarled and mossy, and as he lurched slowly forward, he seemed to be the spirit of Atlantic Canada moving against them.

■   ■   ■

"Hi, folks," said Pierre. "I wonder, Daniel, if you could show me how to clean out the chimneys."

"Sure thing, Pierre," said Daniel, with the fatherly tenderness he'd permanently adopted toward the defrocked priest.

She watched Daniel and Pierre emerge from the shed with a twenty-four-foot ladder, which Daniel climbed.

"Those so-and-so agents," said Pierre beside her on the ground. "They tried to make me give a bigger deposit. What a bunch of crooks. I told them all I had to legally give was one dollar. One dollar." His jowls were shaking in anger, and his Punch & Jingle Show was going full speed, the incident apparently having touched the very center of his religious beliefs. "Those crooked so-and-so's," he fumed. "Excuse my language, Sara, but if there's one thing that gets me hopping, it's a person who can't be trusted."

■ ■ ■

"But, Daniel, I don't trust him."

They stood on the sidewalk, between the real estate office they'd just stepped out of and the red brick newspaper building.

"The mortgage has gone through," he said patiently. "You heard Cookie on the phone with the bank. This is it. We've got to be out in two weeks, and that means we've got to get rid of our things, which means an ad in the *Loyalist*."

"But what if he backs out?" She knew she was behaving hysterically, standing fist-clenched in the middle of the sidewalk. "How can we know he'll keep his word?"

"Sweetheart, you weren't raised Catholic. You don't understand that when a priest gives his word, that's it. Forever."

"He changed his mind once," she said obstinately. "He can change it again."

"He hadn't taken his final vows."

"He hasn't taken these final vows either. He's put down one hundred dollars."

Daniel turned away impatiently. "I'm going into the *Loyalist* office, and I'm going to take out an ad for a yard sale next weekend, and tomorrow and Friday I'm going to bring all my books in and give them to the library."

"All your books?"

"I might leave a few religious works for Pierre."

"Are you really going to get rid of everything?"

"What else am I going to do with it? I'll keep my tools and some clothes."

Unclenching her fists and feeling rather humbled, she followed him into the newspaper office.

■ ■ ■

Jalopies with plastic hood ornaments filled the lane; women came with their hair in rollers; trucks arrived with children and dogs. By 9:00 A.M. the yard sale was going at 78 r.p.m.

Old Burpee, laid low by strokes and no longer able to get even one watch to go on his wrist, was deposited upon a rocker, and there he remained, his venerable bottom covering the price tag, while he dribbled snuff, muttered unintelligible comment, and greeted other old codgers who'd come out of their lairs this fine Saturday.

"How much fer this here bottle cutter?"

"Fifty cents."

"I'll give you a nickel."

Suttle and his wife appeared in his Studebaker, the old man still chuckling at the same private joke that had tickled him when he'd sold them the place; however, his belly was no longer fat enough to shake, and each tremulous chuckle threatened to be his last. Mrs. Suttle was nothing but a brittle stick which the first strong wind would lift and carry away; she held her apple basket over one arm.

"Won't you help yourself to apples," asked Sara, as she had every fall for eight years.

"Will you come back to visit?" quaked the old midwife.

"Of course."

"You'll never be back," chuckled Suttle.

The shrunken pair hobbled to the orchard, where two little boys sat perched on the limbs of two trees, testing Daniel's walkie-talkies.

Old Alf, with his attaché case, did a brisk business in Dr. Fowler, positioning himself near Uncle Burpee's rocker. "Burpee, ma fran, you need a drink . . ."

"Would you like some of my houseplants?" Sara asked Jeffer, who moved through the crowd smoking in silence, Hilton faithfully panting at heel.

"I don't mind," replied Jeffer apathetically. "You got any eight-track tapes?"

"Come down in price on that telescope yet?" asked a gentleman from town.

As she pocketed the reduced price for Daniel's telescope, she happened to glance across at the orchard: The call must've gone out; the beast had risen; at least thirty people were swarming over the apple trees, breaking branches and doing more damage than the bears had done in a century.

"How much fer this here . . . what zactly is it?"

"It's a sterling-handled cake knife."

"Give you twenty-five cent fer it."

"Sorry, as you can see, it's marked three dollars."

The face beetle-browed in suspicion. "Thirty cent?"

She thought over all the others who'd suggested a quarter, and since thirty cents was the best offer, she took it, knowing once again that when it came to money, these people would beat her down every time; generations of poverty gave them a bargaining position stronger than hers could ever be; their ceiling was so low, it was absolute . . . absolutely too low . . . but what else could she do? Dump the stuff in the woods? It's our getaway, she told herself, trying to think of the sophisticated seaside resort she'd been at once for an antique auction, where the people knew the value of life and things, and didn't try to take your grandmother's sterling-handled cake knife for a quarter. And this, she thought, gazing at the hordes of shuffling haggling buffaloes on the lawn, is what I'm cutting loose from, and why I've got to throw away my grandmother's cake knife, or sink forever in the lethargy gallumphing now over the grass.

"I'll give you ten cent fer them rose bushes."

"Sorry, the rose bushes aren't for sale."

"How much you want fer that there sidin on the house?"

She hesitated, sorely tempted to sell the cedar clapboards as a gesture against Pierre Petite. "I'm afraid they're already sold."

In the shade of the flower garden set a trunk filled with small items marked 25¢ *Apiece,* most of which were ultimately going for a penny or two, and into this trunk she'd dumped a variety of things purchased on her mad K-mart binges; there was, for instance, a collection of identically shaped tiny plastic objects, which she'd rubber-banded together in a group, whose purpose was now a mystery to her. To this trunk of cheap oddities, the good people of the province kept returning, crowding round in bovine herds to finger the oddball bargains with a dull-eyed curiosity which, she felt, reflected to perfection her own consumer dream for the past eight years.

"Here's a buck fer this Indian basket," said Pike savagely.

"Just take it, Pike. Take whatever you can use."

"It's marked a buck and I'll give you a buck," he threatened loudly, "and anybody who don't pay the price as marked is a god-damn mean good-fer-nahthin son of a bitch." The red-bereted maverick cut a wide swath each time he pushed through the crowd with another item and fistful of greenbacks, and in his wake there was always a few moments of timorous silence before the goddamn mean good-fer-nahthin sons of bitches made their next heart-woundingly low offers.

By three o'clock, the bones had been picked clean, the orchard stripped, the lawn devastated, and only a wasteland remained, while the vultures and jackals drove up the lane.

She and Daniel lifted Uncle Burpee to his feet, and traded the rocker he'd sat on for a bottle of Alf's Dr. Fowler.

■ ■ ■

"We close with the lawyers in the morning"—she was cutting Phoebe's hair—"and leave tomorrow afternoon."

Phoebe sighed deeply. "And you dunno where yer goin?"

"No."

"I suppose a person can alluys find a place fer the night to lay their head." She sounded not at all sure and, for an instant, Sara saw their venture through Phoebe's eyes and was the slightest bit terrified.

The instant passed. "We can sleep in back of the van till it gets too cold," she replied; they'd traded their truck in on a brand-new van, from a car salesman Daniel said was a Grand Master, thus ensuring the gentleman's grand mastery for another year. She went on clipping Phoebe's hair—rather short—as neither of them knew where Phoebe's next haircut would come from.

"The only thing Daniel hasn't gotten around to doing yet," said Sara, "is wrapping his pennies. Two apple-juice cans full. The bank won't accept them like that."

"You think they would. Get the pennies and the apple cans too." Phoebe sighed. "Anyways, that thing in me ear finally shook loose."

"What thing in your ear?"

"The thing that's been cloggin me hearin fer the past nine'r ten years. Started up with me abscess that there spring when the hen house blowed over. Talk about a wind. Shingles flyin . . ."

"You mean," interrupted Sara, "you've been half-deaf for nine or ten years?"

"I could hear pretty good if you stood on me left side."

"What if I stood on your right side?"

"Not a thing. Betimes I felt an awful fool not knowin what you was talkin about."

Sara put down her scissors. "You mean," she persisted, "sometimes, when you got a kind of vacant look in your eyes, you weren't hearing me?"

"That what finally made me shake it loose. I couldn't abide it."

So that, thought Sara in a blinding flood of light, is what happened to my speech about being a Jew. It went in one ear and flew out with the chicken coop.

So much for my deep psychological analysis.

I was just standing on her wrong side.

"I suppose I should've gone to the doctor," admitted Phoebe. "He might've shook it loose before. But I never did like a doctor."

"You're okay now?"

"The very best," she replied, sweeping her shorn locks up from the floor.

They had been together all afternoon in Phoebe's kitchen, making a final summation on the state of the village, Hilton and Jeffer, Festus, each of the grandchildren, and life in general, while Murvyle and Daniel were at the empty house, loading Murvyle's pickup truck with produce from the garden, from the refrigerator, and with whatever else wasn't attached, rooted, or contracted to go with the place. Now, Murvyle's truck, piled high with possessions, came chugging up the road, and parked in the barnyard.

"Murvyle comin," sighed Phoebe.

The old man's bootsteps stomped onto the shed; he entered the kitchen. "Best get home," he said to Sara. "Daniel's feelin lonesome."

She made for the barnyard where the van was parked, and drove home for the last time, down the hill to the stream, then up the opposite hill to the one-room schoolhouse, and onto their own road;

as she drove down the lane, she was surprised to see a Mercedes parked in the driveway.

She stepped out of the van, and walked into the house.

In the empty echoing kitchen, Daniel stood with their lawyer. The two men slowly turned toward her.

"Three guesses," said Daniel quietly.

"Pierre Petite backed out," she whispered.

"I don't know if you're aware," said the lawyer, "that Pierre Petite has a friend in the mortgage department of the bank, Wayne Gall."

"Does he by any chance have buck teeth and an extremely low forehead?"

"That sounds like Mr. Gall. He wrote a letter for Pierre Petite rejecting his mortgage application."

"But it was approved two weeks ago."

"This new letter is dated this morning."

"I don't understand."

"Your man got cold feet, and Gall wrote him a letter so he could back out without losing his hundred-dollar deposit." The lawyer shook his head. "Slippery. Very slippery."

As he continued talking, she gazed around in shock at the denuded interior of the house; there were pale spots on the walls where pictures had hung, and on the floor where furniture had set. The lawyer's voice echoed in the emptiness. ". . . I'm afraid the summer selling season is over. You'll almost definitely have to wait another year."

"Stay here another year?" she asked in a cracking voice.

"Maybe," said Daniel, "we ought to rent it. That was our idea in the first place."

"I'd demand a five-hundred-dollar damage deposit," said the lawyer, "because the kind of people you're apt to get out here . . ."

"But that kind of person," said Daniel, "wouldn't have five hundred dollars."

"It's not going to be easy. However, a substantial deposit is your only deterrent against people . . ."

". . . like Pierre," she said, "with his chintzy deposit."

"Yes, Pierre," said the lawyer. "We can sue him, of course. We've got a case. Especially if we end up selling for less. But he's a slippery character. Very slippery."

"In other words, it wouldn't be worth it."

"Probably not."

They seemed to have come to an impasse.

"It was kind of you to come out."

"I came as soon as I could. After tendering your deed. You recall you already signed the place over to them." They walked to the door. "Sit down with pencil and paper, and figure out your options. Then come in and see me tomorrow." He got into his Mercedes. "One thing I've learned over the years," he remarked as he started his car, "is never trust a Catholic priest. Or," he added with some bitterness, "a Pentecostal preacher."

They went back into the house, and she looked around again: the final turn of the screw. She sank down onto the floor in the yellow spot which signified the couch. He sank down beside her, onto the phantom rocker, kneeling in its faint yellow after-image.

"Oh God," she said.

"At least we have our health."

"Oh God."

A car's motor sounded, coming down the lane.

They gazed out the window.

"The Petites," he said.

"I am not letting them in."

"You can't keep them standing out there."

"I can too."

"They came to apologize. We've got to treat them like human beings."

The car parked, and the two hated figures stepped out.

"Oh God."

There was a knock at the door; Daniel walked toward it, while she remained hunched on her phantom couch, furious at his kindness. Not only did she want the Petites to stay outside, she wanted them to be struck down by lightning while they were standing there; after which the rain would come and fill the well.

Daniel opened the door; the team echoed in. She refused to look up, but could hear the Punch & Jingle Show getting nearer to her, and then, priestlike tones, "Sara, you look so fra-gile sitting there."

How wrong he is, she thought, contemplating his death by lightning. She saw his socks at eye level, and contemplated hitting his ankle with a monkey wrench. But the monkey wrench was sold. For a nickel.

"I don't know what to say, Sara. We couldn't get the mortgage money. We feel terrible."

"What a blow it was to us," said Celeste. "We were so disappointed. I'm heartbroken."

Suddenly, Sara actually liked Pierre Petite, relative to what she felt toward Celeste. Whereas Pierre was making the effort to put on a show of vulgar sincerity, anguish, and regret, Celeste didn't even bother; she spoke her words as coldly and contemptuously as if she were saying, "What a pair of suckers you are."

Sara raised her eyes to see if Celeste's expression matched the cynicism in her voice, and Pierre, overjoyed at this recovery of the fra-gile Sara, said sorrowfully, "We had no idea you sold your furniture."

"We were supposed to be out tomorrow," she replied. "When did you think we would sell it?"

Daniel quickly stepped forward; she felt his concern that she was about to get nasty.

"These things happen, Pierre. We understand." He still, she saw with amazement, hadn't dropped his fatherly attitude, and Pierre launched into a long song and dance, with accompaniment of jingling change, on the fickleness of bank managers, who had caused them all this untold pain, not to mention funny Maurice, whom they still hadn't the heart to tell.

He jingled and punched his way to the kitchen sink. "We really shouldn't be telling you this, but you could sell the house with twenty acres for the same price as two hundred. You're giving away a hundred and eighty acres."

There was no response.

"That mortgage . . ." he continued. "We never signed anything. I mean that's why they're giving us back our hundred dollars."

"What's a hundred dollars?" asked Sara bitterly, looking around at the empty barn and the enormity of her predicament.

"Yes," agreed Pierre. "That hundred dollars wouldn't help you at all. What's a hundred dollars?" There was an echoing pause, in which the couple's relief was palpable.

"Can we lend you a table?" asked Pierre earnestly.

"Thank you," said Daniel. "That's very kind of you. But we'll make out all right."

Obviously relieved that he didn't have to lend them a table, Pierre followed up with a bolder empty gesture, which he also knew would be turned down. "Do you . . . do you . . . want to come live at our place for a few days?" His tone, in spite of his clerical training, indicated clearly that should anyone appear on his doorstep, he for one wouldn't be home. Celeste stifled a yawn, having handed the show over to her husband, as he mounted the pulpit and punched his pudgy fist in lamentation. "Have you thought of renting the place?" he asked. "Maybe Maurice would rent it."

Sara raised an eyebrow at the absentee offer.

"Maybe *we'll* rent it," said Pierre, with sermonlike fervor, empty of any real content as all sermons are, and Sara began to sense that behind this wild charade, something was weighing heavily on the minds of the Petites.

"You don't have to concern yourselves," said Daniel in fatherly tones. "We'll manage."

"We know you haven't had an altogether easy life here," said Pierre, switching to funeral oration technique. "We know your house burned . . ." His voice caught. "Your baby died . . ." Sara couldn't believe her ears. If only she had the wrench; sold for a nickel. She hadn't known anyone could sink this low. "It's a small world," said Pierre, seeking inspiration in platitude. "It was an aunt of mine who handed that dead baby to you in the hospital when you were taking it home. She said she will never forget that moment as long as she lives."

Sara glanced up. "What did your aunt look like?"

"Oh, big and fat like me. You probably don't remember her."

Sara remembered quite well the thin sparrowlike head nurse who'd handed Daniel the child in its cold freezer package, and she wondered at the incredible confidence that would risk such an obvious fairy tale. Does he think we could possibly forget such a thing? Then she realized Pierre was not truly connected to life, but lived on an invisible altar, from which he continued to pontificate, dwelling at length on death and fire.

Wearily, Daniel interrupted, easing them to the door. "We understand how you feel, Pierre, and we don't blame you." But the Petites, for some reason, wouldn't take the hint, hesitating even at the open door with a little shuffle dance.

Finally, both Petites extended their hands. "We want to wish you all good luck."

Daniel accepted the famous firm and sincere grip of the defrocked priest, and Sara realized she too would have to shake his hand; as a bonus, the pastor rewarded her by sympathetically squeezing her fingers. Celeste's strong handshake, by way of contrast, held no pretense at sympathy, or anything other than her own self-satisfaction at backing so effortlessly out of a difficult situation, the ease of which she obviously felt was due to her own natural superiority.

As the door was about to close behind them, Pierre turned back. "I'm awfully glad we came out and had this little talk and feel warm toward each other again." He gave a light laugh. "We were afraid you were going to sue us."

So that, thought Sara, is what's been in back of their minds. That's the reason for the visit, offers of tables, home, brother, blessing, and funeral oration.

"We've no intention of suing," said Daniel. If she had the wrench, she would've hit *him*. Even if we aren't going to sue, can't he at least let them worry a bit?

Thus assured, the happy couple gaily rushed off.

"Their whole family should die a horrible death," said Sara.

"The new pope died suddenly and unexpectedly during the night . . ."

The van swerved slightly; he quickly righted his hands on the wheel and caught her eye.

"I had nothing to do with it," she said.

"It's certainly quite a coincidence."

"You think my curse went awry?" she asked, in a voice which sounded to him, as Pierre would say, very fra-gile. Throughout the night, he'd kept waking to the noise of her teeth loudly grinding.

". . . This has been Mortimer Astle with today's headlines." The announcer's nasal twang reverberated from the radio, as they crossed the bridge into town.

Daniel parked near the real estate agency, and they walked into the office.

"Daniel . . . Sara . . ." exclaimed the president of the company, rushing to greet them with open arms. He kissed Sara effusively. Since they hardly knew the man, Daniel suspected this overwhelming reception might perhaps indicate that Pierre Petite wasn't the only one in fear of a lawsuit. "Hell of a thing to happen, isn't it? First time we've ever seen it the day before closing. But I'll tell you, all things work out for the best. Coffee? Tea?" He exuded well-being, from his fifty-dollar haircut to his Palm Beach suit and tan, from his twenty-four-carat-gold ingot cufflinks to his manicured nails, and his sense of all being right with the world seemed even to touch Sara. "I'll have a cup of tea," she agreed weakly.

He asked the receptionist to get them some tea, and invited them to join him in the presidential office. "You get a sixth sense in this business. I'll tell you something funny, I never trusted that Petite fellow."

"Neither did I," said Sara.

"Now isn't that funny? There was something about him, wasn't there. But we're all going to work real hard for you people."

"We thought," said Daniel, "we might rent the place."

"Not a bad idea. Nothing like an income property."

"But we'd rather sell," said Sara.

"Now I don't blame you. If you sell a place, you don't have to worry about it." He smiled warmly, and the salesmanship of the man hit Daniel squarely: Everything, he realized, is going to be okay. With this team behind us, we can't miss. True, it's the same team that's been behind us all along, but now Sara and I aren't just any couple of suckers trying to sell their house; we're a particular pair of suckers, who've been taken so badly, the pendulum finally has to swing. For the first time, he felt himself relaxing. Everything was sold; there was nothing left to pack; all they had to do was find a buyer, and if they didn't, if worse came to worst, he'd get to keep the place and stay. But he sensed from the aura of the president's office that now there was no question; there would be a sale, if Ed Brady had to go out and make it himself; who could refuse those cufflinks and that haircut? As Brady chatted on, Daniel reflected on financial success; does it come from a fifty-dollar haircut, or does the fifty-dollar haircut come from it?

There was a knock on the door, and Cookie Norton strolled into the office. "Golly, you'll never guess who I just ran into on the street."

They looked at her blankly.

"Thurston Munbow. He says he'll buy your house."

". . . Thurston Munbow?" asked Daniel.

"The old frigger?" asked Sara.

"But he didn't even look at it," said Daniel.

"I guess he looked at the cellar," said Cookie. "He said it was an awful nice cellar. He offered five hundred dollars less than the Petites."

"We'll take it," said Daniel and Sara together.

Cookie nodded. "I sent him over to see his bank manager."

"Well, well, well," said Brady. "I knew Cookie would come up with something."

"But are you sure?" asked Sara; Daniel saw she hadn't yet realized that when the full Brady team was behind them, miracles were in order.

"Oh, yes," said Cookie. "Thurston doesn't say anything unless he means it."

"I've heard that before," said Sara darkly.

Brady turned to Cookie. "Get a thousand-dollar deposit. A thousand dollars should sweeten the deal."

The suggestion was barely out of his mouth, when the old frigger himself wandered into the office, dazed and grizzled like some long-lost prospector.

"Howdy," he said, taking off his cap; wood chips fell onto Brady's carpet; a handmade cigarette dangled, bent, from Thurston's lips; one suspender button was missing on his pants; and he had the look of having stopped off for a nip at the Society Saloon. "Lovely day," he remarked as if the most desperate business were not at hand, and like all country folk, he seemed about to spend hours exchanging meaningless pleasantries or companionable silence.

But he had two frenzied homeowners, one remorseless real estate agent, and one company president eager to move the conversation forward. "Well, now," said Brady, putting an arm around the grizzled veteran. "Sit right down, Thurston. Can I get you coffee? Tea? Have you had your breakfast yet?"

"Aye."

"I hear," interjected Daniel, "that you're buying our house?"

Thurston scratched his head; a few more wood chips fell on the carpet. "Way I cal'ate it," he drawled, "at the price she's sellin fer, a feller would have to be crazy not to."

■ ■ ■

He moseyed over to the spiritual section of the library, curious to see how they'd arranged the books he'd donated.

Several entire new shelves had been dedicated to the subject. He examined the display with pleasure, then strolled toward the reading room, and sat down with the *Daily Loyalist,* whose interests and his were still joined for another few weeks, or as long as it took the old frigger to get a mortgage.

The pages crackled in his lap; he perused a familiar editorial demanding the death sentence for marijuana dealers, and a major news story on the largest pattypan squash grown in the county.

A small sound nearby, not quite a sigh, but more than a breath, as of someone grappling with a mental problem, made him turn his head.

On the next couch sat the spectral Urantian, holding—Daniel recognized the green cover and the place where he'd stained it with tea—*Tibetan Yoga and Other Secret Doctrines.* As he uttered his almost-sigh, the unemployed Urantian slowly laid the book down in his lap and stared out the window, his eyes lifted toward heaven, his mind obviously blown by this new addition to the library; piled on the couch beside him were other volumes of Tibetan yoga recently acquired; gazing, dazed, out the window, he stroked his throat with an incredible delicacy of touch, clearly a metaphysical response to the heaviest of the heavy.

Daniel regretted the half-mocking tone he'd privately adopted toward the spectral Urantian, as he realized here was the only other mind in town compatible with his own, ready to follow the mad Milarepa through his thousand journeys into the self. This, thought Daniel, would have been a friend.

For an instant, he thought of going over and saying, "Excuse me. I just wanted to tell you these are my books. So hello. And goodbye." But then he realized the fate of the mystical seeker in Atlantic Canada was to be utterly lonely; that was the karma, not to be alleviated even for this brief moment.

■　■　■

Murvyle sat forward on his lounge, spitting philosophically into the stove. "Now you got time to wrap them pennies."

"That's a blessing," agreed Phoebe. She rose, and made her way to the little room where she stored Christmas presents from the children and grandchildren.

"Here's a few things to see yous through the next few weeks, bein as you sold all yer stuff." She emerged with a random selection of twentieth-century necessities, including an electric popcorn popper, electric knife, electric can-opener, vaporizer, and shaving cream warmer.

Murvyle moved to the table, and helped himself to fresh bun and butter. "This entire sit'yation puts me in mind of old Nettlin Goosemire."

"Yes, it does," agreed Phoebe, pouring more tea on the subject.

"Old Nettlin was alluys one fer actin up. Once, I recall, we even had to chain him in the dooryard." Daniel dipped a cookie into his tea, trying to bridge the connection to old Nettlin Goosemire. "Anyways," said Murvyle, "he finally went straight. Married. Family. Went on fer quite the while. Until one day, his wife sent him out to buy Oxydol."

"You can prob'ly use pots and dishes too," said Phoebe. "Jes help yerself from the pantry."

"Well sir," Murvyle continued, "I met him in town that mornin. *Lovely day,* he says to me. I was the last one ever to see him. He went fer Oxydol and kept goin."

"Must be fifteen, twenty year now," concluded Phoebe.

"Didn't he ever come back to visit?"

"Hell, no," said Murvyle. "Why would he wanna come back to visit? We'd only tie him in the dooryard again."

■ ■ ■

"Here we are," she said glumly, as he parked the van in the driveway.

"It's only a few more weeks."

"If any bank will give a mortgage to a retired old frigger without a pot to piss in."

"This province was built by old friggers," he replied, and saw: The front lawn had been the victim of a curious violence. A digging fork had been stabbed into the turf; an Indian basket had been flung upside-down by the steps; a ladder, chair, and other familiar objects had been furiously hurled on the grass.

"Isn't that all stuff Pike bought at the yard sale?" she asked.

Is it some kind of gesture of rejection? he wondered. Is Pike trying to tell me the stuff I sold him is unsatisfactory? Then he realized it was only Pike's inimitable fashion of returning things he thought they might need for their unexpected stay. He picked up the chair, and entered the shed.

A huge washtub heaped with carrots set inside the door. "Who would've brought us carrots?"

"Who bought our washtub?" she answered. Vaguely, he recalled a village woman who, to him, had blended in with the whole grasping crew on the morning of the sale.

He unlocked the kitchen door, and they carried their temporary gifts into the hollow echoing house. He set the chair down on the mottled sun-spotted floor, and Sara set down the electric corn popper, vaporizer, and other necessities for taking up housekeeping once more.

"I'll put the carrots in the cellar," he said, carrying the washtub down, mainly to have a look at what had so taken Thurston's fancy.

Puzzled, he stared at the century-old arrangement of stones, each stone fitted without mortar, by a hand that had passed into the wind, and having passed, had turned back for a moment, to touch Thurston Munbow on the shoulder. It was, Daniel realized, a mystery to him, always had been, always would be; there were forces at work quite beyond his understanding, and none of his analysis or Sara's anxiety mattered, when two old friggers reached across eternity toward each other.

■ ■ ■

He stepped out in the morning sunlight to breathe the fresh autumn air, and saw her figure prostrate in the ivy.

"Sara!" He raced toward her.

"Listen," she replied, placing her finger to her lips, and dipping her ear to the ivy like an audioclairant eavesdropping on elves in the leaves. "Can't you hear it?"

"Hear what?"

"The well is gurgling."

He got down on the ground beside her, and pressed his ear to the ground. "So it is."

"Did you ever," she asked ominously, "hear it gurgle before?"

"No. But I never got down and listened before."

"It's gasping its last," she said, rising to her feet, eyes glazed with months of accumulated worry. She looked around toward the forest, the house, and the fields, her manner furtive as a weasel's, as if on all sides of her, and even below her feet in the ground itself lurked enemies, plotting to keep her in New Jerusalem, plotting against her well-being. Her myopic eyes bore the same paranoid message as Pike's, that the enemy was everywhere, the battle never over, the plot ever thickening. "If the well goes dry," she declaimed à la Cassandra, "Thurston will never go through with the deal."

"At the price he bought this place, he can dig a new well. Or I'll dig it for him."

"We can't spend another cent," she cried. "We can't trust anybody. We can't depend on anything." She stamped her foot above the treacherous well, and gestured in the air, her hands defining spastic circles. She was adrift in free-floating anxiety; everything had turned against her; her reason had started to fail and dark suspicion taken over. Is this, he wondered, the ultimate consequence of a life spent in Atlantic Canada?

■ ■ ■

He woke up in panic, awash in waves of fear which emanated from the upright figure sitting rigid beside him in bed sniffing the air like a frightened ferret.

"What is it?" he rasped in the darkness.

"Smoke," she said. "The forest's on fire."

He sank down, his body slowly relaxing; it was only the same old delusion.

"We'll be trapped in here like rats. Roads blocked. Our only way out the stream, for miles . . ." she predicted, as he rolled over, attempting to find the thread of the dream that had been taking him through the night.

■ ■ ■

Morning streamed through the windows, and he rose and padded downstairs to the bathroom; as his hand touched the doorknob, a shrill voice froze his fingers.

"Don't use the toilet!"

"Huh?" he asked, still dazed from lack of sleep and visions of forest fires which had robbed and ravaged his dreams.

Slippers flapped rapidly down the stairs. "It uses too much water," she stated.

"What should I do?"

"Go in the woods."

Her tone clearly said she meant business. He padded out to the shed, put on his boots, and marched off to relieve himself in the trees.

Standing there, watering the pines, he noticed the Deluded One entering another part of the forest to do the same; while inside the house, tank full, fully functional, was one perfectly good toilet.

■ ■ ■

"Don't make a sound," she whispered.

He glanced up from his book; she was crouched at the cellar door, ear cocked toward the basement, eyes on her wristwatch.

"Sara . . ."

"*Shhhh*," she hissed. "The pump's been going for twenty straight minutes." From the tension in her voice it sounded as if her teeth had been filed for twenty straight minutes; and at that moment, the sound of the pump, which he'd always considered an innocuous, even pleasant sound, began to grate on his own nerves as well.

"What," she demanded, "are you going to do about it?"

With a Phoebe sigh, he laid down his book, and made for the cellar stairs.

He stood in the basement and gazed at the sweating laboring pump. There was nothing he could do. Other than stand there and wait while it lifted water drop by drop from the parched earth.

But as he stood and waited, the anxious question mark in his mind was mysteriously, magically laid to rest, by a faint hoarse whisper, an old frigger's voice in the wind:

Come the new moon, the wells will fill again.

■ ■ ■

Cookie Norton stepped out of the official-looking car, followed by a sawed-off figure who marched importantly toward the house as if his chest were covered with all the medals of a South American general.

Going to greet them, Daniel was slightly taken aback by the style of the gentleman's mustache, a cut which he'd thought had permanently disappeared from the world with the demise of Adolf Hitler; he wasn't sure whether to raise his right arm in *seig heil* or merely extend it.

"This is Mr. Granjeau," announced Cookie, "from the Government Mortgage Office."

"Mr. Granjeau," said Daniel, clicking his heels and extending his hand, a neat compromise, he felt, between the two impulses.

Mr. Granjeau stiffly returned the handshake, and entered the house without smiling; in spite of the ebullient chatter Cookie carried on with him single-handedly, the diminutive civil servant remained dour as an SS officer inspecting a concentration camp, not wishing to make human contact with anyone therein because their lives would all too soon be snuffed out. Even as he had these fantasies, Daniel realized the power of delusion flowering around the foreshortened form of Generalissimo Granjeau was in large part due to the rampant fears and hallucinatory material put into the air by Sara, whose footsteps, at that very moment, sounded on the stairs, in their usual-of-late frenetic pace. Turning the corner, her eyes fell upon Granjeau and his mustache; her figure visibly shrank; she cowered at the foot of the stairs, as Cookie again sounded the death knell, "This is Mr. Granjeau from the Government Mortgage Office."

"How do you do?" asked Sara with forced gaiety, which Granjeau had no trouble overlooking, his eyes already sweeping the room, searching for violations. As she offered a trembling hand, he whipped out his tape measure. Is he, wondering Daniel, going to measure her forearm?

No, he was measuring some esoteric aspect of the floor, and noting it lugubriously in his official book.

"I just love these pumpkin pine floors," exclaimed Cookie, as if she'd never seen them before.

"They should really be sanded," said Daniel.

Floors need sanding, wrote Granjeau in his notebook, and Daniel felt Sara's feverish eyes burning into the side of his head. "Maybe I'll go outside and do some work in the yard," he said, to remove himself from further costly utterances.

From the front lawn, through the windows, he watched the solemn progress of the silent Granjeau, notebook in hand, Cookie and Sara fluttering behind him, cooing and exclaiming to each other over the wonders of the house.

In frighteningly little time, they were coming out again, still fluttering, still cooing, as Granjeau, still silent, measured the exterior siding. Grimly, he closed his tape measure, put his book in his pocket, and walked to his official car.

"Would you care for some apples?" asked Daniel.

"They're fabulous apples," exclaimed Cookie, as if the government were mortgaging the orchard, and Sara rushed off toward the fruit trees. The frenzied caricature of the harvest maiden hurried back with her arms filled with apples, most of which spilled; by the time she breathlessly reached the car, there was one apple left apiece for Granjeau and Cookie.

The inspector, still unsmiling, accepted the bribe, wiped it off, took a bite, and as Daniel, Sara, Cookie, and all of Jerusalem were about to breathe with relief, he proclaimed in stentorial tones, "We may have to come back."

"Why?" asked Sara in a strangled voice.

"There's always something you miss," he replied. "Especially when there's a disagreement on price."

■ ■ ■

"They're only withholding two thousand dollars," said Cookie. "And as soon as Thurston makes the improvements, they'll release the money to him, and he'll release it to you."

"What improvements must he make?" asked Daniel.

"Let me see . . . Mr. Granjeau said he has to put cabinets over the kitchen sink."

"He can't," said Sara. "There are windows there."

". . . And he's got to put a bannister on the stairs."

"He can't," said Sara. "There are bookshelves there."

". . . And he has to lay a concrete floor in the cellar."

"But he's buying the house for the dirt-floor cellar."

". . . And another concrete slab in front of the door . . . and varnish the floors."

Daniel felt Sara eyeing him coldly over the floors.

"I asked him," said Cookie, "if he wanted to deduct the two thousand off the price of the house, but you know Thurston, he said he wants to pay you the full amount."

"He did?" asked Sara.

What a fine old frigger, thought Daniel.

■ ■ ■

"Your worries are over," he told her.

She held up the official, anti-bacterial, sterilized, Government

Mortgage–supplied specimen bottle, and replied woefully, "What if
our water turns out not to be pure?"

"Not pure? Our water is like the healing spring at Chartres. Our
water makes Perrier taste like the Hudson. Our water is the most
delicious water in the world."

"That doesn't mean it isn't crawling with invisible organisms,"
she countered, gazing into the bottle. "Now that the well is so low,
who knows what's being dredged up?"

Like all her delusions, there was a kernel of reality onto which a
worry could latch until it snowballed into a major anxiety, and it
was always this kernel which threatened to catch him; he found
himself thinking: Who knows what's being dredged up?

Through the window, he noticed a small dapper figure emerge in
the lane, a vision from Abercrombie & Fitch, with pith helmet
reflecting the red autumn sunset.

"*Ma fran!*" called the figure. "*Ma fran! Ma fran!*"

"It's your friend," said Sara, still gazing at her bottle of pain.

Daniel went outside to greet his friend, who hailed him with a
wave of his helmet. "When you leave, ma fran?"

"Within the week, if things go well."

"Dat so?" Alf shook his head, and took out a bottle of Dr.
Fowler. "You care fer a dose? De flu goin aroun. Take a man right
out of de ball game." He took a swig, stared at the sky, and wiped
his mouth on his sleeve. "Did you ever figger, ma fran, who it was
dat burn yer house down?" He spoke thoughtfully, and behind the
old man's crazy pickled eyes, Daniel saw the glimmer of some true
thing. "I been in dese woods a good many year. I listen wid ma ear
to de groun. I hear a lot of ting. I tell you, it seem like it could be
only one faller. I bet anyting . . ."

"Never mind," said Daniel. "It doesn't matter anymore."

He saw the clouds passing through Alf's eyes, and then the
gleam fading, the subject closing, as subjects so often did in the
country, by dropping silently into the void.

"Well, ma fran, we never did fine no gole. But by Chri, someday
you come back and we go out again, look some more!" The old
prospector sniffed at the wind, turned, and started off up the lane,
on the scent of the mysterious lost treasure, the unknown something twinkling before him, his safari-clothed figure growing gradually smaller, and finally vanishing into the blood-red sunset.

Daniel stood gazing after him. A car turned into the lane, at the sound of which Sara came racing out of the house to ascertain if it was their lawyer again, to say that Thurston Munbow had backed out, passed away, or been put away.

The car stopped; its door angrily slammed; and the lean lanky figure of Pike emerged, toting a freshly painted canvas; as the painting came toward him, Daniel perceived it was an all-encompassing *Guernica* of province-wide mutilation and sorrow. "Better take this with you," warned Pike. "And remember, if you ever come back, you'll alluys have a roof over yer head. Plenty room in my house."

"I'm wondering," said Sara, "if we ever will get to leave."

"You might," said Pike, his tone as pessimistic as hers.

Daniel gazed from the mad painter's face to Sara's; both brows were knit in darkest suspicion, persecution mania, and dread; not only did her expression duplicate Pike's exactly, but her features themselves seemed to have grown almost identical to his. This, thought Daniel, is the archetype of the rural Canadian artist—a mass of creative libido turned to raving paranoid delusions. I'm getting her out in the nick of time.

He opened the back of his van, took out a sledgehammer, and handed it to Pike. "Anyone asks where you got it, tell them you found it by the side of the road."

Pike laid the sledgehammer on the seat beside him, and offered a gnarled hand above his car's rolled-down window; then he started the motor and set his beret for motion.

"We'll be back to see you," said Daniel, "one of these years."

"When you do, you'll be standin on me grave."

■ ■ ■

The big metal barrel set by the edge of the pond, smoke curling from the container up out over the water. "Quite a lot of paper," remarked Murvyle, throwing in another handful.

"A fellow accumulates over the years," said Daniel.

"I know how 'tis. I got every nail I ever pulled out of me boot."

The fall wind carried the smoke beyond the trees and down into the valley, while the two fire tenders stood in silence; tiny water boatmen came and went beneath the pond's surface, their legs rowing more slowly now that the cold winter of the north had begun to move in; and Daniel felt the urge to make a final speech, on this last evening with his companion, then decided it could wait until morning.

"You oughtta put fish in this pond," said Murvyle. "Clean her right up. Or run a pipe out through that there far end," he added.

"Yes, that's right," said Daniel. "Clear her right up."

". . . Where zactly you headed fer?"

"Just going to travel, I guess."

The next comment belonged to the smoke, which curled up about them and then blew on, following the other plumes across the pond and into the woods. A crow called, and the call was a knock at the door of memory, which swung open upon everything he'd known, the raw material for his final speech: He saw himself in his favorite season, striding along the road, the bright sun casting his sharp-edged shadow on a dazzling white screen of snow; the movie continued to roll, its soundtrack unabashed happiness, the great north woods all around him, his own spacious kingdom; he was headed up the road to Murvyle's, or off on his own to follow the frozen stream, and the crisp clarity of the day was an ornament of crystal whose beauty was his own perception, as pure as the winter air and empty as the wind; nothing profound, a wordless philosophy he'd learned without words.

A bull frog croaked.

"That feller will soon be down in the mud," said Murvyle.

They threw another handful of papers, tax receipts, and charge slips into the flames.

"Awful lot of pitchers gettin throwed away."

"Those are only Sara's rough sketches."

"I'll think I'll jes put a few in me pocket." Murvyle folded up some horse heads and tails. "Yessir," he said after a while, "travelin's all right, I cal'ate. Somethin like Gypsies."

"Glinko?"

"Long before Glinko's time. Mebbe forty-five year ago. Them Gypsies used to come back to the camps. Tinkerers some of them, mended pots and pans. Thieves the rest. I never will forget old Sudwick Sarcomb, foreman of that camp. Had them little Gypsy kids dancin all round him. Old Sudwick took quite the shine to them. Tweren't till their wagon was halfway to Moncton that he discovered they took his watch, his wallet, and his handkerchief. Had his initials on the watch. Or was it his wallet? I don't quite recall, but I knowed initials was part of the loss." He spit a long stream of tobacco juice into the pond, scattering water boatmen left and right. "Hand me some more paper there."

The crow appeared low now over the treetops, called again, and circled down and away, as Daniel tried to print the scene forever in his mind, Gypsies and all, the faded past and the fading present. Can it really be ending? he wondered. The step seemed unreal, one he couldn't possibly be taking, to leave this paradise and its laconic caretaker.

"Did yer well come back?" asked Phoebe.

"Yes," said Sara. "Did yours?"

"Yes, it come back with the new moon." Phoebe went to the kitchen stove, put in a piece of wood, sighed, walked back to the table, sat down, and stared out the window.

Have the silences this evening, wondered Sara, been any longer than usual? No, she supposed, they've always been like this.

"Seen the new cheap sale book?" asked Phoebe.

"It came in the mail this morning."

"Awful prices into it, ain't it?" Phoebe rose again to her feet, and went for the new Sears flyer, which they reexamined together, Phoebe wetting her finger before turning each page.

Tomorrow, thought Sara, it will all be over, this endless sitting and watching a window through which nothing happens. Boredom wafted in waves of heat from the stove, and streamed through the window in twilight; it emanated from the pages of the Sears sale flyer, which would be looked at again and again till the next one came, through the endless months of winter, and then saved for reexamination, through the endless years; the endless insufferable years, she thought, will be over tomorrow. But the tension of the past months were still with her; she felt unable to believe it was true, unable to believe the deal had gone through and there was nothing more to worry about.

"I guess the grandchildren are all well?"

"Yes."

"And Hilton and Jeffer?"

Phoebe sighed.

Sara closed her eyes; they'd discussed it all before, before this evening and every other similar meeting, had wrung it dry as dust.

The flowered kitchen, the gleaming stove, the subjects of children and grandchildren, village and weather, the closely watched window and the silence, rounds of tea, rounds of years and seasons, the boredom wrapped them in like two mummies.

■   ■   ■

The open van was backed up against the shed steps, and she handed the sleeping bag out to Daniel, who placed it in the van between some valises.

Morning sunlight washed over the lawn and the dry, brown flower garden; a sharp wind blew. She handed him a thick brief-case containing maps. "I guess they should go up front."

Murvyle's old truck chugged down the lane.

She went into the kitchen to collect the electric popcorn popper, electric knife, and shaving cream warmer, piling everything into two galvanized buckets.

She came out, handed the buckets to Daniel, and he handed them over to Murvyle. "May as well keep the buckets too," said Daniel.

"Aye."

The three stood in silence. She saw Daniel priming himself, preparing to make his final speech of farewell, just as Murvyle bent over, picked up a pail in each hand, turned on his heels, and ambled off. Stepping into his truck, Murvyle called, "See you next summer."

The truck pulled away, and Daniel stood with his undelivered speech dying, and Sara felt the old man's casual gesture had given Daniel what he needed, the extra edge to make the break with the place he loved.

She walked across the lane to the vegetable garden and field. Beyond the barns, the ridges of hills marched in eternal procession; she paused at the old blue wagon wheels imbedded in the ground, and recalled a distant feeling, a fantasy of many years past, a sense of belonging forever to the land, of children playing and grandchildren playing and cycles of birth and death and generations joined with the earth; and the distant feeling was as strong now as it had been then.

A tear of surprise rolled down her cheek.

She turned around, and saw the overgrown mound where the first house had been, and recalled the night of the fire; and two forgotten ghosts, the cats Patches and Alice, seemed to leap from the spot and bound across the field to her in their brief ecstasy.

She wiped her eyes. If this keeps up, I won't be able to wear my contact lenses.

Quickly, she walked to the house, and entered through the front door, but the house was flooded now with memories, and she felt the pain of the past binding her more than happiness could, and realized she couldn't leave.

She climbed the stairs, and moved through the rooms—the empty meditation room that had once been a nursery; the studio where she'd struggled; the bedroom where they'd shared their darkest dreams; and the sunlight in the rooms danced with suffering, and it held her, inextricably.

She popped out her lenses, slipped them into her handbag, and put on her glasses.

Then she went down, and they locked the door, and drove away.

"Can we stop off at Phoebe's one more time," she said. "I didn't really say good-bye to her."

They drove past the schoolhouse, down the hill to the brook, up, and around the bend to the farmhouse. She could see Phoebe sitting at her kitchen table, gazing out the window at them.

"I'll just run in and say so-long." She got out of the van, and walked toward the door; the smell of baking bread filled her nostrils. She knocked, and went in.

"Have a cup of tea?" asked Phoebe.

"No, we've got to be going."

Phoebe stood up uncertainly.

Hesitantly, Sara put her arm around her, kissed her smooth cheek, and felt the stoic old woman burst into tears.

She turned and ran from the house, away from the suffering that bound her, the thousands of hours of boredom shared, the love that overwhelmed her.

They drove off, and waved at Phoebe in her window standing and waving as she'd done hundreds of times; her naked pink face was twisted in grief, and Sara felt how she, Sara, had been the unexpected thing, the neighbor and friend who'd come into the ghost settlement to share Phoebe's life; and now Phoebe would be alone again.

■ ■ ■

The drug of the highway, the warm sun through the windshield, and the monotonous movement gradually put her into a sort of half sleep, where she felt her mind finally relaxing, going where it wanted, without worries or plans, and as her tension dissolved, she let her head gently rest on his shoulder, and felt time and the past slowly expand.

It came over her, gradually, that it hadn't been all sadness in the place they were leaving, that for a time, in fact, she'd been happy there. Happier than she'd ever been before. And she could pinpoint it easily; it shone clear as a drop of water, that instant, that week which had been the happiest of her life.

It was five o'clock in the morning, pitch black, December, the week before the baby was born. She lay on the floor doing child-birth exercises, while Daniel opened the door to let in the stray tomcat Rumpus, who wove back and forth against her, purring and cold. Just that, she thought: that week of hope, so ordinary; and the memory of cold fur rubbing past is the essence of my joy.